WE DON'T CALL T

(Book 5 of 7 in the N

Author: Jonathan Cox

First published Dec 2017

Publisher: JJ Cox Publishing Limited

All intellectual rights belong to the author.

This is a work of fiction and whilst influenced by the experiences and recollections of the author, no characters are based upon anyone living or dead and any similarities are purely coincidental. This book is sold on the condition that it is not re-sold, copied, or otherwise circulated without my prior consent. All intellectual and property rights belong to the author. This work has been registered with the Writers' Copyright Association.

The Nostrils Series

Book 1 – From Green to Blue

Book 2 – From Black to Blue

Book 3 – From Blue to Brown

Book 4 – When You Wear the Blue

Book 5 – We Don't Call Them Raids

Book 6 – A Necessary Fiction

Book 7 – Purple Cover

Book 8 – Never Yield

Author's note

This book is set in 2003 when David Blunkett was Home Secretary, the Commissioner of the Metropolitan Police was John Stevens and the author a detective sergeant on a Murder Squad based at Earlsfield.

My colleagues were some of the best detectives in London and this claim extends to include that motley crew who referred to themselves as the Onions – but more about them later.

Unlike our predecessors a generation earlier, we had at our disposal cutting-edge forensic capabilities which included the still comparatively new science of DNA analysis; CCTV on practically every one of London's street corners; advanced surveillance capabilities; mobile phone billing and cell site tracking; a financial investigation capability able to track money across continents; and formidable intelligence analysis tools. We also had something called the Home Office Large Major Enquiry System, known simply as HOLMES, an impressive computer designed to draw out meaningful lines of enquiry from thousands of apparently unconnected facts.

However, despite this multitude of technological advances, invariably the success of a case still came down to the ability of junior officers – the constables and the sergeants – to get into the local community to locate, speak to and then convince witnesses to come forward. And unlike what you've watched on *Prime Suspect* or *Inspector Morse* or *Death in Paradise*, our senior officers rarely left the confines of their offices, but that's not a criticism because their job was to control and direct, not to engage.

The account told in this book is fictional, but like any author I have drawn on my experiences to build the story and enrich the characters and, more importantly, to add that vital ingredient of realism which is so often missing from similar tales penned by those who, although far more accomplished writers, have never actually done the job.

This book is a 'whodunit' but also a 'what would actually have happened' and therefore, I hope, a police procedural in the truest meaning of the genre.

Jonathan Cox
Metropolitan Police Officer, 1983–2013

"No greater honour will ever be bestowed on an officer, or a more profound duty imposed on him, than when he is entrusted with the investigation of the death of a human being. It is his duty to find the facts, regardless of colour or creed, without prejudice, and to let no power on earth deter him from presenting these facts to the court without regard to personality."
Anonymous – place and date unknown

"Our day starts when your life ends."

DC – Arbour Square Police Station, January 2003

We don't call them raids

Chapter 1

Friday 10th January 2003, 0900hrs

Murder Squad offices, Arbour Square Police Station, East London

All murder investigations start with a briefing.

My team had gathered in the incident room on the top floor of the striking Victorian building, which a few years ago, before the latest cuts had been a fully operational police station. At one time, the particular area into which we now squeezed would have been the station's attic but the space had been converted to make additional offices. Designed to house about ten, this wasn't an ideal location for a meeting attended by all twenty-five of us but it was the largest area we had available.

Some pushed their own chairs into the room from adjoining offices, others perched on desks, a few stood and a number just made do with sitting on the floor.

There was an air of anticipation; this was the first job we'd had for a few months. Bored frustration was about to be replaced with frantic activity and empty bank accounts replenished with unrestricted overtime payments.

Seated in the middle of the room, and with their backs to a third of the audience, were our DCI, Ben Richards, and another white male, whom Ben introduced as the DI from the 'on call' team. I hadn't seen him before. He was young for a DI, perhaps thirty, but grossly overweight and his every movement seemed to demand of him a gargantuan effort. He made a polite request for silence, which he delivered in the guise of several short coughs.

The low mumble in the room ceased and we all prepared to take notes.

The on-call DI opened an A4-sized red notebook at which, for the next ten minutes, he sporadically glanced.

"We have good reason to believe the victim is one Gary Odiham, a thirty-six-year-old IC1 male with several previous convictions, nothing particularly spectacular, mainly for Theft Act offences and drugs, both possession and with intent. His last known address was a bail hostel in Tottenham."

Police officers always described people in a very specific way: the gender first, then the identity code (IC), then the known or apparent age and then finally, if known the height. The reason was simple: we were taught that if you wanted a criminal records check on an individual, that was how you gave the information to the Police National Computer operator.

"At about two o'clock this morning a black cab pulled into the BP garage in Dock Lane, Dagenham and the cabbie filled up with diesel. He paid at the overnight kiosk and returned to his vehicle. He got into the driver's seat before he realised that the warning light on his dashboard was on, telling him that the rear passenger door was slightly ajar. He turned around to see the victim lying on the floor in the back of his cab.

"The victim was alive and clutching the left side of his head; the cabbie immediately saw he was bleeding heavily, possibly from his ear. The victim asked the cabbie to take him to the nearest hospital – this was in fact the last thing the victim said. The cabbie wasn't too keen as his vehicle was rapidly getting covered in blood and he doubted he was going to get paid, and besides, he was on his way home.

"The cabbie describes the victim going limp and apparently unconscious and he called an ambulance on his mobile phone. In all probability, this is when the victim died. The garage attendant says he saw nothing from where he was sitting in the kiosk. The cabbie and the garage attendant state there were no other customers at the time but that will need to be confirmed by the CCTV and the till receipts.

"The local police were the first on the scene and removed the victim from the back of the black cab and onto the forecourt floor where they attempted to resuscitate him; they continued to do this until a paramedic arrived on a motorbike and took over.

"The paramedic pronounced life extinct at the scene at 02:42 and the victim was taken to the London Hospital; a uniformed officer from night duty is with the deceased to provide continuity.

"There's a special booked for this afternoon but the cause of death is likely to be the head injury, although curiously there's no obvious puncture wound. There are other older cuts and bruises but nothing of any particular note; oh, I nearly forgot, he's got numerous puncture marks consistent with IV drug abuse."

A 'special' was a thorough post-mortem, which went into more detail than a normal post-mortem where there were no suspicious circumstances. A 'special' would take a pathologist anything up to four hours, a straightforward post-mortem could take as little as twenty minutes.

"No next of kin, as yet.

"The cabbie is the only witness and he's gone home but we know who he is and where he lives and we've asked him to stay at home today until someone has interviewed him. He won't have anything to do anyway, as we've still got control of his vehicle. I suggest he be treated as a significant witness.

"Initial enquiries at the bail hostel suggest the victim hasn't been there for over nine months but we've only spoken to the night security guy who wasn't the full, so that'll need checking when the manager comes in this morning.

"The cab is still at the garage but has been cordoned off and uniform are running a log. No other witnesses at the garage and just the two scenes. No suspects, no witnesses to the assault itself and we haven't been able to identify the scene of the attack.

"The victim's property included a set of keys but they're not to the bail hostel, a mobile phone, which doesn't appear to be working, and a plastic cardholder containing a five-pound note and a photo ID for a travel pass, which is how we've provisionally identified him.

"Any questions?"

The briefing had been shorter than most but the DI's delivery had been factual, objective and professional. When I asked my first question, most of my colleagues were still writing.

"What was he wearing?"

The DI looked through his notes.

"A blue puffer jacket, white branded T-shirt, jeans and really old trainers with holes in the soles. Everything's bagged and at the hospital. The clothing is heavily bloodstained and will require drying out before it's bagged."

"So he was attacked outside then? I mean, if he was wearing the puffer jacket," I said.

The DI nodded.

"I assume so," he replied.

"No drugs on him?" I asked.

"No, just what I've described."

"No cigarettes, tobacco, roll-up paper, lighter or matches?" I said, more as an observation than a question.

"No," the DI answered.

"That's unusual," I replied.

That suggested to me that he was staying locally and had just popped out for a few minutes.

"Could he have got out of another vehicle and into the cab?" a colleague asked.

"Maybe; we haven't been able to establish where he came from, so I suppose it's possible he alighted from another vehicle," the DI replied.

"Has anyone listened to the 999 call yet?" someone else asked.

"No, not yet," the DI replied.

"Where's the cabbie live?" another asked.

The DI looked at his notes.

"Barkingside."

"Any previous for violence?" the same guy asked.

Again the DI looked at his notes.

"No, but he flashes 'assaults police' which doesn't make a lot of sense," he replied.

"What was the weather like at the time, does anyone know?" the DCI asked.

"It's been pissing it down all night; stopped about six o'clock this morning. If the scene of the attack was outside, the rain will have washed most of the blood away by now," the DI replied.

I had nothing else to say and from the fairly blank expressions around the room, neither did anyone else.

The information was unusually sparse; in fact, apart from one job last year when all we'd had was a decomposing body that had been found in the deep undergrowth of Abney Park Cemetery in Hackney, I don't think I'd ever picked a case up with less to go on. The cemetery case ended up being natural causes, anyway.

Our DCI opened his own red notebook and started to assign the various tasks – everyone waited to find out what they'd be doing.

My team, which was half of the outside enquiry team, got the second scene – the garage and the car – which was fine as it meant we'd avoided the house-to-house and CCTV, well for now anyway. We also got the 24-hour anniversary appeal, which was great from an overtime point of view but meant it was going to be a really, really long day.

I did the right thing; I paired myself up with Samantha. I would have rather gone out with Nicola, or Pod, but I didn't, I posted myself with the newest member of my team so we could get to know each other better.

Samantha and I made sure we stocked up on the usual – statement forms, exhibit bags, Incident Report Books and plastic gloves – and when we had gathered everything we thought we would need, we set off to the BP garage and the scene of death. I was driving and in the passenger seat was a very masculine, six foot two inches tall, broad shouldered, former Welsh Guardsman wearing a light pink blouse, dark skirt, skin-coloured tights and very discreet heels.

Chapter 2

Exactly twenty-four hours earlier
Thursday 9th January 2003
Flat 127, Attlee House, Bethnal Green

THUD

"This is the police. Open the door," shouted one of my colleagues.

We don't call them raids but the press and the public do. To us, we are 'doing a warrant', 'putting in a door', 'spinning a drum' or just plain 'doing a search'; hell, if we feel like it we might even use the proper term and say we're 'executing a search warrant'. Personally, I always referred to a search warrant as a 'ticket', a term I'd picked up long ago as a sprog at Stoke Newington from my Street Duties sergeant, Bob Bellamy.

To a DS like me, doing a ticket was real bread-and-butter stuff and I'd probably execute two or three a month, more if I were on a local CID team.

Now, an Englishman's home is his castle so you can't just kick the door down, not unless you have to do so to save a life or to prevent a breach of the peace. So you need to get your ticket signed by a magistrate before it's legal.

As a young constable, when you go to get your first ticket it's a nerve-racking experience, but when you're on to your fiftieth, it's a piece of cake.

THUD

"Stand fucking back, you're too close," said another of my colleagues.

You might need to search somebody's drum for a variety of reasons – to recover stolen property, to seize firearms, or to uncover evidence of terrorism offences – but today's ticket was issued for the most common reason of all, drugs.

Doing a ticket was good fun because you never knew what you'd actually find and besides, who doesn't enjoy lawfully snooping around somebody else's house and going through all their belongings?

I'd done firearms tickets with as many as forty of us involved: the firearms team, the search specialists, uniform officers to secure the perimeter, CID to pick up the prisoners, dog units, an ambulance crew in case someone got shot, and the local Sanitation Department to block the drains and capture any stuff the occupants might flush down their toilet. Then there'd be a gaggle of governors to take the credit if it all went right and to find someone to blame if it didn't. I'd even known the deployment of the police helicopter, whose call sign was India 99, in case the suspect escaped through the roof.

In contrast, today's ticket only required four Old Bill: the DS in charge, an exhibits officer and two PCs to do the searching.

THUD

No matter how many times you'd done it, putting the door in and then charging inside was a thrill.

This was the dangerous bit as the suspect could be armed or high, or both. A few Old Bill had lost their lives or been seriously injured going through the door. I knew a geezer called Felix, who did a ticket over in East London, got a face full of acid for his troubles and was completely blinded in one eye. Not long after, he died of cancer, leaving a wife and four teenage daughters – life can be really cruel. Then only last year a poor Special Branch officer from the West Midlands was stabbed to death during what the papers described as 'an anti-terror raid'.

Today, I can honestly say that my heart was pounding as loudly as the banging from the front door.

THUD

"Police, open up."

If we needed to get into an address quickly, we'd take Ghostbusters, a team of civvies who specialised in gaining rapid entry. They used a hydraulic-powered pump to operate an expanding bracket that would spring open the frame and the door would just fall in.

Ghostbusters, however, were in big demand and the team covered the whole of the Met so you had to book their services in advance and if you left it too late, they'd already be busy.

In these cases we reverted to the Big Red Key, a really heavy metal battering ram, which you gave to your strongest guy to literally beat the door down. This less sophisticated method of entry always took longer than you thought and it was really noisy so the suspect invariably managed to lose whatever it was they shouldn't have.

And I knew a few mates who'd broken hands and fingers using it. In the end, the job introduced a course, which you had to complete before you were authorised to wield the implement. No one took any notice but it meant that if you hadn't had the course and you injured yourself using it, you couldn't sue.

THUD, SPLINTER, ACCOMPANIED BY THE SOUND OF HEAVY PANTING

I was on the third floor of a Guinness Trust council estate in Bethnal Green; the occupier was a white male in his late thirties.

I didn't know his name, all I knew for certain about him was that he was a heroin dealer and occasionally scored a bit of puff, but H was his weapon of choice and he made just about enough money to feed his own addiction. I knew he'd just taken delivery of enough gear to keep him busy all day so I made sure I was at his address first thing, because by two in the afternoon there would be nothing left.

THUD, MORE SPLINTERING

"Go, go, go," my colleague shouted to the team.

I'd done so many tickets I couldn't remember them all. This one, however, was different because for once, I was on the wrong side of the front door.

Chapter 3

The fact I was addicted to heroin wasn't my fault; that I'd not got off the gear most definitely was.

As far as I knew, I was the only Old Bill with this particular addiction. I knew more than a few who were alcoholics. I suspected a couple of my younger colleagues might do the odd line of coke and just about everyone admitted to trying weed at some time in their lives, but no one else shared my desire for the dragon. I was also the only H addict I ever knew who could lead something of a normal life, which incidentally included being a DS on one of the Met's twenty-seven murder squads, otherwise known as AMIP, the Area Major Investigation Pool.

In the early days of my addiction, I'd had counselling and loads of medical support. I'd done the methadone piece and when that didn't work, the buprenorphine programme. None of it was effective. The pressure to quit mounted and the job made it clear that the situation couldn't go on indefinitely, so I decided to fake getting off the gear by stopping injecting, choosing instead to smoke the drug.

The deception proved remarkably successful, principally because there were no needle marks anywhere on my body. I also made a real effort to significantly reduce the amount I was taking and within a year, I was down by something like seventy per cent.

I returned to work and got on with my life.

As far as the job knew, as far as my family knew, I was clean.

Let's not kid anyone here – nothing can match the effects of injecting. Injecting gives you the high, anything else just controls the withdrawal symptoms and believe me, you want to avoid those at all costs. As long as I had a fix a day, my bowels didn't turn to water and I had enough energy and motivation to live a normal existence.

Then in 1991, I managed to give up permanently – well, for nearly seven years – before I fell off the wagon. So deep down inside, I knew it could be done. Back in 1998, I'd had a terrible few weeks and just when it was all over, I'd found a needle, syringe and tourniquet all ready to go and simply couldn't resist the temptation.

Whenever I did give up, I was an emotional wreck who shit the bed and felt like I was suffering from the worst case of fatigue ever. I had used irritable bowel and flu as cover stories more times than I could remember. The only person who knew the truth was my doctor because, well, a blood test result is a blood test result. He was a genuinely nice man who kept a watchful eye on my liver's ALT and Gamma GT readings and regularly listened to my heart with his cold stethoscope. He repeatedly expressed the view that I must somehow be manipulating the results. My wife, Jackie, a nurse by trade, might suspect but she closed her mind and never questioned me. Jackie closed her mind to a lot of things where I was concerned. Besides, I was careful, so very careful.

I never kept H at home but in a secret compartment, behind the dashboard in my car, that I'd had a dodgy garage in Finsbury Park fit for me. I admit a dedicated search team might find it but no one else would. The downside was that I could never be bothered with buying a new car and so I'd had the same old Golf for ten years. I was also really careful about when, where and how I took my daily allowance – so much so that the whole process had become something of a ritual. I always made sure that I didn't do anything or meet anyone within an hour of scoring because even though I thought I was acting normally, I was wise enough to suspect that something in my behaviour would give the game away.

I wasn't happy though, I really wasn't. Every single time I opened the bag, I hoped it would be the last time, and over the last few months I'd done really well by gradually reducing even further the amount I took every day – but I was still a drug addict.

I was very conscious that I was at my most vulnerable when purchasing. I therefore made a practice of buying as many bags as I could afford at any one time and on most visits, I'd stock up for at least a week. One of the benefits of reducing my daily measure was that my supply went that little bit further, so I didn't have to visit a dealer quite as often.

To add to the growing pressure for me to quit, and quit for ever this time, were the rumours which were circulating that the job was going to introduce random drug tests for its staff.

And all this explains why, at nine a.m. on Thursday 9th January 2003, I was sitting on a dirty settee in a scummy council flat in Bethnal Green, as four hairy-arsed coppers came charging into the place, all shouting, swearing and sweating.

"Stay right where you fucking are and let me see your hands."

I did as I was told.

When the Big Red Key had delivered its first hammer blow, my dealer had just been on his way out of the lounge and I saw him push my oner down the front of his pants before he commented, almost nonchalantly, "I think we have visitors."

He sat back down in the seat opposite.

I must say my dealer was surprisingly calm, although I distinctly heard him whisper under his breath 'cunts' several times. Wherever he had the gear stashed was obviously pretty secure. Of course, as a punter, I hadn't seen where this was because he'd make sure I was seated in the lounge, before he'd close the adjoining door and go to retrieve my order. This was par for the course and if he hadn't done so, I would have worried that something was up.

If my dealer was the epitome of cool, I was exactly the opposite. Over the years, I had played this scenario out in my mind so many times that I should have been prepared but I wasn't. I knew what I had to do and say to extradite myself but I would also need just a decent dose of luck.

When the officers realised that we were completely compliant and that no one else was in the flat, they quickly settled into their routine. I deliberately kept my head down and avoided making eye contact.

The confident guy I assumed to be the DS was a white male in his mid-forties and he issued a series of instructions to his team. A middle-aged white guy and a young Asian lad were sent to start the search and a third, a quiet and calm thirty-something white female, sat down at the other end of the settee. She was wearing blue plastic gloves and carried in her left hand a large paper evidence bag, which she placed on the floor. In her right hand she was holding a blue book and a thinner white document, both of which I recognised immediately. The first was an Exhibits Book, the second the Premsearch Register.

The DS was talking to my dealer and asking him to sign a copy of the warrant; he clearly knew it was his flat and not mine.

I realised my hands were very slightly shaking, so I placed them under my thighs and tried to control my breathing. My plan would only work if I was super cool.

In the background, I could hear the others starting to open and close furniture doors and cupboards in the nearby rooms. The exhibits officer to my left started writing notes and the DS began questioning the dealer.

"We are searching your flat on the authority of this drugs warrant, a copy of which I've provided for you. Can you confirm that you reside here?"

"Yes," my dealer replied.

"Does anyone else live here?"

"Nope."

"Apart from you two, is anyone else in the flat?"

"No."

"Are there any controlled drugs in the flat?"

"Nope," my dealer replied.

The DS now looked towards me.

"And what's your name, mate?"

Suddenly the expression on his face changed to a frown so severe that the lines on his forehead could have been counted.

"Fucking hell, Nostrils, what are you doing here?" the DS asked.

Chapter 4

I would've sworn on oath that I'd never met this DS before but apparently I'd have committed perjury because he knew me. I glanced across at my dealer, who looked momentarily confused. I only used him sporadically, perhaps once a month, because I wanted to keep on my toes. Come to think of it, I wasn't sure we knew each other by name as we'd met at another dealer's and I always called him 'mate'. Quite frankly, the less we knew about each other the better.

I identified my dealers by a telephone number and location – both of which would frequently change – rather than a name. I don't ever recall anyone knowing anything about me. I wasn't their 'usual customer'. I mean, I was always smartly dressed, clean, and most spectacularly of all for them, on time. I think they thought I worked in a bank or something, an image perhaps reinforced by the fact that I always bought in relatively large quantities.

When I first started buying from these council estate dealers, I remember being convinced they would think I was an undercover cop, but it transpired that I looked too much like an Old Bill to be Old Bill. I mean, what idiot would use a forty-year-old white male in a suit as a test purchaser? Over the years, this counter bluff had worked really well and not once had anyone challenged me for being a police officer. The cold fact was that by 2003, I'd been buying H from East London dealers longer than most of them had been selling it.

Before the DS could say anything that might give my game away, with the tiniest of movements I flicked my head towards the flat's entrance to suggest that I needed to speak to him outside; the DS nodded back. Perhaps, luck was going to be on my side after all.

It was a cold winter's day with a biting wind and a grey overcast sky. The DS and I stood on the balcony, which ran along the front of and provided access to the four flats that were on this section of the landing. We'd actually moved away from the flat itself and were now standing outside the neighbour's to ensure that the dealer couldn't overhear our conversation. There was only a low concrete wall, perhaps four feet high, separating anyone on the balcony from a forty-foot fall to a concrete car park.

"Fucking hell, Nostrils, how are you?" the DS enquired, bringing me swiftly back to reality.

"Good, mate; when did we see each other last?" I said, putting into effect a technique I had learnt to use exactly in situations such as these; it usually worked.

"In the summer, on the First Aid course down at the old Wanstead Training Centre," he replied.

Was that it? He'd remembered me from two boring days sat in a classroom, six months ago? And then the memory started to return: we'd gone for a drink in a pub called the Magpie, which was just down the road from the training centre and which had a stunning garden.

We'd ended up having too much to drink and I got Wendy to pick me up. There were about eight of us and I remember having a right laugh with an eclectic group of officers, only one or two of whom I'd previously met. One of those present, it may even have been this chap, recognised me as the guy who'd got blown up years ago in an IRA bombing. That happened quite often. The thing was, lots of people in the job remembered me because of that incident. So the older ones, anyway, felt that they actually knew me before they'd even met me, if you know what I mean? Fortunately, as the years rolled by, fewer and fewer of my colleagues knew anything about the bombing, which was just fine by me.

"Nick, Nicholas Charles," he said, offering an outstretched hand, which I gladly accepted.

"Hello, mate," I said, with interest and delight that were equally and carefully measured.

I wanted to take the initiative in the conversation and with luck, lay a smooth path along which to extradite myself from this awkward situation.

"You're at Bethnal Green, right?" I asked.

"Yeah, still. Fucking hell, mate, I've put in for SO13 and got a board this Wednesday but they're not taking many on, as everyone who went there on the hurry up after nine-eleven has just stayed on. Fucking hell, mate, I think there are like forty of us going for three places; I ain't that good so I really don't rate my chances. I'm on the Crime Squad, which is fine but the DSs are due for rotation soon and I think I'm next in line for the CJU. The SO13 thing is my last chance to escape the Borough before a year or more of boring, boring paperwork. You're at AMIP, right?" he replied.

SO13 was the Anti-Terrorist Squad, a really sought-after and glamorous posting.

"Yeah, yeah. I'm on one of the teams at Arbour Square," I replied, but my mind was racing ahead of the conversation because I'd spotted a possible ploy which might facilitate my escape route.

"Yeah, fucking hell, mate, that's right, I remember," he replied.

"Listen, I've got a good mate up at SO13; if you like I could have a word? He's a DI and has been there for years; his name's Raymond Stickleborough-Crompton but everyone calls him Alphabet because his name contains more letters than the alphabet. Do you know him?"

"No, mate, what do you reckon, a quick chat over coffee? But thinking about it, there isn't really enough time, my board's in a couple of days. Fucking hell, mate; I wish I'd run into you sooner."

"Leave it with me, I'll get in touch with Alphabet today and see if he's got any information which might be of use. Hell, you never know your luck, he might be on the board," I said hopefully.

"Only if my luck has started to change," he replied, with an air of resignation.

"Fucking hell, Nick. You've gotta be more positive than that," I replied enthusiastically.

He lifted and dropped his shoulders as if the weight of the world was upon them.

"What's the matter, mate?" I said.

"Domestics, you know."

"Anything I can do to help?" I asked.

"No, really. You're a nice geezer but this is a problem without an obvious solution."

"Well, you know, let's get a beer," I suggested.

"Fucking hell, mate; now that sounds like a plan," he replied.

I went to shake his hand but Nick looked a little awkward; he stuttered a little before saying:

"L-Li-Listen, Nostrils, I think I can guess but I gotta ask, you understand. What the fuck were you doing in there with that herbert?"

"Trying to cultivate him, you know, early stages," I replied, with my well-rehearsed line.

"So he's not registered yet?" Nick asked.

It was the right question to which I had to find just the right answer.

"No, no, really early days," I said.

I didn't want to say too much because of course, everything I was saying was a lie and the less you lie the easier it is to remember exactly what you've said and also there's less that can subsequently be disproved.

"How do you want us to play this? Fucking hell, mate; I'd be happy to do you a favour with the herbert, if it'll help? You know, as long as it's not too big an ask," Nick offered.

What Nick was offering was a really nice gesture; he was suggesting that they could lose any drugs they found to give me some leverage over the dealer. I mean they wouldn't make a kilo disappear, not that this dealer could ever afford to buy that amount of gear, nor would they ignore a firearm or anything that serious, but they could gently massage the evidence to my advantage.

It was of course all rather meaningless, as the dealer had no idea his last customer was Old Bill and I had no intention of recruiting him as a registered informant.

"Listen, mate, I appreciate the offer, I really do but just do what you've got to do. He's going to be no good to me and I'd made that decision before you came through the door, and there's no reason to change my mind now. Tell you what, you can even pretend you thought I was a punter which will keep him happy, as he'll think that I haven't compromised him by showing out to you."

"That sounds like a sensible suggestion but I think he noticed that I recognised you so how can I explain that? I mean, fucking hell, mate; I called you by your name."

Nick was right, of course, but that wouldn't fit in with my plan.

"He's as thick as shit, mate. Honestly, if you go back in and never mention me again, I don't think it will ever cross his mind to say anything," I said.

Nick nodded and held out his hand.

"I'll give Alphabet a call and put a word in. Take care, mate; email me with your mobile number and I'll give you a call, as soon as I've spoken to him. We'll arrange a beer or two, too?" I said.

I turned around and walked away a free man when really I should have been led away to the nearest police van in handcuffs.

Chapter 5

Walking back to the car I experienced a series of emotions. I felt utter relief that I'd probably got away scot-free from a situation I'd always dreaded; in fact, I'd had nightmares about being caught buying my drugs. Then I started to panic because I realised I didn't have any heroin, a situation which was almost unheard of. It made me feel vulnerable and weak but at the same time desperate and pathetic. Finally, I experienced a feeling of sheer depression because my life was such a dreadful mess. It wasn't just the addiction, which was bad enough; it was that my private life was a car crash waiting to happen. Then I made a momentous decision.

By the time I turned the ignition key, I had decided to quit once and for all – and for good this time. No more H, no more sneaking around dodgy East London drug dealers, no more constant risk of losing my job, no more stress about Jackie finding out, but above all else, no more of the slavery that is addiction. I had done it once successfully, I knew what to expect; this was going to be difficult but not impossible.

I could never really relax. If I was getting to the end of my supply, I'd worry about when and where I was going to get the next batch. If I had enough for the next week, I'd worry about when and where I'd be able to take my next hit. When I was at work, things were easier as I could always disappear for a bit without anyone even noticing, but if I was at home for a couple of days, I'd have to work out the most elaborate plan to make sure that I got an hour just to myself. It was a ludicrous way to live, or rather exist.

Over the last year or so I had grown slightly more confident about my chances of quitting as I'd slowly but surely reduced the amount I was taking. And so, that cold, windy Thursday morning in January, I made the life-changing decision to never take heroin again.

I think, however, it's only fair to point out that this wasn't the first occasion I'd given up; it wasn't the second or the third but more like the thirtieth, and only once had I made it through the first couple of days. This time, however, I felt something was different but I couldn't quite articulate exactly what that was. I don't know, perhaps I was just ready?

When I got back to my car I checked my phone and noticed several missed calls from an unknown number. I wondered whether we'd picked up a job so I called the office and spoke to grumpy Naobi, an Asian woman who was an indexer, that is to say she copy-typed information into HOLMES and cross-referenced each piece of data with everything else already in the system. It was a really important role and very underestimated. I didn't doubt for one moment that every year a few of London's murders were solved by the dedication and attention to detail of this small band of specialists.

People said Naobi was a great indexer; I thought she was one of the rudest people I'd ever met. I'd also heard rumours from different sources that she was shagging a married guy who was in the job but they were never substantiated and if she was, I don't know why she bothered because the activity certainly wasn't making her very happy.

Naobi told me that the DCI was after me but that it wasn't urgent. I asked her to tell him I was on my way in and to show me a ring on my duty state. Most importantly of all, she confirmed that we hadn't got a new job.

I hung up and momentarily worried that the DCI might be asking me what I was doing in a drug dealer's flat in East London but quickly figured he couldn't have found out that soon and relaxed.

I made my way back to the office and left my car in the car park of a nearby gym.

Every Monday I paid Eric, the old guy that worked there, twenty quid and in return he let me use both the gym and the car park — now that was a good deal, but there was an added advantage. Near the gym entrance was a very rarely used old toilet, which actually looked closed. I discovered that it was unlocked and almost every workday for the best part of three years, I had used this to take my drugs.

No one would ever find me in there and I could relax for an hour in my car afterwards. If anyone saw me chilling in the car, big deal, I was just having a quick power nap.

Even though it was only thirty minutes since I'd decided definitely and forever to give up, the sight of that toilet as I pulled up made me start to question my decision. My mouth started to water and I realised I was clenching and then relaxing my hands. My breathing was becoming quicker and I'd started to be conscious of my heart beating as an unsolicited excitement was starting to build.

My mind raced through where I might be able to buy another bag and then I realised I'd have to find a cash machine first. Then I'd have to explain to Jackie why I'd made two separate hundred-pound cash withdrawals on the same day. Wait a minute; I had my secret building society book in the car that contained my ever-dwindling abortion fund – I could use that but I'd have to go over to the City to get to the nearest branch.

Heroin was a massive part of my life and now I wasn't quite sure that I wanted to be without it. Admittedly, I didn't get the hit I experienced when I first used the gear but it could relax me like nothing else and for a short while after the fix everything was right with the world, even when it really wasn't. Did I really need to give up now?

For fuck's sake, what was I doing?

The mere glimpse of that toilet door had set off such a powerful automatic reaction that made me realise I was no better than one of Pavlov's dogs. I felt like shit.

I won that battle by the simplest but hardest thing I'd ever done. I got out of my ageing VW Golf, locked the door and walked towards the nick.

Chapter 6

The old Arbour Square Police Station now housed three of London's murder teams. The place was closed to the public in 1999 and if you needed uniform assistance you had to go to Limehouse, although there was a black phone at the old front entrance that would connect you to the control room where, if you were really lucky, someone might answer. As a police station, the building had housed its fair share of famous prisoners, including the Kray Twins and numerous IRA suspects. Even more impressively, it was where the enquiry team was set up to investigate the Jack the Ripper murders.

My desk was on the second floor, or third if you counted the basement, and the only guys in the office were two of the DCs, Julie and Nicola – both were on my half of the enquiry team and were very solid and sensible detectives. Over the last two years they had become friends and I tried, wherever I could, to work with one of them.

Julie was white and in her mid-thirties, bottle blonde and attractive with a trim little body; she was seeing Luke, a DC on the Flying Squad at Rigg Approach. She was an East End girl through and through and proud of her roots. She called everyone 'babes', even the DCI, but it was quite endearing.

Nicola was white and probably a little younger than Julie. She was tall, lanky and scatty; an ex-head pupil at Cheltenham Ladies'

College, she was married to an Old Etonian, a barrister who worked at the Temple, and they had a young family, a golden retriever and a live-in au pair.

Julie, Nicola and I were part of that half of the enquiry team referred to as the Cheeses. The others included two of the nicest fellas you could ever meet, Pod and Taff, who were notably older than anyone else.

Why were we called the Cheeses? I think it had something to do with the perception that we spent our off-duty time doing cheesy things, like going to the theatre and having dinner parties. Personally, that couldn't have been further from the truth.

If we were the Cheeses, the other half of the team were the Onions. Hard-drinking, diehard macho detectives who considered themselves quick witted, old-school and streetwise. The Onions spent most of their time in the Peacock, a pub almost next door to the nick, discussing the cases, and we, the Cheeses, spent most of our time out and about solving them. Well, that's not entirely true but there was, at the very least, a seam of truth running through it.

Where the term Onion originated was curious. Those that were the Onions before they were called such referred to us, the gentler side of the team, as the Cheeses. This started after Nicola and her old man had a dinner party before I'd even joined the team. Those that weren't invited derided the event as a very middle-class and boring thing to do and named those who attended Cheeses.

At the time, one of the guys on the team was Luke, the guy going out with Julie. As an ex-military, rowdy, hard-drinking individual, Luke was a natural fit for the Onions, but because he was going out with Julie, he got invited to numerous cheesy social events.

At the next office lunch, the Onions presented him, quite literally, with a block of cheese and an onion and asked him to choose. From that moment on, the respective names were set in stone.

I'd been on the team for about three years and there had always been this 'Cheese and Onion' divide.

Oh, I've forgotten the third half of the team, Samantha, who was neither a Cheese nor an Onion. Samantha was, as far as I was aware, the only transgender detective in the Met and had only just joined the team. Although I didn't know her very well, she and I had one thing in common: we both did the Telegraph crossword.

The old DCI we had was a hard-drinking fella called George Becker, who was always in the pub with the Onions. The most amazing thing about the old DCI was how he managed to get home on his motorbike after eight pints of lager. As a result of their relationship with Becker, when he was in charge, the Onions held the power. The latest DCI, a lovely fella called Ben Richards, however, tended towards a more neutral position and life as a Cheese became easier.

Whichever way the wind blew, I tried to get on with the job and did my bit. I knew the Onions didn't trust me because I'd previously been at the Complaints Investigation Department, but that was no bad thing, as it meant they gave me a wide berth.

In fact, on my first day on the team, one of the older DSs, an alcoholic Scotsman called Jeff Smith, who was definitely one of the Onions, took me to the pub next door to buy me a drink and to sound me out.

"So, Nostrils, we're searching a house and you see me steal twenty quid, you know, find it under a bed and slip it in my pocket? What you gonna do?" Jeff asked, before I'd had my first sip of beer.

"Why, why are you asking me?" I enquired politely.

"'Cos I need to know what sort of man I'm working with, you know; are you going to cover my back?" Jeff explained.

"You steal a score during a search? What am I going to do? Is that what you're asking me?" I said.

Jeff nodded; his pint was already almost gone. I looked him straight in the eye.

"I'll nick you," I said, holding his stare.

He finished his pint, planted the glass very deliberately on the bar and said:

"Then I can never work with you, mate, sorry."

"Okay" I said, with as much *'like I could possibly give a fuck'* put into just two syllables as I could.

He defiantly turned his back on me and shook his head in a manner suggestive of such gravity that any bystander might have thought that I had just admitted to torturing puppies.

Strangely, and, I am certain, against both our expectations, as the years rolled by Jeff and I had actually got on all right. He was no more of a thief than I was, and for him, the question he had asked me had been about trust; for me, it was simply about integrity.

I can also add that Jeff was about the best office manager the Met ever had.

So AMIP Team 2 was a motley crew of seasoned detectives, which included a dozen alcoholics, one heroin addict, one guy who was addicted to co-codamol, a transsexual and more than a few nice, normal people. Whatever the mix, it somehow worked because, with the exception of the murder of a prison officer in October last year, we'd managed to solve every case we'd been allocated in the last three years.

Chapter 7

"Hi, guys," I said to Julie and Nicola as I took off my black 'Petticoat Lane' leather jacket and sat down at my desk.

"Is Ben about? I hear he's after me?" I asked.

"Think he's gone to the Yard," Nicola replied.

I logged on and double clicked to open up my email. The first email was from Wendy. It was just nine words long, repeated the phrase *'I love you'* three times and signed off with three kisses. The next email was from Nick Charles and it contained his mobile number.

I was vaguely aware that the girls were chatting about the concept of ordering clothes online and whether it was worth the hassle of going to a post office sending them back every time they didn't fit.

A good ten minutes passed, when I asked whether anyone was upstairs, by which I meant in the incident room. Nicola told me that Jeff was next door and had been since about two, as were most of the Onions, but that she thought a couple of the indexers were still about.

I stood up.

"Before you go upstairs, can we have a word, babes?" Julie asked, her voice containing a note of seriousness.

"Of course, what's the matter?" I replied.

"It's about your heart-throb," Julie said.

"For fuck's sake, I thought you were being serious," I said.

"No, we are," said Julie, and Nicola nodded.

"Go on," I encouraged them.

"It's about Sam. Someone's gotta speak to her," Nicola said.

"So Samantha is my secret heart-throb, brilliant!" I said sarcastically.

"Look, you're the only one who has any relationship with him, her," Nicola said.

"What fucking relationship?" I replied, genuinely curious to know what they thought was going on.

"You do the crossword thingy together," Nicola replied.

"Oh for fuck's sake, if I'm struggling with a clue I might ask her if she's done it. That hardly makes us a couple. You women should make more of an effort to befriend her, if you ask me," I said.

"We have tried, honestly, but I actually think he's, she's terribly awkward around the girls, even more so than she is around you boys. We have asked her out to lunch, we even invited her to an Ann Summers party but she's really not interested in getting to know us, or so it seems. We really have made an effort though; no one could say we haven't tried," Nicola pointed out.

"So you want me to speak to her about this? Not sure that's going to be the easiest conversation and besides, she hasn't really got to get on with any of you, just do her job," I said.

"Gosh, no, that's not the problem," Nicola said.

"Well, what is it then?" I asked, a little perplexed.

Nicola and Julie looked at one another; there was an unnaturally long pause, which I interpreted to mean that each was waiting for the other to speak first.

"Come on, guys, it can't be that bad, spit it out," I encouraged them.

"It's a toilet issue," Julie said.

"What? 'Cos she uses the Ladies?" I asked. "I don't think there's a lot I can do about that. As far as the job's concerned, Samantha is a female employee."

"She may want to be a lady, she may dress like a lady and she may want to be called by a lady's name, all that's fine, but my goodness, she evacuates like a man!" said Nicola.

"What?" I asked.

"Look, as you know, the toilets here are terribly small, intimate almost and there are three cubicles. If you're going to the toilet, etiquette dictates that you use one of the end cubicles, not the middle one. That way, if anyone else comes in, the 'other' end cubicle is free," explained Nicola patiently.

"And," Julie added, "as a general rule, we don't use the facilities for, how shall I put it? More than the simplest requirement. I mean, in an emergency we'd use the one in the basement, which is a single one. We'd never use the one on this floor for that."

"Am I right in thinking that Sam doesn't understand the rules?" I asked.

"No he, she doesn't. She parks her hairy arse in trap two, with her Daily Telegraph crossword on her lap, and bloody craps like a cart horse. She's in there for anything up to twenty minutes at a time," Julie continued.

"... and goodness me, she can go four times every morning," Nicola chimed in.

"... and she stinks the place out," said Julie.

"... and she doesn't clean up afterwards, clearly needs a course on how to use the toilet brush," Nicola declared, conclusively.

"What do you want me to do?" I asked, although I feared that I already knew.

"You need to speak to her," my friends said simultaneously.

"That's a really shitty thing to ask me to do," I said.

"Very funny but we'd really appreciate it" Nicola said, smiling sweetly.

"Okay, no problem; I can just imagine the conversation; it'll be a piece of cake," I replied, thinking exactly the opposite.

~~~

I went up to the incident room but nothing much seemed to be happening; there were just two colleagues still working, big Alex and little Alexandra. With Naobi, they made up the three indexers on our team and worked for the office manager, the aforementioned Jeff.

The two Alexes were nice people: big Alex was a Greek lady whose old man was a butcher and little Alexandra was a thirty-something, whose claim to fame, or notoriety, was that she was one of the survivors from the Marchioness disaster.

We exchanged a 'hi' but I sensed an atmosphere.

"Who's on call this week?" I asked, to no one in particular.

"I forget; it's on the board," big Alex replied.

"En taxei," I said, using one of a splattering of Greek words that Wendy had taught me.

On the white board to which big Alex referred, someone had written in the most perfectly crafted copperplate writing the unofficial murder squad motto, *'Our day starts when your life ends'*, which, although insensitive, was pretty typical of Old Bill humour. The thing was, when you spent every day dealing with murder, you couldn't connect to the event on a human level otherwise you'd go mental – so you distanced yourself.

What the makers of TV programmes and films never grasped was that, invariably, murder was just an assault that had gone wrong.

I saw that one of the teams based at Edmonton was the on-call team this week, which meant they provided the round-the-clock response to any potential murder.

If anyone was murdered in East London, the on-call team would go out immediately, secure the scene and undertake any urgent actions and we would pick the job up from them within twenty-four hours. Unless it was a very straightforward crime, like a domestic murder, where the on-call team might keep the case.

I remember late last year picking up what appeared to be a really straightforward case. A poor prison officer from Pentonville had been caught up in a robbery at an off-licence in Walthamstow; it appeared the suspect had mistaken him for an off-duty police officer, as he was wearing a white shirt and black trousers and boots, panicked and shot him in the head. Two suspects were in custody for a different robbery at another off-licence a few miles across London, which had occurred about an hour after the Walthamstow murder. Everyone assumed the two events were linked and our team was on call. We picked the job up and the DCI said we'd keep it as the suspects were already in custody. As it turned out, the two people in custody weren't connected in any way to the murder, but it took a week or two to work that out.

At the time, we didn't have the capacity to take on a difficult murder case and a separate robbery but we were stuck with both. As it transpired, we had yet to solve the prison officer murder, which was very unusual and largely because of the fuck-up right at the start in not assigning the case to a team with the appropriate capacity to pick it up. I'd been on a CID course at the time so I'd barely touched the job.

By the look of the board behind Jeff's desk, most of our team were free, or rather 'on in green', so we were in a good position to take the next murder.

The atmosphere upstairs was strained. The two Alexes were unusually quiet and I guessed they'd had a difficult day. There was no sign of either Naobi or the DCI, who had an office nearby, but I didn't ask.

As I turned back from the door I saw the back of one of the Onions walking away from the office and down the stairs. I knew that he would have been in the pub most of the afternoon and wondered why he'd come back and not just gone straight home. When I thought about it, his brief and unannounced visit to the incident room aroused my suspicion, so I discreetly manoeuvred to the window, overlooking the back yard.

Just as I thought, he'd come back to the office to pick up a logbook and keys to one of the pool cars and I now saw him get in and drive off in a red Ford Fiesta. You really weren't meant to take the police vehicles home unless you were on call and had the DI's authority. What's more, he'd have had at least six pints to drink. Should I do something? Yes. Would I? No. I mean, only a few hours before I'd been buying heroin from a dealer – we all did things that we shouldn't.

And that was all it took. Suddenly the addiction bit, and that is the best way to describe it – a bite. While it lasted, probably about a minute, all I could think about was how much I wanted H and where I could get some. In no time at all, my mind had worked it all out: where I'd get the money; what I'd tell Jackie; which dealers lived roughly on my way home; where I could score; where I'd rest up. I had it all worked out to a T. So much for giving up; in fact, fuck giving up, I'd give up another day, or week, or month or year.

I was still staring out the window when I realised the girls in the incident room were switching off and packing up. I glanced at the clock; it was five thirty, but at this time of year, because it had already been dark for over an hour, it felt much later than it actually was.

"You going next door?" I asked.

They shook their heads without saying any more. From their body language they clearly thought it a much better and smarter idea just to head off home.

"Night, ladies," I called out as they left.

I had gathered myself again and knew what I could do to take my mind off the bite. I picked up a phone.

"Hi hon, it's me; how are the girls?" I asked.

After a short conversation with Jackie during which I explained that I'd probably be in about nine because a couple of things had cropped up at the office, I hung up and made another call.

"Hi hon, it's me. Where are you?"

"Wherever you want me to be," the lovely Wendy replied.

Chapter 8

I was very happily married to Jackie.

Jackie was lovely, a great wife and we got on really well. More importantly than anything, we had two gorgeous girls, who were nearly five and three. Why then, for the last five years, had I risked losing them by having a relationship with a girl called Wendy? Well, if I knew the answer to that question, I'd be a smarter man than I was.

Wendy was white but with a beautiful Mediterranean olive skin, which she inherited from her Greek Orthodox mother. Her father was, of all things, a Church of England vicar in a small town in Norfolk. Wendy was twenty-eight, five foot ten inches tall, with a mop of long and wild jet-black hair, possessed the best and longest legs that had ever served the Commissioner, and I absolutely adored her. If I am being picky, the only thing I would have changed about her were her feet, they were a size eight!

One summer evening in February 1998, I'd met Wendy at an awards ceremony at Chigwell Police Club; we'd chatted for about an hour and I thought little more about it. At the time she was a PC at Barking. About a week later, through the internal post system I received an invitation to a *'Meal for Two'* at the Green Man in Toot Hill; the note specified a time but no details about from whom the invitation originated.

I confess to being quite intrigued and was delighted when I arrived to discover my mystery invitation had come from Wendy.

That was all it took; from that moment on we were a couple in just about every sense of the word. I met her friends, who knew I was married, and her family, who didn't. I spent at least two nights a week at her house and we got away a few times a year to B&Bs heated by log fires in secluded, romantic locations.

She lived in her own place in Leyton, a small terraced house just off the Lea Bridge Road. Last year, she'd been promoted and was now in charge of the Community Support Unit at Limehouse.

At first Jackie didn't know anything, then she suspected, and eventually I figured out she knew, but she never said a word. The thing was, we had a really nice little family. Our two girls were wonderful and happy, we had a nice if unpretentious house, just about enough money to live a decent life without having to watch every penny. We got on really well and even had a pretty decent sex life for a couple that had been married as long as we had. I guess Jackie had a simple choice: carry on or risk ending up with us getting divorced. Jackie chose to bury her head in the sand and, in some ways, I did too.

I had two lives and was careful never to let them cross.

Did I like lying to Jackie? No, I hated it. Why, then, did I do it? Because Wendy was just about everything a man could want and who the fuck gives that up?

As a general rule, the working week was for Wendy and the weekends for my family. I switched effortlessly from one existence to the other and rarely made a mistake. As the years rolled on, I acquired a completely new set of friends who knew me only as Wendy's other half. When I went to a work-related social function, I took Wendy, not Jackie, and eventually some people actually assumed Wendy was my wife.

I knew I wasn't doing the 'right' thing but in the strange world in which I'd worked all my adult life, it wasn't as unusual as you might think. Not that that fact made what I was doing right, it didn't, but frankly, I didn't really give a fuck what anyone else thought.

After a few years Wendy told me that she wanted to have a baby, which was going to be difficult as I'd had the snip and actually, more importantly, I didn't want any more kids. The thing was, I hadn't told Wendy I'd had the snip and fortunately there was no physical evidence of the operation. I knew I should have told her but the thing was, once you've not said anything straight away, you're sort of fucked if you declare it later because you look terrible.

If it ever came to the situation where Wendy insisted that she wanted a baby, I could at least for a couple of years pretend I was trying to father her child. For now, Wendy was on the pill anyway.

I'll never forget a conversation we had late one evening when I candidly told Wendy that I wasn't terribly keen on having any more kids. She said that in that case, one day she would have to leave to go off and have a family but that when she did, I wasn't to worry because she would come back to me.

It was difficult not to love Wendy, particularly when you factor in that she was nine years younger than I was and in the looks department well, magnificently out of my league.

~~~

That evening at Wendy's, I was restless and discovered an old bottle of scotch in one of the kitchen cupboards. I had a couple of large glasses and not being a particularly heavy drinker, it had gone to my head and I'd chilled, I mean like really relaxed. It wasn't the same as H but it wasn't a completely different feeling either.

Wendy was surprised, as she'd never seen me drinking scotch before – she wasn't half as surprised as I was.

We watched several taped episodes of *Friends* and had an early night but at three o'clock the withdrawal diarrhoea arrived, so I took two Imodium and made sure I wore my pants just in case.

While I sat on the toilet, I did take considerable solace that I'd managed a whole day without H. I decided that going-forward I needed to make sure that I had some scotch to help me through.

It seemed like I'd only just got back to sleep when I was woken by the ringing of my mobile phone.

With blurry eyes, I checked my watch; it was ten past five.

"Hello."

"Chris, Ben, we've got a job so get your team in as soon as possible, all of them."

From the tone in Ben's voice, I knew this was a pukka case.

"Received," I replied, mimicking the response all police officers use on their radios when they are assigned to a call.

And so our latest murder investigation began.

Chapter 9

I called my team as I drove in; it saved time. I got hold of Nicola and Julie but had to leave voicemails for Will, Pod and Samantha. A traffic report on the radio named several roads in Dagenham that were closed because of a police incident so I took a calculated guess that that was where the murder had happened.

I was first in, well sort of.

I went to the incident room to grab a logbook and noticed the sound of snoring coming from underneath Jeff's desk and returned a few moments later with a coffee for the office manager and then gently shook the duvet to wake him.

"Jeff, we've got a new job. Everyone's on their way in. There's a coffee on your desk and I've put your bottle of vodka back in the drawer."

The smell of stale exhaled alcohol was quite overpowering and while I wasn't bothered, I opened a nearby window so that it wasn't too noticeable when everyone else started coming in.

Jeff grumbled a couple of sentences of which I could make out just three words: 'Nostrils', 'coffee' and 'thanks'.

Over the next hour the team arrived. I don't know how late they were drinking in the Peacock but to their credit the Onions arrived as swiftly and as sober as everyone else. Before long, we'd got wind of the basics of the new job: it was a stabbing in Dagenham and there were no suspects. The on-call Edmonton team had picked the job up and their DI was on his way to Arbour Square to hand it over.

Just before nine we were called up to the incident room and were briefed by the on-call DI from Edmonton; by ten o'clock we were on our way to Dagenham.

Although Samantha had been on our team about three weeks, this was the first time we'd been properly alone together. I was determined to use the opportunity the half hour's drive would provide to get to know the newest and strangest member of my team.

If I am being honest, I wasn't entirely sure that I was all right with the cross-gender thing; I mean, how were the public ever going to take her seriously?

I knew there were some blokes who made very good women but by God, Samantha wasn't one of those. In fact, I'd have made a better woman. Physically, everything about Samantha was both very big and very male. She had, for example, a really square chin and massive shoulders; her hands were huge; her calves were well defined and really quite impressively muscular; and her feet were at least a size twelve. The only saving grace, and it was a very small one, was that her clothes were very understated and wouldn't have looked out of place at church on Sunday.

As I turned right out of the back yard of the nick, I started the conversation.

"How you settling in, Samantha? How long have you been with us now?"

"A month today, it's ... all right," she said slowly, too slowly.

"Oh that doesn't sound good," I said, picking up on the hook in her response, "Are there any problems?"

I glanced across at her; she was sitting with her large handbag on her lap in a very defensive, closed position. She was looking straight ahead and seemed to be mulling over how to respond. I knew better than to talk into the silence.

"Put it this way, Chris, this is the longest conversation I've had with anyone in a month."

How the fuck should I respond? I thought fleetingly about making a joke about us being a team of few words but plenty of action, but that would have just been crass. Should I ask her why she thought that was? But that was pretty fucking obvious. Then a better response came to me.

"That must be really difficult for you."

I took the next left.

"You've got no idea," she said.

"Well let's set that right, right now. Tell me about you, your life, your family, where you live. I want to know everything but I warn you ..." I paused, quite deliberately.

"Warn me about what?" Sam said, right on cue.

"If you pause, hesitate, deviate or repeat yourself, then I'll be in like a flash and bore you to death with the mundane details of my own life," I said. "Deal?"

"Deal" Samantha replied.

Over the next half an hour I learnt all about Samantha Cruikshank. How he'd been born into a military family who'd travelled the world. He'd been to schools in West Germany, Cyprus, Gibraltar and Hong Kong. His father had been the Regimental Sergeant Major in the Welsh Guards, his mother the perfect military wife.

Sam was an only child and wonderfully spoilt, but from the moment of his first consciousness realised that there was something wrong. By the time he was six, he realised what it was: he was a woman in a man's body. Throughout his childhood and adolescence he hid it well; the fact he was especially good at sports helped disguise his true feminine personality.

When he was about sixteen, his mother walked out and never returned – they were in Aldershot at the time.

He did what was expected and entered his father's regiment at the age of seventeen, just in time for the Falklands War, where he was on the ill-fated Sir Galahad when it was bombed by Argentine aircraft and thirty-two of his colleagues were killed. Luckily, he escaped largely uninjured. Well, physically uninjured, but he'd suffered from nightmares for years.

After that, his military career was largely uneventful and he joined the Met in January 1993, almost ten years to the day after I had.

He was a PC at Romford and then a DC at Ilford, where he applied for AMIP and was selected.

"It was then that I made the most difficult decision anyone can ever take. I decided to change my gender and to use the transfer to AMIP to emerge as the new, real me. I was bricking it. The job went into meltdown when I told them. At first, they said I wouldn't be able to have any contact with the public and then they said I could but only in a controlled environment, like at a police station.

"I had a terrific solicitor who fought my cause every step of the way and eventually, after about seven months, the job relented. Apparently, the government might be changing the Disability Discrimination Act to include people who are Trans. Wouldn't that be great?"

"Yeah, sure," I replied, with a tiny bit too much enthusiasm.

"So where were you for seven months?" I asked.

"Sick with work-related stress. I didn't want to be but that was the advice my solicitor gave in case the job were going to refuse my request. In which case, we'd have gone for constructive dismissal and the fact that I'd been sick with work-related stress would have come into play," Samantha replied.

"Listen, Samantha. I've worked with police officers of all colours, genders and sexualities. Most have been fantastic and a few absolutely fucking crap, and whether they were good or bad wasn't a result of anything other than their attitude. Some of the best officers I've known were black; some of the worst were black too. The only thing that really gets on my tits is when someone uses their colour, race or sexuality to blackmail the job. We'll have a deal: you judge me by my ability and dedication, not by whatever else you might hear about me, and I'll return the compliment and do exactly the same with you. Well, what do you say, partner?"

I stole a quick glance across at her face and knew instantly that I'd said the right thing.

"It's really nice to know that you don't have an issue with my trans. If I'm being honest, I wasn't entirely sure how you'd react. I mean you're very …"

Samantha hesitated.

"Very what?" I asked.

"Male," she replied.

"Listen, Samantha; whatever floats your boat, eh?" I replied.

It was really strange because I could almost feel my own attitude towards Samantha actually starting to change, as I was engaging with her.

I desperately wanted to ask whether she'd had any medical procedures to change her physically but I didn't quite feel confident enough. It was nice, though, that she was opening up and chatting. She'd even relocated her handbag from her lap to the back seat, which I took as a very positive sign.

"And are you pleased that you made the choice you've made?" I asked.

"I spent all of my life staring at other women, not because I fancied them but because I wanted to be them. The best way I can describe it is what it must be like to be a woman who can't have kids seeing other women with their babies. Chris, I am thirty-nine but I've never had a relationship with anyone because to do so would have been a lie, and besides ..." Sam paused, struggling to find the right words. "Chris, I've never even had a close friend, you know, someone you can share your secrets with, someone you can confide in, because before I did this, close relationships terrified me. If anyone did start to get close, I just bricked it. Ironically, now I've done it, no one wants to know me."

"Samantha, I hope you don't mind me asking but I'm trying to understand. Are you gay? I mean, do you fancy men or women?"

I immediately thought that I'd said the wrong thing as I felt Samantha tense up.

I pulled up at a red ATS and looked across. Samantha had turned away from me and was looking out of the side window. I guessed she was crying.

I wanted to apologise but a bit of me didn't think I should so I held my nerve. The lights changed and I set off, going up through the gears. The handbag was back on Samantha's lap and she was searching for something inside. She took out a packet of tissues and wiped her eyes.

"I didn't mean to upset you," I said, a good minute after my last question but in the heavy silence, it seemed like a lot longer.

"You didn't," Samantha replied.

I was confused.

"But you're upset," I said.

"No, you idiot, I'm happy," she replied and turned to face me.

She smiled, a mascara stain-striped smile, but definitely a smile.

"Happy? You fucking women are a nightmare. You're crying, Samantha," I said.

Samantha laughed.

"No, you don't understand. I'm happy because you're the first person that's ever asked me that question. You're the first person that's ever cared enough."

It was strange really but I found myself able to empathise with her, I really did. Not because I'd ever changed my gender but because I remembered so vividly my own early days in the job and how difficult I'd found it to be accepted. I recalled on several occasions wondering whether I should just resign. I too knew what it was like to be lonely, and to be blown up. Crikey, it actually seemed we had quite a lot in common.

"Well, you have a friend in me," I said, but as the words left my mouth I cringed because they sounded so corny. I also realised they were awfully close to the lyrics from the Toy Story song.

Samantha laughed again.

"Gee, thanks, Woody," she said, in a cartoon-style voice.

"Oh fuck off," I said, careful to make sure from the intonation in my voice that I was only joking. "I'd be happy to be your first ever friend; in fact, it would be a privilege."

"Thank you," she replied, "that means a great deal to me."

I smiled.

I thought this probably wasn't the best time to bring up her breach of toilet etiquette.

Chapter 10

Although Julie, who was the exhibits officer, came straight to the garage, we couldn't start the forensic examination of the black cab until the arrival of the Lab Sergeant.

The first decision to make was whether to examine the vehicle in situ or get it lifted and removed to a local nick and do the work there. It was under the pump roof but this wouldn't provide sufficient protection if it started to rain, which was a distinct possibility looking at the overcast sky. With that said, the black cab wasn't the scene of the attack, so what evidence was potentially going to be lost?

In any case, I didn't think we'd get much from a black cab. I mean, in the last week the vehicle must have carried a hundred different people, all of whom could have left their prints and other forensic traces; but from the story we'd heard, with the exception of the victim, none of them would have had anything to do with the crime.

I introduced myself to the uniform PC, a young black guy called Duncan, who was keeping the log and checked that the Photog had been and at what time. The Photog was the Photographic Officer. Duncan informed me she was there at five thirty. This was good because the photographs would accurately depict the scene at the time of the incident, that is to say, when it had been dark.

"How long you worked this ground?" I asked the PC.

"Five years; came here from Training School," he replied.

"Any idea what happened here?" I asked.

I always thought it was sensible to pick the brains of the locals; after all, this was their patch.

"He was a druggy apparently, so perhaps he owed someone, or he'd broken into someone's house to get some money for his next score," the PC suggested.

They were both sensible ideas; in fact, I really liked the second.

"Do you get many night time residentials, Duncan?" I asked, picking up on his burglary theme.

"Not really but you'd have to check with the BIU, sarge," he replied.

The BIU was the Borough Intelligence Unit, which when I first joined the job used to be called the Collator's Office.

"Does the victim's name mean anything to you? Gary Odiham?"

"Nothing, sarge."

"Any drug dealers live locally, Duncan?" I asked.

"Of course, this is Dagenham, but don't ask me where," he said.

It was a fair reply.

"Do street dealers frequent this area?" I asked.

"Never seen any; you used to get a few toms about half a mile down the road and they're never far from the drugs, are they? But we ran an op last year to move them on," he replied.

'Toms' was a very policey expression for prostitutes. As far as I knew, no one else used the term.

"The murder happened about two, didn't it?"

The PC checked his log.

"Yeah, the 999 call was at twenty past."

"Apart from the garage, would anything else be open that late on a Thursday evening around here?" I asked.

"No. Oh, perhaps the odd shebeen, they open and close quite often in the derelicts," he replied.

"But the IC3s use the shebeens don't they? An IC1 druggy wouldn't frequent one, would he?" I asked.

"Could do. If you don't mind me saying, sarge, that's a bit of an old-fashioned idea," the PC replied.

This information surprised me but I thought the fact it came from a black PC gave it more credibility.

"Interesting," I replied, "in my days on the beat, shebeens were the exclusive enclaves of the black, weed smoking community."

"Not any more, not in multi-cultural Dagenham," he declared, smiling.

"Cheers, Duncan, let me know if you think of anything else," I said.

"Will do," he replied.

I spoke to the manager of the garage on the phone, apologised for the inconvenience and explained that we would be out of his way as soon as possible. He was fine and said he'd be down by midday.

Julie seized the garage's CCTV tapes, which were in fact recorded on DVDs. We resisted the temptation to review them on the garage's systems because that always carried a risk that you might inadvertently erase or otherwise damage the recording. From the angle of the various cameras surrounding the garage, the footage should reveal the general direction the victim came from, which would be a good start. I dispatched Nicola to the Met Police technical laboratory at Denmark Hill to review the footage. It was only twenty minutes away.

I told Samantha to call the office and ask them to arrange to get several appeal signs made up and delivered – these were the big yellow billboards which ask for witnesses to contact police.

I didn't enter the scene, there was no need for me to do so, but the back door of the cab was still open and even from a distance, I could clearly see a pool of dark blood in the back footwell and a much smaller one on the ground, where the uniform officers must have dragged the victim to try resuscitation. The fact there was much less blood on the ground would suggest the victim had indeed died in the black cab. The body doesn't bleed when the heart has stopped pumping.

We heard the Lab Sergeant was on his way but I'd already taken the decision to relocate the black cab to a nick. I didn't think he'd disagree but I'd wait just in case.

If the victim's identity had been released, by now people would usually have started laying flowers and cards, probably by the short wall that separated the garage forecourt from the pavement. Our guy's name hadn't been published yet because we hadn't traced and notified a next of kin. What's more, with only a single photo ID to go by, we couldn't be absolutely sure that we knew who we had. We were probably right but only fingerprints would give us a confirmed match.

While we were waiting, the team were speaking to people passing by and local shopkeepers. They would be trying to glean any information that might be useful. This was the first time I'd seen Samantha out and about engaging with the general public. She seemed slightly uncomfortable but persevered nonetheless. People's reactions to her varied from slightly bemused to completely aghast, a few even walked off laughing. I felt genuinely sorry for her because she must have known what was going on behind her back but I also understood their reactions, which on another day and in different circumstances, would have been mine.

I wondered what the victim's family would think if they ever met her? Would their perception be that we weren't taking the matter seriously? Would Samantha's presence increase their anxiety even further?

I wondered why she didn't dress as a man at work and as a woman in her private life; surely that would keep everyone happy? I decided that when I got the opportunity to do so, I'd ask her.

Chapter 11

The DCI called us back for a team meeting at nine p.m.

In contrast to the last six weeks, the whole place was buzzing with activity – it was like a massive beast had awoken from winter hibernation. I always thought the first time I didn't get a thrill when we got a new job, it would be time to move on.

Exhibits were piled high on several of the desks and Julie worked swiftly to make sure they were prioritised, copied and logged in. Many of the team were writing on the green message forms and two or three were talking busily on the phone.

The activity was really good because it was helping to keep my mind off the gear. I'd had a few moments of panic and my bowels were really iffy but the fatigue, which by now should be setting in, appeared to be kept at bay by the adrenalin. I did a quick calculation; it was fifty hours since I'd last scored.

I was preparing for the anniversary appeal and completing a briefing, which detailed the information known so far, outlined the aim and parameters for the operation and assigned units to various locations; it was all pretty basic stuff. The hope was to trace and identify anyone who'd been in the vicinity at the time of the murder, which is why it is done twenty-four hours later. As the murder had been at two a.m., we'd take up positions from twelve through to four.

We would repeat the exercise a week later, then a month later and if necessary, a year later.

I always thought that a bit like house-to-house, we had a tendency to treat these anniversary appeals too lightly, to just go through the motions, rather than consider them the potential case solving opportunities they actually were; and I included myself in that critique.

First however, we had the team meeting, and it wasn't unusual for these to go on for ages. So twelve hours after it had all begun, we were all once again seated in the incident room on the top floor of Arbour Square, with most of the team occupying the same positions they had that morning.

Our DCI had attended the special, as he always did, and the meeting started with his update.

"The cause of death was a single blow delivered with force to the left side of his head with a sharp, thin, single-width implement – possibly a screwdriver. The implement entered the head through the ear cavity, which explains the lack of an obvious entry wound. The implement perforated to a depth of 4.25 centimetres, breaking through the temporal lobe and catching the basal ganaglia. There were no other recent injuries, so no evidence of a struggle. There was nothing under the fingernails; a few old scars – the most notable of which was on the left inner wrist, which would be consistent with a self-inflicted suicide attempt to slash his wrist. This wound was at least ten years old.

"He had a small DIY tattoo just above his right knee, three immaturely formed letters, G A Z, consistent with those normally done while in prison.

"Lots of evidence of recent intravenous drug abuse, along both arms and in the vicinity of the groin.

"Poor dental health but still had all of his teeth.

"Pathologist confirms time of death, bloods to tox.

"And the pathologist reckons the victim could have lived at the absolute maximum five minutes with that injury, but believes we should start to work on the basis that he died within ninety seconds. So the scene of the attack is close to that garage, chaps.

"Any questions?"

There were none.

"Right, what do we know about the victim, Pod?" the DCI asked.

Pod had been appointed the Family Liaison Officer so it was his role to trace and then deal with the victim's next of kin.

Pod was in fact Peter Dyson, an absolute diamond of a fella. He was nearing the end of his service and had already relocated his missus, Judith, to a villa on the Costa del Sol in anticipation of his imminent retirement. Pod was, in fact, his initials, his middle name being Oliver. Like most of the nicknames though, it had been established decades before, so no one gave it a second thought, all these years later.

Pod took a deep breath and spoke slowly, choosing his opening words carefully, which I anticipated meant he had made little progress; I was right.

"Not very much yet, I'm afraid, guv'nor. He left the bail hostel nine months ago and they had no useful information. He was paroled there after his last stint in prison, which was a nine-month sentence for burglary non-dwelling. Police Advisers were very helpful but the only relevant information they had was that when he was in prison he gave his mother as his next of kin.

"Well that's a start," said the DCI hopefully.

"Not really, she died when he was inside and the last note on the file before his release was the death message. Mum was a Glenda Beaumont; she was fifty-five years old and died of heart disease and liver failure, she lived on the Costa del Sol and passed away in a Spanish hospital – so if you'd like someone to go and make some enquiries I'd be happy to volunteer," Pod said.

There was a ripple of light laughter around the room. Pod already spent every long weekend and all his annual leave there.

"Do we know who she lived there with?" the DCI asked.

"No," replied Pod. "I've trawled his CRO file for any associates or previous addresses and there are a few actions but there's nothing recent."

CRO stands for Criminal Records Office and a CRO file would include details of every occasion a person had been arrested, charged and convicted.

"Tell me about his last arrest," asked the DCI.

Pod glanced at his notes.

"Burglary non-dwelling. Suspect entered Marks and Spencer in Ilford during opening hours, hid in the changing rooms and then stole suede jackets to the value of two thousand, one hundred pounds. Arrested for handling by an off-duty PC when he tried to sell him one of the jackets in a pub several hours later but admitted the burglary during interview; had four other offences taken into consideration.

"I left a message for the arresting officer and the DC that charged him to call me when they're next on duty."

Big Alex had taken a call while Pod was giving his briefing and I'd vaguely been aware that she was speaking to someone in whispered tones. She hung up as Pod concluded and then said,

"Sir, that was CRO; the prints confirm the victim as Gary Reginald Odiham."

The DCI nodded.

"Any more? CRIMINT?"

CRIMINT was the Met's criminal intelligence database.

"Sorry ,boss, I'll get onto that next, just haven't had a chance."

The DCI looked at his notebook and called out the next item on his list.

"House-to-house? CCTV? Nicola, do you want to start with the CCTV from the garage?"

"I took the CCTV ROM from the garage to Denmark Hill, got some copies run off and I've spent the day reviewing it. There are six cameras around the garage at various angles and the system records a frame from each alternatively, so it's not a continuous film. As a result, when you watch the footage from one camera, the film jumps about two seconds each time.

"You can see the victim in shot for a total of six seconds. He enters the garage through the 'in' entrance having crossed the main road from the opposite footway; when you first see him, he is just crossing the white lines in the middle of the carriageway; he is running and holding his head with his left palm held tight against his ear; he is wearing a big blue jacket, jeans and white trainers.

"The victim climbs straight into the rear of the black cab parked at pump six. When he gets in the cab he leaves the back passenger side door slightly open and thirty seconds later, the cabbie returns and gets in.

"The cabbie didn't notice that the back door is slightly open until he's inside. He gets out a couple of seconds later, walks around the front of the cab and opens the back door, which had been ajar. You see him have a quick conversation with the victim and then he makes a call on his mobile phone, which he gets out of his right jacket pocket. Eight minutes later police arrive and remove the victim from the cab and commence resuscitation."

"Nice work," the DCI said.

One of the Onions spoke next.

"We got all the CCTV within half a mile in every direction but it only covers the main roads. There's a Barclays Bank about two hundred yards west in Dock Lane, so if he's come that way, we'll spot him. But if he's come down one of the two side roads opposite, they're residential, and we've not spotted anything. Nothing yet on house-to-house, guv'nor."

The DCI asked me for an update from the garage, which didn't add anything of particular note and I outlined the plans for the anniversary appeal.

The DCI went round the room but no one else had anything to add. It was probably the shortest 'end of the first day' debrief I'd ever attended, which indicated that we'd not got very far despite twenty of London's best detectives spending the last twelve hours on the case.

It was all rather disappointing but I hoped the anniversary appeal would yield something more tangible.

Chapter 12

Again I paired myself with Samantha and so, for the second time in consecutive days, we were driving back across East London together and we chatted all the way.

I learnt that she was spending a year as a woman, which she had to do before she was allowed to start the sex change procedure; was attracted to men but had never been in a proper relationship with anyone; lived alone in a flat in Forest Gate; had lost contact with her father years ago; and was really quite lonely.

"My life's pretty shit, Chris," she declared.

Her use of the word 'shit' reminded me that I had to discuss something with her, but I just couldn't bring myself to initiate the conversation because she seemed so genuinely happy, so I let the moment pass.

The thing that Samantha wanted more than anything else was to be accepted as a woman. She knew people laughed at her, she knew it was going to be tough but she'd never imagined quite how her colleagues would react.

"When I was a male PC at Romford and a DC at Ilford, I got on with everyone. I am a nice person, genuinely interested in other people. I try to be kind and helpful. I wasn't the life and soul, I wasn't a great storyteller, but my colleagues liked and respected me. We went for a beer after work most days, and during work occasionally. I ran the lottery and was always the one who arranged the social activities and all that. Then I came to Arbour Square and it was like running straight into a brick wall. No one said a word to me, not even a hello or a goodbye – it was vile."

I listened but felt really awkward and very guilty. Sam was on my half of the enquiry team and was my responsibility – that she felt this way was at least partially my fault.

"Listen, Samantha, I'm sorry, I really am. I don't think anyone's being deliberately cruel I just think they're …"

I corrected myself.

"… we were, are, unsure how to act around you. Personally, I was so afraid of offending you in some way, I thought it safer to say nothing. I realise that was stupid. I am sorry but I'm learning too here, every day's a school day."

And then I did something that even surprised me; I put my hand on Samantha's knee to demonstrate that I was completely genuine. Then the memory hit me so hard it took my breath away and I heard myself gasp for air.

A long time ago, when I was a young sprog at Stoke Newington and I felt as lonely and out of place as Samantha now did, a colleague had done to me the kindest of gestures and simply placed her hand momentarily on my knee, and it was the most powerful and reassuring signal I had ever received.

Suddenly, I was back in time at that dive of a pub in Hackney, and my Street Duties instructor Dawn had unexpectedly joined me for a drink after she'd had her nose broken. She had put her hand on my knee and although I didn't realise it at the time, at that moment my life changed.

Now I had passed the gesture on to Samantha and I hoped it changed her life for the better too.

"Chris, Chris, Chris …"

"Sorry, Dawn, I was miles away?"

"Dawn?"

"Samantha, sorry, I'm a complete idiot," I said apologetically.

"No, Chris, you're lovely and I just don't understand why everyone hates you."

The hurt must have shown on my face because Samantha quickly tried to salvage the situation by adding,

"Well, not everyone, not your team, they love you."

I started to laugh.

"You are fucking tactless," I said, hiding very well just how hurt I felt.

"Do you know what they call you behind your back?" Samantha asked.

Oh fuck me, the conversation just gets better and better, I thought.

I started to laugh again, though more out of nervous anticipation about the revelation that I was about to be told than from any amusement.

"Nostrils," Samantha said.

"Yes?"

"Yes, what?" Samantha said.

"Sorry?" I asked.

"Nostrils."

"What?" I enquired, politely but with growing frustration.

"Chris, they call you Nostrils," Samantha clarified.

"That's my nickname; in fact, I reckon about half the people I know in the job don't actually know my proper name. I've been called Nostrils since the day I left Training School," I said.

"Is it because of your broken nose and that scar on your head?"

"For fuck's sake, Samantha, you're killing me. What obviously broken nose?" I asked, a little disingenuously as I did, in fact, have a broken nose."

Samantha dithered.

"Well, you know, the um, the thingy, the bit in the middle, well it isn't, is it?"

"If, my dear woman, you are referring to my displaced lower lateral cartilage, then you are quite correct in observing that it resides in my right nostril."

Samantha laughed, not a silly girlie giggle but a deep manly chuckle, which wouldn't have sounded out of place coming from a strapping six-foot-two-inches guardsman.

"Although I did, as a matter of fact, injure my nose on duty, that is not why I am called Nostrils. I acquired that tag because on my first day on division, a blagger discharged a sawn-off shotgun at my head from about five yards."

It was further than that but every time I'd told the story the distance got shorter.

"Did it hit you?"

"Of course fucking not, you get hit from five yards with the shot from two barrels of a sawn-off, you don't look this fucking handsome," I said.

"So it just hit you in the nose, then?"

"No, it didn't hit me in my nose; it peppered my titfer though."

"Christ, that must have hurt," Samantha said, grimacing.

"What? Why? What?" I asked.

"Being hit in the titfer," Samantha replied.

"Samantha, do you know what a titfer is?" I asked incredulously.

I knew it was a fairly old-fashioned term but surely she knew to what I was referring?

"Well, I assume you're talking about your, you know …"

"Samantha, your titfer is your helmet; P O L I C E helmet," I added, just in case she got the wrong end of the stick again.

"Ohhhhhh," she said.

"So how did you injure your nose?" she asked.

"What?"

"You said you did your nose on duty, what happened?" Samantha said.

"I got head-butted," I said.

"Prisoner?"

"Sergeant" I replied – this really was going to confuse her.

"Samantha, it's a long story. A prisoner got assaulted, well, a bit of excessive force, and the sergeant thought the injuries we'd suffered weren't quite enough so before the FME arrived, he head-butted me. It was a long time ago now, in the early eighties, when things were done differently."

I looked at Samantha to assess her reaction. Had I shared too much about something best forgotten?

"I don't really understand," she said, which was just fine.

"Anyway, so that's why you're called Nostrils," she declared, as if she'd finally reached the right answer.

I didn't have the heart to tell her she was still wrong.

"That's right, that's why I'm called Nostrils," I agreed.

I'd decided Samantha wasn't the brightest member of my team, but as her real personality started to emerge, I actually thought she'd be great fun to work with.

Chapter 13

It was pouring, I mean really heavy, unrelenting rain, which fell all night and the six of us – Julie, Nicola, Pod, Samantha, Taff and me – got absolutely drenched.

We stopped and engaged everyone who passed through Dock Lane; if they were in a car, with the assistance of some local uniform guys, we pulled them to one side and spoke to the driver and occupants. We even stopped the buses and did a quick shout out to the passengers, asking whether anyone had been on the bus twenty-four hours earlier.

At the time of the murder, which we thought was a little after two o'clock, I did what I always did and took a small time out to myself to walk the scene, trying desperately to put myself in the shoes of either the victim or the suspect.

Why had the victim run to the garage? I knew the superficial reason was to obtain help. That was the wrong 'why' question. The right 'why' was 'why had he run to the garage to get help, as opposed to anywhere else?' If he died within ninety seconds running distance, what was the furthest he could be in any direction from the garage? Ten minutes later, having walked in every direction, I had my answer.

If the victim had been stabbed in Dock Lane there were other places he'd probably have gone for help before he got to the garage; to the west was a twenty-four-hour cab office and to the east was an all-night convenience store. Surely he'd have gone into these first, why run past them to the garage? So I assumed for the point of the exercise that the victim wasn't attacked in Dock Lane. That left two residential side roads, Palmerston Road and Gladstone Road, which were very roughly opposite to the entrance and exit to the garage; these roads went south-west and south-east respectively.

I walked down both and noticed that because of an early curve and the building line at the junction, the garage was barely visible from more than a few yards into Gladstone Road. In contrast, the garage could be seen from a long way along Palmerston Road. From this I concluded, if the victim didn't know the area well and was injured and panicking, he'd have more likely come from Palmerston Road than Gladstone Road.

When I got back to the others, I asked whether anyone knew if there'd been a shebeen and Julie said a few people had mentioned the presence of one about a hundred yards down Palmerston Road on the left.

Was that a lead? The victim was white; did white guys go to shebeens? According to the local PC who I spoke to earlier, they did. If our victim was in the shebeen when he was stabbed, then that was our primary crime scene.

I wandered back down Palmerston Road and found what was probably the shebeen, now a boarded-up derelict Victorian terraced house at number 73 – although now there was no sign of life at the premises. I clocked the number and thought I'd have a word with the DCI about getting a warrant. I'd also do some CRIMINT work to see if there were any recent reports linking any named individuals to it.

I called the anniversary appeal off at a quarter past three. We were, to a man, woman or indeterminable other, utterly soaked through.

We'd stopped and spoken to seventy-two people and only twelve had been through the scene twenty-four hours earlier and not one of them had any information to assist our enquiries.

Several of the local residents said they appreciated our presence, especially as it had apparently prevented the shebeen from opening for the first time in several weeks.

When I pulled the plug, everyone scuttled off to their cars and I was just a little relieved that Samantha had jumped in with Nicola and Julie. I thought I was going back on my own when Taff asked whether I was going his way; I nodded and smiled, as I'd be glad of the change of company.

Unsurprisingly, Taff was of Welsh stock. He was in his late fifties and a really nice, genuine guy. He was happily married with several grown-up kids, one of whom was an actor on Eastenders. He was the only uniform officer on the team, having never qualified as a detective, but he was as good an investigator as anyone else, except me of course.

I had a chat with Taff about Samantha and explained how isolated she felt and whether we could all do more to make her feel one of the team.

"I think you've got an uphill task there," Taff said.

"Do you not approve?" I asked.

"Me, no, I couldn't care less, but most of the team are of the opinion that he shouldn't be dealing with the public. They are concerned what a victim's family would think if they knew their son's murder was being investigated by a bloke wearing a dress."

I felt a pang of guilt because I'd shared these reservations.

"What do you think about that?" I asked.

"Well, go back a generation they'd have made the same argument about a homosexual investigating a murder, wouldn't they?" he replied.

"Do you know what they call him?" Taff said.

I shook my head.

"It," he said.

"Sorry?"

"Not Samantha, or he or she, but 'it'," Taff explained, "and they're up to something, I don't know what, but they're up to something and I think Samantha is the target."

"It'll be a prank, right? Any ideas?"

"No, I just overheard a few words here and there."

"Is there anything I can do?" I asked.

"I don't think so, Chris. You'll be the last to know, I assure you. They really don't trust you an inch," Taff said.

"I'm just fine with that," I said.

"I don't blame you," Taff replied.

I was actually quite worried about Samantha. She was such a coiled spring of emotions and I knew the last thing she needed was to be the subject of a cruel, thoughtless practical joke that focused on her trans status. I decided to speak to the DCI in the hope that he would put the word around that they were to stop whatever they were going to do.

We got back to Arbour Square at four, ignoring every red light or other obstruction on the way.

I was absolutely shattered, we all were and wet through, too. I briefly toyed with the idea of crashing at Wendy's because it was half the distance home but that would be a waste of a night away.

We chucked everything on the desks and Nicola and Julie went to the kitchen to make some hot drinks. We still had a few things to write up and I wanted to drop the DCI an email so he knew what had happened, as none of us were going to be back before lunchtime.

I went upstairs to the incident room but resisted putting the overhead lights on as I guessed Jeff would be kipping under his desk. I picked up the top couple of documents that were in the in tray and took them away to have a quick look through while I went to the toilet – I did like having something to read.

The top piece of paper was an action, which Pod had returned as complete. It was to obtain the victim's CRIMINT record, which was attached. I casually leafed through the eight-page printout.

The description page matched what we knew: male; IC1, born 1967 in Whipps Cross, London, slim build, tattoo G A Z on right thigh.

The latest entry on the next page referred to an unsuccessful search at an address in Bethnal Green by the local Crime Squad yesterday. My eyes raced over the details to find the address: 127 Attlee House – a flat with which I was well acquainted.

My stomach turned to water.

Chapter 14

I knew this was a problem, a really big problem. I could feel panic rising and suddenly thought about how much I needed to score.

I reminded myself several times to work through the problem. After all, I had been seriously in the shit a few times in my career but each time I'd managed to survive. What would happen next?

Pod's action result would go to the office manager who, having read the CRIMINT report, would raise further actions. The first and most important would be to examine the victim's home address at Attlee House for evidence to assist the murder investigation. The whole flat would be searched and forensically examined.

I realised that my prints were bound to be in the flat and tried hard to remember what I'd touched. Obviously they would be on four twenty pound notes which I'd given him but that money was likely to be long gone by now. And then I remembered that when he invited me to sit down, I'd picked up a closed laptop and placed it on a side table to make room on the settee. My prints would be on that laptop for sure. I thought again, really focusing, but couldn't remember touching anything else. And then I had another thought and immediately wished I hadn't. The victim's phone could be linked to mine, as it was how I contacted him. Fuck, fuck, fuck and fuck!

The second action Jeff will raise will be to speak to the DS who conducted the search and of course Nick Charles will refer whomever he speaks to straight to me.

If this happened, what was likely to be the consequence?

The job would discover that I was at a drug dealer's flat when a search warrant was executed. They would learn I had lied about cultivating him as an informant to evade being searched and possibly arrested. Having checked my personal file, they would soon realise I was there to purchase a Class A drug, heroin. I would be suspended and medically retired rather than sacked because of the back story to my addiction. I'd likely lose Wendy and with no money coming in, I'd struggle to pay the mortgage, which would seriously impact upon Jackie and the girls.

If things went really badly, I could end up in prison for conspiracy to supply, misconduct in a public office and perverting the course of justice.

This was a fucking nightmare.

If only I'd decided to give up the gear before I went to his flat yesterday? Why, oh why, did I leave it those twenty-four hours? But deep down I knew the answer – I'd only decided to quit because I'd escaped such a close shave.

Then I saw the briefest glimpse of hope. The victim had been in possession of keys, these would be to the flat in Attlee House. They would be at Arbour Square somewhere, perhaps on Julie's desk waiting to be logged in. If I could get hold of them, I could get to the flat before it was searched and make sure that my prints weren't on the laptop – that would at least be a start.

I finished in the toilet and made my way back to the office where the three that remained, Julie, Nicola and Samantha, were sipping steaming tea from polystyrene cups and completing various bits of paperwork. I glanced at Julie's desk, which was piled high with exhibits, but couldn't see any keys. I looked again for any sign of the victim's clothing but to no avail. Maybe the exhibits from the hospital hadn't been handed to her yet?

"You got the victim's clothes yet?" I said to Julie, with as much innocence and nonchalance as I could muster.

"Yeah, they're covered in blood so they're in the drying room downstairs," she replied.

"Is the bus pass there? I was going to have a gander?"

"It's in that pile on Nicola's desk. The bag's not sealed so you can have a look but do us a favour and put some gloves on and photocopy it for me, if that's all right, babes?" Julie said.

It was under Nicola's discarded coat but I found it quickly; it was next to both the phone and the keys. I was desperate to know whether the bags containing the phone and the keys had been sealed but couldn't do so without looking conspicuous. I realised that if they were sealed, my plan would become considerably more difficult.

I photocopied the bus pass as Julie had requested and confirmed the picture on the photo ID was the guy whose address I had been at only yesterday. When I returned to the office I had one intention, to get everyone to go home as soon as possible. It was already nearly four thirty so time was running out.

"Listen, guys, let's call it a night. We're not going to be any use tomorrow unless we get home now and get some sleep," I said, in a voice that indicated this was an order not a request.

"I should get these exhibits done," Julie protested.

"I'll give you a hand," Nicola said helpfully.

"Guys, seriously. Go home. The exhibits can wait."

This was Julie's first job as exhibits officer and she knew she should log the exhibits tonight, but I could see in her tired eyes that my proposal was appealing.

"Go," I implored.

Samantha stood up and grabbed her jacket.

"I don't need to be told again," she said.

"All right," said Julie cautiously.

"Come on, fuck off you lot. I'll follow you out," I said.

"Do you want a lift to your car?" Samantha asked.

"No, I'll be all right. I need to go to the loo again, anyway," I said.

From the small toilet window, I watched as the three girls left through the back yard; it seemed to take them an age.

I went back to Nicola's desk and picked up the phone – the bag was sealed; the keys, however, weren't. This was quite usual as whoever had seized them realised that they'd soon need to be used to open the victim's home address and had done the sensible, but not strictly the orthodox, thing.

The way I saw it, the phone was potentially the biggest threat and had it been unsealed, I would have simply immersed it thoroughly in water to make sure it was beyond repair and therefore incapable of giving up its secrets to a forensic examination. Then I would have dried it thoroughly and put it back. As it had already been established that the phone wasn't working, no one would have been any the wiser.

Now, however, if I broke the bag open and removed the phone and put it into a new evidence bag, the new seal number wouldn't match the original, which would have been recorded several times by now in various indices. It would be blatantly obvious to everyone that it had been tampered with, which would cause grave suspicion; someone might even question why I'd sent everyone home and was the last to leave.

The only option was to take the phone, evidence bag and all. Then we would simply have a missing exhibit, which wouldn't be the first time, rather than one that had been tampered with. I also realised that as I'd picked up the photo ID, I was bound to be asked whether at that time I clocked the mobile phone and I'll say 'no, it definitely wasn't there'. That way, everyone will think it went missing before it got to Arbour Square.

I took the phone, slipped the keys in my pocket and set off. Unlike everybody else, I still had work to do.

Chapter 15

This was going to be tight. By the time I got back to my car at the gym and got going, it was ten to five. I had to get over to Bethnal Green, wipe the laptop clean, dispose of the phone, which would mean a trip into the City, return the keys to the evidence bag and fuck off before the team started arriving at about seven.

I drove quickly but sensibly, as I didn't want a tug from some eager but bored night duty PC. I risked parking on the estate as there was no one about and I was pretty certain there weren't any CCTV cameras in the vicinity.

I checked the landing to the flats carefully before ascending the stairs because I wanted to make sure the coast was clear. It was.

As it had been the day before, the security door gaining access to the ground floor was broken, which made life easier. As I ascended the stairs I took the keys out of my pocket and noticed how brand new they were. Suddenly, I worried that these weren't going to be the right keys, but when I saw the new front door it all made sense. Of course, the police had broken his original door and as no drugs were found, they would have had to get it repaired. These were the keys to the victim's new front door.

I pulled on a pair of blue plastic gloves, never the easiest thing to do, particularly when you're in a hurry.

The lights were on throughout the flat and as I entered I also noticed the heating was on full blast.

I checked my watch as I went in – it was five twenty.

Before I'd left Arbour Square, from the cupboard under the kitchen sink I had collected a duster and polish spray and as I entered, I carefully replayed the events from the day before, almost in slow motion in an attempt to identify anything I might have touched.

The first thing would have been the silver metal doorknocker on the old door but that was now, fortunately, long gone. Apart from the laptop, I hadn't touched a thing in the lounge but I had definitely touched the wall near the kitchen as I'd entered because I'd had to step round a pile of dirty clothes. So I wiped down a large section of the hall wall.

After I did this, I saw the laptop, which had previously been in the lounge, now at the foot of Gary's bed. I gave it the attention it deserved. When I put it down, it gleamed like new.

The whole process had taken no time at all when the realisation hit me. Gary hadn't been arrested because the officers who searched this flat hadn't found any drugs. Yet I knew there were drugs here because I'd just purchased ten bags so the gear must still be hidden in the flat.

There were two basic options: leave now or find the drugs. If I found the drugs, I wouldn't have to worry about giving up for another two weeks, particularly as I could really cut down on the amount I was taking. I decided that was in fact the right way to go about giving up. A small reduction over the next two or three weeks was probably the best medical option to take as my body would have time to adjust.

I could already feel myself getting excited.

I didn't bother going into the lounge as I knew the drugs weren't in there because after I'd given him the money, he'd left the room to get to his stash. In such a small one-bedroom flat, knowing the drugs weren't hidden in the flat's largest room, the lounge, was a good head start. What's more, the officers had missed them yesterday so they weren't going to be anywhere obvious so I could eliminate looking in obvious places like the toilet cistern or under the bed.

It took longer than I thought but I found them, and it was a clever hiding place. The flat was heated by several storage heaters, which had probably been installed twenty years previously. These were solid units and I examined the one in the bedroom, which sat immediately under the only window. I discovered that with the right implement and the removal of two screws, you could drop the bottom metal plate off.

Gary had been clever enough to keep the matching implement, a screwdriver with a strangely shaped, unconventional head, in the kitchen next to an open thirteen-amp plug for a kettle so it looked like he was in the middle of changing the fuse. Only upon closer examination, I noticed the screwdriver would be no use on the plug.

I lay parallel to the bed and on my back to remove the base, which was only six inches above the carpet, so the screwdriver had to be used at a slight angle. Nothing about this was easy or obvious, which added to its effectiveness as a hiding place.

When the base dropped down so did part of a white carrier bag, which had been concealed in the gap. I pulled the bag out and opened it up. Inside I saw hundreds of small clear plastic bags each containing a tenth of a gram. This was quite an amazing discovery. I was looking at thousands of pounds worth of heroin. I knew from experience that drug dealers like Gary just didn't trade in such volumes. I'd have been surprised if he'd had more than thirty bags at any one time.

I felt under once more to make sure I'd got everything and my fingers touched various pipes and wires. As I went to remove my hand, a finger caught against something hard, which moved in response to my touch. I narrowed my hand by pulling together the tips of my fingers, turned it about one hundred and eighty degrees and felt again. I was touching a handgun. I rolled over onto my back and gently tried to manoeuvre the item out. I was really careful as I had no idea if it was loaded or whether the safety catch was on.

After a few twists and turns, the firearm emerged and I studied it carefully. What I had in my hands was a silver handgun with a distinctive star shape on the black plastic handle cover. There were other markings but I couldn't make them out in the light.

I put the handgun down on the floor, shut my eyes and thought.

If I put the weapon back the chances were my colleagues wouldn't find it later in the day. After all, they would be searching a victim's home address, not looking for drugs or other illicit items. Quite understandably, they wouldn't be in the mindset to unscrew the bottom of storage heaters.

For two reasons the weapon had to be found: one, to take it off the street, and two, to enable it to be test fired to establish whether it had been used in any other shootings or murders. But if I left the handgun in a more obvious place, someone might question why the Crime Squad from yesterday hadn't found it? No, hang on, I realised, Gary could have removed the handgun after the police had left. Yes, that made sense.

I was still wearing my gloves so there was no chance my dabs were on the handgun.

I did briefly flirt with the idea of taking possession of the handgun. The Home Secretary, David Blunkett, had just announced a firearms amnesty and I thought that perhaps I could use this to hand the handgun in. In the end I decided against it because I thought of an easier solution. I put it under the pillow on Gary's bed and replaced the bottom of the heater. I put the screwdriver back in the kitchen and stuffed the plastic bag containing the gear into my coat pocket.

I was standing in the hall and about to flick the light switch off when, for the second time in two days, I heard a very unwelcome knock from the front door.

My fingers stopped literally touching the switch. I didn't move but listened carefully. Only a few seconds passed and there was another knock, this time harder.

I checked my watch; it was twenty to six.

Bang, bang, bang

Someone was pounding a fist on the door.

"Gary, you cunt, open the fucking door. We know you're in there, we just saw you through the cunting letter box."

The voice was male and probably white.

"Gary, you'd better open the door otherwise pop, pop, pop, pop, pop ..."

Chapter 16

I was in a really bad situation and time had run out. Unless I fancied being shot by people who were clearly mistaking me for Gary, I had to show out as a police officer. It was the only way I was going to extricate myself from this situation.

Someone was kicking the front door now.

"Open the door, cunt," said the voice.

I heard the letterbox click open and without saying a word, I stepped into the middle of the hall and held my warrant card forward so it would be clearly visible through the letterbox. I saw the letterbox drop shut and heard the sound of running footsteps disappearing into the distance. It seemed like my bluff had worked and I breathed out long and hard.

I decided to give it a good ten minutes, but I actually waited about ninety seconds. I locked the front door with shaking hands and walked very, very nervously to the car. The coast was clear and I figured those that only a few minutes previously had been at Gary's door, were now several miles across town.

I had so many drugs, they didn't fit into my hiding place in the Golf, and so I pushed the plastic bag under the driver's seat.

I then took a small but calculated risk. It was just before six o'clock so I knew the uniform shifts would be changing from nights to early turn, inside knowledge that influenced my decision.

I drove into the City to a deserted London Bridge and pulled over in the bus lane exactly halfway across the river. I tore open the exhibits bag containing the victim's mobile telephone, got out of my car and subtly dropped it over the side of the bridge and into the middle of the Thames. No one was ever going to find that again.

Then I did something that took me completely by surprise. I leaned back into the car, took out the carrier bag full of drugs from under the driver's seat and dropped it over the side of the bridge. Before the bag had fallen far, a gust of wind blew it horizontally for a few seconds, which opened it up and scattered the numerous smaller bags across a wide area of the river, where they gently floated towards Charing Cross on the incoming tide. Finally, I dropped the can of polish into the river.

I jumped back into the car and drove to the south side of the bridge, where I was held by a red ATS. I used the delay to tear the plastic evidence bag that had contained the phone into about ten different pieces and then as I drove on, every so often I threw a piece out of the window.

At six thirty I pulled up at the gym car park and by quarter to, had wiped the keys free of prints and placed them back in their unsealed evidence bag on Nicola's desk.

I sat down exhausted, crossed my arms on my desk and rested my head on them.

The last thing I thought before I dropped off to sleep was happiness, genuine undiluted happiness, because I knew from my unplanned gesture on London Bridge that no matter how hard the road ahead would be, I was off the gear.

~~~

Of course, I woke up less than fifteen minutes later when everyone started coming in. I had a few moments of panic because I realised the keys were still in my pocket but I was able to put them back just in time.

Still half asleep, I relocated to my car, where I started the engine, put the heater on, leaned the seat back, tuned into Radio Two and fell back to sleep for another couple of hours listening to Dawn Patrol with Sarah Kennedy. When I woke, I popped into the gym to have a quick shower, after which I thought I'd relax in the sauna, where I fell asleep for another hour. Fortunately, and because I thought that might happen, I'd left the door slightly ajar so at least I didn't dehydrate and die.

When I came to, I realised I'd forgotten one vital thing; I hadn't spoken to Alphabet, and so I immediately made the call. After a few minutes' conversation, I was utterly convinced I'd gleaned enough information about Nick Charles's up and coming board for SO13 to put him into a lifetime of indebtedness to me.

I called Nick but it went straight to voicemail so I left a message telling him to 'contact me on this number straightaway'.

I went back to the office, very conscious that I was wearing the same shirt and underwear I'd slept in.

I walked in. Taff was already in, which impressed me; he couldn't have got more than four hours' sleep but apart from him, the place was empty.

"Hi, mate, where is everyone?"

"Morning, Nostrils; they're doing the victim's HA; Pod got it off CRIMINT in the end," Taff replied.

I glanced over to Nicola's desk and noticed the keys were gone.

'Fuck me, that was close,' I thought.

I got a text from Wendy asking if I'd be around later and as I was replying I got one from Jackie asking where I was, and was it anything to do with the murder in Dagenham that had been in the news. After I'd texted Wendy with a 'possibly, hon x', I replied to Jackie with a 'yes, hon x'.

I then got a '?' back from Jackie and I re-read the message to realise I'd sent the wrong message to the wrong person which sort of meant I'd be at Wendy's later which would be a third night running away from home. Mind you, wherever I went I wouldn't be home until really late.

At that moment my phone rang.

It was Nick Charles, so I asked him to hold the line, as I needed to take the call in private, and headed back to the yard.

"Hello, mate. Thanks for calling me back," I said.

"Calling you back? Have you called?" he said.

"Yes, I left you a message."

"Oh, sorry, mate, I haven't picked it up yet, I'm crap with messages. Can we meet? I've got a problem," Nick said.

Shit! He'd found out about Gary Odiham. Although I thought it was a positive thing that he wanted to meet me to discuss it rather than just spill the beans.

"Do you know Stefano's? It's just down the road from your place," Nick suggested.

"We can't go there mate, it's always full of Old Bill. How about Victoria Park, the tea hut on the south side?" I proposed.

"One hour, mate?" Nick suggested.

"One hour," I replied.

Chapter 17

"Nostrils," called Jeff, from the top of the fire escape, as I hung up.

"Yes, mate," I called back.

"You want a tea?"

"Yes, mate," I replied.

"I'm making one for the DCI, he wants to see you. I'll put yours in his office."

Normally such a request wouldn't bother me the slightest, but this morning I was a bag of nerves.

I was very lucky. The vast majority of people for whom I'd worked over the years were as good as gold and I included Ben Richards in that assessment.

A white male some six or seven years older than I was, Ben was an experienced detective who'd worked his way up through the ranks. More impressively, he was a rugby union man through and through, a season ticket holder at Saracens and still playing for Eton Manor Vets. The more I worked with him, the more I liked him.

I decided to take the initiative and opened the conversation as soon as I walked in.

"Hello, boss. I gather you had a difficult Christmas."

I was referring to rumours circulating that his girlfriend had turned up on Boxing Day at his home address to confront his wife. He looked up from his desk where he was writing up his Decision

Log and then put his pen down in a gesture that suggested he wanted to focus on our conversation. I realised that if he continued the conversation about his Christmas, I was probably okay.

"I've moved out," he said, and inwardly I breathed a huge sigh of relief.

"How do you feel?" I asked.

Over the next ten minutes, I listened as the DCI recounted a sorry tale, but I did learn that the part of the account that I'd heard about a brick through the window was fabrication, or at least exaggeration. He had moved out of the marital home and was living with a friend. His kids seemed fine, his wife unforgiving and his girlfriend just a little insane. I didn't envy his position but my personal life was pretty precarious so I wasn't one to judge.

And I deliberately didn't ask the identity of his mystery; I thought it much better if I had absolutely no idea who she was.

We'd spoken for long enough for my fears to subside about why he wanted to see me. When he did eventually get to the reason, I wasn't concerned at all.

"Right, I think we have a potential suspect," he declared.

"That was quick! We didn't have a clue a few hours ago, what's happened?" I asked, but I took a discreet look at my watch because in a minute, I was going to have to set off to meet Nick in Vicky Park.

"What's the SP?" I asked.

"The team up at the victim's HA have spoken to his next-door neighbour. She said that someone was in the flat early doors this morning. At first she thought it was the victim, not realising that he had been murdered. She heard an argument of some sorts between the person in the flat, a male IC1, and some other guys who turned up demanding to be let in. Something happened and the guys outside, who the witness says were carrying a firearm, ran off – so I think we can assume the person in the flat pulled a bigger firearm on them in return. Anyway, the guy in the flat then let himself out and it was at this point the witness realised that it wasn't our victim. She watched the guy walk off so we've got quite a good description.

"Anyway, SOCO reckons the flat has been partially wiped clean of prints so this guy was obviously back there to hide the fact that he'd been there before. He was disturbed by the guys with the firearm before he could complete his mission, because while some of the flat's been cleaned, some hasn't. I think we can safely assume that we need to trace and identify this man," the DCI said.

"But the flat wasn't the scene of the attack, was it? I mean, the victim died several miles away," I said, fully aware of course that I was right.

"It could be a kidnap that went wrong," the DCI suggested.

"Are there signs of a struggle at the flat?" I asked.

"No one struggles much if a handgun is pointed at their head, do they?" the DCI surmised. "Why else would someone go back to clean the flat? It would only be someone who 'a' knows for certain that the victim is not at the flat because he's dead and 'b' needs to remove evidence."

"Yeah, but a kidnap? Where was the ransom demand? And to whom? They must have killed him almost straight away?" I said.

"That's why I said 'a kidnap that went wrong'," the DCI retorted.

"Gary Odiham doesn't look kidnap material to me, boss. Unless of course, it was some territorial gang bullshit and the kidnap was to prove a point and stamp authority; but then it was a fairly straight murder, there wasn't any evidence of torture or prolonged abuse, was there?" I asked.

"Not at all; just the one blow to the head," the DCI replied.

"How did this guy last night gain entry to the flat?" I asked, deliberately trying to muddy the waters.

"There was no sign of forced entry, so he must have had a set of keys taken from the victim. Even more reason to think we might be dealing with a kidnapping."

"So whose keys did the victim have? The ones that were in his possession when he died?" I asked.

"Maybe there were two sets of keys?" the DCI replied.

I didn't think the DCI had thought this through but with that said, I did, of course, have the advantage of knowing exactly what had happened and why.

"It's highly unlikely that the victim's going to be carrying two sets of keys and if we have one set, how on earth did the suspect, or whoever it was at the flat last night, get in if they didn't have a set of keys? Perhaps there's a way over the balcony from an adjoining flat? There usually are in those old Guinness Trust places."

I realised the second the words slipped from my mouth that I'd actually fucked up; how on earth did I know it was a Guinness Trust building? Fortunately, the DCI didn't spot it.

"Can you take one of your team and go and debrief the neighbour? Treat her as a significant witness; get a photo fit done if you can."

Oh fuck – not only was I the guy the witness had seen only a few hours earlier, to assist her in case she had even the slightest doubt, I was still wearing exactly the same clothes she'd seen me in.

Chapter 18

I was running out of time and energy. What's more, during the conversation with the DCI, I'd started to get stomach cramps so I had to go to the toilet on the way back to my office. The cramps were really quite painful, they were the worst physical sign of giving up the gear and I'd had them several times before.

As I sat on the toilet, I counted the number of hours since my last fix – it was getting to the stage when I really had to concentrate to work it out; I was impressed. This was the longest I'd gone since California, a couple of years ago. I tried to avoid going abroad because of the problems it caused scoring and to cover up the real reason, I told everyone I was terrified of flying, which was a load of bollocks.

I decided to keep a running total of the hours I'd been clean in the hope that it would motivate me.

When I eventually got back to the office, I had only fifteen minutes to grab someone and get over to Vicky Park. Julie had arrived and was chatting to Nicola.

"Is Taff in?" I asked.

"He's just gone out and about, babes," Julie replied.

I didn't want to ask Julie because she would be busy logging the exhibits.

"You free, Nicola?"

"I'm free," said Samantha, who replied before Nicola could say anything.

I could swear I saw Nicola smile.

"Oh great," I said, with as much sincerity as I could muster. "Get your hat and coat, you've pulled."

"Tell him to bugger off, Samantha, you can do much better than that," Nicola said.

"I've had worse," Samantha replied.

"Really, poor you," Julie said, joining in.

"Any port in a storm," Samantha replied.

"Gosh, I'd rather drown," Nicola said.

"Fuck all of you," I called out, as we left the office.

~~~

I put my foot down and was only a few minutes late getting to my meeting with Nick Charles.

I asked Samantha to give me ten, explaining I had a private matter to sort out with an old friend; she was fine.

I declined Nick's offer of a bacon roll because I knew it would go straight through me and stuck to a cup of tea.

I told him about his upcoming board for SO13, that my old friend Alphabet was the chairman, and ran through the several topics which Alphabet had assured me would come up including:

the guise of Irish terrorism post the Good Friday Agreement; terrorist financing; the emerging threat from Islamic fundamentalism; a scenario the anticipated answer to which was a suspect matrix; and various key sections of legislation which would form the basis for several questions.

Nick listened intently, made notes in a small black book and asked several probing questions which I couldn't answer because what I was telling him was the extent of my knowledge. He seemed pleased but several times made a comment about how stupid he would feel if he failed, despite knowing the questions.

"Listen, Nick, we haven't had this conversation, right? Alphabet was worried because last year someone was thrown off of SO13 for doing just this and giving the questions in advance to his mate."

This was a complete lie but a strategic one, because I wanted to make sure Nick felt obligated to me.

"What conversation?" he asked innocently.

"Now, as you know there's been something of a development since we last met," I said, turning the conversation to the real reason I wanted to meet him.

"You mean Gary's murder?" he replied.

I nodded.

"How did you know about that so soon?" I asked.

"Seyone told me; the young Indian guy that was on the search. Someone told him. You don't want me to tell anyone you were there, do you?" Nick said.

I shook my head. I didn't know what was going on but I thought it was going well, so I resisted every temptation to jump into the conversation. We sat there quietly for a few moments as Nick had obviously thought I was going to speak next, but it was important to know what he knew before I did.

"I am figuring that you didn't have the controller's authority to meet the potential informant and that your DCI is going to go ape if he discovers you were doing it the old-fashioned way."

"Nick, you're spot on, but how the fuck did you guess?"

"I've been around a while. Fucking hell, mate; when we came in your face was a fucking picture and I knew in that instant that you shouldn't have been there," he replied.

Of course, Nick would never think for one moment that I was there to purchase drugs, not in a million years.

"Fuck me, you're good," I said, genuinely impressed at his perception. "Is that why you wanted to see me?"

"No, I wouldn't have said anything, mate. I had guessed what was happening. Who's got the murder?"

"My team," I said, raising my eyes to the sky.

"That's a coincidence, mate. Well fuck me. How did you come across that herbert, anyway?" Nick asked.

"Another snout put me his way, one I've been running for years," I said.

Of course, it was bollocks; for 'snout' I should have said 'one of my dealers' and instead of 'running' I should have said 'buying from'.

"I'm not surprised you didn't want to recruit him," Nick said.

Again, I resisted the temptation to say anything meaningful because I had no idea where he was going with this conversation, so I just said,

"Why's that?"

"The herbert fucking hates the Old Bill with a passion that I've rarely encountered."

"That might explain a few things," I commented, hopefully saying the right thing.

"I mean, he was fine throughout the search; polite, almost deferential. Then as we were leaving and when he knew that we'd found nothing, he said he'd like to say something to us. He made a bit of a thing about it and asked me to gather everyone in the lounge, which I did. Fucking hell, mate; I genuinely thought the herbert was going to thank us for treating him so fairly, not fitting him up and for respecting his property. Then he says, 'I'd just like to say to each and every one of you, I hope you get cancer and die a really painful, slow death'.

"I was like, what the fuck! I wanted to pan the cunt but we had a young guy who was on attachment with us, Seyone, the Indian kid, and I didn't know how he'd react."

"So what did you do?" I asked.

"We walked out. Fucking hell, mate; I was furious, Nostrils, but what could I do?"

"You walked out? What's the fucking world coming to? In my day we'd have beaten him within an inch of his life for such disrespect to the uniform," I said.

But as the words left my mouth I realised I'd misjudged the situation. I was joshing him but from Nick's expression, he thought I was serious. I had to undertake some urgent repairs.

"I'm kidding, mate, I'm breaking your balls."

"Yeah?" he asked tentatively.

"Yes, you fucking idiot. In the old days we would never have given him a beating," I assured him.

Nick smiled.

"Just a bag of herbal," I said.

Nick nodded in a knowing manner that suggested he had shared such experiences; I thought in all probability, he hadn't.

"Listen, Nostrils, the reason I needed to see you was because I've got a bit of a problem and wanted some advice. You were at CIB, right?"

"I was, Nick, but it was a few years ago now," I explained.

"That's why I phoned you this morning. Listen, Nostrils, the info on the flat in Bethnal Green was A1, yet we didn't find any drugs. Something went very wrong," Nick said.

"Go on," I encouraged him.

"The info was so good that we knew one hundred per cent that he had taken possession of a package, from whom he'd got it and when it had been delivered. Now CRIMINT shows us that Gary's a drug dealer, mainly H, but cannabis too."

"Oh," I said, pretending it was all news to me. "Without wanting to compromise you, was your intel informant led?".

He shook his head.

"Oh," I said, this time using the word in the hope that he would provide me more details.

"Listen, Nostrils, I'm pretty certain the intelligence was from the line room. Fucking hell, mate, that's how good it was, that's how we knew when and from whom the herbert got the package. We don't know exactly what gear it was, I mean people don't use words like heroin and cannabis on the phone, do they? But what else was a low-level drug dealer going to be getting from someone who's fucking wired up?"

This was startling news; was my voice recorded somewhere in the system ordering my next score? Then I realised that I might be all right as it all depended who they had the line on.

"Gary was hooked up, was he?" I asked. "He was only a low-level dealer."

"No, I assume Gary's name came up on the line. The main man was someone else. I don't know who, obviously."

"What are you going to tell my team when you're spoken to? You're not allowed to reveal the source when it's off a line, are you?" I asked.

"No, that's right. I'll just say 'intelligence received' and if they push I'll tell them that I am prohibited by law from revealing the source – most people know what that means," Nick said.

I realised this was all playing out all right.

"Listen, Nostrils ..."

"I'm listening, I'm listening," I said, gently mocking his repeated use of that phrase.

"Listen, I know those drugs were there, why didn't we find them?"

"Perhaps they were just too well hidden," I suggested, which of course I knew to be the truth.

"Fucking hell, mate; I'm telling you I ain't happy. I think one of my team found them and nicked them."

"That's a quantum leap, ain't it? What grounds do you have to say that?"

"One of the guys on the team is a coke head, I'm fucking sure of it. He has family who work in the City on like two hundred kay a year and he's told some of the team that they're always putting it up their noses. Well, he's always out socialising with his brothers. I reckon he's had the drugs off."

"Coke heads don't do smack," I said, a little too quickly.

"That gear was there, Nostrils," Nick declared.

"Why don't you go and see the guys from my team who are over there now and get them to really pull the place apart?" I suggested.

"What? And look like a right cunt when they find it?" he replied.

"Besides, we turned that place upside down. That cunt's had it off and I'm going to put in a call on the 'report your mates' thingy what CIB have just set up."

"Nick, don't take this the wrong way but …"

"What?" he asked, a little too aggressively.

"… have you got like, a problem with this geezer? He's not shagging your missus, or anything, is he?"

"He's a cunt, simple. He's got a wife *and* a girlfriend. He's too confident, too flash, too full of himself, drives a Saab convertible; I mean, who can afford one of those legitimately? Fucking hell, mate; the herbert lives in a huge house in Brentwood. The guy's a wrong'un, Nostrils, a bad egg, bent as a nine bob note."

"What's this geezer's name?" I asked.

"Ronnie Edwards, but everyone calls him Buster."

"Like the Great Train Robber?" I said.

"Exactly," Nick said. "What more proof could you want?"

What could I say?

Chapter 19

When I got back in the car it was quickly obvious from her body language and a persistent and annoying huff, that my polite request for Samantha to stay in the car while I spoke to Nick hadn't gone down as well as I'd thought. We drove in silence for a few minutes but I have never been one to tolerate such situations for long so I thought it best to address the issue.

"Why have you got the hump?" I asked, deliberately abruptly.

"Why do you think?" Samantha replied.

"Because I asked you to stay in the car?" I asked.

"Because you were embarrassed to be seen with me," she replied.

Suddenly I realised why she was hurt; it really hadn't crossed my mind that she would interpret events in that way.

"Oh, Samantha, that's just not true, honestly. Nick, the guy I was meeting, is an old friend and he phoned me this morning to say he needed to speak to me urgently about a really sensitive matter. He wanted my advice on something. I couldn't turn up with you; in fact, if we hadn't been on our way to Bethnal Green, I would not have taken anyone but gone on my own. It had nothing whatsoever to do with being embarrassed to be with you, I promise."

Samantha undid the window a little; I suspected that even though I'd taken a shower I might not smell terribly sweet being as I was, in the same clothes.

"You do believe me, don't you?" I asked.

"I think so. You were meeting Nick Charles, right?" she replied.

"Oh, do you know Nick?" I asked.

"Yeah, we used to work together. He's a nice bloke," she replied.

"I don't know him well but he wanted to discuss something really sensitive," I explained.

"What did he want to talk about?" Samantha asked.

I was a little bit taken back as I'd not anticipated such a direct question, but Samantha was probably testing whether I was telling the truth or not.

"He thinks one of the PCs on his team is corrupt," I replied.

"Why?" Samantha asked.

I paused briefly, just long enough for my mind to skirt ahead in the conversation to see whether anything I might say would compromise me.

"Nick's team did a ticket at the victim's address, yesterday morning," I explained.

"Yes, I know. I saw the CRIMINT report. Nothing was found was it? So what?" Samantha asked, quite reasonably.

"Well, for reasons which I genuinely can't go into, Nick knows there were drugs in the flat but none were found, and having turned the events over in his mind, he thinks one of his PCs has had them off," I said.

"Why?"

"Several reasons I think: first, 'cos they weren't found; second, because he thinks the colleague has got a coke habit; third, I don't know, I just think he thinks he's a wrong 'un," I said.

"So Nick is on the Crime Squad at Bethnal Green now?" Samantha asked.

"Yeah," I replied.

"It's not Buster that he's got the concerns about, is it?"

I was flummoxed.

"'Cos if it is, he should be worried. The guy's a thief. When I was a PC at Romford, he was on another relief and things were always getting nicked, you know, money from the tea kitty, a score out of someone's wallet, some drugs out of the property store. A few people reckoned it was him but then he moved to Bethnal Green and no one thought anything else about it. And what happened? You guessed it, the thieving stopped the moment he transferred."

'Perhaps Nick was right?' I thought to myself. What the fuck was I thinking? I'd taken the drugs, not Buster!

"Was it Buster?" Samantha asked.

I nodded.

"See, he's at it again," Samantha declared triumphantly.

~~~

I left Samantha in the car for a second time, while I popped into M&S to buy new underwear and a shirt. I had to leave her in the car so we didn't get a ticket or even towed away.

As I was leaving I had an even better idea and popped into a nearby barber's for a haircut, and not just any haircut; I had a number two all over, which removed a good three inches of hair and, as I had planned, completely changed my appearance. I actually looked a bit of a thug.

Poor Samantha had been on her own for over an hour and when I got back in the car the first words out of her lips were, "Where the fuck have you been?"

"Charming. I thought you were meant to be trying to be a lady," I said.

"A woman, Nostrils, I think my chances of ever being a lady are long gone. Seriously though, a skinhead, why have you done that? You've been gone ages, what was I meant to do? I've had to show my warrant card twice to the traffic wardens. Seriously, where the devil have you been, sarge?"

"Calm down; sorry, I knew I took a while but I did have to get a new shirt and then change, and then the barber's was next door and no one was waiting so I thought I'd pop in but the guy who cut my hair was like eighty and he was so very slow. I apologise."

We were on our way again now, making little progress through the usual heavy traffic.

"But why a skinhead? What is that? A number one?" Samantha asked.

I made up a story.

"It was a misunderstanding. He thought I asked for a number two, but I'd actually said 'how do you do?' Before I knew it, he'd zipped the old clipper from my forehead right back across the scalp. I was like 'what have you done?' but it was all too late by then 'cos you can hardly stick it back on, can you? So I settled for a number two all over. What do you think?"

"You look really hard, what with your broken nose and that scar – a right villain," Samantha said.

She was nearer the truth than she'd hopefully ever know.

~~~

I didn't even bother to pretend not to know where I was going and drove straight to Attlee House, Bethnal Green, but Samantha didn't notice.

The witness we were seeing was the immediate neighbour of the victim and although we would take her to the local nick to get the interview tape-recorded, first I wanted to review exactly what she could see. There was obviously a degree of self-preservation in my actions but it was also the most professional thing to do.

I had removed my three-quarter-length black leather jacket and popped it in the boot. With my coat off, my new shirt and a different haircut, I hoped that I now looked satisfactorily unlike the person she'd seen only a few hours before. Well, that was my intention, anyway. We would soon find out if it had worked.

Several of the Onions were dealing with the victim's address. We spoke to one outside, who informed me that there didn't seem to be much to go on.

"What's this about the place being cleaned?" I asked.

"SOCO's absolutely certain about that. I mean, when you see the state of the rest of the flat, the victim had never polished or cleaned in his life yet there's a laptop that's spotless and SOCO reckons he's never failed to get a dab off a laptop cover. Mind you, SOCO got a great one off the front door, almost a full palm and hand print, but of course it might be the victim's or the guy who fitted the door."

For a moment I panicked; was that my print? No, of course it wasn't, I'd been wearing gloves earlier.

"Oh, I see, anything else?" I said.

"I don't think so. The usual drug dealer's den; you know, same old, same old."

That didn't make any sense. When I left the place only a few hours ago, I placed a silver handgun under the pillow in the bedroom. I could only assume that they hadn't searched the bedroom yet.

I wondered briefly whether I could think of any justification for entering the victim's flat because to do so would provide a wonderful alibi if one of my fingerprints was found in there. Then I realised I couldn't possibly enter without donning plastic gloves and shoe covers at the very least, and to do otherwise would generate suspicion.

"How long you going to be?" I asked.

"A couple more hours. Are you here to see the old girl, next door? She seems to think someone was in here last night. I think she's a bit mad, personally."

"What's her name? Do we know how old she is?" I asked.

"Sophie ... something like that, Italian I think, she's at least eighty," he replied.

"Here?" I asked, indicating the front door.

He nodded.

An eighty-year-old, foreign, short-sighted lady suffering from senility was, at this precise moment in time, exactly the witness I hoped we'd find.

Chapter 20

'Sophie ... something like that' was, in fact, Sophia Amasanti.

'At least eighty' was, in fact, 'eighty-nine'.

And eighty-nine-year-old Sophia Amasanti was a former refugee who had arrived in England in 1938 with her family to escape Mussolini's fascist Italy, only to have her father and two older brothers interned for the duration when war broke out the following year.

Despite residing in the UK for over sixty years, a tiny hint of an Italian accent was still detectable but her English was immaculate and her brain razor sharp.

I explained why Samantha and I were calling and Mrs Amasanti invited us into an absolute palace of a council flat, the like of which I'd never been in previously or since. It was spotlessly clean, furnished to the highest standard and decorated with the style and grace of a Capri villa. And it didn't smell; I mean, every house I'd ever been in during my time in the job smelt – but this one didn't. Admittedly, some of the ornate furnishings really deserved to be sitting in a grander residence but wow, this was some place. Porcelain figurines populated every surface and stylish antiques and objets d'art abounded, yet the flat wasn't cluttered.

"Did you know Gary well?" I asked.

"Not really, officer. Is he all right?" Mrs Amasanti asked.

I suddenly realised that she didn't know he'd been murdered.

"Not really," I replied cautiously.

"So the men that were after him, did they get him? What have they done? Killed him?" she asked.

"Gary was murdered, yesterday," I replied.

"Oh, I see. Well, I suppose that makes sense. It explains why you're all here. Did he owe them money?" she replied.

"We don't know who's done it yet? Or why?" Samantha said.

For the first time, Mrs Amasanti turned towards Samantha and looked her up and down.

"Gosh, what a deep voice," she said. "Are you a man? Why are you wearing a skirt?"

The question completely floored poor Samantha, who spluttered a few incoherent words in response.

"My colleague's name is Samantha. She was born a man but has now chosen to live as a woman," I said, mustering up as much authority as I could.

"Is she a police officer?" Mrs Amasanti asked, the question directed to me as if Samantha was invisible.

I didn't answer and gestured to Samantha, suggesting that she should reply.

"I am a detective constable from the murder squad," she said, and I was sure she was trying to raise the tone of her voice.

"Well, what can I say? Can you imagine what would have happened in June 1944 if the Allied army had stormed the beaches of Normandy all wearing skirts and dresses? I suspect Herr Hitler would have carried the day," Mrs Amasanti said.

"Well, we're not in Normandy and this isn't 1944," I replied.

"Thank goodness for that," Mrs Amasanti declared.

I could feel poor Samantha's embarrassment and wanted to steer the subject back to Gary.

"Mrs Amasanti, you were saying that you didn't know Gary very well?" I said.

"No, not really. He was dealing drugs, of course. That wasn't his flat, either. I think some African gentleman sub-leases it to him."

"Did you speak to him much?" I asked.

"No, officer. We would exchange hellos; he would borrow a jar of milk; I would occasionally get people knocking on my door by mistake," she replied.

"How long has he lived there?" Samantha asked.

I was pleased she felt sufficiently confident to rejoin the conversation.

"Three months, four, five months," Mrs Amasanti replied, with an exaggerated shrug of her shoulders and an open-handed gesture, indicative of her country of origin.

I asked her to show us where she was when she saw what she had told my colleagues about.

She led us into her kitchen, which was the first left as you entered the flat and the window was next to the balcony and immediately next to the victim's front door.

The window had fitted horizontal shutter blinds, which were open and although you couldn't get right up against the window because the sink and draining board were in the way, you could quite clearly see the front door. Anyone who walked along the balcony to that flat would be visible for a good three yards.

I was sure, however, that I would have noticed if she had been watching me as I left and it would have been very dangerous for Mrs Amasanti to have stood observing from the kitchen, while the guys outside were trying to kick Gary's door down.

"Last night, when you saw the incident next door, were the blinds open like this?" I asked.

Mrs Amasanti reached to the right of the windowsill and turned a thin wooden rod that hung down. The blinds turned shut but then she twisted the rod just the slightest turn back and you actually got a reasonable view.

"Obviously, I turned the kitchen light off, officers," she said.

"Do you normally wear glasses?" I asked.

"Only for reading, officer," she replied.

"And please don't be offended, but how good is your eyesight?" I asked.

"I'm not offended at all, officer, that's a very sensible question."

She twisted the rod again so the blinds opened out and pointed across to the flats opposite, which were a good eighty yards away.

"The flat with the red door has the number 132 on it in black," she stated proudly.

I followed her outstretched finger and she was spot on; her eyesight was excellent.

~~~

We took this charming old lady to Bethnal Green and tape-recorded her interview. Her memory was even better than her eyesight, well almost, as it transpired.

Mrs Amasanti was in bed. It was about five o'clock when she heard Gary come in, thought no more about it and went back to sleep. A while later, she wasn't sure of the time but it wasn't long, she heard Gary fiddling at the base of his bedroom wall. He did this all the time – she assumed he was adjusting the wall heater or otherwise trying to get it to work. She explained that her own heaters could be temperamental, too.

A few minutes later she'd heard a commotion at the front door, which wasn't especially unusual, as Gary had visitors at all hours – most of whom were 'pretty rough'. She got out of bed and without turning the kitchen light on, adjusted the blinds, which had been shut, so that she could see out of them at an angle.

There were two males outside whom she hadn't seen before. They were white and both wore woollen hats that were pulled down over their ears, so she couldn't describe either their hair or anything about their facial features. One was taller than the other and both were between twenty-five and forty-five years old.

The taller male was holding what Mrs Amasanti described as a 'pistol' and the shorter male was constantly looking through the letterbox.

The sight of the firearm made Mrs Amasanti nervous and she explained that after seeing the weapon, she was much more careful about not letting them see her.

The shorter male did all the shouting and swearing. She got the impression that Gary owed them money. Suddenly, she heard the two men run off really, really urgently, almost 'like they'd seen a ghost'.

"I had to be a trifle careful that they didn't see me looking, so I could only peek intermittently. I decided to lie low; is that what you call it, officers?"

I nodded.

"It all went very quiet for a while and I decided to go back to bed. Then, just when I thought everything was over, I heard more movement and checked again. The door opened and Gary came out of the flat, except it wasn't Gary, it was that other bloke."

"What other bloke?" Samantha asked.

Then dear, sweet, lovely old Mrs Amasanti dropped her bombshell.

"The policeman from the morning before, one of the ones that did the raid."

"We don't call them raids," I replied meekly.

Chapter 21

On the way back to Arbour Square, we discussed what it could all mean – or rather, Samantha opined at some length while I interjected sporadically.

"So what exactly did the old girl see this morning?" Samantha asked.

I slowly shook my head. I had every intention of slow playing this conversation.

"Why did a PC from yesterday's search, or is it the day before, I get so confused when the days blur into one another, go back to the address in the middle of the night?"

"Samantha, maybe the old biddy has just got it wrong. I mean, she is eighty-nine," I suggested.

"I don't think so, do you? She was as sharp as a soprano's top C," Samantha retorted.

"It doesn't make any sense to me. I think she's just mistaken and confused," I said.

"She wasn't. You do surprise me, Chris. You saw how good her eyesight was and you know that mentally she was all there. Why would she make this up?"

"I don't think she's made it up at all. I just think Mrs Amasanti, who has very little going on in her life, has got a bit carried away. I think she really believes what she is saying. I just wouldn't want to put her in front of a jury," I said.

"But what does it mean?" Samantha asked.

I shook my head.

"Was the PC involved in the murder?" she asked.

Again, I shook my head and this time decided to add, just for the effect, a single and purposeful shrug of the shoulders.

"But that makes no sense?" Samantha said.

"What doesn't?"

"The PC being involved in the murder," she replied.

"Doesn't it? It's too huge a coincidence, isn't it?" I said.

I was being deliberately obtuse.

"Is it?" Samantha replied.

"Look, Samantha, Mrs Amasanti is probably just confused. I'm not saying she's a bad witness, not at all, but a lot happened over a few hours and, whether we like it or not, we will struggle with any case that relies on the evidence of an eighty-nine-year-old witness who'll probably have shuffled off her mortal coil by the time this comes to trial," I said.

We sat in silence for a good five minutes and I was starting to think that, perhaps, I'd muddied the water sufficiently.

"How do you feel about the way Mrs Amasanti reacted to you?" I asked gently.

"Well, at least she had the balls to say it to my face."

"I think it's a generation thing; I can't imagine many people of her age coming to terms with it, can you?" I asked.

"No, I suppose not," she replied.

"Samantha, can I ask you something?" I said.

"Of course," she replied.

"I don't want to offend you or say the wrong thing, but why don't you dress as a man when you come to work and then as a woman when you're at home and, you know, in your private life."

Samantha laughed, but not in any way which suggested she was amused, just simply frustrated.

"Chris, that would be cheating. That would be doing it the easy way, the coward's way. Besides, I don't have a private life so what you're suggesting is that I dress like a man when I'm at work and then put on a dress when I get home and sit there watching TV."

"But Julie and Nicola, they always wear trousers to work. They don't wear skirts and dresses because it's not really very practical," I pointed out.

"Chris, when I wear female clothing, I am making a deliberate statement to both the world and also to myself. It means I am no longer scared to be who I really am. Sometimes, if I have a really bad day, it's the one good thing that can't be taken away or spoilt. Every day that I dress as a woman is a victory," Samantha explained.

"Like an addict who's given up their drug?" I asked.

"Exactly," Samantha replied.

And for just a minute, I completely understood my colleague.

As we pulled into the back yard, and without a hint that she was going to do anything except pick up her bag, collect the cassette tapes of Mrs Amasanti's interview and alight, Samantha suddenly declared,

"It's obvious. The guy from the search who Mrs Amasanti saw, was Buster. This fits in exactly with what Nick was telling you this morning. I thought you were meant to be smart. This is nothing to do with the murder. Buster found the drugs during the search and maybe some cash too. But he left it where it was, got hold of a set of keys and went back in the middle of the night to have it all away. Does your guy know how much was there?" Samantha asked.

"Several grands worth, I think he said," I replied, "plus probably a grand or two in cash. His brothers are a couple of flash City gents, banker wanker coke heads, so he probably sold them the gear."

I was so tempted to explain that people who take cocaine are not the same ones that take heroin, but decided to keep my mouth shut.

"Buster's made three months' money for a few hours' work. If there was anything else in the flat worth nicking, he'll have probably had that away, too. He's had a right touch, except …"

"Except what?" I asked innocently.

"… except that we've caught him bang to fucking rights, thanks to Miss Italy 1940!"

"Perhaps," I said, not wishing to appear too dismissive.

"This Buster, what does he look like?" I asked.

"How old are you?" Samantha asked.

"Thirty-six."

"How tall are you?"

"Five ten," I replied.

"He's male, white, fortyish, brown hair like you used to have until you had it cropped, bit overweight ..."

"Like me," I said helpfully.

"His beer belly isn't as big as yours."

"I'll have you know that flabby bellies are nothing to do with the consumption of beer. I read in the papers only the other day, that it's actually to do with having the wrong kind of genes," I replied.

"Wrong *size* of jeans, more like. What are you? A thirty-eight waist?" Samantha asked.

I shook my head but let the subject go because I wasn't going to win this exchange.

As Samantha got out of the car, I asked her not to say anything to anyone else yet; she agreed. I added that I'd be in in a minute, as I wanted to make a call, and my partner trotted off clumsily on her heels.

I needed a few moments to get my head together and try to work out what the fuck was going on here. To add to the muddle, I was tired, my bowels were uncooperative and I was starting to really miss my old friend, the one that used to make everything okay again.

This is what I figured out.

On Thursday morning, Mrs Amasanti's attention had probably first been drawn to Gary's flat when the police started to demand entry and to batter the door down. At that point, through her blinds, she would have had a decent view of Nick and his two or three colleagues who were trying to get in; one of these was Buster.

She would then have watched Nick and me step outside and have a brief discussion, before I left. The others, including Buster, would probably have been in and out several times over the next hour before leaving, when nothing was found. All this time, Gary would have remained in the flat.

On Friday morning, she was roused when she heard me removing the drugs from the storage heater, which, unbeknown to me at the time, was actually only a few feet, albeit through a wall, from where she slept. She then watched the two males outside, saw them leg it when I produced my brief, and then saw me leave. Now I know I left quickly because I was really nervous, so she would have only seen me fleetingly.

Mrs Amasanti obviously realised she'd seen the person leaving the previous morning during the search but somewhere in her brain a wire has crossed and she thinks I was one of the officers doing the search. Hang on, in her mind I *was* one of the officers doing the search – so she is absolutely right. She just hasn't recognised me when I returned because of my haircut and change of clothing.

People were going to put two and two together and make five by assuming this Buster guy was the common association between both events when in reality, the connection was me.

To make matters even more complicated, if someone was to put Buster on an ID parade, Mrs Amasanti would actually pick him out because she would have seen him during the search.

Fuck me; this was a mess.

To cap it all, because the events at Attlee House were a massive red herring, we were actually nowhere nearer catching the murderer than we had been at the briefing yesterday morning.

~~~

The DCI called it a day at seven and sent us home, as much to save the overtime bill as to allow us any respite. He told us to be back the following morning at nine and that we'd kick off with a team meeting. I realised that I'd have to work out how to play this before that meeting and I'd have to get Samantha on side, so she didn't say anything untoward.

I called Wendy on the way home to say goodnight: she told me how disappointed she was that I hadn't called in and that she would send me a photograph of what I missed.

When I got in Jackie was in her grandma pyjamas and rabbit slippers, her hair was tied up and she had a brown face pack on.

"I've got some interesting news?" Jackie said.

"Go on," I encouraged her.

"Cilla Black is quitting Blind Date."

My phone beeped; I opened a message containing a picture from Wendy and instantly regretted not calling in at hers on the way home for a quick one.

Chapter 22

I was shattered but I had a really bad night, most of which I spent doubled up with stomach cramps. My body was really starting to suffer from the withdrawal. I had been here before, I knew what to expect, but it didn't make it any easier to cope.

To get into the office for nine, I had to get up at six. I was in the car at six fifteen with Sarah Kennedy. I would be early but the alternative was sitting in traffic for hours on the way in. If I was lucky and shot in, I could usually grab another forty minutes' kip in the car.

When I arrived at the office just before nine, I felt better than I had thought I would, but no sooner had I arrived than Samantha told me that she wanted a word. Before I'd even taken my coat off, we were back in the yard.

"Right, what we going to say at the office meeting?" she asked.

"Jesus, Samantha, give me a break. I've only just walked in."

"You look like shit, by the way," she said.

"I love you too," I replied.

"Look, at the office meeting we're going to have to update everyone about our debrief of the significant witness, the one that everyone thinks saw the suspect. In reality, she is a significant witness but to a burglary by a police officer, not a murder. What are we going to say?"

Samantha was right.

"Leave it with me, I'll try to get in to see the DCI before we kick off but if not, I'll just tell the meeting that I need to update the boss separately about the witness and am not in a position to provide the details to the whole meeting."

"That won't go down very well, the Onions won't like it," Samantha pointed out, quite correctly.

I wasn't aware that she knew about the great Cheese and Onion divide, but we could discuss that later.

"Leave it to me," I said.

"Okay," she replied.

I went to walk away but as I did, Samantha said, "Can I just say …"

I stopped and turned back.

" … thanks for the last few days."

"I don't know what you mean," I replied, genuinely caught by the change of subject.

"Yes, you do. For treating me like I used to be treated when I was a man. For being, like, normal and for actually asking me the questions no one dares to."

"Don't be silly. It's nothing. I said we were going to be mates and I meant it," I replied.

"Thanks, Nostrils," she said.

"Listen, Samantha, do me one favour?"

"Go on," she replied.

"My close friends call me Chris."

Samantha smiled.

"Okay, Chris," she said.

~~~

I deliberately didn't get to speak the DCI before the office meeting because I wanted to see what other information had come to light. I mean, if a tangible line of enquiry had emerged where all efforts might be directed, it was just possible the Buster issue might fade.

At the meeting I learnt three potential lines of enquiry had emerged.

First, a crime report had been uncovered from four weeks ago where Gary Odiham had been the named suspect for a theft of a woman's handbag. The woman was having her hair done at a place in Hoxton and Gary had walked in, picked the bag up and walked out. The victim refused to substantiate the allegation, so the case was dropped, but enquiries revealed her husband was a well-known East London villain.

Second, a friend of Gary's had come forward to say Gary owed fifteen hundred pounds to a local loan shark. I suspected these were the men who had turned up when I was in the flat. Gary's medical records also showed that he'd told his GP that he owed money to someone and the anxiety was causing him to have suicidal thoughts. His GP had prescribed a mild sedative.

Finally, only last week Gary had been involved in a fracas with the father of a teenage girl who'd found his daughter in Gary's flat and suspected he was supplying her with drugs.

There was something found at the home address which, while not a motive, was interesting. It was a handwritten note, signed by the victim and dated July 1983, in which he expressed remorse about the death of a young girl called Grace. He'd have been eighteen at the time and the speculation was that perhaps he had killed her in a car or motorbike accident.

I wasn't overly excited about any of the motives.

The handbag theft incident was hardly a sufficient reason to kill someone, was it? Give him a good hiding perhaps, but not murder. And people who were owed money rarely killed their debtors because that way they never saw their money again. Lastly, if the bloke who caught Gary with his daughter was going to kill him, surely it would have been there and then, not a week later?

No, I wasn't buying any of them especially but I could've been wrong; I'd been wrong plenty of times before. I thought it was more likely that the victim was simply turned over for drugs or money. Perhaps he fought back or the robber was a bit of a psychopath and it all went tits up.

The only other matter of relevance was that Julie asked everyone to check their bags, coats, desks and cars because apparently the victim's phone had gone missing somewhere between the mortuary and the office.

At the end of the meeting I loitered outside the DCI's office until he was free and then I asked him for two minutes.

"That's a fierce haircut, Chris," he commented, before I could even sit down.

I told him my story about the old barber and how my misheard greeting 'how do you do' had turned into a request for a number two.

"With your hair like that, your scar's really obvious."

"Is it?" I asked.

I was so used to it, I genuinely didn't see it any more.

"Is that from the bombing?" the DCI asked.

I nodded.

"How old were you?" he asked.

"Nineteen," I replied.

"Fucking hell, Chris – just a kid. Does it ever bother you?"

"It did at first. I think I had a bit of a breakdown. In the aftermath, I did some pretty stupid things, like getting heavily in debt and stuff. But that was nineteen years ago; fortunately, the memory fades," I replied.

I didn't tell him that one of the stupid things I'd done was to steal five thousand pounds at the scene of a sudden death – but that's a different story.

"A young WPC died in the bombing, didn't she? Dawn something?"

"Dawn Matthews, she was my Street Duties instructor at the time," I replied.

I could just feel the emotion rising, from a long way deep down inside me.

"Can we change the subject?" I said.

"You okay?" the DCI asked.

I was breathing heavily now and the sweats were coming.

"So what's this about the significant witness that you couldn't tell the office meeting?" he asked.

I desperately needed to quell the rising storm. In my head, I was back in the debris in the immediate aftermath of the explosion and there was a loud ringing in my ears.

"Nostrils?"

I was struggling to breathe; I could hear myself panting. I could smell something burning. I could see my partner, a crumbled heap of clothing, about fifteen yards away.

"Chris?"

Tears! Fucking hell, I had tears in my eyes.

"Chris?"

I shut my eyes but it was too late, I could feel the tracks running down my cheeks.

What was that smell, that sweet smell?

I felt someone take my left hand and a gentle female voice say, "Chris, it's okay, darling, everything's okay."

I opened my eyes and there was Nicola, kneeling beside me. Her face was close and she was whispering reassuring words. Behind her was the DCI, looking as awkward as anyone I had ever seen. I was suddenly aware of what was happening and very, very embarrassed. I wiped my cheeks and apologised.

Nicola handed me a tissue and stood up.

"What was that all about?" the DCI asked Nicola.

"Did you mention the bombing?" Nicola asked.

The DCI nodded.

"Yeah, best not to," Nicola replied.

"Christ, sorry, Chris," the DCI said.

"Don't be silly, it's me, I don't know what gets hold of me sometimes. I am really embarrassed," I replied.

"Take thirty minutes, this can wait," the DCI said.

"No, let's get on with it. I'll be okay. Thank you, Nicola."

"Yeah, thanks, Nicola," the DCI said.

"Come on, boss. What were we talking about?" I asked.

"What's this about the significant witness that you couldn't brief the team about?" he asked.

I composed myself and told him everything Mrs Amasanti had said but left out my meeting with Nick and the fact that he was saying he thought Buster had nicked the drugs. I concluded by repeating Mrs Amasanti's assertion that the person who was at the flat during the night was one of the officers who had searched the place the previous day.

Was I being a bastard? Not really, I had to tell the DCI. He might even want to listen to the interview.

"Is this old lady credible?" he asked.

"Her eyesight is excellent; she would have had a good view of the area outside the victim's flat, too. But she is eighty-nine and I wouldn't want to put her in the box," I replied, being as objective as I could.

The DCI tapped the desk with his fingertips, as he mulled the information over. I thought I'd give him a nudge in the right direction.

"Whatever this is about, I don't think it's got anything to do with the murder," I said.

"We can't know that for certain," the DCI replied.

"I can," I wanted to say, but of course I resisted.

"We can't ignore this. I want you to take this to CIB. They can pick it up. Have a word with one of your old mates," he suggested.

"Boss, I left there seven years ago, I don't know anyone there any more," I replied.

He picked up his mobile, flicked through a few screens and then jotted down a telephone number on a Post-It note, which he handed to me.

"That's a guy called Adam Stanley, he's a detective superintendent on three. He's as sound as a pound; give him a call and set up a meeting. Provide him with an extra copy of the tapes from the interview and tell him what you've got," the DCI instructed.

"Do you want to come too?" I asked.

He shook his head.

"I'll wait until tomorrow," I suggested, conscious that it was a Sunday.

"Do it now, he won't mind," the DCI ordered.

This situation was going from bad to worse.

Chapter 23

I knew this Buster chap had done nothing wrong. He hadn't stolen the drugs during the search on Thursday morning, he'd missed them, as had everyone else who'd searched the flat. They were cleverly hidden. Gary knew this, which is why he was so relaxed when the Old Bill came charging through his front door. Buster hadn't gone back later to steal them either, I had. Well, not to steal them but to take possession of them and then dispose of them, as soon as practicable, which, incidentally, is a specific defence to a charge of possession under the Misuse of Drugs Act 1971. Now I had to go and make a report to a CIB superintendent which, although accurate in itself, I knew to be utterly misleading.

To make matters worse, the stomach cramps were not abating so I spent another half hour in the toilet. It was my own fault for having breakfast, but I'd been so hungry, I'd started feeling sick. Everything I ate went straight through me.

The time on the toilet did, however, give me an opportunity to think. I decided to play the 'Mrs Amasanti is eighty-nine years old and losing her marbles' card really hard when I met the CIB superintendent. I'd say I was only reporting it because the DCI had told me to do so but that was because the DCI hadn't actually met Mrs Amasanti in person.

I could see a problem. I knew that just as I was leaving the department, CIB were setting up a database of corrupt officers, in the same way that the police had CRIMINT to track intelligence on London's criminals. I think the team collecting this data was called CIBIC, which stood for the Complaints Investigation Bureau Intelligence Cell.

If there was any intelligence on their database about Buster suggesting he was corrupt, which was highly likely after both Nick and Samantha's testimonials, then it would be hard for CIB to ignore what the old lady was saying.

As I washed my hands and walked back to my desk I felt absolutely exhausted. My inability to keep any food in my stomach was starting to take its toll.

Julie was still booking in exhibits but everyone else was out on enquiries. My team had picked up the actions relating to the annoyed father and the handbag theft. We'd also been given some limited house-to-house to do in the vicinity of the victim's flat.

"You know yesterday, babes, or Friday, you know when you photocopied the victim's bus pass photo ID card thingy, did you see his phone?" Julie asked, as I sat down.

I pretended to concentrate on remembering.

"No, it wasn't on Nicola's desk with the other exhibits. Or if it was, I definitely, definitely didn't see it," I replied, with as much certainty as I could demonstrate without over-hamming the performance.

"No problem," she replied.

"It might turn up yet. What type was it? Can you remember?" I asked.

"An old pay-as-you-go Nokia. It was really scratched and the back was missing. The battery was held in place with Sellotape. Not worth anything and not working either, though that could have just been a flat battery," Julie replied.

"So no one's going to nick it, are they?" I said.

"No, I agree. Not that we've ever had a problem like that on this team," Julie replied. "I'm absolutely certain that I brought it back from the hospital. It was bagged and I've got a seal number in the Exhibits Book. It's really weird. As you say, no one's going to steal it. I wonder if it's just been thrown out with some rubbish. Perhaps we should search the bins in the yard? I wonder if there is a mobile number for him on CRIMINT or his CRO? If there is, we won't need the phone itself to retrieve the itemised billing, will we? I'll get Jeff to raise an action," Julie said.

She was almost talking to herself.

"You all right now, babes?" Julie asked.

"Yeah, fine thanks," I replied.

"Nicola told me you had a bit of a moment in the DCI's office."

"I did but I'm fine now; it only lasted a few seconds," I said, hoping she'd drop the embarrassing subject.

"But you've spent the last forty minutes in the toilet, so clearly you're telling porkies," Julie said.

"Honestly, I'm fine, Julie. I was in the toilet because I've got an upset stomach. I didn't realise I was being timed! And I used the Gents," I replied.

"Okay, okay. If you want to go for coffee and have a chat, I am here. That's all."

"Thank you," I said, in a polite but firm manner, which I hoped would bring the subject to a close.

I sat down and logged on.

I turned around to make sure no one else was coming in because when I sat at my desk my back was immediately to the door.

"Julie, I'm not going to be able to speak to Samantha about the toilet issue, it's just too difficult. Besides, I've just started to strike up a relationship with her; she's having a difficult time you know, and I think if I said what you wanted me to say, it'll set her right back," I said.

"Okay," Julie replied, "I suppose I understand. But I want you to know that we are trying to be nice; we've invited her to our girlie lunch next week and Nicola offered to go shopping with her."

"Thank you. I've spent some time with her now and I really think she's all right," I said.

It was a statement that meant a great deal more than it superficially communicated.

"Received," Julie replied.

"And do you know the very best thing about her?"

Julie didn't reply, so I told her anyway.

"Our dear Samantha is definitely not an Onion," I said.

"What the hell does that mean?" asked a deep, gruff voice.

I turned round to see Samantha standing with legs wide apart and both her hands on her hips in just about the most masculine pose she could adopt.

I wasn't sure how long she'd been there but I assumed she hadn't heard anything too derogatory because Julie was smiling from ear to ear.

"Well?" Samantha demanded, a smirk giving her amusement away.

"It's as big a compliment as I can give you," I replied.

Samantha dropped her angry pose and sat down. The thing was, she sat in such an unladylike position, with her knees apart, just like a bloke would.

"What is it about this Cheese and Onion divide?" she asked.

"Julie?" I said, prompting her to explain.

"We'll fill you in next Tuesday, over lunch, babes," Julie said to Samantha. "I'm too busy now; I've got a missing mobile phone to find."

I didn't mention that if she really wanted any chance of recovering the item, she'd need a huge dose of luck and the Met's underwater search team.

Chapter 24

On Sunday the team made little progress.

The annoyed father was traced and eliminated when he provided a cast-iron alibi. Besides, his anger about the incident had clearly subsided.

There was no trace of the 'loan shark' and very little chance of finding them either. Such arrangements weren't documented.

The good news for me was that the house-to-house on the Bethnal Green estate hadn't identified any other witnesses to the events in the early morning of Saturday.

Curiously, Pod was yet to trace a next of kin. He'd gone through all the exhibits from the mortuary and the flat, examined the victim's various police and prison records but found nothing except an address for his mother in Spain. He could raise a request through Interpol, but they were notoriously slow and we wouldn't expect a result for maybe three months. It would actually have been quicker and easier for him to jump on a cheap flight and go and make the enquiries himself but the job's process for authorising non-urgent overseas travel was about as slow as making an Interpol enquiry.

Just before we clocked off, Pod took me into the yard to make a proposal. It was amazing how much business was conducted in the back yard.

"About tracing anyone who might have known the victim's mother. Look, we live about fifteen minutes' drive away. What do you think if I get the missus to drive over and just knock at a few neighbours' doors? I mean, she's not trying to investigate anything, or arrest anyone, or even identify any witnesses, just trying to locate a next of kin."

It seemed a sensible idea.

"Why will she say she is asking?" I asked.

"She'll just say she's a family friend," Pod proposed.

"I can't officially sanction it, but why not? Besides, if she doesn't give her surname, I don't see how it can backfire," I said.

"I'll give her a call. She was in the job years ago, in the days when plonks left when they had a baby," Pod said.

"I agree. Listen, as you've nothing to do as FLO, why don't you come out with me tomorrow. I've got an action to TIE Mr and Mrs Pascal."

TIE stood for trace, identify and eliminate.

"Oh, the guy whose missus had her bag nicked by Gary?" Pod asked.

"Yeah, do you know him?" I asked.

"I've heard the name, of course. In fact, I've heard the name quite recently, I think. What do you know of him?" Pod asked.

"I first came across him when I was up at CIB. He was an East London blagger who made good but he must be in his sixties now.

There wasn't any form of villainy he wasn't involved in, but the one I liked best was this. He ran a number of big warehouses where people with really expensive and vintage cars stored them. For a fee, Tony's boys would look after them, keep them valeted, make sure the battery was fully charged, turn the wheels, get them MOT'd and serviced; you know, all the stuff you have to do to make sure your investment holds its value. If you wanted to sell your car, he'd do that for you too.

"What he didn't tell the owners was that he was also leasing the vehicles out to City boys and the like who wanted to hire a Ferrari for a few days. He'd charge like a thousand quid for a weekend's lease. It was a beautiful scam until one day, an owner saw his precious Bugatti being driven down the King's Road in Chelsea by some young kid. He gave chase in his everyday Porsche and the whole charade ended up with two poor women being wiped up at a bus stop.

"That's when he first came on the radar at CIB as a corrupter of Old Bill. He was using contacts within the Met to find out who the witnesses were and where they could be found. There was good intelligence to suggest that he had a relative, a nephew or brother-in-law or something, that was a DC somewhere. As it transpired, Tony Pascal threatened or bought off witnesses and the case never even got to court.

"The last I heard he'd specialised in supplying Class A to stockbrokers, traders and investment bankers, you know, those working in the square mile."

"So do you know where we can find him?" Pod asked.

"Yeah, he lives out in the wilds of Essex, Chipping Ongar," I replied.

"That's a long way from a hairdresser's in Hoxton?" Pod said.

"You can take the villain out of East London but you can't take his missus out of the hairdresser's which she's used for the last forty years – or that's what I'm guessing," I replied.

"Does this Tony Pascal know you?" Pod asked.

"God, no. So you up for it?" I asked, knowing full well what the answer would be.

~~~

I called into Wendy's on the way home, giving her about thirty minutes' warning, which was enough time for her to get ready for my arrival. I was entertained to a very erotic strip to the Verve's *Bittersweet Symphony* and then the full works. Then there was that really awkward after-sex bit where I just want to get home and Wendy wanted me to stay.

It was really unusual for us to see each other at a weekend so this was an added bonus, but I had to get home. The thing was, I would stay with Wendy tomorrow night: it was a Monday, and I always stayed on a Monday. In order to keep Jackie happy, I needed to get home this evening and spend at least a little time with her.

My life was a constant balancing act, trying desperately to keep everyone happy and usually I did quite well, but I knew one day it would all come tumbling down. So real was that event to me that I'd given it a name, Armageddon. Now I knew I was probably overplaying it, that when it all went tits up it wouldn't actually be the end of the world, but for me it would be a seismic event.

To her credit, Wendy spotted that I was stressed, which she put down to the pressures of the job, but the real reason was because I was starting to feel panicky about my decision to give up. I found I was really agitated and I could hear my heart beating so forcefully that even my teeth vibrated in time with the cardiographic rhythm.

I spent a restless hour post-orgasm at Wendy's and then made my way home, where Jackie warmed up a lovely roast dinner that she had made earlier.

Then I spent twenty minutes on the toilet losing it; what a mess I was in.

Chapter 25

Monday was going to be a busy day. First, I had to get over to Essex to interview Tony Pascal and then I had an appointment in Putney with the superintendent from CIB. We had a six o'clock team meeting and then at eight, I was taking Wendy home, going out for a meal and staying the night.

I was in early and saw Julie undertaking a systematic search of the vehicles in the yard, looking for the missing phone. I joined in; it was the least I could do. Of course, we found nothing. As we walked in through the back door and up the stairs to the office, I noticed Julie had split her trousers along the seam and you could clearly see her lacy black knickers. I didn't know what to do. If I told her, that would mean I was looking at her arse, which I was but not really in that way, if you know what I mean? If I said nothing, she'd be really embarrassed when she realised, particularly if she'd been out and about all day.

I decided to tell her; she was fine and went off to sort it out.

~~~

An hour later Pod and I were driving over to Chipping Ongar.

Pod was a specialist Family Liaison Officer and probably the best I ever worked with. He was older, that always helped, and he had a calm, unruffled character. What's more, he picked his words carefully, never reacted quickly and naturally possessed and, more importantly, expressed oodles of empathy. If I ever lost one of my family, heaven forbid, I would want Pod to be the FLO.

I'd known some real FLO disasters over the years: the one who told the family that they were 'lucky' to have his team investigating the case – trust me, the last thing a murder victim's family want to hear when they've just lost a loved one is that they're 'lucky'; then there was the FLO who told the family the name of the suspect before he'd been either arrested or charged – the victim's father managed to find the suspect before the police did and shot him dead two days later in a pub in Belgravia; and another infamous FLO from South London who specialised in seducing the merry widows.

En route, I filled Pod in on the handbag theft. It was what we used to call a 'walk in theft' and once upon a time had been a really common crime, particularly in the factories and warehouses of the East End. Technically, it was a burglary because the thief was a trespasser, as he had no right to be in the building for that purpose.

This particular walk in theft, slash burglary, had occurred on 14th December at three fifteen p.m. at a hairdresser called *The Other Whitechapel Cutter*. The suspect had entered through the front door and stolen a Versace handbag, which had been left under the coat rack. A part-time employee called Ashley Carter recognised Gary and gave his name to the police officers that attended the hairdresser's. The victim provided a list of the bag's contents, none of which were of any particular value, with the exception of a pair of Armani ladies' sunglasses. No money was reported stolen. The victim told the police officers she didn't want to make a formal statement or go to court.

When he turned up to sign on the next day, the officer in the case arrested Gary on the off-chance that he would put his hands up and that he could proceed without a victim, but when Gary no commented the interview, she had no option but to NFA the case.

Gary said he was sleeping rough and his address was recorded as No Fixed Abode. In a serious case, they'd have put a surveillance team on him to find out where he was living, but in a job that wasn't going anywhere anyway, it wouldn't be worth it.

Chipping Ongar was much further than either of us had thought, but eventually we arrived at a really imposing gated residence. The house itself was lying out of sight and well back from the road.

Pod had been driving, so I jumped out to push the buzzer next to the gate. I waited just long enough for me to start to think that no one was in, when, without engaging in any intercom conversation, whoever was inside released the gates and they started to open.

I jumped back in the car and we drove slowly along a gently rising and twisting rhododendron-lined driveway and then entered a gravelled area in front of a really impressive late-Victorian, red-bricked detached house, which would have looked perfect as the setting for an Agatha Christie murder story.

Parked to the right was a seven series BMW, next to a silver Mercedes SLK, and both bore expensive three letter, single digit number plates. To the right of the Mercedes was a Suzuki GSX 750, which I recognised immediately because our old DCI George Becker had one, which he drove to work and parked in the back yard.

"His and hers, how sweet," Pod said.

Pod had just applied the handbrake when a grey-haired white male emerged from the garden to the right of the house; he was accompanied by two untethered German Shepherd dogs that took one look at our car and ran towards us barking.

We sat briefly like prisoners, as the male approached.

"Fuck this for a game of soldiers," Pod said.

I agreed.

Simultaneously, we opened our doors and stepped out. The dogs looked momentarily confused and backed off, but their barking intensified.

I'd never been particularly worried about dogs, though I knew some of my colleagues, like Julie, were terrified of them.

Many years ago, I'd spent a tour of duty walking around the Indian Embassy with a dog handler and his charge. We chatted all night and he taught me everything I ever needed to know about dogs, or so it felt like. I learnt that because it is a hunting animal, a dog only bites from the rear, and that for the same reason, a dog very rarely barks before it bites; and that the most dangerous dog was not one that barked but one that snarls, raises its top lip and circles behind you.

Based on this extensive training, I reckoned we were safe, but more importantly, by getting out of the car we were demonstrating to this guy that we weren't going to be intimidated or fucked about.

"Mr Pascal?" Pod asked, raising his voice above the ridiculous din.

Mr Pascal called the dogs off and only had to repeat himself the once before they were back at his side and silent. This was really impressive and in stark contrast to several dog handlers I'd seen. In fact, years ago I'd been bitten in the arse by a police dog when he mistook me for a burglar at the rear of some shops in Stoke Newington. Fortunately, the incident hadn't left a mental scar, just a few puncture hole wounds.

"Rozzers?" the man asked.

"Mr Pascal, I presume," I replied.

"What's your fucking name, rozzer? Stanley?" he asked.

"Chris, Chris Pritchard and this is DC Peter Dyson. We're from the murder squad," I said.

"You got a warrant?" he asked.

"Nope. We're not here to nick you, either. We're just looking to have a few words, if that's all right?" Pod said.

"You'd better come in then," Mr Pascal replied, in a tone that suggested that he appreciated Pod's candour.

Pod had a good manner with people and his age occasionally gave him an advantage, so I decided to take a back seat.

Mr Pascal opened the front door with a key, kicked off his boots and called out to 'Josie' in a loud but friendly manner.

"Shall we take our shoes off? asked Pod politely.

"No, you're all right, rozzer, leave 'em on. You won't be here long."

We followed him through an impressive oak-lined hall to an enormous kitchen at the back of the house, the floor area of which was larger than the entire downstairs of my own house.

A woman appeared wearing a white dressing gown and slippers; she was in her late fifties and slightly overweight but her hair and make-up had been the subject of much time and attention.

"Hello, Mrs Pascal," Pod said.

"Tea, boys?" she asked cheerfully.

"Please. Thank you," we replied together.

We stood around what I can only describe as an island of units in the middle of the enormous room.

"What can I do for you two likely lads?" Mr Pascal asked.

I let Pod do all the talking.

"Thank you for inviting us in. We are investigating the murder of Gary Odiham, who was stabbed a few nights ago in Dagenham."

"What's that got to do with me?" Mr Pascal asked.

"We think Gary stole your wife's handbag a couple of weeks ago when she was having her hair done in a hairdresser's in Hoxton."

"I have no idea what you're talking about?" he said.

Pod looked at Mrs Pascal.

"Some young lad nicked my handbag, Tony. One of the young girls that works at the place, you know sweeps up the hair, makes the tea, she recognised him and called the police. I would have forgotten his name, but it was Gary something. I told the police I didn't want to press charges."

"Was this at Sasha's place?" Mr Pascal asked his wife.

"Yes, of course. I was with mum, I always go with mum."

"My wife told me absolutely nothing about this theft," Mr Pascal declared definitively.

"Did you, darlin'?" he asked her, seeking confirmation.

Mrs Pascal shook her head.

"I never said a word to Tony," she confirmed.

"What was nicked? How much money did you lose?" Mr Pascal asked.

"I didn't have any money, honey. Well, just enough to pay for me and mum's hair," Mrs Pascal replied.

Mrs Pascal was pouring out the teas when a stunning young lady, probably in her mid-twenties, glided into the kitchen wearing only a white towel. Her dark brown hair was tied up and she appeared to be just about to get into a shower or bath. She ignored us completely and walked over to Mrs Pascal.

"Make me a tea, mum, please," she said.

"Lauren, get some clothes on, can't you see we have company?" her father said, clearly agitated by her presence.

Lauren glanced over her shoulder at us.

"Hello, boys," she said, almost seductively. "I'm assuming you're police officers?"

"Lauren, get the fuck out of here, now."

Her father was very clear and unambiguous.

I was a little surprised that he swore at her but then I had been slightly taken in by the grandeur of the residence; after all, Tony Pascal was at heart just another East London villain.

"Is this about Tim?" she asked.

Mr Pascal pointed a finger at his daughter and she turned on her heel and walked off without another word.

"So why the fuck didn't you tell me about this robbery?" Mr Pascal asked his wife.

"Tony, all I had in it was a few quid and some make-up. My purse was in my big handbag at home. Sasha was really embarrassed and didn't charge me for the cut and blow dry. It really was no big thing, and besides you'd have only got annoyed."

She put our teas on the island with some milk in a jug and a sugar bowl.

"So you thought I might have something to do with the murder of this lad? And over a fucking handbag? Which I knew nothing about anyway?" he asked.

"We needed to eliminate you," Pod said, with the slightest of smiles.

"Guys, I ain't gonna spend the rest of my life in prison for something as petty as that, am I?" he said.

I was tempted to point out that his wife obviously didn't trust his reaction, otherwise she would've told him in the first place, but I kept quiet.

"Have you heard about the murder?" Pod asked.

"Thirty something, scaghead and minor drug dealer stabbed in the ear with an ice pick in Dock Lane, Dagenham?" he asked.

"That's the one," Pod replied.

"No. I've not heard anything about it at all," Mr Pascal replied.

And with that, we all knew we weren't going to get any further with our enquiries in Chipping Ongar.

Chapter 26

Several hours later I was sitting in an office in Jubilee House in Putney, an eight-storey office building overlooking Putney Bridge and the Thames.

Ben's superintendent friend at CIB was Adam Stanley, a large white male in his early forties with a patchy beard, wearing a brightly coloured waistcoat. From his mannerisms and manicured speech, I assessed him to be an ex-Special Branch eccentric intellectual; the job was littered with them and generally they were really nice guys and a bit different from the rest of us.

"You were here a few years ago, were you not, old sport?" he asked.

"From eighty-eight to ninety-four, but we were at Tintagel House then," I replied.

"Did you work with Linda Potter, that superintendent that ended up kidnapping that young DS?"

I really couldn't be bothered to talk about that sordid affair and it was clear that Adam hadn't drawn my file; otherwise he wouldn't have asked that question.

"Yes, I did," I replied, without giving anything else way.

"Where were we? Oh, that's right, Ben says you have got something that we should know about. Something about a significant witness in one of your enquiries suggesting the involvement of a serving officer."

"That's right. Have you already spoken to Ben?" I asked.

"Briefly, yes. He's filled me in on the murder. Thirty-six-year-old white drug dealer, stabbed in the left ear somewhere in Dagenham; died in the back of a cab."

As awkward as it felt, I took Adam slowly through the events of the last few days. I filled in more details about the murder itself, talked about our search of the victim's flat, including the fact that the SOCO believed the place had been deliberately cleaned, covered the fact that Bethnal Green had searched the flat on a drugs warrant the day before, and then discussed the evidence provided by Mrs Amasanti.

I have to admit that every time I thought about the flat, I pictured the handgun still sitting under the pillow in the victim's bedroom and wondered why the Onions hadn't found it. Then I reminded myself that the search they conducted was to find evidence that might help to solve the murder. So they weren't looking for anything specific, like drugs or stolen property or, for that matter, a handgun. They would have been searching for a diary, a notebook, a computer, a mobile phone or sim card – anything that might contain a suspect's name or contact details. Perhaps it wasn't therefore particularly surprising that they hadn't searched a bed.

Throughout my diatribe, Adam kept making notes and didn't say a word. I concluded by handing over the tape of the Mrs Amasanti's interview and a copy of the Premsearch Register, which was in the system.

"And, old sport, please be so kind as to impart the name of the officer who is suspected of being involved in this?"

"I don't know," I lied, "but if the witness is right, he's a white male who's on the Crime Squad at Bethnal Green. There were only four of them on the search," I added, "maybe five," as quickly as I could, to suggest a less precise answer.

"The witness, the old lady, is eighty-nine?" Adam asked.

"Yep."

"Compos mentis?" he asked.

"Honestly, I think she's extremely credible but …" I paused for effect, "hand on heart, I think she's confused. I wouldn't convict anyone on her say so."

It was Adam's turn to pause, and then he left the room. I had no idea what was going on. He was gone a good forty minutes; so long, in fact, that I'd started to get really bored, so I'd decided to go through my phone and tidy up my contacts. Eventually, the door swung open again and he returned carrying several pieces of paper that were stapled together.

"Terribly sorry to keep you waiting, old sport. Chris, please read and sign. It's an NDA, a non-disclosure agreement, and it means that if you breathe a word of what I am about to tell you to anyone, you will commit a serious disciplinary offence, which could result in your dismissal. Do you understand?"

I was tempted to reply 'cross my heart and hope to die' but resisted and instead just said, "Yes, sir."

I flicked through the several typed pages until I found my printed name below a typed line where I signed and added the date. Adam took the document back and signed next to my name.

"You see, what you do not know, Christopher, is that this morning I had a call from a detective sergeant from Bethnal Green; this chap runs the Crime Squad. He made a very strong case to suggest that one of his DCs, a Ronald Edwards, is corrupt. And Detective Constable Edwards was on the drugs search of the victim's flat. In fact, your two stories marry very well indeed."

I thought I'd play dumb.

"I don't understand?" I said.

"It looks like this DC Edwards chap did find the drugs during the original search but rather than seize them, left them in situ so that he could go back later and steal them. He obviously didn't know these hoodlums would come calling, which drew the attention of your significant witness."

"Oh, I get you," I replied.

"There is something else though, something which does not make sense. A couple of years ago, the job had a problem with a thief over on Romford Borough. Things were going missing during searches and also from the locker room and places like that. Operation Tips was set up, PG Tips, tealeaf, thief. The ITU was in its infancy and it was an ideal scenario for them to run a few tests."

"ITU?" I asked.

"Integrity Testing Unit, old sport. Intelligence analysis identified three likely lads, so to speak, and the ITU ran integrity tests on each of them. Now I don't know what you know about integrity tests but they take forever to plan and implement, I mean months each. DC Edwards and another guy were on the Crime Squad there, and analysis suggested that they were the two most likely to be involved.

"A UC purporting to be an illegal from Eastern Europe rented a flat on the ground and spent two weeks filling the place with everything you would expect a Polish chap would need: you know, Polish cigarettes, Polish food, newspapers, currency, a passport, everything. Meanwhile, hidden cameras and microphones were placed everywhere. There wasn't anywhere in the flat that you could go without being videoed and recorded, even the WC.

"Then when we knew both targets were working, we put a phone call in to their DCI saying that the occupant was in custody in Manchester for possession with intent, saying that we were from the local CID and we asked them to do a quick Section 18 for us.

"In two locations of the flat, in really easy places to find, were two items which were the bait: the first was two hundred pounds cash in the top drawer of the bedside cabinet; the second was on the coffee table in the lounge and was a hundred quids-worth of US dollars.

"The two of them accepted the job from the DCI and with the Section 18 warrant in their little mittens, went round to the address and put the door in, which we'd deliberately set to be just about as easy as possible to break down, without being suspiciously so.

"It was beautiful except, my old sport …"

"Except what?" I asked, genuinely interested to learn what could have gone wrong.

"Neither of them stole a thing. They found both pieces of bait, sealed them up and booked them in back at the nick."

"Did you tell them?" I asked.

"No, you never tell a target who's passed a test, it's just the way it goes," Adam replied.

Of course, neither Samantha nor Nick would have been aware that Buster had passed this integrity test and if they had known, perhaps they wouldn't have had such a downer on him.

"Do you think they smelt a rat?" I asked.

"It's possible, of course, but the thing was, the following weekend the third suspect, a PC from Romford called Chris Panagopoulos, was caught stealing from a handbag at the Warren and Operation Tips was closed. I don't think there were any more thefts, so everything worked out all right in the end. I mean, old sport, the integrity test means Edwards isn't a thief, which contradicts the scenario about him going back to have the drugs off, doesn't it?

"Mind you, I found a really old vetting report from when he joined the job which identified that Edwards had some pretty dubious relatives on his mother's side, but then he was born and bred in the Elephant and Castle, so that's hardly a surprise, is it?"

"So what next?" I asked.

"We might do albums with Mrs Amasanti. That's one option. It shouldn't be difficult to cobble something together from warrant card photographs, even if some are a little dated. If that's not successful, we'll get a team behind him for a few days and then arrest DC Edwards and search his home address while there's still a chance that he's got some of the gear. Then we'll put the chap on an ID parade with your witness."

I didn't know what to say; all I could think was 'what a poor cunt'.

Chapter 27

It was six by the time I got back to the office, which was a hive of activity. I was only in a few minutes when Nick rang saying he wanted to meet me urgently and asking whether I could 'pop next door' to the Peacock.

As you entered the Peacock the bar went both right and left. My team usually took up positions to the right, where Jeff and two of the Onions were already putting the world to rights. I therefore made sure Nick and I sat round to the other side, the left, and in the corner.

I nodded to my colleagues, bought a couple of beers from the lovely barmaid Siobhan and joined Nick.

"What's the matter, dude?" I asked, as casually as I could under the circumstances.

"Right, first thing this morning I contacted the Right Line, or whatever it's called, and told them about Buster. Next thing I know, I'm talking to a detective superintendent called … I can't remember, but really posh. I told him what I told you and we chatted for ages. I didn't think any more about it, then about …"

Nick checked his watch.

"… just over an hour ago, fucking hell, mate, he calls me on my mobile and asked me to find out who boarded the flat up after our search and who had the new keys."

I listened carefully but didn't say anything.

"Well, it only took me about a minute to find out because I asked Seyone, the guy on attachment who was with us. He said he'd stayed behind at the address until it was boarded up and that the bloke what came out gave a set of new keys to Gary and a set to him. I asked Seyone why he thought he needed a set and he shrugged his shoulders and said he assumed they always did that. Anyway, I asked Seyone where that second set of keys were now and he said he didn't know what to do with them so, fucking hell, mate, he left them on Buster's desk with a note."

"So what are you telling me?" I asked.

"That Buster had a set of keys to the flat," he replied.

"And that's relevant because …?" I asked, conscious that Nick's thinking was that Buster had stolen the drugs during the search.

"Well, okay, if this guy from CIB is asking what happened to the keys to the flat after we left, I assume that he's thinking maybe Buster went back after we'd left and stole the drugs."

My mind was racing to keep ahead of what the fuck was going on here, who exactly knew what and particularly how much I should say, and to whom. I was pretty certain that I alone knew everything, which gave me a small advantage but I was genuinely concerned that every twist and turn events took, this Buster guy was looking guiltier and guiltier.

Was it possible that he could actually get in trouble for doing something he hadn't done? In this day and age that seemed absolutely impossible because there were just so many checks and balances. What's more, how far could I let this run before I intervened? And what guise would that intervention take? Finally, would I actually be prepared to sacrifice everything I had to save some guy I'd never met from being wrongly convicted? I wasn't sure I was either that good or that strong.

"Look, Nick. I might know more than I can tell you. I've had to sign a non-disclosure agreement, so I have to be really careful what I say. Apparently, if I tell you anything, I could lose my job," I said.

"Fucking hell, mate; so there is more to this than you or him can let on?" he said.

"Why don't you go back to CIB? The guy's name is Adam Stanley …"

"So you are involved?" he said, interrupting me.

"Have you told Adam what you've found out about the keys?" I asked.

"No, not yet. I wanted to speak to you first. Fucking hell, mate; I wanted to make sure that I wasn't in any trouble," Nick explained.

"Look, I don't think you're in any trouble. Give Adam a call; arrange a meet, he might be happy to share a bit more information with you. But please, please, don't say anything about me. I shouldn't have agreed to meet you today, and he doesn't know about our rendezvous in Victoria Park either. I've really tried to keep your name out of everything, but then you went and put yourself in it by making that call."

I was, of course, completely manipulating the story but Nick was lapping it all up.

"You're as sound as a pound, Nostrils, good old-school Old Bill. I promise that your name won't pass my lips."

"Cheers, dude," I said.

We were finishing our pints and I thought with this business concluded, we'd each go our merry ways. I was wrong, Nick seemed keen to have another drink and when he returned with two and sat down, I discovered that he had something else on his mind.

"Nostrils, you got Sam Clarke on your team?" he asked.

"Samantha Clarke," I corrected him. "Yes, why?"

"We were at Romford together years ago, on the same relief," he said.

"Go on.",I said, as there was clearly something he wanted to tell me.

"Fucking hell, mate; I thought I saw him in your car the other day, up at Vicky Park."

"You did," I replied.

"I couldn't fucking believe it when I heard. You'd have never met anyone less likely to be gay, let alone a tranny."

"I'm not sure that's quite the right term, I think you're meant to say 'trans'," I said.

"Of course, I heard the rumours when he went off sick, I was absolutely astounded," Nick said.

"She seems all right," I said tentatively.

I didn't know quite where this conversation was going.

"Sam, fucking hell, mate, he's as sound as a pound. Really good thief taker, really busy bee, never took any shit from anyone. Good company, heavy drinker, in fact he was the relief social secretary for years. Brave little warrior too: on one occasion in uniform he took on three herberts in a back alley and one of them had a knife and he nicked two of them. Got a Commissioner's Commendation for that."

He wasn't describing the Samantha I knew.

"I'll tell you something and I can give no one a higher compliment: I'd follow him in the box any day."

That was praise indeed for a colleague.

"Fuck me, Nick, you're not dating her are you?" I asked.

"Very funny, Nostrils. So how's he getting on now?"

"I think she's struggling to settle in but I'll do my best to help her."

I kept emphasising the 'she' in my sentences in the hope that Nick would pick up on the hint. My plan wasn't working.

"Difficult, isn't it? But he's all right, Nostrils. When you see him, give him my best and tell him I'm there for him if he needs to talk," Nick said.

That was a nice thing to do and say. My opinion of Nick just rose up one large rung.

"I will. I think she might take you up on that. I'll tell you what, let's go out for a drink with her, next week. I think that would really mean a lot."

"A drink? Next week? In public? With a tranny?" he asked incredulously.

Chapter 28

There was a small triangle of roads almost opposite Limehouse Police Station where, shortly after eight, I parked up to collect Wendy. She emerged through the front entrance a few moments later, crossed the busy road at a nearby pedestrian traffic lights and jumped into the passenger seat. She had been followed only seconds later by a young white man in his late teens and I noticed that at the crossing, he and Wendy exchanged a few parting words, so she obviously knew him. As he moved off, I looked more closely at him. There was something familiar in his manner and walk and I wondered whether I'd previously nicked him.

Wendy was wearing her white police blouse, a long dark blue uniform skirt and flat black shoes. Over the shirt, she wore wore a denim jacket, which meant she was technically wearing what we called 'half blues'.

"Hi, darling," she said, as she sunk into her seat.

"Who was that lad?" I asked.

"What lad?" she replied.

"The one that followed you out the nick, he said something to you by the crossing. I'm sure I recognise him."

Wendy paused, looked blank and then simultaneously shook her head and shrugged her shoulders. Clearly, I'd mistaken what I thought I'd seen. I didn't give the matter any more thought and we set off for Leyton. We chatted all the way and I was surprised when Wendy suggested popping into the pub on the way, because usually she'd have wanted first to get changed out of what was left of her uniform.

"Are you sure?" I asked.

"It's too late to go home and then go out again; let's go to the Bird, no one will take any notice of me dressed like this in there."

The Bird, or to give the hostelry its full title, the Blackbird, was our local. Although the pub was only a mile from where Wendy lived, we still took the car because Wendy didn't drink, so getting home was never an issue. We knew the landlord and his wife quite well and several of the regulars had over the years become good friends.

We were seated on our usual stools, with our usual drinks, when Wendy started a conversation with those words that no one really wants to hear.

"There's something I need to tell you and I'm not sure how you're going to react."

"Ah, so this is why we're in the pub; safety in numbers, eh?" I said, with more joviality than I felt inside.

She looked serious.

"Are you leaving me?" I asked.

"Oh God no; I'll never, ever, ever leave you," she replied.

"Well then, don't be afraid; out with it, wench," I demanded.

"The lad you saw leaving the nick, the one I spoke to at the crossing."

"The one you denied speaking to at the crossing," I corrected her.

"He's your son," she said.

"I'm sorry, what did you say?" I asked.

"He's your son, he's Matthew Star."

"What?" I said.

"He's your son. The one Sarah had, years ago. Well, eighteen years ago, to be exact," Wendy explained.

"Okay," I said slowly.

"He wants to meet you, to get to know you," she said.

"Wendy, darling, and please don't take this the wrong way, but what's he doing talking to you?"

"His mum wouldn't tell him anything about you until he got to eighteen. Then she told him that she had an affair with you, when you were both police officers together at Stoke Newington. I mean, he didn't even know his mum had ever been a police officer; that's how guarded she was about that part of her life.

"She told him that you'd been badly injured by an IRA bomb and that your colleague had died in your arms. She told him that he was named after, and in memory of her, hence the name Matthew. She also told him that you'd been awarded a gallantry medal for rescuing someone from a burning house and that you were one of the best and most honest police officers she'd ever known.

"Matthew said he was fascinated by the news and that he knew he had to find you.

"Although she didn't know it, Sarah assumed you were still in the job. Well, Matthew is clearly a young man with a lot of initiative. He had a friend whose brother had just joined the Met. He got his mate's brother to look you up on Aware and found out that you worked at Arbour Square. He went there yesterday but discovered, of course, that the place is closed to the public, so he picked up the phone by the door, you know, the one that connects you with the control room at Limehouse.

"Gazza answered it, you know gay Gazza, the civvie who always does ten to six in the control room. Anyway, Matthew asked to speak to you. Gazza didn't know where you were working now so naturally he put Matthew through to me in the CSU, telling him that I was your 'other half'.

"I was really busy yesterday and as you know, we had the Deputy Assistant Commissioner visiting the unit. Anyway, I wasn't really focused on anything the poor lad was saying and the line was really bad, so I told him to come to the station today and ask for me at the front counter. I didn't realise it was anything to do with you and just thought it was related to one of my cases. I'd completely forgotten about him when I got a call about six this evening to say I had a visitor at the front counter. I've just spent the last two hours with one of the nicest young men I've ever met. Chris, he wants to meet you, to get to know you."

I didn't know what to say so I took a deep glug of beer instead.

"What's he doing with his life?" I asked eventually.

"He did his A levels in the summer and has taken a gap year before going to Exeter to study geography. Rather than go travelling round the world, he's stayed at home and been working with his dad because one of the things he wanted to do, was to see if he could find you and if you were happy, to get to know you."

"What's his mum up to?" I asked.

"She's married and he's got two younger half-sisters."

"What did you tell him?" I asked.

"I told him that I'd speak to you to see if you wanted to meet him. He understands that you may not want to be involved with him; he also knows that Sarah left you and wouldn't let you have anything to do with him. He's not angry, annoyed or upset. He just wants to find his real father, Chris."

I nodded and took another drink of beer.

"Anyway, he's staying at a B&B in Putney, so he's about for the next couple of days. Listen, Chris, you're a lovely dad to discover you've got. I mean, a hero policeman, one of London's top detectives …"

I laughed. "Many claim that status," I said.

"No, I'm looking at it from his point of view, not the reality."

"Thanks a lot," I said, laughing out loud.

"One of London's top detectives, medals for bravery and a lovely man, to boot. What more could a son wish to discover about his long-lost dad?"

A 'lovely' man? I was doubtful. Not from where I'm sitting, more like 'drug addict, burglar, perverter of justice and bigamist' man!

Chapter 29

I had a nice evening with Wendy, but the subject of Matthew dominated the conversation and if I was being honest, I really needed time to think things through without being bombarded by my girlfriend's views and opinions.

Besides, how was I going to explain to Matthew the 'Jackie and Wendy' aspect of my life? Would he want to meet his half-sisters, Pippa and Trudy? How would Jackie react to him? Very few mothers welcome their father's additional offspring into the nest, that I knew for sure. The lad seemed to have done pretty damn well without me; I mean, he'd got A levels and was going off to a decent university. What value could I add to his life? Besides, the timing of his appearance was really bad, not that that was his fault.

After a decade of comparatively uneventful life, I had suddenly found myself in a pile of shit. I didn't know how this was going to play out and whether as yet, I'd end up going to prison and losing my job. How pleased would my son be then, that he'd found his long-lost father? Especially if he'd just started to get used to me being around?

No, there was definitely a lot to consider before I was going to commit to meeting Matthew.

I got a feeling that Wendy was really enjoying the fact that she had a grip on something that wasn't Jackie-centric. This was a part of my pre-Jackie life and was potentially part of my future and Wendy sensed a rare advantage over her rival. What's more, this was an opportunity for her to be involved with one of my children, albeit one I'd never met and didn't know at all.

The whole episode had disturbed me and I felt some resentment towards Sarah, too. Who was she to decide to suddenly do this to me? Had she asked me first? Like fuck, she had. Just like when all those years ago she decided to disappear out of my life and take my unborn son with her. She'd never bothered to ask me then what I thought or whether I would like her to do something different.

As I thought about those old dark days at Stoke Newington in the mid-eighties, other memories started to come back. The fact that Sarah had sacrificed her own career to make sure her then-boyfriend and his mate didn't fit me up for something I hadn't done. How she'd written me a really touching and heartfelt letter to explain what she'd done and to say goodbye.

With so many thoughts and memories swirling around my head, I was really unsettled during the night and kept tossing, turning and going to the toilet. I don't know whether it was the Buster issue or the appearance of Matthew, or both, but I was awake until gone three.

I decided I'd try to look on the bright side of my life, the best part of which was that it had been one hundred and twenty hours, or nearly six days, since I'd last taken heroin.

Chapter 30

Tuesday started with our third office meeting of the campaign and one by one, we went through our actions.

Pod updated everyone about our meeting with Tony Pascal and our thoughts that he'd probably not had anything to do with what had happened. One of the Onions suggested that the murder could have been 'one of Pascal's minions who were trying to impress their boss', which actually wasn't a bad suggestion.

The house-to-house in Dagenham was all but complete, with absolutely no leads, which was extremely rare. The CCTV analysis had been similarly unremarkable and hadn't uncovered the victim, other than when he entered the petrol station, or any sightings of potential suspects. This actually supported my own supposition that the victim had run down one of the residential roads that were opposite.

We were still waiting for toxicology, but in all probability that was only going to tell us exactly what drugs the victim had taken.

There was still no next of kin and this was the first murder investigation I'd ever been involved in without a next of kin.

Julie apologised to the DCI for losing the victim's phone, which I thought was a very brave thing to do, because sometimes the Onions could be unforgiving bastards, but to their credit, they didn't exploit the moment. Of course, I did feel a pang of guilt knowing that I was the guilty party, not Julie, but dwelling on the issue wouldn't solve anything nor bring the phone back. The DCI asked for a report on the incident.

Julie then informed everyone that SOCO confirmed the flat had, at the very least, been partially cleaned by someone after the murder but before the Onions had searched it. She explained that a common brand of furniture polish had been found on swabs taken from the laptop and a few other places in the hall. She pointed out that not only was that brand of polish not kept in the flat, no polish or cleaner of any make or type had been found anywhere on the premises.

Understandably, the DCI was convinced that the cleansing of the flat was really significant; he explained,

"Team, I think we can assume that whoever murdered the victim knew where he lived. Bearing in mind that the victim was murdered a good distance from his home address, this must mean that there was a significant pre-existing relationship between the two. This was not, I repeat, not a chance meeting, such as unplanned robbery or other random violent attack. Do you all agree?"

I looked around the room; everyone was nodding in agreement, except me.

It was now my opinion that because of my actions, this murder was going to be almost impossible to solve.

Julie said that despite somebody's attempts to forensically clean the victim's flat, prints had still been found in the lounge. She said there were seven prints lifted which weren't the victim's, and CRO had identified four different people. The first was a palm print from the front door and it belonged to a Duncan Monroe, a licensed door security man and former prison officer who had one previous for a GBH on a prisoner, when he was a screw at HMP High Down.

Two others were females who resided on the Attlee House estate, a Sonia Rider and a Susie Watson, and four were unknown because their owners hadn't got a criminal record. It did cross my mind that one of these prints might be my own, but I'd have to worry about that later. And then I realised that they may belong to the officers that were on the Crime Squad search but decided to keep my thoughts to myself for fear that I might say a little too much.

My team got the actions to interview the two females on the estate and the Onions were told to trace and eliminate the former prison officer.

We were all used to these office meetings lasting for hours; it was indicative of the lack of leads that this one had taken no more than thirty minutes.

Samantha, Pod, Nicola and Taff set off to trace the two females. I stayed in the office. I had a quick word with Taff and asked him to make sure Samantha wasn't left on her own; he said he understood and asked me to leave it with him.

The Onions had decided to arrest their ex-prison officer, a decision with which, incidentally, I agreed. It seemed likely that he wasn't there to buy drugs but as a debt collector. If he had nothing to do with the murder, he was more likely to tell you what he was doing there, if he was arrested. Being arrested for murder tended to focus the mind.

I spent the rest of the morning writing up some actions, reading through the statement bundles, looking through the messages and reviewing the documentary exhibits, particularly those which had been seized from the victim's flat. I was desperately trying to find some hint or clue that had been missed. I found the handwritten poem and read it several times:

When I closs my eyes, I see you.
You're smile is so honest and free.
You were always happy and so full of love.
But you left becuase of me.
Without you here, the darkness falls.
The nightmares rome and Lusifer calls.
Forgive me, Grace, I miss you so.
I'll join you soon, of that I no.

It was signed and dated 30th December 1988.

There were a few spelling mistakes but the sense of loss was certainly there, and he'd kept it all these years; but it was fifteen years old, so it couldn't be anything to do with the murder?

I dug out a copy of Gary Odiham's criminal record, which I studied carefully. There was no suggestion of any arrest related to a death and the rest was typical for a thirty-six-year-old low-level drug dealer.

I then had another look through his CRIMINT record – there was nothing of note and what few lines of enquiry there were had already been actioned.

I wandered down to make a cup of tea and noticed Jeff standing on the fire escape balcony smoking, so I joined him. No one I knew had investigated more murders than Jeff.

"What do you reckon then? 'Cos quite frankly, you old cunt, I haven't got a clue," I asked.

Jeff smiled at the sheer abruptness of my question.

"You're a fucking nightmare, Nostrils," he said, "no wonder everyone hates you."

"What are you talking about? My team loves me," I said, smiling broadly.

"That's true; you're like marmite, Nostrils. People either love you or hate you. Personally, I think you're a bit of a tosser."

It was my turn to laugh.

The curious thing was, it wasn't an unfriendly exchange.

"Well, what happened to our victim? Have you ever known a case with fewer leads?"

Jeff flicked his cigarette on to a nearby roof and immediately lit a second.

"I'll tell you what happened. Gary Odiham was at a nearby address buying his weekly supply to sell. Someone was waiting for him to leave, rolled him for the drugs and he got stabbed because he fought back, or ran, or because the robber didn't give a fuck. The only connection Gary will have to that part of London will be to a nearby dealer, who by now and because of all the attention from the Old Bill, will have upped sticks and moved on."

Jeff's logic was sound enough.

"But what about the victim's flat being cleaned?" I asked.

"It doesn't make sense and personally I don't think it'll be important. A red herring riding a white elephant, Nostrils."

"Perhaps," I replied cautiously.

"You got a better idea?" he asked.

"I sort of agree; it's got to do with drugs," I replied.

My phone went. It was the DCI who was upstairs in his office and he wanted to see me immediately.

I felt nervous; what the fuck had happened now?

Chapter 31

"I didn't realise you were here, I assumed you'd be out and about," Ben said, before I had sat down.

"My team's on the estate but I had some corres to do. I also wanted to read through what we've got so far," I explained.

"Your witness, the old Italian girl, she was spot on," he said.

"In what way?" I asked.

"They nicked Duncan Munroe this morning. During interview he said that he went to the address with another male to collect some money that his boss was owed by the victim. He said his mate was looking through the letter box and saw a police officer."

"Was he in uniform?" I asked, playing along.

"No, I don't think so," the DCI replied.

"How did they know he was a police officer?" I asked.

"Munroe's mate says he thought he saw a police badge; I assume he means a warrant card but has been watching too many American cop programmes," the DCI replied.

"What? Through the letter box?" I asked.

"Yes, no, I'm not sure but he says the guy in the flat, who they thought was Gary Odiham, showed them his brief. The guy who was with Munroe was wanted for failing to appear, so they gave it legs. I admit, it's all a bit confusing."

"Do we know who the other male is?" I asked.

"He won't say," the DCI replied.

"What's the description of the guy in the flat?" I asked.

"They never really saw him. They'd assumed it was Gary but when they realised it wasn't, panicked and scarpered. Munroe actually said that after they'd fucked off and thought about the whole thing, they came to the conclusion that it may not have been a real police officer."

"So no description at all?" I asked.

"No, white, male, early forties and that's it."

"I don't suppose he mentioned the name of his boss, did he? The one Gary owed the money to?" I asked.

The DCI shook his head.

"Do we know how much money it was?" I asked.

Again, the DCI shook his head.

"Was the officer on his own in the flat?"

"He doesn't know; he only saw one officer but assumed there were others," the DCI replied.

"What are they going to do with Munroe?" I asked.

"Release him on bail. They don't think he's anything to do with the murder and of course, his account is corroborated by the old girl next door. Munroe says he'll speak to his mate, who'll probably give himself up. Apparently, the reason he didn't want to get arrested on Thursday night was because it was his daughter's birthday Friday and his missus would have gone ballistic if he'd missed the party."

"And I thought the old girl was mistaken," I replied.

"Your witness was spot on, Chris. Did you speak to Detective Superintendent Stanley?"

"Yes, boss, yesterday," I replied.

"What did he say?"

"I've signed an NDA, boss, I can't tell you," I replied.

"So there's more to this, then? Have we crossed an existing covert op?" he asked.

"I can't say," I replied.

"We must have done, otherwise you wouldn't have had to sign an NDA. If everything you'd told them was new, they'd have simply submitted an intelligence report and undertaken some development enquiries. What you told them must have dovetailed into something else they knew or were already up to. Get hold of Adam, ask him to see us both as soon as possible."

"Yes, boss," I said.

I went to stand up but the DCI indicated that I should remain seated.

"What does it all mean?" he asked.

Before I could say anything, the DCI went on,

"We have an officer who was part of the search on the Thursday morning, a simple drugs warrant, where no drugs were actually found. That night, or rather in the early hours of Friday, our victim is murdered in Dagenham, about six miles away from the flat?"

"About that," I replied.

"Then within twenty-four hours, the officer who was at the search is back at the flat, forensically cleaning it, when he is mistaken for the victim by a couple of guys to whom the victim owes money. When challenged, the officer shows out and then, presumably, makes his exit."

"So what's the connection between the victim and the officer?" I asked.

I didn't want to say anything but I was walking a very thin line here and had to make the whole conversation appear as natural as possible.

"I'd say informant and handler, but if that was the case why would the officer have gone back to the address? Let's get that checked out, though. Ask Jeff to raise an action to see if the victim was an informant," the DCI directed.

"Will do," I replied obediently.

"But let's assume there's no informant angle to this. What's the fucking relationship?" the DCI asked.

"Friends, family, old school mates, dealer and purchaser? I wonder if the officer had arrested him, you know, previously?" I suggested.

"Okay. I like it, raise an action to research all old arresting officers and cross-reference against the Premsearch Register."

"Will do," I replied.

"Even if the victim was serving up to the officer …" The DCI paused, mid-sentence. "No, that doesn't make sense, he's hardly likely to get involved in doing a warrant at his own dealer's address, is he? Unless, of course, he tipped him off, which would explain why no drugs were found. Fuck me, that's it," the DCI said with excitement.

"I'm not quite with you," I said, which was partly true.

"Look. It doesn't matter what the nature of the relationship was, but I think it's safe to say that there was some pre-existing relationship between the victim and the officer on the search. When the officer learns that they're going to do a warrant at the victim's flat, he tips the victim off, which explains why nothing was found. Then, when he learns that the victim's been murdered, the officer goes to the address to clean any forensic evidence that he's ever been there and, possibly, remove the drugs. At which point, Munroe and his mate turn up and disturb him."

"But that doesn't work," I said.

"Go on?"

"Why would he go back to hide forensic evidence when he'd just searched the place; I mean, his prints can legitimately be all over the flat," I pointed out.

"Okay, good point. Maybe he'd gone back for another reason? No, this doesn't make any sense at all. Why would he clean the flat?"

"And another thing, we didn't release the victim's details until yesterday, did we? 'Cos we hoped to notify a next of kin first. So how would the officer from the search know that quickly that he'd been murdered?" I asked.

"Perhaps he didn't need to hear it from us because he murdered the victim, that's how he knew he was dead, that's how he knew that he had to go back to the flat and that's how he also knew the coast was clear – that's an explanation," the DCI replied.

"It's one explanation, not the only one, boss. There are just too many assumptions," I replied.

"I agree, it's just useful to talk these things through sometimes. Give Adam a call; let's get over there as soon as we know he's free. Hang on a second …"

The DCI had just realised something.

"… you already know the identity of the officer who was in the flat, don't you?"

I nodded slowly. The fact was, I wasn't lying.

Chapter 32

We met Adam at Jubilee House, but this time, instead of being taken to a small interview room on the second floor, we were led to the canteen on the fourth floor where we were treated to posh filter coffees and several Danish pastries. Ben and Adam chatted about old times at Special Branch, I sat quietly asking myself how the fuck we'd got to this state of affairs. Adam found us a table in one corner, well away from the few others who were about, but no sooner had we sat down and started to discuss the case than I saw Dave Walby sitting at the far end of the room.

Dave and I had been DSs together at CIB years ago and he had quite literally saved my life. He was a DI now; we had remained friends for many years, but as is so often the way, our lives had taken different paths and we hadn't spoken for ages.

Dave caught my eye, came bounding over immediately and shook my hand. I noticed straight away that he'd put on about two stone.

"Chris, you old bastard, are you working back here? Why didn't you tell me? You taken promotion yet?" he said.

"Hello, Dave, no and no. How's the missus? How's Kerry-Anne, how old is she now? I asked.

"She's twenty-six now. Getting married in the summer, you must come to the wedding. What do you mean no and no?" he asked.

"No I'm not working back here and no I haven't taken promotion, I am still a DS. Where's the wedding, I'd love to come?"

"It's in a little Wiltshire village called South Wraxhall; she's living down there now with her fiancé – he's a pilot for BA. How's the lovely Jackie, she caught you out yet, you old shagger?"

"Dave, I've got a bit of business. When I'm through, I'll come and find you. Okay?"

We shook hands again and I watched him walk away. Apart from saving my life, he was the only person in the whole world who knew about and understood my addiction to H. As soon as Dave was out of earshot, the DCI spoke. He was upbeat, excited and really enthusiastic; in contrast, I felt physically sick.

Adam got him to sign a non-disclosure agreement and then filled him in on the Buster connection, on which he'd hitherto been unsighted.

Adam said that he had established that Buster had retained the second set of keys to the replacement front door and that this was how he'd managed to gain entry in the middle of the night.

When Adam heard about Munroe's statement and the flashing of the warrant card, it was clear Buster's fate was sealed. Although there was no one anywhere near us, Adam lowered his voice and leaned forward.

"We have had DC Edwards under surveillance for the last forty-eight hours."

"Anything of note?" the DCI asked.

"Not at all, old sport. The usual life of a Met detective – work and then home to either wife and kids or girlfriend. What is it about these chaps, why in God's name do they want to complicate their lives so much?"

Both the DCI and I looked down awkwardly.

"Anything else?" the DCI asked again.

"Only one thing, Benjamin. I think we will need to set up a joint investigation team, based here. Perhaps DS Pritchard and half a dozen of your best men ..."

"Officers," I interjected, correcting his gender assumption.

"... yes, yes, of course, Chris. Half a dozen of your best officers, one of whom will need to be the exhibits officer."

"That's a DC *Julie* White." I said, emphasising her female first name.

"I'll need to run that suggestion by my OCU Commander," replied the DCI.

I detected just the slightest hint of frustration in Ben's voice; clearly he was disappointed at the prospect of losing control of the case.

"Is it on HOLMES?" Adam asked.

"Of course," we replied.

"That's okay, we've got access to account managers here. They can throw a switch and we'll be able to pick it up," Adam said.

"I can't see any way that this DC Edwards is not somehow involved in the murder. DC Edwards looks as guilty as a puppy sitting next to a pile of fresh poo," the DCI said.

"I agree, my old friend," Adam said.

"And just make sure you don't fuck up, Adam, because you're just about to take this case away from London's most successful murder squad," the DCI said quietly.

"Don't worry, we'll put DC Edwards on the sheet for you and we will keep you in the loop, I promise. Let's get Chris over first, I'll find an office but it might have to be off-site. If ..."

Adam quickly corrected himself.

" ... when I need your advice and guidance, I'll be in touch straight away."

Adam's voice was conciliatory.

"I will still need to speak to my DCS, I don't have the authority to just hand the whole job over," the DCI said.

"A serving police officer wanted for murder; I don't think anyone's going to argue, do you, old sport? But I understand that you will have to speak to your bosses."

I could see it all from their point of view, I really could. Buster was bang to fucking rights, everyone knew it, no doubt about it, except of course, he wasn't because the poor guy had done absolutely nothing wrong. The problem was, only he and I knew that.

I knew I couldn't let that happen and would have to come clean, but don't think for one moment that any part of me wanted to do so. It would be the end of my career and this job was all I had done since I was a boy.

A woman popped her head around the canteen door and, having spotted Adam, gestured for him to join her.

Adam politely excused himself.

The DCI turned to me, lowered his voice and said, "This Buster guy has obviously been on their radar for years, did you hear that? They did a job on this DC two years ago."

I nodded, although clearly I'd been so engrossed in my own thoughts that I'd completely missed that conversation.

"Are you all right, Chris? You look really grey," the DCI asked.

"I don't feel great, boss, I've had the shits for a week," I replied.

The DCI went to speak but at that moment Adam came back to the table and sat down. It was clear from his expression that something significant had happened. I wondered if they had worked out that it was me who they should be after and not Buster.

"We've got a small problem," he said.

'Here we go,' I thought.

"DC Edwards and his wife and kids have just got on a plane at Gatwick and are, as we speak, in the air and on their way to Madeira."

"How long have they gone for?" I asked.

"Initial enquiries with the airline would suggest a week, but that's not confirmed yet."

I had seven days to solve the murder, stop Buster getting nicked and save my own career.

Chapter 33

Even though I only had a week to unravel this awful mess, I really couldn't leave Jubilee House without catching up with Dave. So when we'd said goodbye to Adam, I told the DCI I'd catch up with him later and that I'd make my own way back to Arbour Square. The DCI said that he had to buy a birthday present for his wife so he was going to have a gander down the High Street; we agreed to meet in reception in an hour. I thought the fact he was still buying his missus a present suggested they weren't irreconcilably parted and was a good sign, but I decided not to trigger a conversation by commenting about it.

Ten minutes later, Dave and I were sitting in a coffee shop opposite one of my favourite pubs, the Spotted Horse. I was certain the place we were in used to be a small wine bar, but the residents of Putney were clearly starting to prefer caffeine to alcohol.

I noticed Dave chose a table in a dark corner, out of sight of the main part of the premises.

Dave was in his early fifties with unkempt wispy grey hair that had a will of its own.

Many years ago, Dave had got me out of a spot of bother and I felt affection towards him, which I imagined was similar to how you would feel about your favourite older brother. He'd also gone out of his way to look after me when an old girlfriend, Carol, had dumped me, and I'd even spent one Christmas with him and his family. But more importantly than any of this, Dave and I shared two secrets – the biggest will remain a secret to my dying day but the second was that I was on the gear a lot longer than I pretended to the job.

We'd only just sat down when he asked me – no, he ordered me – to roll my sleeves up, and I realised why he'd wanted to sit here.

Had it been anyone else in the world asking me to do that, I'd have told them to go fuck themselves, but not Dave. Dave had earned the right to ask that of me a long time ago, and for ever.

I did as he requested. He took each arm in turn and studied it closely.

"Good, good. Are you clean?"

"I am," I replied, completely honestly.

"When did you last?" he asked.

Fuck! I really didn't want him to ask that question because I wasn't in the mood for a lecture, but nor would I lie to him.

"One hundred and sixteen hours," I replied, completely honestly.

Dave put his head in his hands.

"Oh, Nostrils, for fuck's sake."

I didn't know what to say or do; Dave's reaction was straight from the heart.

I could tell him that he didn't understand how hard it was, I could explain that I had actually given up and that one hundred and sixteen hours was 'giving up' but he would think both sentiments were bullshit and of course, he'd be right.

"Does Jackie know?" he asked.

Dave thought the world of Jackie. He'd been there when we'd started going out, had been to and even made an unprompted speech at our wedding, and was probably one of the few people left in the Met who had actually met her.

"No," I replied.

My mind formed a sentence in my defence but my brain knew it was bollocks, so I said nothing.

"I should get up and walk out of here," he said.

I looked down in shame.

"Give me one fucking reason why I should stay?" he asked.

"Because I think so much of you, because I don't want you to, because I told you the truth, and most importantly of all, because if you walk out now there's more chance of me getting back on the gear," I said.

I felt deeply ashamed; a tear rolled down my left cheek.

"Does the job know?" he asked, his head still clasped in his hands.

I shook my head.

He looked up and saw me crying.

"You stupid cunt," he said.

"I know," I replied.

"But you did give up, didn't you?" Dave asked.

"I did. I gave up in 1991."

"When? Why?" he asked.

"I was clean for six, seven years and then something happened, but I've got no excuse. I was at Tottenham at the time, in the CID office."

"So you've been back on the gear for five years?" he asked incredulously.

I nodded.

"But your arms are clear, so you're not injecting, right?" Dave asked.

"No, I don't inject, ever. I usually smoke and I really don't do much, and I've been really cutting down over the last couple of years," I said but the more I explained, the stupider I felt.

I wanted to be anywhere else, but I wasn't leaving.

"Nostrils, what am I gonna do with you?" Dave said, with genuine affection.

"Thank you for caring. I know you probably think this is bollocks but I gave up on Wednesday, that's six days ago. You might think that's nothing but for me six days is the longest I've been clean in years."

"I've never met a heroin addict who hadn't just given up," he said, and he was, of course, absolutely right.

"You have now," I said.

"So why now?" he asked.

"Last Thursday I was buying from a dealer in Bethnal Green when the local Crime Squad came through the door. I managed to talk my way out of it but it was the last straw and I decided to quit. Believe me or not, but if I'd wanted to lie to you I would have just told you I'd not scored for years, wouldn't I?"

"Um," Dave replied.

I took out a tissue and wiped my face dry.

"You know they're going to introduce intelligence-led drug tests for officers, don't you?"

"I've heard. Well actually, I thought it was going to be done randomly," I replied.

"They're going to do both. Intelligence-led when they receive specific information and random for officers undertaking what they deem to be critical roles," he explained.

"Critical roles?"

"You know, carrying firearms, UC officers, close protection for the royal family. If you've been on the gear for so long, how come you're still alive, Nostrils?" he asked.

"That's what my doctor wants to know. But as I said, I have been reducing the amount significantly. I probably take about a quarter, maybe even a fifth, of what a normal addict would take," I replied.

"So why didn't you give up earlier?" he asked.

I shrugged my shoulders because there really was no answer to that.

"Can we talk about something else?" I asked, indicating the closeness of the people behind us.

"So you reckon you can finally get off the gear this time?" he asked.

"Because I was off it for years, I know it can be done," I replied.

"Can we change the subject, please?" I implored him; I really didn't want everyone in Putney to know I was a scaghead.

"The guy in the canteen with Adam Stanley, was that Ben Richards?" Dave asked.

"Yeah, he's our new DCI. Well when I say new, I mean he's been with us about three months. He's a nice fella," I replied.

"Isn't he the one that's seeing the Indian indexer?" he asked.

"I've no idea who he's seeing," I replied honestly.

"Between you and me, we had a DCS here that used to be on AMIP. He had a bee in his bonnet about some of the guys who worked at Arbour Square. He was convinced they spent their time in the pub next door."

This was sounding rather familiar.

"Anyway, one of the first things he did when he came to CIB was set up a camera above the dry cleaner's opposite. It was on the back gate and it recorded everyone coming and going. Anyway, one of the guys from the team he was targeting was at Denmark Hill looking through some CCTV when he noticed playing on the next machine a video of the back of Arbour Square nick. The shit hit the fan because of course the DCS didn't have any directed surveillance authority. It was a right old mess."

I realised this was nothing to do with my team after all.

"What was his problem with the guys he was after?" I asked.

"They'd nicked him years ago for assaulting his missus," Dave explained.

Suddenly I knew the DCS he was talking about. I once worked with a guy who'd told me the story about a senior officer who used to slap his wife about.

"I know about that, well, the domestic violence bit," I said.

"Everyone in the Met knows about it. How he's still in the job I don't know," Dave replied.

We sipped our coffees and although I was facing the wall, I was vaguely conscious that other people were sitting down at the table immediately behind us. I looked down and wiped my face again because I didn't want anyone else to see I'd been upset.

"I bet you wish you were sitting here," he said.

"What?" I asked, caught by the sudden change in conversation.

"The woman that's just sat down behind you is fucking gorgeous," he whispered.

Dave had always been a bit of a nightmare where the other sex was concerned. In fact, during one search we'd done, he'd actually stolen a pair of the female occupant's knickers. I can honestly say that where the other sex was concerned, Dave had much more ambition than ability, and normally ended up looking a complete arse, but his attempts to pull were frequently amusing.

"Is she with a bloke?" I asked, vaguely aware that I'd thought it was a couple.

"More like her kid brother," he replied.

It was the first time Dave and I had stopped talking. From behind me I heard a very familiar voice say,

"I've spoken to your dad. He actually saw you yesterday as we were walking out the police station."

Chapter 34

I froze.

"What's the matter, Nostrils? You look like you've seen a ghost," Dave said.

I didn't say a word but I was conscious that my head was shaking slowly from side to side as the situation sunk in.

"What is it? For fuck's sake, Nostrils."

Dave's voice was louder this time and I went to shush him but it was too late. I heard the chair behind me slide backwards and felt more than saw Wendy appear to my left.

"Chris, darling," she said, her voice full of genuine surprise, "what are you doing here?"

"Hello, hon, I was at Jubilee House with some business when I bumped into an old colleague, er, friend," I corrected myself quickly.

"Wendy, this is Dave, Dave is the guy that came to Thailand when I was in that spot of bother with Linda Potter."

"Hi, I'm really pleased to meet you. Chris has told me all about you, many times," Wendy said, in a manner that immediately suggested to Dave we were more than just good friends.

Dave looked slightly confused but he stood up and shook Wendy's outstretched hand.

Wendy turned towards me and lowered her voice.

"You do know who I'm here with?" she asked, her face in a comical grimace.

"I can guess, I heard a bit of your conversation just then," I replied.

"What you going to do?" she asked.

If I was going to meet my son for the first time, these were not the circumstances I would have chosen but it appeared I didn't have a choice. Without replying, I stood up and turned around.

Sitting starring into a huge mug of tea was a young white lad with blond hair who facially looked exactly like I did at that age; the similarity was so striking it took my breath away. I was looking at Chris Pritchard on his first day at Training School but with blond hair; it was like seeing a ghost from the past.

Matthew clearly hadn't realised exactly whom Wendy had got up to speak to; his eyes darted up from his tea and met mine.

"Hello, son," I said, and held out my hand.

Wendy relocated quickly, moving from Dave to beside Matthew and bent down slightly to put her arm around him – it was a nice thing to do.

"What?" he said.

"I'm sorry, Matthew. I had no idea your dad was in here," she said.

"Dad?" he said, as the situation started to dawn on him.

"Yes, son. Apparently, chance had decided that we were going to meet. Now stand up and shake my hand," I smiled, as warmly and gently as I could in the darkest corner of a Putney coffee shop.

Wendy's hands were holding his upper arms and she gently encouraged him to stand up. The poor lad seemed in a state of shock.

"Come here," I said, coming around the side of the table, and Wendy guided him into my arms.

I hugged him but he didn't return the gesture, he just sort of flopped into me.

I raised my eyebrows to Wendy and indicated that she should take him back, which she did; I was most grateful. She sat him down again.

"I'll leave you to this," said Dave, who was understandably keen to extricate himself from such an awkward situation.

I nodded an acknowledgement.

"I'll catch up with you next week," I called after him.

Wendy took charge of the situation.

"Chris, go and get some more drinks, I'll have a coffee and Matthew a tea."

I did as I was told, guessing that she wanted a few moments to compose Matthew and for once in my life, I was glad that there was quite a queue. As I walked away I could hear her asking him how he was. I made sure it was a good ten minutes before I returned ,and when I did, I met a different young man. Whatever Wendy had done and said had worked.

We sat and chatted. I asked about his mum, Sarah. She was married to Matthew's proper dad, a man called Sebastian, and together they ran the family farm near Tetbury in Gloucestershire. Matthew had two sisters, called Holly and Emily, who were twelve and ten.

"When did you know your dad wasn't your birth dad?" I asked, curious to learn how the fact of my existence had emerged.

"Gosh, well, Pop didn't meet Mother until I was four and I vaguely recall a time without him. I was a page boy at their wedding, although I can't remember much about it."

"Has he been a good dad?" I asked, but the emotion that I experienced when I asked the question caught me by surprise and ridiculously, I could feel myself getting upset.

"Pop's been brilliant," Matthew replied.

"And does he know you've come to find me?" I asked.

"Of course, he's helped me a lot actually: he booked the train tickets and the hotel."

"How do you think he feels about you doing this?"

"He's cool," he replied, and I sensed Matthew had a real love and respect for him.

"Mother only told me about you a short while ago."

I desperately wanted to impress him by quoting back at him the month of his birth and the information was there, logged somewhere deep at the back of my mind, but I couldn't recover the data in time and I knew that to guess wrongly would be much worse than saying nothing – so I chose that option.

"Tell me about your sisters," I said, keen to keep the conversation on topics with which he would feel comfortable.

"Oh, they're a real pain, but I love them; they're both utterly into horses."

"Oh, they ride?" I asked, rather feebly.

"They've both got their own horses; Holly's is a fifteen hands called Tiffany; she's a real handful and needs lots of exercise as she used to do cross country."

"I hated cross country, I don't blame her giving it up," I replied.

"Holly didn't do cross country, Tiffany did," Matthew replied.

I felt really stupid.

"Emily's still at the pony stage, she's got Perseus. Now she's an outstanding rider, a complete natural; she'll ride for Great Britain in the Olympics one day, everyone says so," Matthew said.

"Great," I replied.

"And what are you into?" I asked, hoping that he would reply 'rugby'.

"Well, I really enjoy my hockey, but it's a hobby rather than a passion."

"And what's your passion?" I asked.

"Polo," he replied.

"Sorry? Water Polo?"

"No, polo. Last year Pop bought me two ponies for my eighteenth."

"Great," I replied.

I didn't really know what to say; he was speaking English but talking a different language.

"And where do you keep all these horses?" I asked.

"In the stables," Matthew replied, trying desperately not to smirk at my ludicrous question.

That was it; I decided not to ask another horse-related question.

"Has your mum still got the modelling agency?" I asked.

"How do you know about that? Mother said you'd not been in touch for, like, ever?"

"I met someone who knew your mum, a police officer who was on attachment to the Met; it was years ago. She said your mum had set up a child modelling agency."

"She did. That's where she met Pop; he was into photography at the time. The modelling agency was doing really well but some American company bought her out. I think she got eight million," Matthew said casually.

"Pounds?" I said, with way too much incredulity.

"It wasn't guineas, so I suppose it must have been," he replied innocently.

Guineas? What was he talking about? Eight fucking million! Suddenly I felt really small and insignificant. Wendy must have sensed my discomfort because she reached out under the table and squeezed my leg.

"Great," I said again.

"Oh, my middle name is Christopher," he said, as if he'd suddenly remembered.

"Wendy told me that you know why you're called Matthew," I said.

He nodded and reached into a leather bag, which was on the floor next to him.

Matthew took out a scrapbook, a good old-fashioned scrapbook the like of which I hadn't seen since I was at school.

"Mother kept this and gave it to me for my eighteenth birthday. It was an even better present than the polo ponies."

Matthew opened the scrapbook up and we leafed through the pages together. They contained every piece of information that had ever been written about me. Mainly there were newspaper cuttings; the first seven or eight pages were about the bombing. This happened before I'd met Sarah so she must have really gone out of her way to find them. There were a couple of bits about my QPM, most came from The Job, the monthly internal Metropolitan

Police staff newspaper. There was an extract from something called the London Gazette, a publication I'd never seen before. There were also several pages about the Old Bailey trial of the corrupt officers at which both Sarah and I had given evidence. There was even a newspaper picture of the room in Bangkok where I'd briefly been kept prisoner.

The trial of the corrupt officers in 1990 was the last time I'd seen Sarah. I was terribly hurt because she'd totally ignored me; in fact, that still wounded me. I just didn't understand her unwillingness to speak to me.

On the final page was a photograph of Dawn's grave. Dawn was my friend and colleague who'd been with me when we got caught in the bomb explosion at the shopping centre. She had died in my arms and was buried in Buckhurst Hill. Matthew was named after her because Dawn's surname was Matthews.

I felt completely and utterly blown away.

Chapter 35

I exchanged mobile numbers with Matthew and we agreed to meet again the next day. I left him with Wendy, who was revelling in her newly found role of stepmum. I must say, she was really good with him.

I made my way back to Jubilee House to meet the DCI.

Leaving both the Metropolitan Police and Chris Pritchard had obviously turned out to be a very wise decision for my ex-girlfriend. I was genuinely pleased for Sarah and delighted that my son Matthew had benefited to such a fabulous extent. He was so much better off than he would have been if he'd lived with me.

Sarah had also made the right decision when she decided that I was not to have anything to do with him. It troubled me at the time but it was certainly for the best. To cap it all, Sebastian sounded like a wonderful chap. Deep, deep inside me that fact upset me; I knew it shouldn't have, but it did.

It really pleased me that not only had Sarah given him Dawn's name but she'd also given him my name, too. That was a nice thing to do, an acknowledgement of the past and the fact that once and briefly, I had been an important part of her life.

En route I received a text from Wendy to say that Matthew had checked out of the Putney B&B that his father had booked for him and was going to stay with her for the rest of the week. I wondered what she'd told him about our relationship and whether Matthew knew I had a wife and two girls twenty miles down the road? I texted her and asked her to call when she had a few minutes to herself. I wasn't meant to be seeing Wendy until Thursday and I wondered whether she would now be expecting me that evening.

I felt life was starting to run away from me, and it didn't matter what I did or how fast I ran, I couldn't keep up.

I had a week to solve the murder of Gary Odiham, yet as far as I could tell, we had fuck all to go on. No witness to the attack, no next of kin to help us piece together the victim's lifestyle, no primary scene, undefined motives and not even the merest hint of a suspect. To make matters worse, the enquiry was about to go charging off in the wrong direction; that is to say, the involvement of poor Buster, who had nothing at all to do with the murder.

The enquiry office was empty; everyone was either in Dagenham or Bethnal Green, so I went up to the incident room.

"Any developments, Jeff?" I asked hopefully.

"Tox is back. The victim's blood contained traces of …" he picked up a typed report from his in tray, "… alcohol, heroin, cannabis and barbiturates. He had Hepatitis B and Hepatitis C and was HIV-positive. It seems all our suspect did was bring his demise forward by a year or two. Boss says we might be losing the job anyway, to your old mob."

"Apparently, not certain it's the right decision though," I replied honestly.

"What's the SP then, Nostrils? Why's the dark side getting involved? I don't get it? Is it because of the geezer with the warrant card? We don't even know for sure he wasn't impersonating, do we?" Jeff asked.

"I agree," I replied, but I didn't want to get drawn into a long debate.

"Any next of kin yet?" I asked, deliberately changing the subject.

"Nope, but what do you make of this?"

Jeff handed me an action result that Samantha had written out. It detailed her conversation with a woman called Sonia Rider who resided at another address on the Bethnal Green estate. This was one of the actions that emanated from the fingerprints found at the victim's address.

Sonia said she was a friend of the victim and had known him for two years. She would meet him most days and they'd watch Jeremy Kyle together. The victim had told her that his mother had died recently but that they hadn't spoken for years. She last saw the victim on Thursday afternoon when he told her that he was going over to Dagenham that evening but didn't say why.

She didn't know whether he had any friends in Dagenham, but he had started to go there quite frequently lately. She had no idea who might have murdered him and she didn't know anyone who had a grudge against him.

I was a little disappointed; Sonia was potentially a really important witness but Samantha didn't appear to have realised and the comparatively short message was inadequate under the circumstances. It might be different if we had someone in custody who'd put their hands up, but when we had nothing, this report was hopelessly insufficient.

Jeff could tell that I'd finished reading.

"Well?" he asked impatiently.

"Leave it with me. I'll just a take a copy," I replied.

"Thanks, Nostrils. It's not good enough," Jeff said.

"I know, mate. I'll deal with it. Thanks for bringing it to my attention."

I went downstairs to call Samantha but she was now back in the office and sitting at the desk next to mine.

"Hi," I said.

Nothing.

"You all right?" I asked.

Nothing.

I looked closer; Samantha was really upset.

"Fucking hell, mate, what's the matter?" I asked, before realising that my use of the gender specific term 'mate' was probably inappropriate.

232

My mobile phone rang; it was Wendy, I pushed to divert her call to voicemail.

Samantha's handbag was on the desk in front of her and she reached in; I assumed she was going for a tissue but she drew out something black and placed the item on my desk. I looked closely and then picked up a small pair of lacy black knickers, which I immediately recognised. Although I didn't deliberately look, I could see that they hadn't been recently laundered.

"I don't understand," I said.

"Someone's put them in my handbag."

"They're not yours?" I asked innocently.

"A size ten? Don't be ridiculous. And the same thing happened yesterday. When I got home I discovered that someone had put a similar pair in my handbag."

"I don't understand," I said, although that was a lie because I had an idea what was going on.

"Some bastard is putting them in my handbag. You know, they think it's funny. They're probably all involved, all laughing at me behind my back."

I looked across at Julie's desk and by the pedestal was a pink Nike gym bag.

"Yesterday I thought 'maybe there's been a mistake' but I was just being stupid. Why would it be a mistake? Of course it wasn't, it was just someone being spiteful and absolutely horrid. And when does it stop? And how am I meant to react? If I say anything, well that's probably what they want. If I say nothing, then I'm just a mug."

Samantha was, of course, right.

"I'm sorry. What do you want me to do?" I asked, but I desperately hoped she would say 'I don't want you to do anything'.

"I don't know," Samantha replied. "Chris, who do you think it is, you know, who's doing this?"

I had an idea; this had the trademark of the Onions, and one or two in particular, but I had to be careful because I didn't know and any guess might end up coming back to bite me.

"I don't know, Samantha. It won't be one of us, so ..." I replied, without completing the sentence.

I realised, of course, that this had been the prank that Taff had warned me the Onions were planning. I had intended to speak to the DCI but the issue had gone completely out of my mind because we'd been so busy.

Samantha nodded and started to pull herself together. She put the underwear back in her bag and glanced across at the piece of paper I was holding.

"I see you've got a copy of my message," she said.

For the second time in as many days, I chickened out of having a difficult conversation with Samantha. I should have told her that the message of her meeting with Sonia wasn't anywhere near good enough. I just didn't have it in me to upset her even more than she was already.

Chapter 36

I called Wendy as I drove home but she was obviously in the car with Matthew because she couldn't say a lot. We agreed to meet in the Bird. I was half an hour behind them in the rush-hour traffic which was bumper to bumper.

I pulled up in a road opposite called Forest Avenue and texted Wendy to get her to meet me in the car, which she did. I asked her a few questions that quickly established that Matthew knew nothing about Jackie and the kids.

"I'm going to tell him everything," I said.

I thought Wendy might object but she didn't; all she said was that she wanted 'to be a part of this'. I agreed, of course.

"And I want to be there when you tell him, you know, about Jackie and the girls," she added.

Again, I agreed.

Matthew was sitting to the right by the window, which was almost back on yourself as you walked in. He was halfway through a pint of Guinness, which I immediately saw as a good omen. I ordered the same, got Wendy another diet tonic water with a slice of lemon, all she ever drank, and a packet of bacon fries, her favourite bar snack. After the precursor of courtesies, I cut straight to the point.

"Matthew, there are certain things we need, here and now, to get out in the open."

"You don't want to get to know me, do you?" he said, getting completely the wrong end of the stick.

"Pop explained that you might find this difficult to deal with. It's all Mother's fault for not letting you have anything to do with me for eighteen years. I'm sorry ..."

"Be quiet," I said, firmly but pleasantly.

"First, your mum did absolutely the right thing by keeping us apart until you were old enough to make your own decision. Second, I am very happy to get to know you, an experience which will be both an honour and a pleasure. But there is something you need to know and if I don't tell you now, the longer you go on not knowing, the more deceived you will feel."

"Golly gosh, that sounds serious," he replied.

"Don't panic just yet, it really isn't that bad, but you do need to understand the situation. Wendy here, is my girlfriend ..."

Underneath the table I squeezed her knee with my right hand.

" ... but I also have a wife called Jackie, and you have two more half-sisters, Pippa and Trudy, who are my daughters."

"These are daughters you've had with Jackie, not Wendy?" he asked.

"Yes," I replied.

"We haven't got any children yet," Wendy added: a little unhelpful but I thought 'hey, why miss an opportunity to make that point?'.

I waited for him to react.

"Are you divorced?" he asked.

"Nope," I replied.

"Are you separated?"

"Nope."

"So you are having an affair?" he asked.

Wendy hated that expression, so I squeezed her knee reassuringly.

"It's more than an affair, Wendy and I are a proper couple," I explained, picking my words carefully.

"Does this Julie, your wife, know about Wendy?"

"Jackie, yes and no. She suspects, I am sure, that I am seeing someone else, but she hasn't met Wendy," I explained.

"But why doesn't she divorce you? Mother would never put up with Pop doing that to her."

I decided not to inform Matthew that his mother had been the 'other woman' for several years.

"When you have things like a mortgage and children and guinea pigs, life becomes quite complicated," I said, although it wasn't really much of an explanation.

"How long have you and Wendy been going out?" he asked.

"Five years," Wendy answered.

"That's it, Matthew. That's what you needed to know. Are you all right with that? Are you still comfortable getting to know such a morally corrupt person?"

He nodded.

"Anyway, I have something I need to tell you. It's nothing as huge as that," he said, which made me shift uncomfortably in my seat.

"I agreed with Pop that I would never call you 'Dad'," he said.

I was tempted to laugh, but this was obviously an important thing for him.

"I understand, completely. What would you like to call me? Chris is fine," I replied.

"I've been talking to Wendy; we think I should call you 'father'. If that's all right?"

"That's just fine, and are you comfortable if I call you 'son'. Or would you rather I called you Matthew?"

"Son is fine," he replied.

"Is that it? It that all you've got to tell me?" I asked.

I realised Matthew was trying to think of something else, as if, because I'd asked, he wanted to oblige me.

"I smoke," he said guiltily.

I laughed.

"Do mum and dad know?" I asked, the corner of my lips turning up and into a conspiratorial smile.

He shook his head.

"See, we both have each other by the balls," I said, before realising this probably wasn't the most appropriate thing to say to your long-lost son.

Matthew laughed; I just got the feeling he wasn't used to someone as rough around the edges as me.

"So what do you think of London then? Have you visited often?" I asked.

"A few times with school, a few times with Mother and Pop. We come every year to the Royal Opera House, we're all huge fans of Darcey Bussell, so we go whenever she's performing," he replied.

"I'm afraid I don't know anything about opera." I replied.

"It's not opera; Darcey Bussell is a prima ballerina," he explained.

Horses and now ballet! I wondered whether, apart from a similar physical appearance, we had anything at all in common.

"What do you think of Putney?" I asked.

I was about to say how nice I thought it was and how, if only I could afford it, I'd like to have a flat there.

"If we're being completely honest, it's quite the roughest place I've ever been. I mean, goodness me, I'm all for the benefits of a multi-cultural society, I mean I'm reading geography at uni in

September, but I never realised just how multi-cultural the poorer parts of London were."

"Putney? The poorer part of London?" I asked incredulously.

It appeared my son, bless him, had experienced a very sheltered upbringing. I checked my watch; it was ten past seven.

"Drink up; I'm going to show you what I do to make a living," I said.

"I need to go to the toilet first," he replied.

"Off you go," I said, nodding towards the Gents.

Quite accurately sensing an adventure, Matthew stood up, grabbed his coat and headed towards the toilets.

"What on earth are you doing?" Wendy asked.

"I'm going to take young Matthew for a lesson, well lesson's not the right term, an experience, a life experience," I replied.

"What are you talking about? Seriously, Chris, what are you going to do?"

There was an air of panic in Wendy's voice.

"Relax, it'll be all right," I replied.

"Seriously, what are you going to do? Are you going back to the office to show him where you work?"

"No, not that. I've got some enquiries to make with a witness. It'll be harmless enough; he can shadow me. Besides, it'll be an hour round trip so we'll have a chance to get to know one another, and trust me, the way work is shaping up, it might be the only chance I get to see him this week," I said.

"Do you want me to come?" she asked.

"No, really, we'll come back to yours when I'm finished. I can't explain why, Wendy, but I just need to do this and as I said, I probably won't ever get another opportunity. Anyway, let's just see what happens," I replied.

Wendy nodded. She knew me well enough by now to know that I'd made my mind up.

"Listen, hon, why don't you take a couple of days off and look after Matthew for me, if you don't mind. You're always moaning that you've got too much annual leave. What do you reckon?"

It was precisely the right thing to say because Wendy's face absolutely lit up.

"I'd love to," she replied.

Matthew emerged from the toilet and joined us.

"Now, son, you ready to see the real London and real Londoners?" I asked.

"Yes, father," he replied.

Chapter 37

Sometimes I think there is actually no better way to get to know someone, anyone, than to spend an hour in a car with them, because it forces you to talk without putting you face to face, so conversation flows more easily. By the time we'd got to Bethnal Green, Matthew and I were no longer strangers.

My original suspicions had been accurate; my long-lost son was a very bright, articulate, impeccably mannered member of the English upper middle class. His father was a product of Harrow and Cambridge who dabbled through his twenties with a funded photography business before assuming the reins of the farm, which had been in the family since time immemorial.

And what did the farm produce? Milk? No. Dairy? No. Meat? No. Crops? No. Game birds, bloody game birds, you know, pheasants, grouse, partridge. I'd never even realised that such farms existed but Matthew informed me there were hundreds of them in the UK. Pop, he declared with pride, was the General Secretary of the Game Farmers' Association.

My other thoughts about Matthew having had something of a sheltered upbringing were also right. Driving through ever more run-down areas of London, I watched Matthew's expressions display a myriad of emotions from interest, through fascination, and then from confusion to fear. I am a persistent storyteller and every few hundred yards I was able to recount another tail of crime or disaster which had occurred in a nearby building or on a passing street corner. If he thought Putney was multi-cultural, I have no idea what he thought of Dalston or London Fields, but whatever it was, he kept his views to himself. When we were less than a mile from our destination, I decided to tell him what we were doing and why.

"Right, Matthew. My team is investigating the murder of a white, male drug dealer called Gary Odiham. He lived on the estate we're going to but he was murdered in Dagenham."

"Estate?" he asked, with an element of surprise.

"I don't think it's the kind of estate you're thinking of, son. This is a *council* estate," I replied.

"When did the murder happen?" Matthew asked, and I silently gave him a mental tick for asking a sensible question.

"In the early hours of Thursday morning. Now one of my team has interviewed someone who lives near the victim and knew him quite well; her name is Sonia Rider. I need to speak to Sonia in case I can get more information out of her about the victim than my colleague did."

"Why? Why do you think you might be more successful?" he asked – another sensible question.

"I just might; I'm quite good at talking to people. Of course, now I've told you that, I bet Sonia will tell me to fuck right off," I said.

Matthew laughed, slightly nervously.

"You're not used to swearing, are you?" I asked.

"Golly gosh; not from an adult, no, sorry, father."

"No, I'm sorry, mate. I don't always swear, really. I don't swear in front of the girls. It's just that, well, I'm not making excuses but I'm in work mode now. Anyway, if anything happens, if it kicks off, get the fuck, sorry, get out of the flat immediately. Do you understand? Get a black cab back to Leyton and on the way, call Wendy," I said.

Matthew nodded.

"I have got a yellow 'Observer' jacket in the boot, which you can wear if you want. It's been in there since last summer when we had some Church of England bishop come out with us for a couple of days so he could get close to the real community of London. It's probably easier not to bother with the jacket, you could pass for twenty-one so you could be a young constable on attachment from Street Duties, it's quite feasible. It's up to you."

"Will they not want to see my police identity card?" he asked; three sensible questions in a row – this was actually one smart kid.

"No, as long as they see mine and it's obvious that you're with me," I replied, "so keep your mouth shut, don't touch anything and fuck off if anything happens."

"Is anything likely to happen?" he asked, uneasiness clearly evident in his voice.

"No, it's really not. I wouldn't have brought you along if I thought there was any risk. Now, are you happy to do this?" I asked.

I had just pulled up and applied the handbrake.

"Yes," he said.

"And one final piece of advice: if we are offered tea or coffee, politely decline unless you want to take something more tangible than sweet memories back to Gloucester."

Matthew looked slightly confused.

"Just don't drink, eat or touch anything," I said.

He nodded.

Matthew looked around at his first sight of a London council estate, the repugnance evident in his facial expression. I thought I'd give him one final word of encouragement.

"It'll be fine, I promise. Welcome to my world, it sucks but you'll love it," I said, stealing my favourite line from an early episode of *Friends*.

"Where are we?" he asked.

"This, my son, is Bethnal Green, home of the infamous Kray Twins, and it's the proper East End of London."

~~~

The flat, which was number 29, was on the top floor, of course. We took the lift, I wouldn't normally but I just wanted to see Matthew's face. The unlit, graffiti-, slow and clunky lift was truly something to behold.

"What the devil is that stink? Gosh, it smells like urine," Matthew said.

"That'll be urine," I said.

"I'll have to take my shoes off if we go into the flat," he said.

"I'd just wait and see," I suggested.

The lights were on inside the flat and I had a quick glance through the letterbox but the view was blocked, so I rapped the heavy iron knocker several times. A few moments later the door opened a few inches and was held at that distance by a heavy metal chain. I could vaguely make out the partial face of a white female.

"What?" she said curtly.

"Police, can you open the door please, Sonia?" I said.

"You got a warrant?" she asked.

"No, of course not," I replied, in a manner which suggested that was a really stupid question.

"I've already spoken to one of your lot," she said, making no move to open the door any further.

"Sonia, darling, do us a favour, just open the door. We're not gonna try and come in, I promise," I said, in my nicest, politest 'I'm the best mate you've ever had' voice.

"Hang on," she said, and then she shut the door.

About a minute later the door opened again, but again the chain was on.

"Show me your thingy, your ID," she demanded. "In fact, put it through the letterbox."

"I can't fucking do that, can I? What if you take it and then shut the door; I'm going to look a right fucking stupid cunt," I said, but my voice was friendly.

I definitely saw Matthew grimace at the word 'cunt'.

"Hang on," she said.

This time the door only closed momentarily before it opened further. We were confronted by a painfully thin woman of indeterminate age; she could have been anything from twenty-five to forty. She wore an old baggy brown woollen jumper and torn jeans and had untidy, unwashed mousey brown hair down to her shoulders, a pale, almost yellow, complexion, and she possessed only a few teeth, which were randomly scattered. Most distractingly, in each corner of her mouth she had white lines of condensed spit that extended and contracted as she spoke – it was difficult to look at anything else.

"Thanks for opening the door," I said.

"Listen, you two, I've already spoken to one of your chaps, a big hairy geezer in a skirt. I told him everything I knew, now you're just harassing me, d'ya know wot I mean, mate?"

"I know it feels like that but I promise you, Sonia, it's not our intention to harass you, or to cause you any more distress and anguish," I said, putting both my palms up and forward in an obvious gesture of defence.

"It's still basic harassment, mate, d'ya know wot I mean?"

"Sonia, darling, we're here for only one reason, to try to find out who murdered Gary; you were a good friend of his, right?"

"Mate, if Gary was here he'd tell me to tell you to fuck off, I promise ya, mate."

"Please help us," I said quietly.

"Fuck off, he'd say."

"Sonia?" I said, raising my voice and changing its intonation to one of inquisitiveness.

The alteration confused her momentarily.

"Wot?" she asked, an inquisitive look on her face.

"Can we come in?" I asked.

"I don't think so, mate" she replied, and closed the door a few inches to indicate that she meant it.

"Sonia, darling. I don't care what you've got in your flat. I promise you, unless there's a dead body with an axe sticking out of its head, I won't nick you or ask you about anything in your flat."

She hesitated.

"Stolen gear, drugs, hooky cigarettes, snide designer training shoes, I don't give a flying fuck."

I don't think any Old Bill had ever spoken to her like that before.

"I, err, well, err ..."

"I want ten minutes of your time, just to see whether you know anything that might help us to find out who killed your friend. Please, Sonia, please," I said.

"You ain't gonna nick me?"

"No," I replied definitively.

She stepped back and opened the door. I indicated and Matthew went in first. Before she closed the door, I saw Sonia turn the plastic numeral '2', which was fixed to the front door by a single screw, upside down. I'd been around enough drug dealers to know what the sign meant: it was telling anyone about to call at the address to fuck off, normally an indication that the occupier had sold out of drugs.

I looked at Matthew's face as he entered the lounge; it was one of utter and absolute repulsion.

Chapter 38

The place was exactly what I would expect it to be. The furniture would have been old twenty years ago: threadbare orange and brown carpet, a 1970s pine coffee table, walls stripped of paper but devoid of paint, white net curtains stained to the deepest shade of grey and an atmosphere of stale tobacco smoke with a trace of sweet cannabis. And this flat had never been cleaned, hoovered, dusted or otherwise made better in any way, ever.

To a police officer, or a social worker or a district nurse, such places were commonplace, but to my eighteen-year-old son whose life experience was a game bird farm in deepest Gloucestershire, such living conditions must have been utterly repugnant.

We stood politely in the lounge waiting for an invitation to sit but when none was forthcoming, we planted ourselves awkwardly at each end of the sofa; Sonia sat on the floor in front of an old gas fire with her knees raised and both arms wrapped around them defensively. On the coffee table between us was an expensive mobile phone, which was plugged in and charging. Although the ringer had been muted, as we sat down the phone vibrated to indicate an incoming call.

"What da ya wanna know?" Sonia said.

I got the distinct impression that I wasn't going to get long here and therefore every question had to count. I was also conscious that one wrong question and Sonia would close up. Normally I would start by asking some gentle, non-confrontational background questions about their relationship, where they'd met, how long they'd known each other and questions like that, but I got straight to the point.

"What the fuck was Gary doing in Dagenham?"

"Meeting a mate, basic." she replied.

"Do you know who?" I asked.

"Probably some guy called Bigga."

Then she added quickly, "Bigga ain't the one what killed him, no way."

"Who's Bigga, Sonia? Where can I find him?"

Sonia frowned momentarily and I feared that she already thought she'd told us too much.

"Some Jamaican fella, lives over Dagenham. Only been in the country a few months," she replied.

"Got an address?" I asked, with more hope than expectation.

She shook her head.

"Don't go fucking mad …"

"What?" she said cautiously.

"… did Gary get his gear from Bigga?"

I knew it was a risky question.

Sonia shook her head.

"Gary had a business arrangement with Bigga," she replied, saying the words 'business arrangement' with a different intonation, suggesting to me that she was directly quoting Gary.

The mobile phone vibrated again.

"Sonia, darling, was the 'business arrangement' drugs related?" I asked.

Sonia nodded with the slightest movement of her head, as if such a deft action could never amount to betrayal.

"Why are you so sure Bigga didn't hurt Gary?"

"Basic, mate, why would he? It was a business relationship, d'ya know wot I mean? He was doing good business with my Gary, especially since …"

Sonia stopped mid-sentence.

"Especially since what?" I asked.

Sonia looked at the carpet but said nothing.

I dropped my voice to almost a whisper.

"Why were Gary and Bigga suddenly doing good business?" I asked.

"Gary came into some money, d'ya know wot I mean?"

"Did he inherit money? I know his mum only died recently," I asked.

"No, they hadn't spoken for years, they was like estranged, d'ya know wot I mean?" she replied; again her different intonation on the word 'estranged' strongly suggested that she was actually quoting Gary.

"So where did the money come from?" I asked.

Sonia shook her head. I interpreted that gesture to mean that she knew but wasn't prepared to impart the information to me.

"If you knew how I could get hold of Bigga, would you tell me?" I asked.

Sonia shook her head in a similarly negative gesture.

"Does Bigga know who did this?" I asked.

Sonia shrugged her shoulders.

"Do *you* know who killed Gary?"

"No."

"If you did, would you tell me?"

"I dunno," she replied.

I identified a significant level of honesty in her replies. She may not tell me the answer to a question but she would tell me that she wouldn't tell me, rather than deceive me with a lie. This was really important and I needed to exploit the opportunity.

"Guess?" I said.

"I don't know. Maybe he was mugged. If he didn't have any gear on him, maybe he was robbed of it, d'ya know wot I mean?"

"Maybe, I have thought of that," I replied slowly.

"What actually happened to him?" Sonia asked.

"Do you really want to know?" I asked.

The mobile phone vibrated again.

Sonia nodded.

"At two o'clock last Thursday night, Friday morning, very near to a BP garage in Dagenham, someone stabbed him in the head with what we think was a screwdriver. He died almost straight away."

"Poor cunt," Sonia said, her voice suddenly bursting with emotion.

And then she went to pieces, starting to sob and cry.

We sat in silence for a good minute while Sonia wiped away floods of tears with the sleeves of her woollen jumper.

I looked across at Matthew who met my eye.

"You all right?" I mouthed.

He nodded back.

"I'm sorry, Sonia. I really want to find out who did this," I said sympathetically.

Although she was crying, she laughed.

"What?" I asked.

"Gary would have hated you helping him, d'ya know wot I mean?"

"Really?" I asked.

"He hated cozzers, he called you cunts, ya know, 'I was stopped and searched by the cunts' or 'the cunts are on the estate', d'ya know wot I mean?"

"Why?" I asked.

"You killed his dad," she replied.

"What? When?" I asked.

"I dunno. He reckons you beat him to death, ya know, in the back of a police van. He was like ten, d'ya know wot I mean? He fucking hated you guys, cunts he called you. Fucking hell, mate, basic, if he fucking saw me now talking to you, he'd be like 'babe, what you fucking doing?' – d'ya know wot I mean?"

"That must have been twenty years, more, ago," I said.

"Yeah, but he said you was all bad, all cunts."

Sonia was sobbing intermittently now. It was actually quite a sad scene because she'd obviously really felt for him.

"Were you two a couple?" I asked.

"Sort of, d'ya you know wot I mean? I loved him but he was a fucking nightmare."

I smiled.

"Men, eh?" I said.

My comment triggered an immediate reaction.

"Who the fuck was that bloke you sent to speak to me earlier? He was dressed up like a woman, were you taking the piss? Basic mate, no one's gonna talk to cozzers anyway, no fucking chance mate if it's a tranny, basic innit? D'ya know wot I mean?"

"The guy's name was Sam. He's living a year as a woman to see whether he wants to have a sex change. Live and let live, eh?" I said.

"Whatever floats your boat, mate, whatever floats your boat. But not as a cozzer; it ain't good, mate, basic innit? I'll tell you something, mate, the people on this estate ain't talking about what happened to Gary, they're talking about the fact that a massive, like, police officer is walking around the place dressed as a bird. Basic, mate, d'ya know wot I mean?"

"Sam's a friend of mine. I am loyal to my friends," I said.

The mobile phone vibrated yet again.

"Respect," Sonia said quietly.

"You know Gary's flat was searched by police, you know, the morning before he was murdered."

Sonia nodded.

"The police never found any drugs, did they?" I asked.

"No," she replied.

"Did he have any?" I asked.

She nodded.

There was that honesty again; I was actually starting to like Sonia.

"Did Gary give you drugs to sell?" I asked.

For the first time, Sonia looked really awkward, but I'd guessed.

She nodded so deftly the movement was almost difficult to detect. Sonia started to cry again, gently this time.

She shook her head.

"We can't shift the stuff quick enough, basic. We were like a team, d'ya know wot I mean? Anyways, Gary had started working over Dagenham way; Bigga found him some new business locations, d'ya know wot I mean?" she said.

I felt I pushed my luck about as far as I could without risking our most tentative of relationships.

"Sonia?" I said.

She wiped her eyes and looked up.

"Thank you for seeing us. I know how upset you are. Can I call in again? Would that be okay?"

She nodded.

"You're all right, you are. But your partner there, handsome, he doesn't say a lot," she said unexpectedly.

Matthew looked suitably embarrassed.

"He's still learning. We'll see ourselves out. I'll drop the number two back down."

She smiled because we had connected. I knew that might be really important in finding out what had happened to our mutual friend, but these kinds of relationships take a while to nurture to fruition.

Chapter 39

"Well, Matthew, what do you think of my world?" I asked, as we drove off the estate.

"Gosh, people actually live like that?"

"An awful lot of London lives just like that. They would feel as lost in your world, probably more, as you do in theirs," I replied.

"So, Sonia, she doesn't work, right?" Matthew asked.

"No, not like you mean. She has never had a proper job but then, what you've got to understand is, neither did her parents or anyone else she knew when she was growing up. Her parents, if she had two, because she probably just had a mum, wouldn't have been bothered whether she went to school, or if she did, what grades or qualifications she achieved. No one she knew would ever have actually got out of bed in the morning and gone to work. No one she ever knew would have done anything other than live off the state. Quite frankly, Matthew, our Sonia there never really stood a chance to escape the council estate, benefit culture into which she was born."

"You sound like you feel a bit sorry for her," Matthew said.

"I do, sort off," I replied.

"But she's a real scallywag, isn't she?" Matthew said.

'A scallywag?' Fuck me; I had to seriously resist the temptation to laugh out loud. What sort of eighteen-year-old ever used the expression 'scallywag'?

"You see, when you get to know them, they're all right. Like all of us, they're just trying their best to make their way in the world," I said.

"Sonia seemed to take to you, well a bit."

"Yeah, I know how to talk to people like that, lots of Old Bill do, not all, but the good ones."

"But you didn't get much information, did you?" Matthew said.

I smiled.

"Gosh, I've got that wrong, haven't I? Sorry," he said, correctly reading my reaction.

"I think we learnt a great deal. I suspect Sonia was the victim's girlfriend and therefore his next of kin, which we've not known up until now. We almost certainly know why the victim was in Dagenham, to buy or sell drugs from or to a recently arrived Jamaican Yardie called Bigga. Sonia may still in contact with this Bigga. She's clearly dealing, drug dealing, from her actions at the front door by turning the '2' and the constant ringing on her mobile phone. While she won't tell us, she may know where Bigga is and she may well visit him, which gives us an opportunity to find and interview him because we can put a surveillance team behind her.

"Bigga isn't necessarily involved in the murder but he might well know who is and is an excellent line of enquiry. Bigga's location in Dagenham could well be the scene of the attack. If we identify the location, we might be able to trace eyewitnesses.

"We also learnt that the victim hated police and why, which will have to be researched. This makes the connection of a corrupt police officer, something which has been suggested but which I don't buy into by the way, unlikely.

"Finally, we didn't stay too long, we didn't piss her off and we got an invitation to go back. No, all in all, I think it was a useful little chat."

"Gosh, I never thought about it like that," Matthew said.

"Why would you? No, I suspect that when we solve this murder, this evening's conversation might prove to be an important part of the enquiry."

"Do you think you'll solve this?" Matthew asked.

"Of course. Look, the Met is pretty crap at a lot of things. I mean, we've lost control of the streets, largely thanks to the installation of CCTV everywhere. We're not great at solving a burglary or a robbery but by God, we are fantastic at solving murders," I explained.

"How come?" Matthew asked.

"Simple, really. We throw resources at them. In London, if you get murdered you'll have a team of thirty experienced detectives working to solve the crime for maybe two months. You put those sorts of numbers into the game, you're probably going to win. A few years ago, I did some work with a guy who was over from the LAPD ..."

"Who?"

" ... the Los Angeles Police Department. Their murder rate there is like ten times higher than London. Anyway, each LAPD murder squad detective had about eight murders to solve on his own!"

"No wonder you feel confident," Matthew said.

We'd just entered Lower Clapton and were slowing down in traffic as I saw the car ahead of the car ahead, indicating to turn right across the oncoming traffic. The car immediately ahead, however, didn't react and ploughed straight into the rear of the car turning right. The impact speed must have been about twenty-five miles an hour.

Nothing happened for a few moments and then both cars pulled slowly over to the left and the driver of the first car, a white female in her fifties, got out clutching her neck.

"Have you got to do anything?" Matthew asked.

"No; it doesn't look too serious," I replied.

Having started to pull over, the second car, an old Ford Escort, suddenly swerved right and accelerated passed the first car and set off towards the Lea Bridge Road roundabout.

"Fuck," I said aloud, "doing nothing is no longer an option, son."

I set off after the Escort.

Now I was in my own car so I wasn't permitted, nor did I want, to get involved in a chase, so I had to be careful and make sure the Escort's driver didn't notice that I was following him. I didn't make it obvious, I didn't flash my lights or sound my horn; I just drove at a discreet distance behind him.

"Driving steadily, isn't he?" I commented.

"What are you going to do?" Matthew asked.

"See where he's going and if he stops and I can lay hands on, I'll nick him," I replied.

"Really?"

I laughed, inside more than out.

"You got your phone on you?" I asked.

"Yes."

"Dial 999 and ask for the police. Then say exactly what I tell you to say."

The Escort was held at a red pedestrian ATS and to the left was the turning which took you to the Nightingale Estate. There was one car between us, which was perfect.

"I haven't got a signal," Matthew replied.

"Keep an eye on it, as soon as you get anything, call," I said.

The lights changed and we set off. If anything, the Escort was driving slower than other traffic and as a result a small queue was forming up behind us. The driver obviously wasn't stupid; that was quite a shrewd tactic to try to avoid drawing attention to them. The car between us turned right and then the Escort slowed and indicated to pull in to park.

"He's going to pull up. Stay in the car …"

As I spoke, I heard Matthew say, "Police, please."

A few seconds later, I heard Matthew giving the operator his mobile phone number.

The Escort pulled up on the left, outside a small parade of shops, and I stopped about twenty yards short. A white male in his mid-fifties got out and I noticed immediately he was wearing half blues, that is to say black shoes, black uniform trousers and a white shirt under a civilian jacket.

"Where are we?" I heard Matthew ask.

I was quickly considering my options, which I have to confess included telling Matthew to apologise and hang up. The thing was, if anyone on the murder squad found out that I'd arrested an off-duty PC for a traffic matter, my life would be a nightmare.

It appeared the driver was going to buy something from the shop. I could just wait for him to return but my eye caught a side door by the shop entrance, which I assumed would lead up to the flats above where, of course, the driver could live.

"Father, the lady wants to know where we are, I said Hackney."

"We're in Lower Clapton Road. Tell them an off-duty DS wants transport for a prisoner."

I jumped out of the car and closed the distance between us more quickly than I'd expected because fortunately, the driver had decided to return to his vehicle, having apparently forgotten something.

"I wanna word, mate," I said, as I neared him.

"What?" he asked aggressively.

In that one word, I knew he was pissed.

I showed him my warrant card.

"You've just driven into the back of a car and failed to stop. We've followed you to here."

"I don't know what you're talking about," he said.

We were both now standing at the rear of his car.

"Are you in the job?" I asked.

"What job?" he replied.

"What do you do for a living?" I asked.

"I'm an ambulance driver at the Homerton hospital, so why don't you just fuck off, mate."

I could smell the alcohol on his breath and his speech was very slurred. I hadn't nicked anyone for drink drive in fifteen years but somewhere deep in my subconscious I was aware that you had to be in uniform unless you made the arrest for 'being drunk in charge of a vehicle', which was a slightly different offence to 'driving over the prescribed limit'.

The guy opened his boot and reach in to get something out. I took hold of his right arm but he pulled back and we ended up in a push and tug tussle. I looked across at Matthew, who was a few yards away on the phone.

"Tell them I require assistance with a violent prisoner." It wasn't quite the truth but it would mean they'd run to me on blues and twos and besides, all my experience taught me that a situation like this takes no more than a second to go from a bit of push and pull to a full-blown battle.

The guy was older than me and not as fit, and he was pissed. After a short struggle I could feel his strength wavering and somehow I managed, with the help of some distant muscle memories which I would have thought long forgotten, to put him in an arm lock. One of the disadvantages of the position I now got him into was that the guy was literally breathing on me. Goodness knows how much he'd had to drink.

A few of the passers by had gathered to see what was going on, which presented a small risk in case anyone of them knew the driver or even worse, was related to him.

"Listen, mate, stop struggling. We were behind you when you hit the woman. We saw you go to pull over but then you suddenly changed your mind and drove off. We've followed you all the way and I suspect there's damage to the front of this car that'll match the rear of hers; what do you say?"

He didn't say anything but went to pull away, harder this time, so I ended up pushing him almost into the open boot, but I still had the lock on, just.

I could hear the cavalry now, always a welcome development in these situations.

I glanced across at Matthew, who was still on the phone; 'good lad' I thought, because that was what I hoped I'd see. The operator had obviously decided to keep him on the line in case there were developments. I was getting tired now.

One minute there were no police officers and less than a minute later, there were at least seven. I must say I was grateful for their swift response. I knew the arresting officer well, his name was Steve and we'd been PCs together years ago.

They sat my prisoner in the back of the van and I discussed various options with Steve. My memory had been right and out of uniform I only had a power of arrest for the 'drunk in charge' offence. The only small sticking point was that technically I should have gone to Hackney, booked the prisoner in and provided my evidence to the custody sergeant. Last time I had done that the process had taken four hours and I was really keen to avoid a repeat scenario. I explained to Steve that I was out with my son, whom I only saw once in a blue moon, and please could he take over for me? He was a star, an absolute star; he took my mobile phone number and said he'd get the custody officer to call me so I could give my grounds for arrest orally. I have to confess, I'd never heard of anyone doing that before, so that would be a first.

Steve said he'd actually taken the call to the 'fail to stop' RTA so he was only half a mile down the road when our call came out. The woman in the car that had been hit was apparently in quite a bad way and his colleague was staying with her until an ambulance arrived.

I got back in the car with Matthew and we set off on our second attempt to get back to Leyton.

"I've decided I don't want to go to uni, that's just a lot of flimflam," Matthew declared.

"Oh, don't say that, Matthew. It's a wonderful opportunity and you must have worked really hard to get those A level results, Wendy told me you got three As."

"Yeah, but uni's not real life, is it. It's just more sitting in a boring classroom and reading tedious books."

"So if you don't go to uni, what are you going to do?" I asked.

"I want to be a policeman," he replied.

Chapter 40

It was late by the time we got back to Leyton. I dropped Matthew off but stayed in the car to phone Jackie to let her know what was going on.

I always tried to stay as close to the truth as possible so I told her about the drunk driver in Lower Clapton and said I was back at Hackney dealing with the prisoner. She actually suggested to me that it would hardly be worth coming home, which I appreciated. I said I'd do my best to get home the next day. She said she understood. Did I feel guilty? Oh my God, yes. Would I change my behaviour? No.

When I got in, Wendy had spent the last two hours preparing a really impressive meal, and cooking was a talent that really didn't come naturally to her. In fact, over the years her inability to produce a decent meal had become something of a joke between us. Well, in fairness, I thought it was funny, I'm not so certain Wendy did.

She'd also made up the bed in the spare room for Matthew.

I don't think I'd ever seen Wendy happier. She really enjoyed looking after us both and made such a fuss of Matthew, you'd have thought it was her long-lost son rather than mine.

Matthew was absolutely full of the events of that evening; he chatted excitedly about Sonia, her flat, her attitude, and it was obvious that he'd never met anyone like her before.

"Gosh, she lived in absolute poverty, Wendy. Everything about her, everything about her apartment was ..."

The young lad was momentarily speechless, but I resisted the temptation to assist him.

"... well, gosh, um ..."

Matthew glanced around Wendy's place as if the word he was seeking was written on the walls.

"... poor, tired, worn out, destitute," he said, as his brain filled with suitable adjectives."

Wendy smiled kindly.

"But forget all that, what did you think of her as a person?" she asked.

Matthew frowned.

"Gosh, she was very rough but she seemed to like ..." Matthew nodded towards me, apparently momentarily forgetting what we'd agreed he should call me.

"Yes, your father can be a bit like that," Wendy replied, with a smirk.

"What Wendy means is that really low-lifey women find me really attractive. That's why she can't resist me," I said.

"Oh, Wendy's not like Sonia, gosh, Wendy's lovely," Matthew replied, with way, way too much honesty.

Matthew recognised his little indiscretion and for a brief moment a cloud of embarrassment hung in the air. I decided the best thing to do would be to completely ignore the comment.

"Oh, tell Wendy about the failing to stop accident and your first arrest," I said, encouraging him to forget the awkwardness. Matthew seized the opportunity and talked Wendy through the fail to stop and the subsequent arrest.

Wendy insisted that Matthew phoned his mum, despite the lateness of the hour, and he did as he was told. I politely suggested that he didn't mention his change of heart about going to university unless he really wanted a swift recall to Gloucestershire, and he agreed.

"Where are you going to say you're staying?" I asked.

Clearly, Matthew hadn't thought this through, as he hesitated, his right foot on the bottom stair.

"With your girlfriend?" he asked cautiously.

"Yeah, that'll be fine," replied Wendy, on my behalf.

Matthew disappeared into the guest bedroom and Wendy came over and gave me a warm, all-embracing hug.

"He's such a lovely lad," she declared, as if she'd known him all her life.

"He's a nice lad," I replied, returning her hug and then pushing her away very subtly.

"What's the matter, Chris? You're pleased to see him, aren't you?"

"I think so, it's just all a bit of a shock. Now he's saying he doesn't want to go to uni, he wants to join the job instead. His mum and dad won't be impressed and quite frankly, he's not ready for it. He's so young."

"Is anyone ever ready for the job?" Wendy asked.

"Probably not," I replied.

"We both joined at nineteen. Christ, my first call was to some poor lad that had jumped out of the window of a sixteenth-floor council estate flat. Nothing can prepare you for that," Wendy said.

She was, of course, right.

"I'm going to do as you suggested and take the rest of this week off and look after Matthew. I'll show him a bit of London and we can meet up with you after work. I'll talk him back into going to university," Wendy assured me.

"I'm going to be busy, the new job's gone mad; you know, the drug dealer stabbed in the head in Dagenham," I said.

"I know; I understand, and I'll make sure Matthew does too. Is it a good job? Any suspects?" she asked.

"No; there's sod all to go on, really. I mean, there's some suggestion that it's linked to police corruption but I'm really not convinced," I said.

"What's the link to police corruption? If you can tell me," Wendy asked.

It was a valid question and as Wendy used to work at CIB and was about the most discreet person I'd ever known, I decided to tell her.

"There's some suggestion that a DC from Bethnal Green might have known the victim, even had something to do with the murder, but let me state for the record, I don't buy into the theory."

"Bethnal Green? Who is it?" Wendy asked.

"Not a word …"

"Of course."

"Some guy called Buster, his actual name is …"

" Ron Edwards," Wendy interrupted me.

"You know him?" I asked.

"You know him too," Wendy replied.

"I really don't," I replied.

"Yes, you do. Ron is Carrie's husband. Carrie Edwards, my old friend from Training School; they live in Brentwood. Carrie's got ovarian cancer and they're waiting to see whether the treatment has been successful. The blood tests aren't looking very good but sometimes there's a delayed reaction to the chemo; that's what they're pinning their hopes on. Three girls under ten."

Of course, with every piece of information, I realised that I did know 'of' Buster. We'd never met but I had heard about him sporadically and vicariously through Wendy.

"Have you met this Buster?" I asked.

"Once or twice but only to say 'hi' to. He's a lot older than Carrie and last time I spoke to her she said she thinks he's having an affair. I think he's quite a handful. They've gone off on holiday to the Canaries or somewhere and when they get back they should know whether the treatment has been successful. I spoke to her last week; she was being very brave but got upset because she said it might be the last holiday they ever have as a family."

I had already pretty much decided that I would come clean before seeing a blameless man get in trouble for something he hadn't done, but now there was absolutely no doubt in my mind.

"Chris, Chris, Chris …" Wendy was saying.

I jolted back to reality.

"What?"

"Matthew's calling you."

I went upstairs and into the spare room where Matthew was sitting on the bed.

"Mother wants a word."

I hadn't spoken to Sarah since before she'd done a bunk and gone to CIB back in 1985, so I was a little nervous when I took the mobile phone from Matthew.

"Hello, Christopher, my darling. Thank you so much for looking after my Matthew."

The last time I had heard her voice, there was the definite hint of a nasal West Midlands accent; now, all trace of her roots had disappeared and, although I could still recognise her, her accent was manicured and crisp.

"Hello, stranger, are you going to tell me off?" I said, fearing she'd be annoyed that I'd been out working with Matthew.

"Well, it's hardly your fault that off duty you came across a fail to stop RTA, is it? Of course you had to do something, I understand the victim was really injured."

I smiled because only Old Bill or ex-Old Bill would use the term RTA to describe a car accident.

It was really strange to be talking to Sarah, but I was really pleased that Matthew had clearly not told his mum that we'd actually been on our way back from seeing a witness on a murder enquiry, so 'well done, Matthew' I thought.

"I understand he's staying with your girlfriend, did he say she was called Wendy? Please say thank you to Wendy for me; I'm sure he's in safe hands, is she in the job too?" Sarah asked.

"Yes, she is; she's a sergeant at Limehouse," I replied.

Then Sarah hesitated and I thought for a moment the line had gone dead or we'd lost the signal or something.

"Hello."

"Hello, I'm still here, Chris. I, err, this is a little awkward …

"Go on, Sarah. We haven't seen each other in years, what could possibly be awkward?" I asked.

"I treated you badly, Chris, all those years ago. I know I did but I so wished you'd spoken to me at the Old Bailey; it broke my heart when you ignored me."

Well, that was a turn up for the books; for the last seventeen years I'd been having exactly the same thought! I now had one hurt less that I'd have to carry around with me.

Chapter 41

I was in early, as usual.

I wrote up the action with the details of the meeting with Sonia, obviously omitting the fact that there was someone else with me. I made much emphasis of the fact that the victim vehemently hated the police, the inference being that he was therefore most unlikely to be in a relationship, let alone a friendship, with a member of Her Majesty's finest.

The obvious line of enquiry would be to trace, identify and eliminate this guy called Bigga. I spent ages on CRIMINT trawling through the name and doing dozens of searches linked to 'drugs' and 'Dagenham' and 'Jamaica', but I was overwhelmed with responses and none of them was an obvious match. Apparently, Bigga was a very common name for black, male Yardie drug dealers.

I was also very conscious that if as Sonia said, this Bigga had only recently arrived from Jamaica, it was highly unlikely that he would have had sufficient time to leave a criminal footprint in the UK.

I decided the only sensible way to find Bigga was to put a surveillance team on Sonia and hope that she met with him. This would mean the usual mountain of paperwork by way of the RIPA application but more importantly, the process would probably require making Bigga a suspect for the murder. I thought I could make a case but I'd have to convince the DCI ,who might decide there were insufficient grounds.

One of the Onions came into the office and asked me curtly where Julie was? I replied that I thought she'd be in shortly and politely asked if I could help?

"You can give her these," he said, and dropped a pair of black knickers onto my desk.

He walked out briskly but as he did so, my mobile rang. It was Nick Charles, and he wanted a word at 'the usual place', which I took to mean the tea hut in Vicky Park. I felt nervous; had he worked out what the fuck had happened? I hung up, put my head in my hands, took a deep breath and closed my eyes.

When I opened them Julie was standing to my left and Nicola to my right and both had a look of complete disgust on their faces.

"What?" I asked innocently.

"What are my bleeding knickers doing on your desk?" Julie asked.

"I don't really know …"

"So they were there when you came in this morning?" Julie asked, interrupting me.

She was absolutely furious, and I can't say I blamed her.

"Listen, I was sitting here minding my own business when the spikey-haired Onion came in and dropped them there and said I could give them to you. He seemed pretty pissed off," I explained.

"What the bleeding hell was he doing with my knickers?" Julie asked, sweeping them off the desk in front of me.

I was in a bit of a dilemma because of course I did know something about Julie's knickers, that someone had put them in Samantha's handbag, but I really didn't know whether I should say anything about that yet. Besides, I genuinely didn't know how they'd got from Samantha's handbag to the spikey-haired Onion.

"I don't know?"

"Why didn't you ask him?"

"I didn't have a chance. For fuck's sake, girls, go upstairs and ask him. This is nothing to do with me," I said.

They turned on their heels and marched out, almost colliding with Samantha, who was on her way in.

"Morning, Nostrils," she said.

"Morning, Samantha. Have you …"

Before I could complete my sentence, one of the Onions, a guy called Tom, came bouncing in and asked, "Does anyone know who put a pair of Julie's knickers in Anthony's lunchbox? Apparently, his wife found them and went absolutely berserk; she chucked him out and he spent the night on my sofa. He's fucking fuming and on the warpath."

I shook my head and looked as innocent as I could.

As Tom walked back out, I noticed the grin on Samantha's face was as wide as that on the Cheshire cat.

"What the fuck have you done?" I asked, my voice lowered.

"Serves them fucking right," she replied, "taking the piss out of me! Let them explain to their wives what they're doing with a pair of knickers."

We sat in silence for a few minutes; I really didn't want to get involved, and then Julie walked back in.

"Sorry I was cross earlier, Chris. My enquiries have revealed that this is nothing to do with you. I've just read about your meeting with Sonia Rider."

"She was one awkward cow; really didn't like police at all, had a right attitude," Samantha said.

I suspected Julie was talking to me, but of course, Samantha didn't know I'd been to see her late yesterday evening.

Julie looked confused.

"I, 'um, bumped into Sonia on the estate late last night; she, 'um, opened up a bit. I didn't get much out of her and it was a very short conversation," I said, in a slightly faltering attempt to stave off any attitude from Samantha.

I needn't have bothered and entirely to her credit, Samantha said, "She didn't like me; I don't think she appreciated my trans status. I thought she'd probably respond better to someone else. I was going to mention it this morning but just hadn't got round to it yet."

"Didn't you ask her for the victim's phone number?" Julie asked.

I was momentarily taken back. Of course I should have asked for it but I had genuinely forgotten. I wondered whether on some level my subconscious was at work because of course, that was the last thing I wanted.

"I'm sorry Julie, I clean forgot. I'll cover it off the next time I'm on the estate. She was spikey though so perhaps it wouldn't have been the right thing to ask at that stage," I replied.

"No problem, babes," Julie said.

Her phone message alert sounded.

"Why is that twat texting me? What is Anthony's problem?" she asked.

I didn't have the heart to tell her that the spikey-haired Onion wasn't the only person to have taken a pair of her knickers home.

~~~

It actually took less effort than I thought it would to persuade the DCI that we needed to get a team behind Sonia. I asked Samantha to prepare the RIPA forms but she clearly hadn't done them before, so in the end I did them myself. By midday, the detective superintendent who was based over at Edmonton had signed them off.

We were in luck; there was a surveillance team available tomorrow. This was all coming together rather well.

I was frustrated when I got a call from the DCI telling me to cancel the surveillance team because CIB were going to provide one. I phoned a DS called Toby, who said we'd have to meet at a neutral location and that he'd brief his team, as we weren't allowed to meet them in person. I can only assume that was because they were worried that one day they might want to deploy them against us.

Samantha and I then went over to the estate to find an OP (observation point). Normally, such enquiries have to be made very carefully, but not in this instance – if Sonia saw us calling door to door, so what? She would just assume we were making more house-to-house enquiries.

We found an old couple living on the ground floor almost opposite Sonia's address and from their bedroom window we had a really good view both of Sonia's front door and the stairwell where she would come out if she wanted to leave the block. It was just perfect and I genuinely think the couple were delighted to be doing something so public spirited. I lied; I said we needed to keep observation on a drug dealer, because if I told them it was in connection with a murder then they might not be so keen to help. They were a nice couple, both in their nineties and on life's lap of honour, so to speak.

I planned to run the operation from midday because I just didn't see Sonia as a morning type of person. The thing with surveillance teams is that they won't sit on a dead plot, that is to say ,one where there hasn't been any movement in over four hours, so timing was everything. It was no use getting them there at eight in the morning if Sonia didn't get out of her pit until one in the afternoon.

For all I actually knew, Sonia may not have been planning to see Bigga for another week, so the whole thing was a bit hit and miss; as so often is the case, the special secret ingredient to success was luck.

I'd spent the last five hours with Samantha and not once did I ask her about Julie's knickers. I thought the best thing was simply not to know. I suspected that in an act of vengeance, she'd popped them in the belongings of those whom she suspected were responsible for putting them in her handbag, but of course the problem was she didn't really know who'd done it and besides, such an act of spite might have serious domestic repercussions for her victims. She shouldn't have done it and I suspect that she quickly realised that too.

I was getting to know her a little more and I have to confess, she was all right. She wasn't the brightest, or the funniest, but she was great company because she was fun to be around and unlike some, she actually seemed to take a genuine interest in other people, so she would ask questions about my family and, in particular, my girls, and she would remember things too, like their names and their ages and little details like that.

By four, I'd dropped Samantha back at Arbour Square and was making my way to Vicky Park.

Chapter 42

I'd spent the whole day worrying what Nick wanted to see me about, but I needn't have bothered, it was nothing to do with the murder case, Buster or the drugs search. He wanted to thank me and handed me a Sainsbury's carrier bag; a glance inside revealed a bottle of malt whisky.

He'd had the interview for SO13 brought forward to four o'clock yesterday and every question I'd pre-warned him about, came up. The board chairman, my mate Alphabet, concluded the interview by welcoming him to the department.

Nick was cock-a-hoop but I took the opportunity to remind him not to tell a soul that Alphabet and I had made sure he knew what was coming, not because I was unduly concerned about that in itself, but the agreement to keep this a secret underlined our previous conspiracy to keep quiet about me being at Gary Odiham's house.

When we'd finished, it was still early but I wanted to go home. I hadn't seen my girls in days and I felt shattered.

I phoned Wendy and discovered she was still out with Matthew. They'd done Scotland Yard and the Old Bailey because apparently those were the places he really wanted to see. What Wendy said next really took me by surprise.

"I took Matthew to Stoke Newington, to Dawn's memorial plaque, and then we went and laid flowers at her grave in Buckhurst Hill."

"Did he want to do that?" I asked.

"Of course. I told him that you were only a few months older than he was when you and Dawn were blown up; he was quite taken aback. We met Dawn's mum at the grave," Wendy said.

"Good God, she must still go there every day. She used to visit for at least an hour and just sit there chatting to Dawn. I can't believe she still does that nearly twenty years later. Can you?" I said.

"I can understand. She sends her love and asked why you never contact her," Wendy said.

Now I felt terrible. After the bombing, Dawn's mum and I had got quite close and we had kept in touch for years but as the years had rolled by, our contact had reduced to the annual exchange of Christmas cards.

"Now I feel awful," I said.

"She was fine, darling. I introduced her to your son and explained that he was named after her daughter, well sort of, you know what I mean," Wendy said.

"What did she say?" I asked.

"She was really, really touched and gave him a huge hug. She's nice, isn't she?"

"Mrs M is lovely. I really must get over and see her soon. Did she say whether she's still living in the same place?" I asked.

"Not specifically, no. But she did say that you'd know where to find her, so I assume she must be. Oh ,and remind me to tell you something else she said; I can't talk about it at the moment."

We said goodbye and I agreed to meet them both tomorrow evening, subject, of course, to something significant happening at work.

The journey home was the usual ball ache but I was in with sufficient time to spend an hour with the girls and to read to them when they went to bed.

As soon as I got in, Jackie jumped in the car to go down the shops and buy some milk, apparently we'd run out – it took her ages and I started to worry that something had happened.

When she returned, Jackie seemed a bit distant so I decided to cheer her up with a proposal to book a summer holiday.

"What do you reckon; where would you like to go?" I asked enthusiastically.

"Chris, I'm leaving you," she replied, "and don't pretend you don't know why."

I felt like I'd been kicked in the stomach.

"I don't know what to say?" I replied, never having said a more honest sentence.

"Seriously, Chris, what do you expect?"

I nodded, of course I understood, but somehow I hadn't expected this.

"I'm not putting up with it any longer," Jackie said.

"What if I stop?" I asked.

Though I had to confess, whatever I told Jackie I had absolutely no intention of breaking up with Wendy.

Jackie laughed sadly.

"I don't believe you can," she said quietly.

I did wonder what had brought this to a head this evening but then remembered how many nights I'd recently spent at Wendy's.

"What can I do to fix this?" I asked.

"You can't, darling. It's gone on for too long, and I've come to realise that our life is never going to be just normal. It'll always be there."

"What about the girls?" I asked.

"They'll be fine. We'll stay here, you can have regular access, and you know, whatever day suits you best. I know it's going to be hard but it's time that I went back to work anyway, the girls are getting older, so I'll pick up some agency nursing, it pays really well."

I really didn't want to be one of those dads who sees their kids every Wednesday and every other weekend.

"Have you seen a solicitor?" I asked.

"Not yet, but I've just spoken to my dad."

I felt another kick in the stomach.

Christ, I needed to get a fix to handle this news. Suddenly I could feel my stomach cramping.

"What did your dad say?" I asked.

"He told me to stay with you; in sickness and in health, he said."

"I've always liked your old man," I said, with a wry smile.

"Oh Chris, I love you so much. Why do you do it?" Jackie said, with genuine warmth.

What was I meant to say? That Wendy was simply so gorgeous and devoted that no male human being on the planet would be able to resist her? I'm sure that would go down really well!

"I'm sorry," I replied, "mea culpa."

Jackie started to cry; I could see her eyes filling up with tears but I resisted the temptation to go to her.

"I love you," I said.

"I know you do," she replied.

"Is our life that bad?" I asked.

She shook her head.

The tears were rolling down her cheeks now and she was catching each in a small white tissue.

"You don't have to do this," I said.

"I do, Chris. I'm sorry."

"What if I stop? What if I change?" I asked.

My mind was racing with a multitude of thoughts. Could I leave Wendy? Should I leave Wendy? Should I just accept that my marriage was over and go off with Wendy?

"But you can't, Chris. It's been going on for too long," Jackie said.

"Have you known all along?" I asked.

I was starting to feel like a real shit.

"Of course, a wife knows these things," Jackie said between sobs.

It was the nights away – that's what had done it.

"I'm sorry, darling." I said. "What do we do now?"

Jackie shook her head.

"How about counselling?" I suggested.

I heard about an organisation called Relate that provides marriage guidance.

"We've been here, Chris," Jackie said.

I was a little confused; I definitely didn't remember going to marriage counselling with Jackie.

"What about if I promise to …"

Jackie interrupted me, "… and we've definitely been here before."

Something wasn't quite right, I'd never before promised not to see Wendy.

I was confused and a lifetime of experience told me that in such situations, you should keep your mouth shut. So I kept quiet.

"I want you to move out?" Jackie said.

"Tonight?" I asked.

"I just can't do it any longer, Chris. It's not fair on me, not fair on the girls 'cos everything's just a big, fat lie."

"Sorry" I replied, for about the zillionth time.

"You're clearly not happy here or you wouldn't do it," she protested.

"I am happy here, I really am, darling," I replied.

"Here, you might as well have it back," she said.

She threw a small clear plastic bag onto the coffee table.

I picked it up and turned it over a few times. I recognised it immediately as being one from Gary Odiham's flat because it had a distinct but thin red line running parallel with the opening.

"Where the fuck was this?" I asked, with genuine amazement.

"Don't give me that, Chris; it was in the car. I found it under the driver's seat, when I put the seat forward."

My mind jerked to the sudden realisation that this conversation wasn't about Wendy; it was about me being on the gear. I never saw that coming.

Chapter 43

Samantha and I met the DS from CIB in a hotel lobby near Heathrow airport at ten.

He was a pleasant enough guy, a white male called Toby in his mid-forties with deliberate, perfectly timed movements. Detective Superintendent Adam Stanley had already given him the back story, so I only had to provide him with a photograph of the subject (Sonia Rider), which I obtained from her CRIMINT file, and a briefing sheet with the address of her flat and a map of the estate. I explained that we had a good OP which had been up and running since nine. The OP reported that in the last hour there had been three callers to the flat and that the subject had answered the door to each dressed in a brown dressing gown. Each caller had left the premises within minutes, circumstances that suggested she was dealing.

Tony gave us two CIB radios, one for me and Samantha in the arrest car, and the other to be taken to the OP, so that when Julie and Nicola saw the subject leave, they could give the off directly to the surveillance team rather than having to relay the message through our murder squad radios, which operated on another channel.

Just as we were about to part, I got a text from Nicola to say that there was another punter at the address and that on his departure, they'd seen the subject turn the number 2 figure on her front door upside down, which suggested to me Sonia had sold the last of her drugs. If that was the case, she certainly hadn't had much. I immediately shared the update with Tony and also expressed my concern that if I was right and she had run out of drugs, this might mean her departure was imminent.

Tony stepped outside, made a quick call and came back to inform me that he'd told his team to go directly to the estate; he estimated that they'd be ground assigned in thirty-five minutes, which was very good going from Heathrow and could only be achieved if they went on blues and twos, which was an option Samantha and I didn't have as our vehicle wasn't equipped with these.

Despite all our best efforts to get there, ten minutes later Sonia went out while the surveillance team was still fighting its way through Earls Court.

The OP reported that she was wearing black leggings, black pumps and a grey woollen jumper. We relayed the information to Tony, who said they'd keep running to cover the address in the event of her return. I was really pissed off as I felt we'd almost certainly missed our chance, and all for the sake of thirty minutes. I moaned to Samantha that I knew everything had been going too well.

"Why didn't you get the surveillance team in earlier?" she asked.

"Clearly I should have, but that's easy to say with hindsight. We've only got the surveillance team for four hours on a dead plot so you've really got to be lucky with your timing," I explained.

"Four hours? That's ridiculous. Don't they work an eight-hour day like the rest of us?" she replied.

"You haven't done a lot of work with surveillance teams, have you," I replied.

"You don't get a lot of demands for them on the Community Support Unit at Ilford," she replied.

My mobile rang; it was Nicola with the excellent news that the subject had just returned carrying some shopping. I relayed this information to Tony. I drove on to the estate and parked up out of sight of Sonia's flat and asked Nicola to come to the car to collect the CIB radio, which she did, a few minutes later. She got into the rear passenger seat.

"How's it going?" I asked.

"Yeah, fine. She was clearly dealing earlier but it's been quiet for the last hour. She was only out of the address for a few minutes, so I don't think we've missed anything. There's no sign of anyone else in there."

"How are your hosts?" I asked.

"They're fine; supplying us with tea and biscuits every hour, on the hour. We'll have to get them some flowers, or something,"

Nicola said. "And what the fuck is going on with Julie's underwear? The poor girl is really pissed off," she added.

For the first time, I turned around to face her and as I did so I caught sight of Samantha's face; she was looking suitably sheepish.

"I've no idea, mate. Colin came marching in this morning and put a pair of her knickers on my desk. That's all I know," I replied.

"Well, she's going to take it further. She says she feels abused," Nicola said.

"Ask her not to do anything until I've spoken to her," I said.

"No problem, see you later," Nicola said as she alighted.

"Knickergate; that's the scandal you've created," I said to Samantha as soon as Nicola got out.

"Oh, what have I done?" she said despondently. "But I didn't take them in the first place, that was someone else. Who do you think it was?"

"Well, it certainly wasn't either of the guys you planted them on," I replied.

"How can you be so sure?" she asked.

"Because no one has yet worked out that it's you that relocated them and they'd know it was you if either one of them was responsible for planting them in your bag in the first place," I said.

"Unless it's a double bluff," Samantha suggested.

"Possibly, but I doubt it," I replied.

"Shall I speak to Julie?" Samantha suggested.

"Leave it to me, hopefully I'll be able to straighten this out. But I want a favour in return?"

"What's that then?"

"If we don't get anywhere here today, how do you fancy a little trip to Dagenham?"

"What for?" she asked.

"Listen, I've asked the DCI for his authority to get a ticket for the shebeen in Palmerston Road but he says there's not enough to go on. What about if we go back later and see if we can, you know, look through a window or something.

"I mean, what if the place is covered in blood? What if that is our primary crime scene?"

I knew I was taking a bit of a risk, because when I said 'look through a window' I meant 'force entry', but if Nick Charles was right, and underneath his insecure facade beat the heart of a seasoned police officer, I reckoned she'd be up for it. What's more, by proposing to do this with her I was demonstrating that I trusted her. If she didn't like the sound of it, she could always say no.

"I'll bring the jemmy and a chisel, you get the UV light and a decent torch." Samantha said.

Chapter 44

I was pleased with Samantha's willingness to get involved in this little piece of skulduggery; she hadn't hesitated for even a second and for the first time, I saw in her the real police officer.

When we were a few minutes away, I decided to lay down a few ground rules to make sure we covered ourselves.

"Let's play this really low key. We'll start by questioning the neighbours about the shebeen and who was running it. Then we'll see if we can get round the back. We'll only go in if we can do so quietly. Remember, plastic gloves at all times, we don't want to leave our own fingerprints in there. If the shit really hits the fan, we'll say we thought we heard someone shouting for help from inside and entered to preserve life under our Common Law powers. Then we'll say it must have been a neighbour's TV that we heard. But I really don't want to have to explain that to the DCI because he's no fool; I've already asked him for permission to get a ticket, so he'll guess what we've been up to."

"What if we do find a bloodstained scene? What do we do then?" Samantha asked.

"Good question. Then we'll leave immediately and I'll make an anonymous phone call to Crimestoppers to say that I'd heard that a drug dealer was stabbed in the address last week," I replied.

"Oh, very clever," Samantha replied.

"Don't tell me you haven't used that before? Crimestoppers is the oldest trick in the detective's book."

"I can honestly say, that's a new one to me," Samantha replied.

I was overplaying the whole thing a little bit. I had used Crimestoppers several times but mainly to submit information I'd picked up when buying my gear. For example, I might see another punter who'd obviously just robbed someone. In such a case I would submit as much information as possible, perhaps his first name and a very good description, to Crimestoppers.

No sooner had we arrived outside 73 Palmerston Road than the heavens opened; it seemed like it always rained in Dagenham. Fortunately or unfortunately, Samantha had a small, very ladylike, pink umbrella, which she deployed with a ping as soon as she stepped out of the car – so much for going in under the radar!

The front of the shebeen was properly secured with a steel bar, which was padlocked into several brackets in the frame in a manner that local councils used to prevent squatters breaking into vacant premises. The lower windows were boarded up. Whoever had been using the shebeen had somehow got their hands on the keys to these padlocks.

We knocked at 75 and a young black lad answered the door; he might have been sixteen. I showed my warrant card and asked to speak to his parents, explaining immediately that nothing was wrong and I just wanted to ask a few questions about the house next door.

The polite young lad told us that both his parents were out: his mother was at church and his father, who was a bus driver, was at work.

"Well, I wonder, would you be able to help?"

"Of course, officer," he replied, inviting us to step inside.

I questioned him about the shebeen, how long it had been there, whether he knew any of the people involved in running it, had he spoken to them, could he describe them, etc. He couldn't tell us a great deal: the shebeen had been there about three months; the main man was a black Jamaican who, from the description, could have been Bigga; no, he'd never spoken to them and nor had his parents but his mother had complained several times to the local council.

"The smell of cannabis would be awful and they played music so loudly it was impossible to sleep," the young lad said.

"No wonder your mum has complained," Samantha said.

"Did anyone complain directly to them?" I asked.

"You wouldn't do that. The main man was a Yardie, a dangerous and unpleasant individual. He had a really strong accent and both mum and dad told me to avoid him at all costs."

"Who used to live there?" I asked.

"Mrs Henderson, but she died last year," he replied.

"Did she own it?" Samantha asked.

"No, these are all housing association. Mum reckons someone at the housing association has rented it out unofficially and taken a backhander," the young lad explained.

"I think your mum might be right. Can we have a look from the back?" I asked, confident that my request would be met.

"Of course, but it's really overgrown next door. I don't think anyone's done the garden for years," he replied.

We went through the hall and then the kitchen and utility room, turned left into the garden and then followed the young lad as he took us to the fence which separated the two houses.

"Over you go, then," I said to Samantha, who had put up her pink umbrella as soon as we'd got outside.

Samantha gave me the look. As the DS I was quite entitled to tell her to climb over the fence but if I was being honest, I wouldn't have asked Julie or Nicola, if they'd been with me.

"You don't have to climb over, it's fallen down just behind that apple tree. Just duck down and there's a gap you can get through," the young lad said.

I did and he was right; getting into the garden was easy but working one's way through the undergrowth of nettles, brambles and holly was bloody hard work. I was just glad it wasn't summer, otherwise everything would have been a couple of feet taller.

Samantha followed me, at one stage complaining that her tights were going to be ruined, which was quite amusing.

The young lad had started to follow us too, but I politely sent him back, saying we were just going to check the place over and would he mind making us a cup of tea, as we'd only be a few minutes.

At the rear of the house were piles of black bin liners filled with empty beer cans, wine bottles and those from other alcoholic beverages.

I turned the back doorknob and it came off in my hand. I showed it to Samantha who stepped forward and shone her torch through the kitchen window.

I leaned in with my shoulder and immediately noticed that most of the door and its wooden frame was rotten. I leaned harder and it popped open with the application of very little force. We were in.

When you're a uniform PC, searching a house in the dark is a surprisingly common occurrence. In those cases, you were usually looking for a dead body. That was a truly horrible thing to have to do. Now we weren't looking for a body but a blood-splattered murder scene, which was better but still pretty creepy.

We worked the house together, none of that Scooby-Doo 'you go to the cellar and I'll do the attic' bollocks. That way, at least we felt the reassurance of another human being.

We did the downstairs and at regular intervals, we turned the torch off and used the UV light. There was nothing of any note. The place had obviously been used as an informal drinking venue and there was even a bar set up in the back room with optic measures and plastic glasses. There was also an impressive sound system by the bar and two gigantic speakers.

Then we went upstairs, where there was evidence that the rooms had been used as some sort of drugs den: mattresses covered most of the floor space and there were old syringes, crack pipes and tinfoil everywhere.

There wasn't any sign of a serious assault or a struggle. Equally significantly, there wasn't evidence of any attempt to clean any particular room or area. I was disappointed.

I was able to close the back door enough to suggest it hadn't been forced and we made our way back through the bramble and undergrowth.

The young lad had made a pot of tea and we stood in the kitchen chatting amiably. I discovered that he was the same age as Matthew but he'd clearly had less of life's advantages. No public-school education or polo ponies for him. He was really keen on joining the job so I wrote down my contact details on a piece of paper and told him I'd help him to draft an application, if he wanted.

As we were leaving, I suddenly remembered a question which I'd have kicked myself if I'd forgotten to ask.

"The people who visited next door, were they always black?"

The lad looked awkward and I suddenly realised that he may have misinterpreted my question.

"I'm trying to establish whether the guy who was murdered, he was white, might have visited next door on the night he was attacked," I explained.

"So you're here about the murder, not the illegal drinking den next door?" he asked.

Samantha replied, "They're connected. We do need to know about the place next door, which we told you when we arrived, but we need to know because we're trying to establish whether it's connected to the murder. The victim, his name was Gary Odiham, died at the garage …

"Yeah, I've seen the yellow signs," the young lad interjected.

" … but he was stabbed somewhere nearby and we thought it might have been next door. That's why Christopher is asking about the ethnicity of the people who used to frequent the club next door."

"Oh, I understand," the young lad replied.

"You see, in my day, only black people would visit a shebeen, that's what we used to call illegal drinking places, like the place next door," I said.

The young man frowned.

"Were you in last Thursday night? Did you see any coming and goings?" Samantha asked.

"Yeah, no. I mean, yes I was in, no I didn't see anything; my bedroom's at the back. As for the colour thing, yeah, it was mainly black guys but I definitely saw the one white guy going who used to go in, bald head, covered in tattoos."

Was that significant? I thought so, or was I just clutching at straws?

Chapter 45

Thursday evenings were Wendy evenings, but this week that also meant they were Matthew evenings.

I was late getting away, of course. I wasn't on the way to Wendy's until nearly nine, so I phoned ahead and told them to meet me in the Bird. I needed a drink; well I actually needed a fix, but I'd make do with a drink.

I realised that I'd gone over a week without my old friend – now that was really going some.

Just as I was arriving, my mobile phone went. I really didn't want to answer, so I checked the screen hoping it was a withheld number so that I could justify to myself hanging up. It was Pod, so it was a call I would take.

"Hello, mate. You all right?" I said.

"Think so, Chris," he replied hesitantly.

"That doesn't sound good, go on."

From the tone in his voice I knew something was troubling him.

"You know we saw Tony Pascal?" he said.

"Yeah."

"What name did his daughter say when she came into the room?" he asked.

"I didn't pay much attention, mate, I was too distracted by the stunning towel-clad body," I replied.

"I think she said 'Tim'?" Pod said.

"I'll take your word for it, why?" I asked.

"Well, Tim was the name of the prison officer from Pentonville that was shot during that robbery last year, the one in Walthamstow," he replied.

"Yeah, so?" I replied.

"Well, the victim was Tim Hughes, and one of Tim Hughes's many girlfriends was, wait for it, Lauren Pascal, Tony's daughter."

"Was she, or he, a suspect? I don't think I had anything to do with that job."

"No," Pod replied, "it was just an off-licence robbery that went wrong, or so we've always thought."

"Tell me a bit more about it," I asked.

"Tim was a right ladies' man and had literally half a dozen women on the go. Two were married, most were single and all thought they were the only one in his life. He had been a prison officer for about eighteen months but was suspected of working as a doorman and as it happens, was about to be suspended."

"Isn't that allowed, I thought they all did it?" I asked.

"They used to allow it years ago but since the rave scene in the nineties, the role of doorman has been so synonymous with drug dealing the prison service put a stop to it. Anyway, he was about to be suspended but was murdered before they actually did the deed. On his way home from work, Tim went into an off-licence in

Walthamstow to buy who knows what. In behind him walked a guy who was wearing a full-face motorbike helmet and gloves, who shot our victim in the back of the head. We assumed because the victim was wearing half blues, the robber mistook him for Old Bill," Pod explained.

"CCTV?" I asked.

"No. The off-licence owner is the only witness," Pod replied.

"Was anything stolen?" I asked.

"Don't think so."

"Let's take another look at that murder in more detail. Cheers, mate, good call. We'll speak tomorrow," I said.

I ended the call and met Wendy and Matthew in the pub. They told me about their last two days and all they'd been up to. Yesterday, they'd been to Buckhurst Hill and Stoke Newington, but today they'd been doing more traditional sights, like Buckingham Palace for the Changing of the Guard and Madame Tussaud's.

Wendy was the mother hen but I don't think Matthew viewed her in a reciprocal light because several times I caught him looking at her breasts. She didn't seem to notice. Then when Wendy went off to the toilet, young Matthew watched her every step of the way.

"You all right there?" I said, to bring him back into the room.

"Yeah, um, sorry …" he spluttered.

I thought that was the end of the matter but Matthew added, "She's absolutely lovely; gosh, I know it's completely wrong but I don't think I've ever felt like this before."

"Matthew! Come on, son. She's, like, twelve years older than you. And besides, she's your father's girlfriend; I don't think you're allowed to find her attractive."

"I know, but I can't help it," he replied sheepishly.

I was suddenly very aware that although he was my son, I really didn't know the young man sitting opposite me. What's more, I hadn't seen this coming and wasn't quite sure how to deal with it.

"When are you going home?" I asked, perhaps a little tactlessly.

"Sunday; Wendy's going to drop me off at Paddington and then I have to change at Swindon."

"Are you looking forward to going home?" I asked.

"No; I would love to stay and find a job here in London, you know, before I go off to Exeter. I mean, I'm on my gap year, surely I should be experiencing life a bit and not wasting my time working with Pop on the farm, I mean, I've done that all my life," he said.

Wendy joined us.

"Have you told Chris that you want to come and work in London?" she asked.

I wondered exactly whose idea this was.

"Just now," Matthew responded.

"Well what did he say?" Wendy asked.

"He," I said, "hasn't expressed an opinion yet. What's important is not what I think, but what Matthew's mum and dad think. Has anyone told them?"

"Not yet," Matthew replied.

"Do you want Chris to talk to them?" Wendy asked.

"I'm not doing that; if I was them, that would incense me. Matthew, you need to think this through properly; first, you need to get your mum and dad on board, then you need to find a job, then somewhere to live."

"He can live with ..." Wendy managed to say before I kicked her under the table to stop her completing the bloody sentence.

I was annoyed with Wendy because I felt ambushed. I was really tempted, there and then, to invite Matthew to meet Jackie and my girls, just to spite her, but I didn't.

"Matthew, have you spoken to mum, today? Well, step outside and call her now, because I want a few words with Wendy."

He did as he was told.

"For fuck's sake, Wendy, what's going on?"

"Nothing is going on. I looked after your son because you were too busy, don't you remember asking me to?"

"But you were going to say he could move in with us, I mean you."

"No I wasn't," she replied, "I was going to say he could share with my friend's brother when he starts his internship in February. As you know, he's got to find someone to live with him."

I realised that I might have jumped the gun a bit.

"You do know he's got a big crush on you?" I asked.

"Of course," she replied coolly.

"Listen, Chris. He's a lovely lad, I mean a really great kid. He's super bright, three grade As, did you know that? But more than that, he's just really nice. A bit naïve perhaps, but only because he didn't join the Met when he was barely out of nappies like you and me. Get to know him, 'cos I've done everything I can to make sure that he knows what you're all about, even though you've hardly been here."

"We got a new job, Wendy. What was I meant to do? Go sick?" I said.

"No, you should have taken a few days off. Told the DCI there was a family crisis or something. But no, not you, your long-lost son appears and you just act as if nothing's happened. You're job pissed, Chris, you really are."

How could I explain that unless I had a remarkable stroke of luck, I wouldn't be in the job, let alone job pissed, for much longer?

"Oh, before Matthew comes back. Dawn's mum told me something I think you should know. She took me to one side, oh, by the way she did say that facially Matthew was the spitting image of you."

"She took you aside to say that?" I asked impatiently, because Matthew would be back at any second.

"No, you idiot; she took me aside to tell me that she's just made a will of which you're her sole beneficiary. So if you are ever going to leave Jackie for me, I suggest you do it before she dies, otherwise she'll be entitled to half of what ever Mrs Matthews leaves you."

Callous though this sounded, it was, in fact, remarkably shrewd advice.

Chapter 46

The Onions had done last night's anniversary appeal and at the office meeting, held exactly a week after the handover briefing, they had a significant update.

A witness was found who stated that shortly after the murder and just over a mile away from the scene, he'd nearly hit two white males who ran across the road in front of his van. The descriptions were understandably sketchy, both men were in their thirties and average height and build, but one of the men was wearing a long red coat, the type and colour often worn by postmen. The information opened up a new line of enquiry with regard to CCTV. Of course, it might have been unconnected but it was well worth a try and the long red coat should be easy enough to spot.

More alarmingly, off her own back and probably because she felt guilty about losing it, Julie had visited Sonia and got Gary's phone number. She said she would submit the requisite applications later but anticipated getting an itemised billing within the next three or four days and cell site analysis in stages over the next couple of weeks.

I felt sick. The itemised billing would show an incoming call from my mobile, less than twenty-four hours before the murder. How on earth was I going to explain that? It was hard to concentrate on the rest of the meeting but I don't remember anything else of significance.

We had the surveillance team for a second day running but Sonia didn't leave the flat all day and had only one visitor, a young white female with a child. Either she'd decided not to deal until everything died down or, far more likely, she'd run out of gear and money.

I was a mess. I was so stressed I didn't know what to do with myself. My heart was racing all the time and my head felt like it was going to explode.

The bloody mobile phone billing was going to be my undoing, unless I could solve the murder so quickly and so definitely that no further action was required, anywhere by anyone. But in eight days, we'd really got nowhere. Still no primary scene, no suspect, no meaningful witnesses, no motive and no bloody idea what actually happened.

And on top of that I had to deal with the Matthew issue and the fact that my wife wanted a divorce because I was a drug addict, except ironically, I actually wasn't.

That I'd now gone nine days without a fix was the only light in a sea of shit. My diarrhoea had stopped and the yearning was definitely subsiding. I mean, I still got the bite, hard and deep, but instead of every hour, it was every couple of hours.

I knew a PC once, a bloke I worked with at Tottenham, who had a mental breakdown and just disappeared. His domestic life was in turmoil and he was heavily in debt and couldn't see any way out. They found him when he tried to set light to himself with a can of petrol and a box of matches. He'd been sleeping rough under one of the piers at Brighton. I was starting to understand why he lost it. The concept of just disappearing was becoming quite attractive and several times I found myself genuinely contemplating such a move. The primary obstacle was that I couldn't let this Buster guy get done for something he didn't do, and disappearing wouldn't solve that insurmountable problem.

I hadn't spoken to Jackie since she'd told me that she wanted a divorce. I thought that any attempt to tell her I'd given up the gear after she'd just found the bag in my car would be pointless. Last night I'd spent at Wendy's anyway, but Jackie would normally have texted or called me at some stage. Her silence was deafening.

Although it was gone seven, most of the team were still about as they'd come in late, having been out the previous night on the anniversary appeal. I went to the incident room where I was surprised to see Jeff still sat at his desk.

"Hello, mate," I said.

"Nostrils," he replied.

"You not solved this yet?" I asked, not really expecting him to reply.

"This is a real stinker. We got a couple of stills of the IC1 males which the geezer nearly ran over but they're really pixelated and there's such a lack of clarity that quite frankly, it could be you and me," Jeff replied.

"Handsome buggers, were they?" I asked.

He smiled and looked up from his keyboard.

"Not my problem any more, though. The DCI says that unless there's a significant development soon, CIB will be picking this up. You and your team are going across for six weeks," he explained.

"Where are we going to be based? Jubilee?" I asked.

"I suppose so," he replied.

"Listen, Nostrils, what's the connection to Old Bill? Why are CIB interested? Is it because the old girl next door said she recognised the guy who was there in the middle of the night as being one of the guys who'd done the search?"

I nodded.

"I assume so, but I don't buy it," I said.

"There's got to be more to it. Is there?"

"Look, Jeff, I've signed a non-disclosure thingy but I can honestly say, with my hand on my heart, that I don't think there's any police involvement in this murder."

"Um," he replied, "take a look at this 'cos it might explain the move."

He handed me an unregistered docket, a brown cardboard folder, which was used to pass information between departments and individuals. The front cover was simply marked 'Confidential'. I opened it up and read a short report, which appeared to be some sort of press release; it read:

As a result of new evidence, police are to reopen the investigation into the death of Reginald Odiham, who died while in police custody at City Road Police Station in 1986. The Police Complaints Authority will supervise the investigation, which will be conducted by Assistant Chief Constable Richard Bovis of the Wiltshire Constabulary.

"Fuck me," I said.

"I know. Could it be connected?" Jeff asked. "Or did you already know that? You didn't, did you? I can tell by your face."

"Didn't have a clue, mate," I replied.

The detective in me didn't like coincidences but my instinct told me this wasn't connected to his death. Perhaps if Gary had been murdered at home, in his bed, in circumstances that made it look like a drugs overdose, perhaps. But not stabbed in the head in the middle of the night in a Dagenham street.

I always had to smile at the conspiracy theorists that thought the security services had assassinated Princess Diana. If they had really assassinated her, they would have chosen Kensington Palace, not a tunnel in Paris, where, incidentally, she had just stopped over on an unplanned visit.

So no, I didn't think our victim had been assassinated because he was loosely linked to an incident of alleged police brutality, which had occurred over fifteen years ago. Like the police corruption angle, it was yet another dead end.

I headed home and called Wendy on the way to have a quick chat and to tell her I'd come round tomorrow. She said she'd had a good day with Matthew but they'd stayed local, as they were both shattered, and had done a visit to the Millennium Dome. She also said that they'd turned the house upside down looking for Matthew's bank card, which he'd lost, but the upside was that she'd found an old warrant card of mine, one which I had, in fact, previously reported lost.

Between Wanstead and Woodford, I stopped for a pee in the forest at a lay-by just off the A11. I confess that I was somewhat hesitant about going home and what Jackie would say to me. As I got back into my car, I felt around under the seats to make sure there were no other bags lying around and as I did so, I felt a small, thin object, which was obviously Matthew's missing card.

It would only take twenty minutes to return it to its rightful owner, so I drove all the way around the next roundabout near the Winston Churchill statute and drove the three miles back to Leyton.

I parked immediately outside and momentarily thought about just putting the card through the letterbox, but realised that would be somewhat insensitive.

I'd had a key since about the second month of our relationship, so I let myself in.

There was just a step-through hall, so within two paces you were in the lounge. I was somewhat surprised not to hear the television on but I could hear noises and voices coming from upstairs, coming from Wendy's bedroom.

They were sounds of sex.

Chapter 47

I stood frozen to the spot. No, surely? I must have got this wrong. I listened harder.

I could hear Wendy saying 'come on, darling' over and over again, I could hear Matthew panting and I could even hear the headboard knocking, something I knew from experience it did during sex unless one of you actually used your hand to push it hard up against the wall.

For a few moments I was genuinely confused. I knew what was happening but I didn't know why. Nor did I know how to react.

Through the panic, I was genuinely surprised that my first instinct wasn't to go upstairs and confront them. If I wasn't going to do that and, quite frankly, what was that going to achieve except a lot of embarrassment, then I needed to get out of there before my presence was detected. That would also give me time to work out exactly how I was going to deal with this situation.

I slipped out, making as little noise as possible. With that said, the noise from upstairs had increased to such a level that I could have been playing the bagpipes and I don't think they'd have noticed me.

I jumped in the car and pulled away, not revving the engine too much as Wendy's bedroom was at the front of the house. I drove almost in a daze. My mind was replaying the thirty seconds, which

I'd spent in the house, over and over again. I was incapable of actually thinking about anything else. Without knowing quite how I'd got there, I had once again pulled over in the lay-by in the forest.

I needed to think. Had I just lost Wendy? Had I, in fact, in less than a week, lost both Jackie and Wendy? Did I want to keep her, anyway? Where could I get some gear? How could Wendy do that to me? And with my son, for fuck's sake! Where around here could I get some gear? How could my son do that to me? Did Wendy really find this eighteen-year-old kid so fucking attractive she had to fuck his brains out? And in our bed! Where the fuck could I buy some gear? Should I go back and confront them? Should I go home and try to save my marriage? Could I even speak to Jackie when this was screaming through my brain? What had Jackie done with that bag of H? The last time I saw it, it was on the coffee table, but that was two days ago. She wouldn't have left it there because of the girls, but if she'd thrown it in the bin, then I might yet be able to find it.

I was normally really good at thinking a problem through, but this had me completely stumped because I couldn't get to the thinking logically stage, I just kept asking questions and replaying the whole hideous scene.

Wendy and I had often talked about faithfulness within a relationship such as ours. I mean, Wendy would quite rightly point out that as I was sleeping with Jackie, I could hardly demand fidelity from her. She was right, of course, but there was an understanding that she would be faithful as long as I didn't stray any further. In which case, she always made it clear she would dump me like nuclear waste. I had always said that I could understand her being unfaithful as a one-off, when the circumstances were just right and the guy simply irresistible. I always said I'd actually be more hurt if she started committing to someone else emotionally, even if she hadn't actually slept with him.

If these were the rules we lived by, sleeping with Matthew made no sense whatsoever. I couldn't believe that she found him desirable; I mean, I knew the type of guy she fancied and it wasn't Matthew Starr. Nor was there an emotional commitment between them, surely not? He was a nice kid but he was eighteen! And he was my son, albeit not really, biologically at least.

My phone went, it was Wendy – fuck!

What was she doing calling me? We'd said goodnight and besides, she wouldn't ring me, because she'd have thought that I would have been at home by now. Should I answer it? If I did, should I be arsey? Could I act cool, even if I wanted to? And despite the total and utter confusion that was my state of mind, I knew that it was never a good idea to say or do anything when your emotions were running quite as high as mine were at that moment.

The call went to voicemail. Would she ring back?

I got an answer to one of my questions, the last, and it was 'yes'.

"Hi," I said, trying desperately to hide any intonation in my voice.

Wendy didn't say anything, which seemed strange. I knew she hadn't heard me when I went in or when I left. Even if she had, she'd have actually called me earlier, not now, a good fifteen minutes later.

"Wendy?" I said.

I checked the phone screen to make sure we were still connected – we were.

I pushed a finger into my spare ear because it was quite noisy in the lay-by with vehicles speeding by every five seconds or so.

I could hear her breathing; I thought I could actually hear her crying.

"Wendy, please speak to me."

I was really surprised by the calmness in my voice.

"I'm sorry," she said, sobbing. "Please come back. I mean, I understand if you don't want to but please come back. We need to talk about this; you need to understand. I know that if you don't come back now you'll never come back and you'll never see your son, or me, again. Please, darling."

I had absolutely no idea how she knew, but clearly she did.

"Where's Matthew?" I asked.

"He's in the shower. He doesn't know anything. I'll ask him to go out for an hour; I'll give him a tenner and send him down to the Duke. Please come back, Chris. I can't do this without you."

I thought that was a strange thing to say, can't do what without me?

"Don't send him to the Duke, why don't you come and meet me in the Bird?"

"I can't. I'm really upset, darling. I'm shaking, I'm so nervous. Please come back."

Wendy had distinctly lowered her voice halfway through the sentence so I assumed Matthew had got out of the shower.

"Come back, park up in the next road and I'll text you when he's gone out."

Wendy was whispering now.

"Please darling, I love you. Please come back, please."

"Okay," I replied.

"You're not going to finish with me, are you?" she said.

Wendy was sobbing again.

I felt like shit but I didn't know why. I even felt guilty, like I'd done something wrong.

"Let's talk about it when I get there," I said.

I heard Matthew call something out and Wendy hung up.

What the fucking hell was I going to say?

Chapter 48

By the time I'd parked in the adjoining street, I'd got the text from Wendy to say that Matthew was out of the house.

The thing was, I didn't feel angry, and that didn't make any sense to me. I felt gutted, confused, betrayed and scared, but not angry. Did that mean I didn't really love Wendy? Did that mean I didn't really care if she slept with my son?

When I arrived, the front door was on the catch, and about forty minutes after I'd walked into the shock of my life, I walked back into a completely different scenario.

Wendy was sitting on the settee, wearing a thick white woolen dressing gown with her knees folded up to her chest. In her hand she held a white tissue, which she used to wipe away a stream of tears and to occasionally blow her nose. I took off my coat, kicked off my shoes and sat down at the other end of the settee.

For a minute, probably longer, possibly shorter, we didn't speak. I think we both wanted the other one to go first.

"I'm sorry," Wendy said, at last breaking the silence.

"Matthew?" I asked, with incredulity, "Not some DI from work, or one of the Sarries rugby team, or your best friend's husband, or fucking anybody, but my son. Seriously? Matthew? You were attracted to Matthew?"

"No," she replied.

"No, what?" I asked.

"No, I wasn't attracted to Matthew. Not for one second," she replied.

"What? I just heard him fucking your brains out," I said.

"No, you didn't," she replied, wiping more tears from her eyes.

"I'm confused, Wendy, who were you having sex with upstairs?"

"You're missing the whole point. Do you really not know me at all? Do you think that I was having sex with Matthew because I fancied him? Jesus, Chris," Wendy said.

She'd stopped crying and if anything, she was frustrated, almost annoyed with me.

"Sorry if I'm being stupid, but I only have sex with women I fancy."

"I want a baby," Wendy shouted.

I was taken aback, not by the statement itself, which wasn't news, but by the fact she'd shouted. I'd never heard her shout, or even raise her voice. She was just from that sort of family that, well, didn't.

"I was having sex with Matthew because I want to have a baby. I am ovulating this week, I am at my most fertile time of the month and I have a limitless supply of fresh, young sperm. Yes, I have had sex with Matthew, but only because circumstances had suddenly presented me with a perfect opportunity to father a child related to you!"

"I, err ..."

"And you've lied to me, Chris, for years. You've had a vasectomy. You can't father children. Christ, I've been off the pill for two years; if you were capable of having children I would have been pregnant by now, the amount of sex we've had."

I didn't know quite how to play this. Should I deny having had the snip? If I was going to, I had to make that denial now.

"And I know you've had a vasectomy, and do you know how?" Wendy asked.

She was really fired up now. I didn't reply.

"Because I was at last year's CID Christmas do and Peter Sheriff was there; you know, the DS you used to work with? He told everyone a story about an OMPD trip you did with him, up to Liverpool. You stayed in the Adelphi hotel and shared a room to make some money on the overnight allowance. Anyway, only a few days before the trip you'd had a vasectomy and one of your testicles was the size of an orange. Peter said you even showed it to him! Can you imagine how I felt? Jesus, Chris. I was so upset. No wonder I couldn't get pregnant. You bastard."

Wendy paused but I felt no inclination to say anything. I couldn't quite work out how all of a sudden I was the one in the wrong.

"So since then I've been trying to have a baby on my own."

"What do you mean? How?"

"There's a company specifically set up for lesbian couples who want to have children. It's called *Women Only* and they deliver you a specimen of sperm which you insert yourself," Wendy explained.

I had actually read an article some time ago, probably in the *Daily Telegraph*, about the company but there were lots of ethical issues being raised and there'd also been some concerns over the level of screening of the sperm donors. I'd also remembered something else: the success rate was really low, like three per cent, and there was some carefully worded suggestion that the whole process was little more than a scam.

"The screening cost me twelve hundred pounds and then I pay four hundred pounds for every specimen. I've been doing it for ten months and I've run out of money."

Wendy started crying again, really sobbing her heart out. I found myself closing the gap between us, then I realised I had my am around her. She sunk her head into my chest and mascara lines started to roll down her face and onto my shirt.

"Christ, Chris, I do everything I can. I even take folic acid tablets every day and only ever drink decaffeinated tea. I'm so sorry, but don't you see, Matthew was my last hope of ever getting pregnant without having to end our relationship, and I love you so much that I can't imagine my life without you. Please, Chris, I know I've done wrong, I really do, but how wrong was it to want to have the next best thing to you, your baby?"

What could I say?

For a start, I believed her completely because the whole thing made sense. I even knew she was short of money because only a few months ago I'd heard her on the phone to her dad asking for a loan. I thought at the time how strange that was as Wendy was usually so financially well organised.

"Why did you lie to me about having a vasectomy?" Wendy asked.

"Because I didn't want to lose you," I replied. "Have you got any money left?"

She shook her head.

"Every penny of savings I ever had is gone. The thing is, I've had three different donors and every time you get a new one, you have to pay for them to be screened – that's seven hundred pounds," Wendy explained.

"Why did you have three different donors?" I asked.

"Because they leave, or they don't want to do it any more or because they move abroad, or something."

"Oh, so this company tells you that your old donor is no longer donating?" I asked.

Wendy nodded.

I could start to see how some might perceive this whole process as something of a confidence trick.

"Do you know who the donors are?" I asked.

"No, but you get to pick them from, like, a list and although you don't know their identities, you do know their physical descriptions and, like, what they do for a living."

I really didn't know what to say, so I said what every Englishman would say in such circumstances.

"Do you want a tea? Shall I put the kettle on?" I asked.

What I was really doing was telling Wendy that everything would be all right.

She nodded. "And get me more tissues; in fact, bring the box in."

When I returned a minute later, the atmosphere had lifted.

I knew we'd both fucked up here. Of course, I should have told Wendy that I'd had the snip and not let her find out like she did. She shouldn't have had sex with Matthew, but I genuinely understood why she had. And the thing was, it wasn't sex, not like all the sex I'd ever had.

"One question, though: how did you know I'd been round?"

"Because you left Matthew's bank card on the table as you came in. I saw it as soon as I came downstairs. We'd been looking for it all day so I knew it hadn't been there earlier. For a moment I was confused and then, of course, I realised that it must have been in your car, you'd found it and popped in to drop it off," Wendy replied.

She took it out of her dressing gown pocket and placed it on the settee between us.

"Don't be annoyed with Matthew," Wendy said.

"How can I be? I'm not his father; I'm a bloke he's just met. There's no bond between us. I don't blame him. There's no way at his age my common sense would have been able to dissuade my penis that having sex with you wasn't a good idea. What do they say? A rising cock has no conscience? No, I don't blame Matthew, not at all. In fact, for the first time, I see something in his character that I recognise," I replied.

"Thank you, Chris. You are lovely. You're the only man I know who wouldn't have just gone berserk."

"I'm just not wired that way, I suppose."

"That's why I want to be with you for ever," Wendy said.

I moved across to kiss and embrace her, but my phone, which was still in my jacket pocket, started to ring.

Wendy sighed.

"Go and speak to your wife, darling. I wish I didn't have to share every bloody moment with her," she said, with a wry smile.

I almost told her that the chances were that she wouldn't for much longer, but held back, just in case I could yet salvage my marriage.

It wasn't my wife calling; it was a manicured female voice and I immediately recognised the familiar sounds of a police control room in the background.

"DS Pritchard?" the voice said.

"Yes, speaking," I replied.

"DS Pritchard, it's the control room at Stoke Newington here."

"Hello, Stokey," I said, with such enthusiasm the woman must have thought I was mad.

"DS Pritchard, are you dealing with a murder in Dock Lane, Dagenham?"

"I am," I replied.

"We have a unit, Golf November two, at an address on the Neville Road Estate."

"Just behind the nick," I interjected, just to show off my knowledge of the ground.

"The female occupier at the address is very drunk but she seems to be saying that she wants to talk to someone about the murder. It is possible that her husband committed the offence, though I say again, she is very drunk. Can you attend?" she asked.

"Yes, yes; but I'm currently in Leyton so running time from there, and I'm not on blues and twos as I'm in my own car. I'll have to pick up someone, oh, and speak to my DCI. I'm going to be at least an hour, probably two," I replied.

"Do you require directions?" she asked helpfully.

"No, I used to work there, many years ago now. I know the ground," I replied.

I hung up and turned around.

Wendy was standing there at the bottom of the stairs.

"You gotta go?" she asked.

"I have, it's work," I replied.

"I know. Sorry, I thought it was wifey. Are we all right, Chris?" she said.

"We will be," I replied.

"You gonna be okay with Matthew?" she asked.

I nodded. She shrugged her shoulders submissively and smiled.

"I'm still ovulating. Do you know what I'm saying?"

I knew exactly what she was saying.

~~~

I couldn't get hold of the DCI so I left a message.

I also had to decide whom to call out to come with me. It was probably going to be easier to arrange to meet at Arbour Square and pick up a job car, if there were any left.

I did what I thought was the right thing and called Samantha because I wanted her to really feel like she was involved in the thick of things. If I was being honest, I didn't really want to return to my old ground accompanied by a bloke wearing a dress, but I realised these were my prejudices and if I couldn't completely eliminate them, I could actually challenge them and work against them. I'd be lying if I said I wasn't a little bit relieved when Samantha said she'd had nearly a bottle of wine and felt quite pissed.

It was quarter to ten and I realised that this might be an issue at this time of night. Next I called Nicola, but only got a voicemail. Then I tried Julie, who answered within two rings.

"Hi, Chris," she said, sounding sober.

"Are you able to come back to work?" I asked.

"I'm in bed but yes, of course. Arbour Square?" Julie asked.

"Yep."

"What is it?" she asked.

"It's all a bit unclear but uniform officers are at an address in North London with a very drunk female who dialled 999. She says her husband committed our murder and wants to tell us all about it. How long are you gonna be?"

"Forty minutes, babes," she replied.

I hadn't hung up for more than a few seconds when the DCI called me back. I updated him and he agreed with my proposal to get control of the potential witness as soon as possible.

When I got into Arbour Square I called the control room at Stoke Newington to see whether there'd been any developments and to tell them that we were still a while away. Night duty had taken over so I spoke to a different person, but they confirmed the late turn van crew would remain on scene until we arrived.

Julie seemed to take ages to get in so I used my time going through the statement binder, which was remarkably thin. The last statement was from the pathologist. The head wound was described as being of equal thickness throughout and the use of a standard knife with a blade that thickened in width along its length could therefore be discounted. This was unusual and I'd not come across it before. Did this mean that it was a case of 'instant arming'? That is to say, that the suspect had grabbed the nearest thing at hand which he could use as a weapon?

When Julie arrived, we didn't waste any time and got going straight away.

On a normal run, the journey from Arbour Square to Stoke Newington would take about thirty minutes but we could probably get there sooner. When she'd been in uniform Julie had been an advanced driver so I let her drive, as her skills would make easy work of the late evening traffic. Not two minutes into the journey, her mobile went off. It was in her handbag on the back seat.

"Can you get that out?" she asked.

I hesitated.

"What, you want me to go into your handbag?" I asked.

The thought of doing so went against all my natural instincts.

"Are you sure?" I asked.

"Oh for God's sake; you've got a wife and a girlfriend, there's nothing in that handbag that's going to come as a surprise, babes," Julie said, frustrated by my hesitation.

I smiled. Having found Julie's phone beneath a pile of tampons, I looked at the screen.

"It's Luke," I said.

Luke was Julie's other half. When I first joined he'd been a DC on the team, but he'd transferred to the Flying Squad after about a year. Since then, I'd seen him only at the occasional social function. He was a nice bloke and he and Julie seemed really well suited, particularly as neither of them particularly liked or ever wanted to have children.

"Well answer it," Julie said.

"Hello, mate, it's Nostrils. She's driving," I said.

"Hello, Nostrils. I swear I spoke to her only half an hour ago and she was in bed. You got another job?" he asked.

"No, just a possible development in the one from last week. Do you want me to get her to give you a ring? We're on a run to Stoke Newington at the moment."

"No, don't worry, Nostrils. It's actually quite handy that you've answered, as it'll save me some grief from the old girl. Can you please tell her I'm going to Belfast first thing tomorrow and I'll be gone about a week? We've had some information that one of our outstanding suspects is hiding out over there. I'll call her from

Heathrow in the morning before we board. I am with the DI and we're on the nine o'clock BA flight."

"Okay, mate, will do. Happy hunting," I said.

I relayed the message to Julie, who moaned because she and Luke had theatre tickets on Saturday to Cirque du Soleil. I thought I'd better stick up for Luke.

"It's the job, though. Bit like tonight, you know. It's the way it goes," I said.

"I know, but you don't know Luke. It really annoys me; he didn't want to go anyway. I wish he'd just told me that in the first place before I booked the tickets. Do you and Wendy want to go?"

I shook my head.

"I couldn't think of anything worse," I replied, "but thanks anyway," I added, a little too late and a little too awkwardly.

"How's Wendy?" Julie asked.

For a moment, just a moment, I thought about telling Julie what had happened with Matthew but that was probably more of a conversation for Nicola. Nicola and I had shared a few secrets over the years.

"She's all right," I replied.

"We've invited her out for lunch on Tuesday."

"Oh, the one that Samantha's going to? That's nice of you," I replied.

It was strange really, but the girls on the team had taken Wendy to their heart and treated her almost as if she was one of our team. It was perhaps a curious stance to take; I mean, most of these girls were married so you'd think that they would see Wendy, the mistress, as the enemy, but they didn't. I know Wendy appreciated being invited along but she said she felt a bit out of it when the conversation turned, as it always inevitably did, to the latest murder case.

Then I remembered there was something that I needed to talk to Julie about, her knickers.

"Nicola told me you were pretty pissed off about what happened earlier, you know, with your underwear," I said.

"Apparently someone has been down my gym bag and removed two pairs of pants which they've planted on two Onions to make it look like I'm having an affair with them. It's not right, babes. Do you know what I mean?" Julie said.

"Someone planted them in Samantha's handbag, you know, trying, no doubt, to be funny. Samantha didn't know they were yours but she was trying to get her own back," I explained.

"So Samantha planted them on the Onions then?" Julie asked.

"Yes, but only because she wanted to show them she wasn't afraid to strike back," I replied.

"How does Samantha know it was them two? It could have been any of them," Julie said.

"She doesn't, she just guessed. I don't think she was thinking particularly logically. In fact, when she did it, I don't think Samantha thought they necessarily belonged to anyone on the team, just that someone had brought them in to do the prank on her."

"Oh I see, I get it now. In that case, I don't blame Samantha, but I'd better get a lock on my gym bag. That's really out of order, Chris," she said.

"I agree," I replied.

"If I told Luke he'd go mad," she said.

"I don't blame him. But why don't you let it go. I'm not saying it's right, I'm really not, but hopefully whoever did instigate this will realise that it has somewhat backfired. What do you say?" I asked.

She nodded.

Our conversation meandered and we did too, through the streets of north-east London, until we pulled up next to a police van which was parked stationary and unattended in a quiet residential street. We were on the Neville Road estate, a low-level housing complex built after the last war and situated only a few hundred yards west of Stoke Newington Police Station.

I checked my scribbled note to confirm the number of the house and we made our way to number 87, which was probably the largest on the estate. As we approached the front door, which was ajar, I could hear a right hullabaloo coming from within and noticed that every light in the house was on. As we passed across the threshold, the sheer scale of the commotion inside struck me. There was a baby crying, but not just crying, screaming. A two-year-old boy, wearing only a nappy, was playing aeroplanes and running from room to room with his arms extended in make-believe wings.

An older boy, perhaps ten, was sitting in front of a precariously balanced TV screen set up halfway up the stairs and playing a 'shoot 'em up' computer game with the volume at full blast. An older girl, who was about twelve, was standing in the kitchen shouting into a mobile phone in a heated conversation, which regularly featured the words 'cunt', 'stiffed' and 'dissed'. Another girl, perhaps sixteen, was in the back room consoling a younger sister of about seven, who was sobbing quietly and rubbing her right knee.

It was midnight yet the kids were in their daytime clothes and even though it wasn't a school night, I would have thought the younger children would be in their beds long ago. There was no sign of the police officers.

"Hello," I called out loudly, several times.

"Up here," a female voice called back.

Julie and I went upstairs, passing the lad playing a computer game and leaving the mayhem behind us on the ground floor.

On the landing we met a male and a female uniform officer who took us into the main bedroom. Both the officers were black which, even in 2003, was quite unusual. On the bed was a white female, a few years younger than me. Unlike her children, she was wearing pyjamas and a dressing gown and was fast asleep. From the smell in the room and the empty bottle of vodka by the side of her bed, it didn't take Sherlock Holmes to realise that she was very drunk.

The female officer spoke.

"Her name is Tracey Manning; she lives here and they're all her children."

"How many of them are there?" Julie asked.

"Six, from five different fathers, apparently," the WPC replied.

"Nice," Julie said, nodding her head slowly.

"Tracey passed out about an hour ago but before she did, she told us that her husband had killed a chap called Gary in Dagenham last week. She said he stabbed him with an ice pick."

"How does she know?" Julie asked.

"Apparently, her husband told her," the WPC replied.

"What do we know about the husband?" I asked.

"His name is Danny Manning. We've done a CRO check and he's got stacks of previous and links to organised crime; he flashes the full house: violent, drugs, assaults police, weapons and firearms," the WPC replied.

"Do we know which OCN this Danny is linked to?" I asked.

I anticipated that the WPC would reply 'Tony Pascal'.

"The Kiracs," she replied instead.

The Kiracs were a Turkish crime family whose network spread out from Mile End across much of East London. It was even rumoured that their influence now stretched as far north as Tottenham. They'd made a fortune in the eighties trafficking heroin and had diversified into a variety of businesses, many of which were now completely legitimate. They were London's top organised criminal network and in comparison, the operations run by the likes of Tony Pascal paled into insignificance.

"When did Tracey last see her hubby?" Julie asked.

"Last week. She says the Kiracs are hiding him," the WPC replied.

"Do we know where?" Julie asked.

The WPC laughed. "No. I did ask her but I think I must have touched a nerve because she called me a fucking fat coon. And said something about heaven."

"Charming," Julie said.

"I mean, I don't mind the 'fucking' and I can live with the 'coon' but I draw the line at fat!" the WPC replied, with good grace and humour.

"Has she got any previous?" Julie asked.

"Nothing, not even a parking ticket," the WPC replied.

At that moment Tracey started to snore and the door burst open with a ten-year-old in tears because his younger brother had knocked over and broken the TV screen, which had been balanced on the stairs.

"Get out," I growled. He did.

"How many kids are there? Did you say six?" I asked.

"Six, oh, and a dog in the garden," the WPC replied.

"Because of the Kirac link, we have to get them all out of here and we have to do it now," I said.

Julie looked at me in disbelief and said, "You gotta be bleeding kidding, babes?"

Chapter 49

I stepped outside to phone the DCI and Julie came with me. Several times his phone went straight to voicemail, so I left him a message telling him what we were dealing with and what I intended to do. As I was talking I could see that Julie was eager to speak to me and suspected she was going to try to talk me out of my plan. I wondered whether she was already stressing about the thought of having to look after six kids. I hung up and turned to her.

"Don't turn round, Chris," she said.

Of course, when anyone says that to you your first instinct is to do just that but I resisted the temptation.

"What is it?" I asked.

"About forty yards away, there are two white males sitting in a black Range Rover and they appear to be watching this house."

"Did you see them when we pulled up?"

"Yes. They were here when we arrived but I just assumed they were having a chat or something and would have gone by now," she replied.

"Could they be Old Bill?" I asked.

"They could be, yes. But if they were keeping the eye on this address, if Danny was their principal target, they'd have an off-street, wouldn't they? Would be easy enough to find one in a road like this, wouldn't it?" And another thing, if they are Old Bill, they'd either be much further down the street or if they were that close they'd be facing away from the address and using their mirrors to maintain the eye," Julie replied.

"I agree. Shall we just go and ask them?" I suggested.

Julie bit her lip while she mulled over my suggestion.

"I don't like it, babes, I don't like it at all, Chris. I mean, if they are not Old Bill, how come they're not worried by the fact that we're here? You'd have thought that with this going on they'd have just disappeared. Why aren't they bothered?" she replied slowly.

I'd never heard Julie like this before.

"They are definitely watching us, babes."

"Definitely two of them?" I asked.

"I can see two but there might be two more in the rear, I think the rear windows are darkened but its hard to tell because the street light's reflecting on the car."

"Any chance we can get the index and get one of the uniform officers to do a check?" I asked.

"No chance, not from here and not without showing out," she replied.

"What if we get in the car and drive round the block?" I suggested.

"That might work," she replied.

"Or I'll pretend to make a call and you go and get our uniform colleagues and we'll just turn them over?" I suggested.

"Sounds like a plan."

I was standing with my back to the Range Rover looking the other way along the street.

"I'll stay here, you go and get them, Julie."

She nodded.

I took my mobile phone out of my pocket and pretended to make another call. I stole a brief casual glance along the street and could see the Range Rover parked on the other side of road facing the address, and yes, there were two white males in the front seats.

I had an imaginary conversation with the DCI until about a minute later the two PCs emerged. They were walking quickly and with Julie, they exited the house and turned right towards the Range Rover. I turned and followed on behind them.

We were closing the distance to the Range Rover quickly and were only about thirty yards away when I heard the ignition turn and the engine start. The headlights flicked on and a second later the front wheels turned left. We were only twenty yards away when the car jerked forward and into the road. As soon as the front tyres straightened up, they spun quickly trying to find grip on the damp road surface.

The WPC bravely stepped into the road to block their path.

"Get out of the fucking road, now," I shouted, with such ferocity and authority that I surprised myself.

I was determined not to let another female officer die on my watch. She stepped back in between two parked cars just as the Range Rover sped by; it was the closest of calls and I would later learn that the side of the vehicle actually clipped the officer's sleeve button.

I stared hard into the vehicle to try to get a description of the occupants, but in the nanosecond that the circumstances afforded, all I could definitely say was that they were both male, white and in their thirties.

As soon as he had passed us all, the driver braked really hard and the Range Rover skidded to a stop. I thought for a second that the driver had had a change of heart and decided to stop after all. I also wondered whether the driver had mistakenly thought he had hit the WPC because he was that close to doing so.

For a second the road was silent, and even though it was dark and the surface damp, I could see smoking skid marks on the road surface.

We started to walk back towards the house and the Range Rover when the passenger window lowered, an arm reached out and pointed towards the house. The hand was holding a firearm, a handgun, and as soon as the arm straightened I heard half a dozen shots ring out, accompanied by the sound of breaking glass and the distinctive ping of bullets bouncing off brick and concrete.

If it had happened slower, I think we would have all hit the floor, but the speed of the event overtook our actions and instead we stood momentarily frozen to the spot, helpless spectators, as several young children, who had previously been in our charge, were placed in mortal danger.

When the sound of a gunshot was replaced by the click of an empty chamber and even before the arm retracted, the Range Rover accelerated away again, performing another wheel spin.

The PC was speaking on his PR. "Golf November; active, urgent."

"Go ahead, four one two," a calm voice responded.

"Shots fired from a black Range Rover part index VX51 or possibly VY51. The vehicle is now north in Neville Road, towards Albion Road. Two white male occupiers; approach with caution; I repeat, approach with caution. And I need LAS to the address in Neville Road, urgently. And I need assistance, urgent assistance. The occupants of the Range Rover have just fired shots into the address …"

While the PC was still speaking, I could hear two tones from about three different directions as units responded to the call even before the officer had finished talking. I knew their first reaction would be to locate the vehicle and arrest the drivers, even though every one of those officers who were responding was unarmed.

"... I repeat, the occupants have just fired numerous gunshots into the address in Neville Road; casualties unknown at this stage. Please stand by."

I glanced at Julie; her face was ashen.

"Are you all right? Is everyone all right?" I asked.

We looked at each other in utter disbelief. My hands were shaking and my knees were wobbling with that strange sensation you get when you have been in a car accident.

We started back towards the address, slowly at first, but within a few paces the walk had turned into a jog and then a run, but when we arrived at the threshold of the house we all paused, petrified about the potential carnage we were about to witness inside.

Chapter 50

"Let's go," Julie said.

Her words jerked us all into action. I should enter first; it was the unofficial role of the DS at any search to be the first one in, but I stopped briefly to examine the bullet marks on the outside of the house because something had caught my eye.

"Hang on," I said.

"Chris, let's go," Julie urged.

My dithering meant the uniform officers were, in fact, the first in while I was still outside, studying the front of the house.

"Chris, if you can't face it, I understand, I really do. You stay here, I'll report back in a minute, babes," Julie said.

"They're okay," I said, almost to myself and in little more than a whisper.

"What?" Julie replied.

"Look, most of the shots have hit the bricks above the window and the two shots which have gone through the glass have done so right at the very top of the window."

I looked more closely and counted six different bullet contacts: four definitely against brickwork and yes, one in the upper left bay window which had left a clean small round hole and another had apparently struck the upper middle bay window because this was smashed.

I walked in, slowly, hopefully but cautiously.

The PC was coming down the stairs.

"They're all okay, sarge," he said.

"Thank fuck for that," I replied.

I went into the front room.

There was a bullet clearly embedded in the ceiling and the other appeared to have struck the ceiling at a more obtuse angel and ricocheted to land elsewhere in the room.

"None of the children were in the front room at the time," Julie said.

I hadn't even realised she'd joined me.

"That was lucky," the WPC said.

"This was a warning. If they'd actually wanted to shoot anyone, they would have aimed much lower. We need to get this family out of here now. We need witness protection and an armed team. I don't know who the fuck this Danny Manning is, but he's got some fucking horrible friends. Is Tracey conscious?" I asked.

"Nope, she slept through the whole episode," the PC replied.

"Are any of the kids in shock or anything?" I asked.

"Sarge, I don't even think they know what's happened. The older girl, her name's Leigh, she heard the shots but assumed it was coming from the TV next door. She was in the kitchen at the back of the house changing the baby's nappy. Two of the boys were actually in the loft trying to get out an old TV screen to replace the one that got smashed and the other two were in their bedrooms at the back. They have all been extremely lucky," the WPC replied.

"Should I cancel LAS?" the PC asked.

"No, let them come. We should get the kids checked over anyway; I don't think they'll mind under the circumstances," Julie replied.

Then the detective in me kicked in.

"Let's close this room off and treat it as a crime scene; that goes for the front of the house too," I said.

We got the children into the dining room, which was at the rear of the address, all six of them. Even the older two girls, who must have been sixteen and fourteen, seemed oblivious to the significance of the events that were taking place, but I didn't resent them their ignorance. Then it occurred to me that from what I'd seen, perhaps mayhem usually prevailed in the Manning household?

The WPC's radio had been going mad, as one would expect under the circumstances, but then a message came through which drew our attention.

"Golf November, one nine nine. I think I've got the Range Rover; it's stationary and parked parallel and close to the east footway facing north in Bethune Road, it's about fifty yards south of the junction with Amhurst Park; the lights are off."

"Who is one nine nine?" I asked.

"A probationer, I think, but this is night duty, they're a different relief to ours," the WPC replied.

"One nine nine, this is Golf November One, do not approach the vehicle. Please acknowledge."

Golf November One was the Duty Officer, the inspector in charge of night duty and he was understandably worried that an unarmed PC was about to come across two armed and highly dangerous suspects.

"Golf November One, received," the young PC replied.

"Golf November, Golf November; this is MP. I understand you have a major incident; you are now on channel one. All other units with communications unrelated to the Golf November incident, please use channel two."

MP was the Metropolitan Police central control room based in Scotland Yard; they would now effectively take over command of the situation from the local control room based at Stoke Newington. All this was pretty standard procedure, but I rarely got involved with this side of the job any more.

"MP, India Nine Nine."

India Nine Nine was the police helicopter. Even when not up in the air, their crew would monitor the radio and take off if anything significant occurred.

"Go ahead, India Nine Nine, MP over."

"We are airborne and will be ground assigned in five minutes. Understand you have a firearms incident with shots fired and suspects at large."

"India Nine Nine, MP, all received. Your sitrep is accurate. Please advise when ground assigned; out."

"MP, MP, Yankee Tango, urgent."

Yankee Tango was the call sign for the Tottenham control room. Tottenham's ground joined Stoke Newington's on the northern border.

"Go ahead, Yankee Tango."

"We have shots fired at a mobile unit, Yankee Tango five four, in Cornwall Road N15; the unit is in pursuit of a silver Ford Mondeo, part index Sierra Golf 52, with two white male occupants."

"Yankee Tango from MP; all received; putting the link in now. Please keep the commentary going."

"I've lost them, last seen west in St Anne's Road towards Green Lanes," said a very out-of-breath female voice.

Our suspects had apparently dumped their Range Rover and got into a Mondeo, which a keen-eyed Tottenham unit had tried to pull over.

"Four one two, Golf November One?"

"Go ahead, sir," the PC standing next to me replied.

"I am outside the address at Neville Road, where are you?" the Duty Officer asked.

"We'll come out and meet you," the PC replied.

"Stay with the kids, keep them at the back of the house, you know, just in case they come back," I said.

"Yes, sarge," the WPC replied.

"Tell the inspector that I'll be out in a moment, I am going to see if we can wake Tracey up," I said to the PC. "Julie, come with me. We have got to move her out of the front bedroom."

"Yes, sarge," she replied.

Julie never called me Sarge!

Tracey was in the recovery position; whether she had done that naturally or the uniform officers had put her there, I didn't know, and she was on the bed rather than in it.

On a bedside cabinet was a picture of Tracey and a man in swimwear, obviously her husband. The bloke looked a right hard bastard and was covered in tattoos; he even had a huge spider-type tattoo on his bald head.

She'd stopped snoring. I shook her shoulder quite roughly and called out her name. She stirred, opened her eyes and mumbled "wha" several times.

"Tracey, I am a police officer, my name is Chris, it's really important that you wake up."

"Wha' do ya wan'? Go awa', Go awa'," she replied.

Her speech was really slurred.

"Tracey, wake up now," I said, with as much authority as I could muster.

"'Fuck off; leave me alon'," she replied.

"Tracey, I'm not going away. You need to wake up now, Tracey," I said.

I shook her shoulder again.

"Ya don't understan'. My husban's got murderin' hans, murderin' hans. And sometim's he touc's me kids wit' his murderin' hans."

"Who did he murder?" I asked.

She started to fall back to sleep.

"Tracey, who did your husband murder?" I asked, my mouth right next to her ear.

"Just fuck off," she replied.

"Tracey!" I shouted, as I shook her shoulder really quite aggressively.

Her eyes opened momentarily.

"I ca't cope wit' it. It's doin' me hea' in. Doin' me fuckin' hea' in'. Now fuck offffff."

Julie came into the bedroom.

"Be careful when you go down the stairs," she said.

"Why, what's happened?" I replied.

"Someone let the bleeding dog in and it's shat everywhere."

Chapter 51

By two o'clock in the morning, the Manning clan had been relocated to Stoke Newington Police Station. There was absolutely no chance of getting a meaningful response from Hackney Social Services until the morning so we had purloined several mattresses from the cells and turned the parade room into a dormitory so that the children could get some sleep.

Julie got a uniform unit to give her a lift so she could get four hours' kip but I thought someone should remain, so I settled down in cell six. In fact, Tracey ended up sleeping in the cell next door as the Duty Officer was worried about her level of intoxication and thought she would be safer where the jailer could keep a regular eye on her.

I had already noticed that the oldest daughter, Leigh, seemed to have assumed the role of surrogate mother so the fact that Tracey was sleeping elsewhere didn't seem to bother the other children.

The two scenes, the house and the Range Rover, had been secured and we had uniform officers protecting both. The Onions would pick up the forensics and exhibit recovery in the morning, when it was light.

The Tottenham units had been unable to trace the Ford Mondeo.

I'd spoken to the DCI and taken him through the events. I explained that I thought the shots were fired as a warning to Tracey to keep her mouth shut, rather than a deliberate attempt to kill and maim. The DCI told me to stay with the family, get them into more suitable accommodation and liaise with Witness Protection and to debrief Tracey as a matter of urgency.

This would be another long weekend for everyone, but I was sure they would appreciate the enhanced overtime.

As I drifted off to sleep, I got the feeling that I had missed something, something really important, but no matter how closely I turned the conversation over in my head, I couldn't spot it.

~~~

My phone woke me up, not because anyone was contacting me but because the battery was running out and it kept buzzing to remind me to put it on charge. I looked at my watch; it was eight thirty and I'd had four hours' sleep – I was actually quite impressed. A young PC was walking through the cell passage and he greeted me with a smile and the gift of a lovely cup of tea, which I gladly accepted.

Fuck me, after all these years I was back at old Stokey. This is where it had all started. I wondered whether there was anyone left from the old days but decided there probably wasn't. Of course, the old nick had long gone and been replaced with a modern police station. I am sure it was a much more efficient building but it lacked all the character and history of the old place.

I wandered out of my cell and into the main custody area, which was quiet; no prisoners were waiting to be booked in. A custody sergeant was typing into a computer behind a high desk.

"Morning, sarge, thanks for the cuppa, much appreciated."

"Morning, mate. So you're the infamous Nostrils are you? I'd somehow imagined someone more …" He hesitated, so I completed the sentence for him.

"Impressive?" I suggested.

He laughed.

"Do you know where my friend is, the drunken woman who was sleeping it off in the cell next to me?"

"Her and her brood are having breakfast in the canteen; its fucking mayhem. I'm glad I'm in here today, that is one out-of-control family. I gather they're witnesses to some murder? Is that right?" the sergeant asked.

"I think so, I hope so," I replied.

The young PC who'd given me the tea popped his head around a partitioned-off area:

"Are you DS Pritchard? It's your office, they say your phone's going straight to voicemail."

I took the call. It was Jeff.

"Nostrils, there's an answerphone message on the Incident Line from Sonia Rider. She says she wants to speak to you, urgently."

"Is that all it says?" I asked.

"Yep."

"When did she leave it?" I asked.

"At one o'clock this morning," Jeff replied.

I had a bit of a dilemma. I knew I should stay and deal with Tracey but then I really didn't want to send anyone else to speak to Sonia, not only because we had established something of a rapport, but because I didn't want anyone to learn that I'd taken Matthew with me the last time I'd gone. I started to regret that decision, even though at the time I'd got a real thrill out of showing him what I did.

"I'll get over there straight away. Is Pod in? Can he meet me on the estate at nine thirty? Get Nicola, Samantha and Taff over to Stoke Newington as soon as possible. Tell them to bring several cars, we've got a family of seven to find a home for. Is the DCI in?"

"Not yet, but he phoned me first thing. You've briefed him already, haven't you?" Jeff asked.

"Yeah, I spoke to him last night. This witness, Tracey something, is saying her husband did the murder," I explained.

"I know, he told me about the drive-by; fucking hell, Nostrils, it was lucky no one was killed or at least seriously hurt."

"Yeah, it was, Jeff, but I think it was a warning for her to keep her mouth shut rather than an attempted murder."

"The DCI wants our team to deal with both the house and the car, but the guys are scattered all over the place dealing with other enquiries, a couple have a prisoner," Jeff said.

"Who's been nicked? Is it for this murder?" I asked.

"It's the debt collector; the bloke who was with the ex-prison officer when the police officer showed out in the victim's address, the night after the murder. He's also wanted on a no bail warrant so he gave himself up first thing so that he could get everything sorted out at once. He's over at Sutton so two guys are dealing with him and three others are doing a Section 18 at his HA."

"So who the fuck's going to deal with the scenes here?" I asked.

"As soon as they've done the Section 18 warrant, they'll be over. The DCI's spoken to the DCI at Stoke and they're happy to hold your scenes until we're able to do them."

"Fuck me, we've got more scenes than Hamlet," I observed.

"The scene's the thing, in which we'll find the conscience of the king," Jeff replied.

"And you know the good news?" he asked.

"Of course, we're all on double time."

"Kerching," he replied.

"Jeff, can you let me know what the bloke at Sutton says? It might be relevant when we question Tracey."

I was lying. I didn't see how it could be relevant at all. The thing was, I was nervous that he might be able to reveal more about the 'police officer' who showed out at the victim's address and wanted to stay ahead of the game if he did.

"No problem, laters," Jeff replied.

I hung up.

I heard the combination lock being activated on the custody suite doors and Julie walked in; she looked smart and fresh. I really don't know how she did it, she couldn't have got more than three hours' sleep and probably less.

"Christ I'm knackered, my head is thumping. Tell me this is just a bad dream," she said. Before I could say a word, she went on, "and those kids are uncontrollable. Have I really got to spend all day with that family? Tell me I'm still asleep and this is all a dream, or rather a nightmare. Then, please, please, wake me up."

I laughed.

"Good morning, Julie. And how are you this wonderful morning?" I said, completely ignoring her mini rant.

"And you can fuck off," she said.

"Potty mouth," I replied.

She smiled.

"Christ, Chris. Did we nearly die last night? What the hell was that all about?"

"The Onions are going to pick up the house and the car later. They're tied up with a prisoner at Sutton. I've asked Taff, Samantha and Nicola to come here and help with Tracey and her kids. Can you just get them to a hotel somewhere? I'll liaise with the DCI and we will need armed protection. We'll worry about debriefing the witness when they're settled somewhere."

"Where are you going?" she asked, agog.

"Sonia Rider, the victim's girlfriend, says she wants a meet urgently," I replied. "Besides, I've never been good with kids. See you later."

"I hate you," Julie called after me as I quickly keyed in the pass number on the combination lock to get out of the custody suite.

Chapter 52

I borrowed a car charger for my mobile from one of the guys in the CID office and at just after nine thirty, set off for Bethnal Green.

On the way, I made a number of calls. They were talking about making it illegal to use a phone in a car. If they ever did, that was going to be yet another law I'd find it really difficult not to break.

I called Pod and confirmed that he was going to meet me on the estate.

I had a quick chat with Nicola and let her know the mayhem she was about to encounter. Nicola had two young children so I hoped she'd be better with kids than Julie was – besides, she'd be with Taff, who'd had kids, albeit they were all now grown up.

I spoke to the DCI, who agreed that we needed an armed team to protect Tracey and her family. He said he'd make the necessary phone calls and that we weren't to move them from the nick until the coverage was in place. I knew instantly that such an operation would take a good twelve hours to plan and implement, by which time I'd be back at Stoke Newington, so I really wasn't going to miss much by taking an hour or two out to meet Sonia.

The DCI wanted us to do a quick interview with Tracey while we were still at the nick, just to get on tape the basics of what she had to say. It seemed a sensible approach, especially as the job was about to spend tens of thousands of pounds to protect her and her family.

I called Wendy briefly, just to let her know what was going on and to make sure she knew I wasn't going to be arsey about what had happened. I think Wendy was relieved that I'd called. She implored me to see Matthew before he went home but I explained what had happened last night with the shooting and everything and I think she understood. We agreed that I would try to get across on Sunday morning and have breakfast with them. If I'm being honest, I thought it was probably best if we didn't see each other before he went. I mean, the last time I heard him he was fucking my girlfriend! I took a little solace that he'd obviously inherited some genes from me, even if it was an inability to keep his cock in his pants.

I phoned Jackie; she didn't answer but I left a message saying I'd spent the night at Stoke Newington and asking her to give the girls a hug from me. I wondered whether she'd done anything towards actually getting the divorce. I felt my marriage slipping away; I really, really didn't want it to, but I was so genuinely busy there appeared to be nothing I could do about it. I found it slightly ironic that she was divorcing me for being on the gear when I'd actually been clean for over ten days, the longest I'd gone without a fix since I'd become addicted.

I then phoned Nick Charles because he'd been trying to get hold of me while I was on the other calls. He greeted me like a long-lost brother and told me that he'd got confirmation of his successful application to SO13. I was genuinely pleased for him. Then he asked me if I fancied a drink next week; I agreed in the almost certain knowledge that I'd have to cancel because of work commitments.

I cut Nick off to take a call from an unknown number. It was a geezer called Barry, who was a DS from the SIS. The SIS were a team who specialised in long-term operations against OCNs (Organised Criminal Networks). When he introduced himself, I assumed he wanted to talk to me about the Kiracs, but it soon became clear he was working on Tony Pascal. I said that if he wanted to meet me in person, he'd have to come to Stoke Newington.

I hung up and immediately took another call from the DCI, who wanted to tell me what had been agreed with SO19, the firearms unit. I let him know that SIS were interested in speaking to me about Tony Pascal.

"You've obviously hit a flag. They've probably got a job on Pascal. Do you think he's anything to do with our murder? Wasn't he the guy whose wife's handbag the victim stole?"

"Yeah, that's right, and no, I don't think he's a suspect. Pod and I saw him a few days ago. He didn't seem to know anything about the theft because his wife hadn't told him."

"I'm not sure the job needs to go across to CIB now. Let's wait and see what this Tracey says about her old man's involvement, the motive etcetera. She might be able to eliminate any suggestion of police corruption, mightn't she?" the DCI said.

When I hung up, I tried to gather my thoughts before I arrived in Bethnal Green. It seemed that after the slowest of starts, this case was really gathering pace and in twenty-four hours, we'd gone from having absolutely no idea who'd done this, to having two witnesses potentially able to tell us. If I had to bet, I'd place my money on Tracey's husband, but the motive was, as yet, a mystery.

I pulled up on the estate immediately next to Pod and got out of my car and into his. I wanted to give him a quick briefing on what had happened the last time I met Sonia. When I had done so, Pod said, "I've done a little digging around the off-licence murder."

"Oh, well done, any connection?" I asked.

"It is definitely the same Tim Hughes; he was going out with Cassandra Pascal at the time he was murdered. But she had just found out he had also gone behind her back and asked her best friend out, a girl called Tabatha White. Cassandra was pretty devastated, apparently. Tony Pascal wasn't interviewed, either as a suspect or a witness, and I couldn't see any reason why he would have been either. Tim was also seeing loads of other women."

"He didn't have a fling with Cassandra's mother, did he? Because that might explain why he was shot," I suggested.

"No, there's nothing to suggest that he did," Pod replied.

"How did Cassandra and Tim meet?" I asked.

"Tim was doing some work as a bouncer for a security firm that Tony Pascal runs."

"Wasn't that Munroe chap, the one who left his prints on the victim's door, an ex-prison officer? Is that relevant?" I asked.

"I'll check, but Munroe was HMP High Down and Tim Hughes was at Pentonville. Also the Munroe chap is in his forties and Tim Hughes was twenty-three. I think that might just be one of those coincidences," Pod replied.

"I tend to agree," I replied.

"The thing was, everyone assumed the robber at the off-licence mistook Tim Hughes for a police officer, panicked and shot him. The photos from the scene are on my desk, have a look; you would think the victim was in half blues. He was in the wrong place at the wrong time," Pod explained.

"How many shots were fired?" I asked.

"One, at point-blank range into the back of the victim's head. Bullet was a nine millimetre; apparently ballistics reckon the shot was fired from a Tokarev."

"A what?" I asked. I knew nothing about firearms.

"It's the handgun that they used to issue to Russian officers. You know, like German officers used to get Lugers," Pod said.

"Do we know anything about the suspect?"

"No, really poor quality CCTV and the owner said he was wearing a full crash helmet and gloves. I don't think we were even able to ascertain a colour, and even the fact that he was male is largely conjecture," Pod replied.

"How did he get away?" I asked.

"No eyewitnesses, although a neighbour did say she heard a motorbike accelerating away from the scene a few moments after she heard the gunshot," Pod explained.

I turned it all over in my mind several times.

"So let me get this straight. The murder of the prison officer during a robbery at an off-licence is linked to the murder of drug dealer by the fact that months after the first murder, the victim of the second murder stole a handbag belonging to the prison officer's girlfriend's mother?" I said.

"That's about the strength of it. It's just a coincidence, Chris," Pod said.

"I don't like coincidences," I replied.

Chapter 53

When we knocked at Sonia's door, she opened it almost immediately. I noticed the number 2 was already inverted, telling her customers that she was out of the gear. She was wearing an old dressing gown, pyjamas and slippers and looked shattered.

"Same rules?" she asked, holding the door only open a few inches.

"Same rules," I replied.

She opened the door the rest of the way and stepped to one side.

"This is Pod, a colleague. Pod, this is Sonia; she was Gary's very good friend."

"Pleased to meet you Sonia; so sorry for your loss," Pod said.

"Thanks," Sonia replied, as we followed her into the lounge.

"Same rules? What rules, do I need to know these?" Pod asked.

"Yeah, you do," I replied. "Sonia and I have an agreement. Unless there's a dead body in here with an axe sticking out of its head, we won't be nicking her. Just while we're chatting, we won't 'see' any drugs or 'notice' any dealing."

As I completed my sentence I heard Sonia say 'fat chance' under her breath.

Sonia flounced down on the floor in front of the fire and crossed her legs.

"Fair enough," Pod said, as we sat down on the settee opposite.

"I understand that you left a message on the answerphone," I said. "It sounded important, we've come straight round."

"It's wrong, mate, they're saying Gary was a grass. It's fucking wrong, you gotta do something," Sonia said.

"Who's saying that?" I asked, hoping desperately that there was more to this.

"Fucking everyone on the estate; it ain't right, Gary hated you lot; it just ain't right. They're disrespecting him; d'ya know wot I mean?" Sonia explained.

"Are they saying anything else?" I asked.

"They're saying he was talking to you lot; they're saying some billy big banana ordered his murder. It's fucking wrong, basic, d'ya know wot I mean?"

"Who is saying this?" Pod asked.

Sonia shook her head.

"A friend of mine, mate, a good friend. Came round to see me last night 'cos it was top priority, d'ya know wot I mean?"

"Sonia, is it more than one person, or just one person who says they're telling you what everyone is saying?" Pod asked, trying to squeeze out an answer.

"What?" she replied, as if she'd just be asked a question on *University Challenge* about quantum physics.

"Gary wasn't a grass, definitely not; and I've actually checked," Pod explained.

He was telling the truth, we had just explored that line of enquiry.

"Well, why is they all saying it then? It's wrong ain't it, basic wrong. D'ya know wot I mean?" Sonia persisted.

"What do you want us to do?" Pod asked.

"Tell them?" Sonia replied.

"How?" Pod asked quietly.

Sonia hesitated; clearly she hadn't really thought this through.

"Did you see they've opened a new enquiry into his father's death?" I said.

"'Bout fucking time, mate. D'ya know wot I mean? Gary said they would."

We sat in silence for a good thirty seconds.

On this visit, there was no sign of Sonia's mobile.

"Have you seen Bigga?" I asked.

"He's disappeared, mate, fucking thin air," Sonia replied.

"Maybe he's been nicked, or deported," I said.

Sonia shrugged her shoulders.

"I ain't got no money," she said.

I guessed that with Gary's death, her own regular supply of gear had ceased. I wondered whether she'd sold her mobile to get the money to buy some drugs.

I took out a score and put it on the coffee table that sat between us. Sonia acknowledged the gesture with a nod. If I'd been with another officer, I might not have dared such a move, but Pod was old school and wouldn't bat an eyelid.

"There's another twenty if you can tell us something useful?" I said.

There's nothing as sad and desperate as a drug addict who has no money to buy the next hit, which I understood better than most of my contemporaries. Sonia looked down at the carpet. Pod and I remained silent but let the offer hang in the air, just within her grasp. Ten seconds passed, nothing. Thirty seconds went by, not a word.

"Just before Christmas, Gary got into a bit of trouble," Sonia said.

Pod and I didn't say a word.

"I don't know much but he'd upset someone, someone he didn't want to upset."

"Go on," I said.

"Basic innit? He was worried, really fucking worried, d'ya know wot I mean?"

"Go on."

"He had this lady's bag off but laters found out she was married to some proper geezer, like, you know. Gary was like 'fucking hell', he was shitting a brick, mate; d'ya know wot I mean?"

"Do you think this geezer might have murdered him?" I asked.

She shook her head.

"Thing is, Gary said he sorted it; that it was all sweet, d'ya know wot I mean?"

"How did he sort it?" I asked.

"He went to see the geezer, didn't he, basic, ya know. Go see him before he finds you. Like say 'sorry' and 'didn't know it was your missus' and 'I'll pay you back' and all that, basic; Gary was proper clever sometimes like that; d'ya know wot I mean?"

I had cottoned on to something Sonia had just said, but so had Pod who asked the question I was about to.

"How much money was in the bag? How much did he steal?"

"He had a right touch, fucking thousands, mate; but then when he found out about the geezer, he was like 'I'm fucking dead, man'."

"So Gary went to see this guy?" I asked.

"No, ya don't go and 'see the guy'," she replied, as if this was the stupidest question she'd ever been asked, even though she'd used that exact terminology a few moments ago.

"What happened then?"

"He spoke to someone, who spoke to someone, who had a word with the geezer; d'ya know wot I mean? He didn't have to pay the money back, nothing, he said he'd had a right touch."

"What arrangement did they come to?" I asked.

373

Sonia clearly knew but didn't want to say.

"What was the name of the geezer?" Pod asked.

Sonia shook her head.

"Basic mate, that's all I can tell ya. You're the police, you figure it out."

"Did Gary get nicked for the theft?" Pod asked.

Sonia nodded. "But the woman wouldn't press charges."

"What did Gary do with all that money?" I asked.

"Basic, mate," Sonia replied.

"He bought more drugs, is that why he met this Bigga? Because his old supplier couldn't get him the quantity he wanted?" I asked.

"I'm not with ya, mate. He did business with Bigga, d'ya know wot I mean?"

"Do you know who introduced him to Bigga?" I asked.

"No. It was just business, Gary used to say it was all about supply and demand, d'ya know wot I mean? 'Cos he had more money, he could buy cheaper but still sell at the same price. Basic, innit? And he had more to shift, mate. He used to say expand, he was clever, mate, smart, d'ya know wot I mean?"

"Exactly how much money was in the handbag?" I asked.

Sonia held up a hand with all four fingers and her thumb extended.

"Large?" I asked.

"Large," Sonia replied.

"Fucking hell," I said. "Did he invest it all?"

Sonia shrugged her shoulders.

"Please tell us where we can find Bigga?"

"Bigga was in Dagenham but he's disappeared. He took Gary to a new 'business location' over that way. Opening up 'new business opportunities', that was what Gary said. D'ya know wot I mean?"

"So Gary had started to deal in Dagenham, as well as here on the estate?" Pod asked.

Sonia nodded.

"Did you ever meet Bigga?" I asked.

Sonia shook her head.

"Sonia, did Gary have any tattoos?" I asked.

"He had G A Z on his knee; he did that himself when he was inside," Sonia replied.

"Did he have any others?" I asked.

She shook her head.

I took out another twenty quid and put it on the table. Sonia nodded an acknowledgement. I mirrored her gesture.

"Sonia, darling, does the name Danny Manning mean anything to you."

"No, mate," she replied without hesitation.

"Does the name Kirac mean anything?" I asked.

"What, the Kirac family? Of course, everyone's heard of them, D'ya know wot I mean?"

"Did Gary have anything to do with them?" I asked.

"No way, mate," Sonia replied convincingly.

"There's a third twenty quid if you can tell me what favour Gary did for the geezer?" I said.

Sonia definitely considered my proposal but unfortunately elected to stay shtum this time. Whatever the favour was, it was big, bad and too dangerous for Sonia to mention, even for another score.

Chapter 54

As we drove to Stoke Newington, Pod and I talked it all through.

"So now we have a good motive for the murder," I suggested.

"Now we have two good motives," Pod replied.

"Only if Tony Pascal was lying and actually did know how much money had been stolen. I thought he was telling the truth," I said.

"It could all have been a big act," Pod replied.

He was, of course, quite right.

"In fact, we have a third lead here, not a motive but a possible link," I said.

"Go on," Pod replied.

"Well, was Gary killed doing this favour for Tony Pascal?" I said.

"Yeah, like it," replied Pod.

"So let's just run through it all," I said. "Gary steals the bag that actually has five grand in it. He spends the money on drugs, effectively moving up a couple of leagues in terms of dealers. At about this time he meets Bigga, who gets him selling in Dagenham. I bet that was at the shebeen, by the way."

"Motive one, he pisses off some established Dagenham drug dealers," Pod said.

"Quite right. Motive one, a rival dealer. Motive two, Tony Pascal learns how much he's nicked, can't be seen to lose face and has him murdered in retaliation."

Pod nodded.

"Motive three, while doing a favour for Tony Pascal, a favour that's worth five thousand pounds no less, he gets killed," I concluded. "We have to establish whether Mrs Pascal told her old man how much was stolen."

"That ain't going to happen, is it?" Pod replied.

"But it all turns on that, doesn't it? I mean, if Tony Pascal didn't know anything at all about the theft, then …"

I suddenly realised I'd fucked up here.

"… hang on; his missus didn't have to tell him 'cos Gary told him anyway. You know, he spoke to a bloke, who spoke to a bloke. So even if Mrs Pascal had in fact said nothing, Tony would have learnt about the theft and possibly how much had in fact been stolen from the thief himself through intermediaries," I said.

"I gotta another question," Pod said.

"Go on, mate."

"What has all this got to do with the murder of the prison officer, Tim Hughes?"

"Has it got anything to do with the prison officer murder? I mean, I really don't like coincidences, but he's the father of the one of the victim's girlfriends, not a suspect, surely? And the theft of the handbag occurred a couple of months after the murder, so at the time of the murder of Tim Hughes there was absolutely nothing connecting Gary Odiham and Tony Pascal. They live miles and worlds apart," I replied.

"Okay, I agree. It's highly unlikely that the two murders are connected," Pod declared.

"Then, again …" I replied jokingly.

"And where does this Tracey's husband, Danny, fit into all this?" Pod asked.

"I ain't got a scooby, mate," I replied.

Pod's phone rang and from the initial conversation, I realised that it was his missus calling from Spain. Impossible though it was, I tried not to listen. My attempts were aided when my own phone rang. It was Jackie, so I asked her to hold on a minute while I pulled over and stepped out of the car.

"Hello, darling, how are the girls?" I said.

"Oh, all right. Listen, are you ever coming home because we need to sort things out?" She sounded different, almost clinical.

"I spent last night at Stoke Newington Police Station," I replied honestly.

"Whatever, Chris. I don't care where you were, all I want to do is sit down and discuss things, like the divorce, the finances, maintenance, living arrangements, access to the girls…"

I took a deep breath; I really wasn't ready to give up on my marriage quite yet, but it seemed that Jackie had taken control of things.

"Let's see how much we can agree before going to solicitors, it'll save time and money in the long run if we can sort most things out between us first," she explained.

"Okay. Is your only reason for wanting a divorce the fact that you think I'm still on the gear?" I asked.

Jackie hesitated.

"Jackie, are you still there?" I asked.

"We need to talk face to face, I'm not doing this over the phone," she replied.

I could sense this wasn't just about me being on the gear. Maybe it was about Wendy, too.

"Listen, hon. The bag you found wasn't mine. We'd searched a victim's home address and recovered a load of drugs. I transported the property in my car and a bag must have dropped out."

"I don't believe you," Jackie said.

I wouldn't have believed me either.

"All right. You're a nurse, use your knowledge and buy or get hold of a drug testing kit. I think you can actually buy them at chemists, or go online. You can test me. If there is any trace that I have recently taken drugs, you can have the house, the car and two thousand pounds a month. What do you say?" I asked.

Again, the line went quiet.

"I swear on the girls' lives, I am absolutely clean, hon," I declared.

I knew that Jackie would believe that statement.

"Jackie, are you there?" I asked.

"I've met someone else, Chris. I still want a divorce whether or not you're still taking. I don't give a damn about any drug testing kit."

"You've met someone else?" I asked incredulously.

"I have," she replied, crisply, clinically.

"How, when, who?" I asked.

"Is that really important?" she replied.

"No, I mean yes. Do I know him?" I asked.

"Yes, well sort of, it's George," she replied.

"Who the fuck is George? I don't know a George," I replied.

"You do. George who owns the gym."

I'd given up my membership of the local gym years ago because I never got the chance to use it, but after the girls had started at school, Jackie had been going regularly. And yes, I did know George: the fit-as-fuck gym owner and the driver of a large white top-of-the-range Mercedes sports car; George who took several fitness classes every day; George who I occasionally saw at school because our eldest children were in the same class; fucking George! Or rather to give my wife's new partner their full name, Georgina Gibson, about the fittest woman, in every sense, who had ever lived and worked in Loughton.

I hung up.

Running through my head were a thousand thoughts, all at once. Divorce? Divorce! Met someone else? Met someone else! Well, I could hardly blame her, could I? I'd spent the last five years with Wendy, after all. But this was going to mean someone else would be bringing up Pippa and Trudy, and that would break my heart. Okay, I could move in with Wendy, but that was going to mean starting all over again with a new baby – who actually might turn out to be my grandson. When did life ever become this complicated? Come to think of it, when did my wife suddenly like to drink from the furry cup? She kept that fucking quiet! And in the meantime, I had to carry on like none of this was happening, and solve this fucking murder.

I got back in the car and heard Pod telling his missus that he had to go; he concluded the call by thanking her for her help.

"My wife went and knocked on a few of the doors of the victim's mother's neighbours," he said.

His voice focused my wandering mind.

"Oh yeah," I replied, without conviction.

"You all right, mate?" he asked, obviously picking up on the change in my attitude.

"Yeah, just domestics, go on," I said.

"Which domestics? Jackie or Wendy?" he asked.

"Both, but please go on, you were saying?"

"Judith went and knocked on a few doors as we discussed. Our place is only a few miles away, on the other side of Estepona. She found a friend of Gary's mum, a woman called Meryl, Muriel or Meriel or something. Apparently, Glenda Beaumont had mentioned that she had a son called Gary but hadn't seen him for fifteen years and he'd never visited her in Spain. Glenda had said Gary was a drug addict and that she'd thrown him out because he kept stealing from her. Gary was also involved in the death of a young girl called Grace; he'd sold her some drugs but she overdosed because the gear was spiked with kitchen cleaner or something."

"Okay, that links to the poem they found in the victim's flat. He wrote a poem to a girl called Grace. We assumed she'd died in an RTA, but now we have enough to open another line of enquiry," I said.

"Fuck me, Nostrils, that was sixteen years ago. No motive for murder is ever that old," Pod replied.

Chapter 55

Pod and I popped into Arbour Square to write up the meeting with Sonia Rider. The enquiry team office was deserted but the incident room was busy and Jeff and the two Alexes were busily working away. Pod and I went for a late breakfast at Stefano's instead.

We didn't get back to Stoke Newington until mid-afternoon, where earlier I'd left Julie as officer in charge of Tracey and her family. Never in the field of police work had anyone done a poorer job. Stoke Newington Police Station was a war zone. The babies were screaming and the children were running amok. Tracey had got hold of a bottle of vodka, which she had drunk in record time before Julie found it. The whole party had been joined by a small, yappy, equally uncontrollable terrier, which uniformed officers had had to collect from the house. To cap it all, Social Services said they couldn't assist because they didn't have the capability to rehouse seven people.

Julie looked dishevelled, Tracey was drunk, the two youngest children desperately needed changing. To cap it all, the eldest daughter had just come on but had none of the necessary provisions. Samantha had just arrived to help.

I really needed Taff and Nicola who, between them, had raised or were in the process of bringing up five kids. Although all three had been sent to assist us, they'd been diverted to deal with the scene of the shooting at Tracey's house. Apparently, the Onions, who had been on their way, had been reassigned to a new case, which was fucking ridiculous. We hadn't had a new case in six weeks and then two had come along within a week.

I had the most splitting headache and wanted to steal another hour's kip in one of the cells. I told Samantha to call me when the guy from the firearms team arrived and walked back across the yard to the main police station building. I paused for a few seconds to remember the faces of a bygone era and the memories came flooding back.

I could remember my first day as if it was only yesterday, reporting to Sergeant Bellamy in the portacabin, which to my complete surprise, still stood in the same spot by what used to be the admin block. It looked worse for wear and the years had taken their toll on this flat-roofed, temporary box structure.

I had felt so lonely and so lost in those first few months when I couldn't do right for doing wrong. My Street Duties instructor, Dawn Matthews, had despised me and everyone else had regarded me with such indifference. Everyone, that was, except Andy Welling, who took me under his wing – I really don't know if I'd have got by without him. Now, twenty years later, both Dawn and Andy were long gone and this was a different world of computers, stab-proof vests and CS gas. I looked up at the window of my old section house room and wondered who lived there now? I remembered so vividly the time I looked up from just this spot and saw Sarah's boyfriend, Paul Pollack, looking down at me just a few minutes before he blew his brains out in the toilet. This place was so full of ghosts for me.

A young uniform PC mistook my daydreaming for confusion and asked politely if he could assist me.

"No, I'm all right thanks, mate. I used to work here, a long time ago now. It was my first nick, so there are lots of memories," I replied politely.

"Are you Chris Pritchard?" he asked.

"Good God, have we met before?" I asked.

"No, never; it's just that the sergeant who took parade told everyone you were here," he replied.

"Oh, I see," I replied, somewhat meekly.

I was a little confused but assumed it must just be to do with the shooting last night, because that was quite a major incident, even for a nick as busy as Stoke Newington.

"We have a service every year to Dawn Matthews, by the memorial plaque in the station lobby."

"Sorry?" I replied.

"Your colleague, WPC Dawn Matthews, there's a plaque in the station lobby to her. Your name is on the plaque too, as being with her when she died. That's why our sergeant told us you were here. They still talk about what you did."

I wanted to tell him that I was lucky, nothing more, and that I did what any one of them would have done for an injured colleague, but I didn't. Not because I wanted any undeserved recognition, but simply because it might besmirch Dawn's memory.

"I did very little, Dawn was the hero," I said.

"But you got the QPM for gallantry," he said.

I could have corrected him and explained that the QPM was for saving an old man from a burning building, but that might come across as bragging. I decided the safest response was a polite smile.

"You have seen the plaque?" he asked.

"I haven't, actually," I replied.

I was vaguely aware that it was erected when they rebuilt the police station in the early nineties. I think its formal opening happened when one of the girls was due to be born, but I had declined to attend anyway. I remember there was a proposal to name the police station Dawn Matthews House, but Dawn's mother had refused to agree because the people that planted the bomb had never been brought to trial, due to some legal technicality. I remember being impressed by her integrity.

"Would you like me to show you?" the young PC asked.

I shook my head and laughed gently. "No, thank you," I replied.

The smile and laughter was a charade; if I got within sight of that memorial, I knew I'd be bawling like a baby.

The young man put out his hand and we shook; it was a surreal moment.

"It is an honour to meet you," he said.

I said, "Thank you," but felt really embarrassed.

Let me state for the record, I did nothing at the scene of the bombing or at the burning building that any other police officer anywhere in the world wouldn't have done.

A few minutes later, I was trying to drift off to sleep in cell six and turning over in my mind the conversation with the young PC. Giving up the gear, now that was a brave thing to do – and I'd now been clean about two hundred and forty hours, well something like that.

Then it hit me: if they still insisted on nicking poor Buster I'd have to do another extremely brave thing and put my hands up. I simply couldn't live with myself if I let a completely innocent person get convicted for something I'd done. In that moment and, if I am being honest, probably for the first time, I actually knew I was no longer bullshitting and whatever the consequences, I could not let an innocent man be convicted in my place.

Chapter 56

I didn't get to sleep. The thought of losing my job and pretty much everything else I valued was causing me too much anxiety. I knew I'd get quite a lot of credit for coming forward; I also realised that I could arouse sufficient sympathy surrounding the circumstances of my addiction that a criminal prosecution, let alone a custodial sentence, would be highly unlikely.

I felt sorry for what I was about to do to my girls, to my wife and to Wendy. I was about to let them all down terribly. That Jackie was about to leave me didn't make me feel any better. I didn't think Wendy would cope very well at all; she came from such a respectable and Christian family that she would find this impossible to explain. What's more, once the story hit the papers, it was all going to come out about me being married as well.

Staying off the gear when my life hit rock bottom was going to be hard, which would be such a shame because I really thought I'd cracked it.

I flirted with the idea of finishing the relationship with Wendy before the shit hit the fan, but realised that would be a bit pointless, as the end was rapidly approaching.

My only hope was to solve this case and get Danny Manning on the charge sheet before Buster and his family returned from their holiday on Tuesday. Even then, I'd have to hope I could convince the DCI and Adam Stanley that the Buster connection wasn't worth pursuing; and also pray that nobody spotted my telephone number when they got Gary Odiham's telephone billing.

I thought my chances of getting out of this mess in one piece were no more than ten per cent.

It was dark when my phone rang and I only just managed to dig it out of my pocket before it cut to voicemail. It was a guy called Bill from SO19. He urgently required, he said, photographs of all the family and completion of the requisite forms, including a full risk assessment that he had sent via email. Then he required a full briefing to be delivered at a neutral and suitable venue, preferably a local hotel.

"Please tell me the forms can be done easily, I haven't got to write War and Peace, have I?" I asked.

"Um," he hesitated, "they're pretty comprehensive, buddy."

I knew the Metropolitan Police well enough to realise that unless I was careful, I'd be spending the next week doing this paperwork.

"Bill, do me a favour? Can you come to the nick and I'll show you what we've got. Then, perhaps, you can give me a hand with the forms? What do you say? I'll buy you coffee and a cake to express my undying gratitude."

"I'll be there as soon as I can," he replied.

I was extremely grateful.

When I went over to the parade room, the Manning family had been joined by their dog, which was barking relentlessly, so I suggested we put it into one of the kennels in the yard, at which point Tracey went apoplectic.

"You're not lockin' me bab' in a fuckin' pol' cell, you bastar's. I wan' him here wit' me. He's a part of me fuckin' famil'."

I tried to explain that both she and I had in fact spent the night in a 'fuckin' pol' cell', but you can't reason with a drunk, so I soon gave up, lied and said I was going to take her pooch for a walk in a nearby park, and I put him in the kennel anyway.

An hour later, I met Bill from SO19 in the canteen. He was a fairly typical firearms officer, obviously ex-military, very precise in his manner and bearing.

"What's the SP then?" he asked, sipping the cup of coffee I had just purchased.

"Where do you want me to start?" I asked.

"Who are we going to be protecting, why and what's the threat? I did hear about the incident from last night, but can you explain how it fits into the bigger picture?"

"My team are investigating the murder of Gary Odiham, a low-level drug dealer from Bethnal Green, who was murdered in Dagenham on the tenth of this month.

"We have Tracey Manning, a thirty-four-year-old woman, her six children, ageing from sixteen down to six months, and a dog. The woman's husband is Danny Manning. He's got substantial previous and links to organised crime; he flashes violent, drugs, assaults police, weapons and firearms."

"Organised Crime? Who, exactly?"

"The Kiracs," I replied.

"Last night, Tracey Manning called 999 and told officers who attended her home address that her husband, Danny Manning, had murdered our victim. When we were at her address, the drive-by shooting occurred."

"Do we know where Danny Manning is now?" Bill asked.

"In hiding, according to his missus, who, incidentally, has been drinking for days and is completely pissed," I replied. "Oh, and Social Services won't touch them with a bargepole; so the DCI wants them put in a hotel until we can arrange something more permanent. I've left a voicemail with the CPJU."

"Is that Witness Protection?" Bill asked.

"Yes, that's right. I think their full title is the Criminal Justice Protection Unit," I replied.

"Sounds like you've got your hands full, buddy," Bill observed.

"About that paperwork?" I asked.

"I'll give you a hand, we'll be able to get it done within an hour. Then, I'll have to get the authority signed off but that can be done verbally in these circumstances and I'll fax the authority request across because …"

As he was talking, my mind was wandering. I had a stinking headache, caused by lack of sleep. Out of nowhere, I got a yearning for heroin stronger than I had ever experienced, anywhere and any time.

" ... then I'll have to brief the team. I can't do that until you've arranged a hotel because obviously, we'll need to know where you're going. I'll also need some other things from you; first ..."

I was nodding and pretending to listen but my mind was shutting out the conversation.

Then we jumped, we both literally jumped.

The fire alarm that was attached to the canteen's ceiling, only a few feet above our heads, had gone off.

Julie ran into the canteen, looked around urgently, picked up a fire extinguisher and exited without saying a word.

Chapter 57

It was only a small fire but the alarm automatically went through to the Fire Brigade, so they responded, and because it was activated in a large multi-storey residential premises, Stoke Newington Section House, we didn't just get one fire engine, we got three. Fortunately, Julie's quick thinking had extinguished the fire before it had a chance to take hold, but the poor guys asleep upstairs because they were on night duty had to evacuate into the back yard, and they were less than impressed.

What had happened? Using his mother's lighter and because he was bored, the ten-year-old lad had set fire to the curtains, so technically we had an arson with intent to endanger life, albeit that the 'suspect' was only just old enough to be criminally responsible for his actions. Fortunately, both the Duty Officer and the Fire Brigade Station Officer were happy to let the criminal aspect go unreported.

The only positive, apart from the fact that the whole place hadn't burnt to the ground, was that the incident seemed to have sobered Tracey up a little, so I decided to take the opportunity to conduct a quick tape-recorded interview and get the outline of her statement on tape.

I got Julie to help Bill with the forms for the firearms team because she'd been there last night, so she knew all about the shooting incident.

It was seven thirty and dark by the time I took Tracey over to the main building and found a small interview room. I should perhaps have got a doctor to examine her first, and I wasn't entirely sure she didn't need an appropriate adult, but I decided to go ahead anyway. I mean, even if what she said was later deemed to be inadmissible, it wouldn't be the end of the world.

Tracey was a tired, white female who looked a decade older than her thirty-four years; her hair was a lifeless, unwashed greyish brown, her complexion sallow and she had deep dark rings around each eye. Her belly was really swollen, but the rest of her body painfully thin. She spoke with a hard, lazy East End accent and habitually abandoned words halfway through, in a manner that made their final syllables obsolete.

I tried unsuccessfully to strike up some rapport as I loaded the tapes into the machine but Tracey was an inebriated wreck. I pressed the record button and waited for the long buzz to stop, which indicated that the tapes were working correctly.

"Tracey, my name is Christopher Pritchard; I am a police officer investigating the murder of Gary Odiham. We are in the interview room at Stoke Newington Police Station. Please state your full name and date of birth.'

"Trace' Joanne Mannin', the first of June ninete' six' nine."

"Tracey, have you had any other surnames?"

"When I was bor', I was Saunders, then I was Jac'son, then Kin' and after I married Danny, Mannin'," she replied.

"So you were born Saunders but are now Manning?" I asked.

She nodded.

"Tracey, this is being taped recorded so can you please say 'yes' or 'no'?"

She nodded again.

"Is that a yes?" I asked.

"Yeah," she replied, clearly agitated by my request.

She huffed, folded her arms on the desk and rested her head on them.

"I'm tired," she said.

"I know you are; this won't take long, I promise; but I need you to answer a few questions," I said patiently.

Tracey lifted her head up.

"I wan' to go hom'. I've change' my mind. Can I go?" Tracey asked.

Technically, of course, Tracey was free to walk out whenever she wanted but I wasn't going to let that happen.

"You need to speak to me first," I replied.

"I don't wanna. I don't know nuffin. I am not talkin' to ya. I wanna go home."

Tracey had transitioned from drunken bum to petulant child.

"I know you do, Tracey. I understand, I really do. Just tell me what you know about the murder of Gary Odiham," I said.

"Nuffin, mate, nuffin. I ain't gonna say nuffin; not a fuckin' word, mate. I ain't a fuckin' grass, mate; I wanna get the fu' ou'a 'ere."

Petulant child had become East End criminal. I ignored her protestations.

"Did Danny Manning kill Gary Odiham?" I asked.

Tracey nodded and put her head back down on her forearms. It was a clear 'yes' but of course, the gesture wasn't picked up on an audio tape.

"Did Danny kill Gary Odiham?" I repeated.

Tracey didn't move; instead, she moaned as if in pain.

"Arrrrrrhhhhhhh."

I decided to say and do nothing.

A few seconds ticked slowly by.

"ZZZzzzzzzzz."

"Tracey," I said loudly.

"ZZZzzzzzzzz."

I shook her firmly by the elbow.

"Wot?" she said indignantly.

"Did Danny kill Gary Odiham?" I asked.

"' off; I'm tire'; I need to slee'."

"Did Danny kill Gary Odiham?" I persisted.

"Stabbed him in the hea', said he coul' feel it inside his skull," she replied.

"Why? Why did Danny kill him?" I asked.

"It was a commercial decision," she replied.

She'd spoken the last answer so clearly, pronouncing every syllable. I was quite taken aback.

"Was Danny paid to kill Gary? Is that what you're saying, Tracey?"

She shook her head.

"For what reason did Danny murder Gary?"

"Dunno," Tracey replied, shrugging her shoulders and reverting back to her former self.

She was so pissed; the interview wasn't going to be any good evidentially, but it might provide some leads.

"What did you mean when you said the murder was 'a commercial decision'?" I asked.

Tracey blinked several times; perhaps she was trying to focus on me?

"Did Gary owe Danny money?" I asked.

"Wot?" Tracey asked, as if I was really stupid.

It was the first proper reaction I'd elicited; did I have to get her annoyed to get anything out of her? If I did, that was fine by me. I decided to play stupid.

"So how much money did Gary owe Danny?" I asked.

My strategy worked; Tracey actually sat up a little and for the first time, she spoke towards me.

"Wot sor' of cun' are ya? He didn't fuckin' owe 'im nuffin. Gary was sellin' coke on his patch, weren't he?"

Sometimes when you do an interview, you get just the answer you want. It actually doesn't happen all that often but when it does, it feels fucking great. This was just such a moment. The hard part is taking the answer in your stride and not reacting to it in any way.

"So Danny killed Gary because Gary was selling gear?"

"I ain't sayin' anymor'. I wanna go hom'," Tracey said.

"Where exactly did he murder him?" I asked, keen to identify the principal crime scene.

Tracey defiantly shook her head, then her face turned to a frown and I knew something was coming ,but all she did was belch.

"Was gonna puke, sorr'," she said.

She breathed out heavily and the stench was revolting; I could actually smell vomit. My eyes glanced quickly around the small room until I saw a round metal waste bin. If it looked like Tracey was going to be sick, the bin would be her bucket.

"I wanna' drin'," she said.

"You can't have a drink yet. I need to know more about the murder," I replied.

Tracey shook her head slowly.

"Who does Danny work for?" I asked.

"I ain't sayin'; I wanna drin'; I wanna go home. Where are me kids?"

"They're here. They're safe, but they won't be if you go home, Tracey. Last night, remember, someone put six bullets into your living room."

Tracey frowned; evidently she had no recollection of the incident.

"Tracey, we will look after you and your kids, but you need to help us."

"Bullets?" she asked.

"Last night, someone shot six bullets at your house, two entered your lounge where, only a few minutes before, your children had been. You were asleep upstairs. It was a miracle none of the kids were killed," I said.

"Wot ya talkin' about?" she asked incredulously.

"What do you know about Tony Pascal?" I asked.

Tracey shook her head, her expression completely blank.

"For the purposes of the tape, Tracey has just shaken her head to indicate a negative answer. Do you know the Kiracs?" I asked.

Tracey nodded.

"That's a yes, then? Is that who Danny works for?" I asked, a little too eagerly.

Tracey's body language closed up and I suspected I'd pushed a little too hard.

"Where is Danny?" I asked, lowering my voice to a less challenging tone.

Tracey shook her head.

"Are you saying that you don't know or that you don't want to tell me?"

"He's with them," Tracey replied.

"The Kiracs?"

"They're hidin' him. I don't know where, the fuck koon in heaven," she replied.

She was talking nonsense. I thought it was time to bring the short interview to a close but wanted to try one last shot at establishing the scene of the attack.

"Tracey, exactly where did Danny assault Gary?" I asked.

She frowned and I hoped she was trying to remember.

"In the 'ead, in the ear," she replied.

No, whereabouts in London?" I asked.

"Dagenham," she replied.

I decided that I'd got enough and was about to close the interview when Tracey said, "I hear him sometimes."

"You hear Danny? Does he call you?" I asked.

"Wot?" Tracey asked.

"You said you hear Danny sometimes. Is that when he told you about the murder?" I asked.

"No, I hear Gary," she replied, her voice no more than a conspiratorial whisper.

"Did you know him?" I asked, trying to clarify exactly what Tracey was saying.

"No," she replied.

"I don't understand," I said.

"I hear Gary's voice in me 'ead," she whispered.

"When?" I asked.

"All the time," she replied.

This time it was my turn to put my head in my hands.

Chapter 58

I took Tracey back to her kids, rendered the tapes unplayable and threw them in a large metal waste container used by the canteen staff to dispose of unwanted food.

I stood in the yard and phoned the DCI and told him that I'd spoken to Tracey but that she was too drunk to conduct a meaningful interview.

"But you have taped your conversation?" he asked.

"She flatly refused, boss. What could I do? And besides, she's still pissed and her voice is really slurred. It wouldn't have been wise to have taped the conversation; I think that could have undermined the integrity and credibility of our investigation," I replied, trying to sound confident.

"As soon as she's sober, I want her interviewed," the DCI said.

"I understand," I replied.

It was clear the DCI was less than impressed with me, but that was the lesser of two evils, because he really didn't want to be told that our key witness thought she heard dead Gary talking to her and that this had been recorded during a formal tape-recorded interview, which, of course, would have to be disclosed to the defence before any subsequent court case.

"Did she say anything?" the DCI asked.

"She's very drunk but she says her husband, Danny Manning, told her that he stabbed Gary in the ear because he was 'selling gear on his patch' – those were her exact words. She also says that Danny is being hidden by the Kiracs; so I don't think it's unreasonable to assume that Danny is licensed by the Kiracs to sell their gear, although she closed up when I asked that as a direct question," I explained.

"For fuck's sake, Chris. Why didn't you get that on tape?" he asked.

"Sorry, boss. I made the wrong call, I apologise."

"I did tell you to get that on tape, didn't I? I did tell you?" he said.

"You did. I'm wrong, I'm sorry. I meant well but fucked up," I said, hoping that such an unambiguous statement would pacify him.

"So this is a turf war? Do we know who Gary was selling for, or whether he was selling for anyone?" the DCI asked.

"Okay; some guy called Bigga is involved and it's just possible that he was working for Tony Pascal," I said.

"Who? Bigga?" the DCI asked.

"No, well yes. I mean, we think Gary was selling his gear to Bigga and we know Gary was connected to Tony Pascal, but whether Bigga and Tony Pascal are connected, I haven't got a scooby," I said.

I was getting a little flustered; I was even starting to get confused myself.

"I'm sorry I had a go at you, Chris. I do appreciate that you've been working flat out for a week. I can hear how tired you are," the DCI said sympathetically.

"Put it this way, I slept last night in cell six here at Stoke Newington. I'm shattered, boss," I said.

"I know; keep going, Nostrils, I need you," the DCI said.

His words touched me.

"Okay. Anything else come out of the chat with Tracey?"

"No, I'll get her on tape as soon as she's sober."

"Right, we've got a small problem," the DCI said.

I swear my heart actually missed a beat.

"The witness Sonia Rider died last night. They're convinced it's an overdose, probably heroin, but this makes me feel very uncomfortable. I've asked them to treat the death as suspicious until we know otherwise."

"She didn't die last night, boss. Pod and I were at her address first thing this morning. She'd left a message saying she wanted to see us and Jeff rang me first thing."

"What time were you with her?" the DCI asked.

"From nine until about half past. We weren't with her long," I explained.

"She was found dead at midday but the assumption was that she'd died overnight," the DCI explained.

"Is that the other job which we've picked up?" I asked.

"Yes. I sent the guys that were going to do the scene of the shooting to her address in Bethnal Green. If it ends up being a straightforward drugs overdose, then it won't take long to deal with, but if it's something more sinister, we'll have a tight grip on it from the off."

"That makes sense," I said.

"The thing is, the person who found her, her best friend, someone called Susie, said that she'd seen Sonia at eleven last night and that her death couldn't have been an overdose because Sonia was complaining that she didn't have any money to buy any drugs and that since Gary's death, she'd been skint," the DCI said.

"Okay," I said tentatively.

Of course, I knew differently. I had given her forty quid only four hours ago, which she obviously used to go and buy some gear. I might need a quick conversation with Pod but I had every confidence he wouldn't drop me in it.

"Of course, that makes it a death following police contact. You'll have to notify the dark side," I pointed out.

"Of course; thanks, Chris. I must confess I'd not considered that because I thought you'd seen her a couple of days ago, which would be over the forty-eight hours. I didn't realise you'd seen her again, there's nothing in the system."

"I saw her on my own on Tuesday evening, but as I say, Jeff called me early doors because she'd left a message on the incident room voicemail," I reiterated.

"What did she want to see you about?" he asked.

"She was upset that there were rumours circulating on the estate that Gary was an informant. She wanted us to do something about them but we explained that wasn't particularly practicable," I explained.

"That's exactly what this Susie girl says she had gone to see Sonia about. To tell her that the word on the street was that Gary had been killed because he was a grass," the DCI replied.

"It was bollocks, really. But we did manage to get the information about the connection with Tony Pascal out of her, so it wasn't a waste of time. In fact, with what's happened, it a very good job we did get round there," I said.

"How was she this morning?" he asked.

"Okay, I think. She seemed no different to the last time I'd seen her. She is, was, all right actually. I mean, a low-life council estate heroin addict, but underneath that pile of shit, she was pretty honest and, I think, genuinely wanted to help find who'd killed Gary."

"Did she appear worried?"

"Not at all. Just frustrated that people were saying her Gary was an informant when apparently, and because he blamed police for the death of his dad, who died in custody years ago, he hated Old Bill with a passion," I explained.

"I'll get on to CIB and report the death after police contact; I can't imagine there's going to be any aggravation. I mean, you and Pod were there on legitimate business, after she'd asked you to go round. I'll make sure that Jeff saves her voicemail message as evidence. Now listen, Chris ..."

"Go on, boss," I said.

"It's eight o'clock. First thing tomorrow, I want Tracey Manning on tape telling us exactly what her old man told her about the murder. Do you understand?"

"Yes, sir," I replied obediently.

I was just about to hang up when I unexpectedly heard the DCI say something else, so I put the phone back to my ear.

"Chris, you still there? Can you hear me?"

"Yes, boss, I'm here," I replied.

"Is there anyone from the firearms team there yet?"

"We've got an SO19 guy who's here helping us to do the forms, but he's not the team," I replied.

"I think there might be a bit of a delay. There's been a big Trident operation today in Lambeth and of course there's also been a state visit, the President of Uganda. The team will be with you as soon as they can but it probably won't be for a while," the DCI informed me.

It's difficult to describe quite how pissed off I was by this news. Fucking hell, we'd been waiting for the firearms team all fucking day and by the sound of it, they were still nowhere near coming to our aid.

"I need to get this family out of Stoke Newington police station, boss. They can't spend another night here; and neither can we. I'll move them without the firearms team, we'll put them in the back of a carrier," I suggested.

"Chris, I know you're tired. I know it's not what you want to hear but you will not move that family without the firearms team and you will not move that family until you have an operation order fully signed up and authorised. Too many people are dying and getting shot at; not going to happen any more. Do you hear me?" the DCI said.

I took a deep breath.

"Chris? Are you still there? Chris?"

"I'm here boss, I hear you," I replied. "Can you call them and find out what the fuck's going on, boss?"

"I'll call you straight back, don't go anywhere," he replied.

I knew he was trying to be funny but I wasn't in the mood so I hung up.

I stood in the yard and watched the guys going about their business. I suspected the job hadn't changed much, if anything. Drunkenness, domestic disputes, suspects on premises, crime reporting, robberies, offences against the person, threatening behaviour, possession with intent, RTAs, the odd FATACC – in other words, shit, shit, shit and then more shit, but at that very moment how I'd have loved to swap places with them.

My phone rang; it was the DCI.

"The firearms team will be with you at nine o'clock tomorrow," he said.

I could have cried.

Chapter 59

This death of poor Sonia meant that we'd lost an important witness who could link Gary Odiham, Tony Pascal and Bigga.

I was also genuinely sad, which was really quite unusual. As a result of this job, I'd become desensitised to murder and death so my feelings about Sonia surprised me. In her own way, Sonia had been all right. I mean, I wouldn't want to date her but when the chips were down, she'd done everything she could to help us and I was quite convinced that given more time, I'd have been able to find out more about her boyfriend and why he'd died. We'd lost an important line of enquiry.

I knew there was a slim chance that they'd pick up Matthew's fingerprints at her address, but as he had no previous convictions, in the short term at least, this wouldn't be a problem. The more I thought about that evening, however, the more I actually didn't think he'd touched anything as he'd spent the entire time with his hands plunged deep into his pockets. Besides, when the post-mortem established a heroin overdose as the cause of death, further enquiries in connection with her death would stop.

I wandered back towards the parade room and as I was about to enter, noticed a serene silence from within. I pushed open the door with a little trepidation, as I figured something must be seriously amiss. I saw Tracey and the three younger children fast asleep, and the three older ones playing cards with Samantha. In the far corner Julie was curled up on a two-seater settee, fast asleep.

Apparently, Mary Poppins, in the guise of a six-foot-two-inches transgender woman, had arrived and taken control. I stood momentarily transfixed by the tranquillity.

Samantha looked over.

"Well done, thank you," I mouthed.

Samantha smiled back; I realised that I'd never seen her smile before.

I walked quietly over to Julie and tapped her gently on the shoulder. She opened her eyes and I indicated that she and Samantha should join me outside.

"I've got some bad news. The firearms team isn't going to be here until tomorrow morning," I said.

"No," Julie said defiantly.

"We're going to have to keep them here another night."

"No," Julie said again, this time almost argumentatively.

"I proposed moving them in a carrier but the DCI has said no. I'm sorry," I explained.

Julie was fuming and I understood why. The poor thing had spent the last sixteen hours looking after them and the thought of another twelve hours was beyond what her patience could take.

"I need to have a word with the Duty Officer to explain what's going on," I said.

Julie was shaking her head. In a nice touch, Samantha had put her arm around her.

"Where are the others?" Julie asked aggressively.

"The Onions are dealing with Sonia Rider. She's dead; looks like she overdosed after Pod and I had seen her this morning," I replied.

"You didn't do your usual trick and slip her a few quid did you, babes?" Julie asked.

I could have killed her. Fortunately, the exchange seemed to go over Samantha's head or perhaps she didn't want to understand and thought it best to play dumb.

"Taff, Nicola and Pod are dealing with Tracey's house and the Range Rover."

"Okay," Julie replied, her voice belying that she had started to come to terms with the situation.

"You two go and get a meal, there's a few decent restaurants in Church Street; it's becoming really trendy, or so I'm told. I'll look after them, honestly, take your time."

They didn't need to be asked twice and had their coats on and were out of the nick before I could say 'can you bring me something nice back?'. It was fine; I'd largely managed to avoid my share of babysitting duties so it was only fair that they both got a break.

I returned to the converted parade room to discover them all now asleep with the exception of Tracey, who sat quietly looking completely bewildered. For the first time, I felt genuinely sorry for her.

I sat down beside her.

"How are you doing?" I asked in a whisper.

"I need a fag," she replied.

"Come out into the yard; I'll get one off one of the guys. Will the kids be all right?" I asked.

She looked around at her children and nodded.

"You haven't left any matches or a lighter lying about, have you?" I asked.

Tracey shook her head and I detected the tiniest trace of a smile.

I managed to get nearly half a packet of Rothmans from one of the PCs coming on for night duty. I'd only asked for one but he insisted on giving me what he had, saying he could soon get some more. Tracey smoked it slowly, savouring each draw and I deliberately avoided asking her any questions to allow her a few moments to enjoy the respite.

"So what's your name?" she asked, as if it was the first time we'd met.

"My name is Chris, Tracey. I spoke to you earlier, in the interview room, do you remember?" I replied.

She nodded, but I wasn't entirely sure she was telling the truth. I was really tempted to remind Tracey that she'd already told me that her old man had admitted stabbing Gary Odiham in the head but I resisted.

"How do you feel?" I asked instead.

"Shit. I need a drin'," she said.

"I can't do that for you," I said gently.

"Either get me a fuckin' drin' or I'm ou' of 'ear. I onl' live over there."

Tracey pointed towards her house, which was indeed only a few hundred yards away.

"I know, but you can't go back there. The Kiracs have already tried to kill you and your children. You have to stay with us now. We'll look after you, we'll find you somewhere to live."

I tried my best to make my voice sound calm, confident and convincing.

"I ain't gonna court. No way, nooooo way," she declared.

"Fair enough," I said.

Tracey eyed me suspiciously.

"We'll take one step at a time; gently does it, eh?" I suggested.

"They wil' kil' me, ya know. Danny calls it 'stiffed'. If I giv' evidence again' them, I am as goo' as dead."

Tracey looked at me; I guessed she was trying to work out whether I'd understood what she'd said. Just for a moment, there was a flicker in her eye.

"No one is asking you to give evidence against the Kiracs. All I'm asking you to do is to tell us what Danny said to you about the murder of Gary Odiham, no more, no less. It won't be easy for you, I know that. But since they shot up your house, I really don't think you've got any choice and Tracey …"

I put my hand on her shoulder.

"… I promise, I will be with you all the time. I will never let you down. I will never lie to you; I might tell you something you don't want to hear and you'll hate me, but remember, I will never lie to you. Do we have a deal? Will you work with me on this?"

Tracey nodded and I knew that the journey to turn her from gangster's moll to prime prosecution witness had begun.

Chapter 60

Sunday 19th January

I intended to spend my second night sleeping in the cells at Stoke Newington, but when Samantha and Nicola returned from their meal, they sent me home on the grounds that I desperately needed a shower and a change of clothes.

I didn't want to go to Loughton because I couldn't face a deep and meaningful with Jackie, so I headed for Leyton. Usually, under these circumstances, I would have surprised her, but I thought I'd better text first just in case I once again found her and Matthew at it like a pair of rabbits. I also warned her not to come within a mile of me until I had freshened up.

As it was, I didn't get there until gone one and they were both in bed. I showered, cleaned my teeth and snuggled up next to Wendy. Only seconds later, it was eight thirty in the morning and from downstairs in the kitchen where I'd left it on charge, I could hear my phone ringing. Of course, I didn't answer it in time but I picked up a voicemail from the DCI telling me that he was on his way to Stoke Newington to supervise the transfer of the Manning family and that I could take the day off. My initial reaction was annoyance because he'd cost me at least twelve hours at double time, but that feeling was soon replaced by deep joy when I realised I could get back into bed and have another two or three hours kip.

"Who was that?" Wendy asked, joining me in the kitchen.

"The DCI. I've got today off, you know, like you asked," I replied.

It was a lie but I thought, why waste the perfect opportunity to score a few brownie points?

"I'll put the kettle on," Wendy said.

"Let's go back to bed, hon. I need a couple more hours, I feel knackered and beside, well you know, I haven't, we haven't, in ages," I replied.

Wendy smiled and moved in for a cuddle; we embraced.

"Sorry, darling, we need to get up and going. Matthew's got to be at Paddington at quarter to eleven, so breakfast and off. No going back to bed for you. Matthew's getting in the shower, I'll start the sausages and you can help me."

As it turned out, it was less awkward than I'd feared. Matthew had no idea that I knew what had been happening and Wendy was her normal bubbly, happy self. She did dote over Matthew though, but in a maternal way, no other. It was so obvious Matthew was completely besotted with her. The one thing I did notice was that having spent the last week having sex with my girlfriend, Matthew could no longer stomach calling me 'father' and I became 'Chris' to him, which was just fine.

Wendy drove to the station, I was in the front passenger seat and Matthew in the back. Matthew leaned forward in between the front seats and asked me a question I hadn't anticipated.

"Chris, what do you want me to tell Mother about your ..." he hesitated, "... situation? I really don't want to lie but I don't think she'll be terribly impressed and I don't want her to say that I can't come and visit again."

"Tell her the truth; I think she might understand; after all, she was in the job once, too," I replied.

"I don't think she'd approve. Mother and Pop are ..." again he hesitated while searching for the most appropriate word or phrase, "... very old-fashioned."

I had to smile but only inside. The Sarah I had known had made two pornographic films before she'd joined the job so I suspected that, at heart, his mother was a lot less old-fashioned than Matthew thought.

"Matthew, son, do what you think is best. Sometimes you have to lie; it's not the end of the world. Either way, I think your mum will understand. Whether your dad will is another matter 'cos I've never met him. But your mum, I used to know quite well," I replied.

"If I don't tell them, then that's hardly a lie, is it?" he suggested.

"Not telling someone what they should be told is sometimes worse than lying," I said.

The moment the words left my mouth, I realised that I'd been less than tactful and one look at his face confirmed that I'd definitely said the wrong thing. Even if I hadn't known about him and Wendy, I would have guessed everything from his expression of sheer guilt. Fortunately, I thought quickly of something to move the conversation on.

"When you go home, tell your mum that I often think about her; tell her, and this is really important, Matthew, that I will never forget what she did to protect me."

I was referring to the time that she learnt her boyfriend was about to get himself out of a pile of shit by planting a load of cannabis in my car.

"I will," he replied.

"What's your dad like?" I asked, just trying to keep the conversation rolling.

"He's great. He's the best. When I have children, if I can be half the father he has been, then my children will have the best Pop in the world."

That was a lovely thing to say.

"Make sure you tell him that," I advised kindly.

The journey held one last comical twist. Somewhere on the final approach to Paddington, *Bittersweet Symphony* came on the radio and Matthew immediately commented how much he loved that song and how it would always remind him of the last week. I looked across at Wendy who was driving; at least she had the decency to look suitably contrite.

"I thought you'd be more of a Girls Aloud kinda guy, they're your sort of age, aren't they?" I asked.

Girls Aloud had won a TV talent show called Popstars and were at number one with *The Sound of the Underground*, and my comment was a gentle dig at Wendy, who mouthed 'sod off' to me.

"I don't know, Chris. I think I prefer older women," he replied, completely oblivious to the irony of his comment.

Wendy smiled.

After we said our farewells and dropped Matthew off at the station, Wendy and I drove back to Leyton. En route and much to her annoyance, I made a call to find out what was going on.

The Mannings had been relocated to the Holiday Inn in King's Cross, which was a bit of a surprise as that was right smack in the middle of the busiest part of London. It was, however, the only place that could be found at such short notice that had four double rooms together. The armed protection was going to remain in place until we moved them out of London to a more permanent location.

Tracey had been interviewed on tape and confirmed what she'd already told me. Apparently, however, she had the raging hump because I'd promised to be with her throughout and then gone and taken the next day off. She did have a point. As no one mentioned her previous claim of hearing Gary's voice in her head, I assumed she'd not mentioned it this time.

I knew Wendy was getting agitated so when I hung up, I apologised and said that I wouldn't make another call today. Within two seconds, my phone rang. Wendy huffed. It was Samantha with a really excellent idea of getting a caravan or chalet on a holiday park somewhere for the Mannings to stay. As it was January, she explained, the option would be much cheaper than a hotel and, if she found the right one, there should be facilities to keep the kids amused. It was a corker of an idea and I asked her to see what she could locate.

As soon as I terminated the call, Wendy politely suggested I turn my phone off. I agreed but switched the device to silent instead.

"Who was that?" she said.

"Samantha, the new girl on my team," I replied.

"Oh, the transsexual. His, her voice was really deep."

"Yeah, I know. She's lovely actually, having a bit of a hard time, as you can imagine," I said.

"I know you told me about him, her, when she joined. I'll tell you who used to work with him, Carrie's old man."

"Buster?" I asked.

"Yeah, Ronnie," Wendy replied.

I remembered that Samantha had told me she knew Buster.

"They didn't get on at all. I remember now that Carrie said that Ronnie and Sam came to blows at an office lunch. Ronnie's brothers had turned up, stockbrokers or investment bankers or something, and they'd started doing coke in the toilets to which Samantha took great offence. It was a couple of years ago now," Wendy explained.

"They actually came to blows?" I asked.

"Apparently," Wendy replied.

The vision of Samantha standing there in her pink dress and heels going toe to toe with some hairy arse DC flashed through my head. Of course, I realised that at the time Samantha was living as a man.

My phone buzzed, which Wendy heard.

"I need to talk to you," she said, clearly indicating that she didn't want me to take the call.

"Go on," I said, pressing the button to divert the call to voicemail.

"If, in a month's time, I tell you I'm pregnant, how are you going to react?"

I didn't reply immediately because I knew how important my next few words were going to be and needed a moment to make sure what I said honestly reflected what I felt. If I am being truthful, the biggest issue I had would be the fundamental change it would make to our relationship. For the last five years, I'd been the entire focus of Wendy's life, but that would disappear with the arrival of a baby. And I know it was selfish, but I kind of liked the attention. What's more, there'd be no more nights out, popping down to the Bird or the Duke or our favourite restaurants; instead we'd be 'nappy smelling' to quote my favourite Squeeze song.

"Thanks!" Wendy said, interpreting my silence as a negative response.

"I'm just thinking it through," I replied quickly. "Listen, I know it's what you want with all your heart; of course I'll be okay with it."

"That's not enough, Chris. You'll be 'okay with it'?" she asked.

"Give me a break, I'm coming to terms with quite a lot here. Not least of which is that I could become a grandfather and a stepdad all at once."

I smiled; it was an act of conciliation.

"I am pregnant; I'm certain," Wendy declared.

"Oh, don't be ridiculous, what's it been, like five days?"

"My sister always says she knew straight away; I spoke to her last night. I've had stomach cramps, like period pains, and my nipples are tingling. It's exactly what happened to her. I'm not stupid, I'm not saying that I'm going to get to full term; hell, I might lose it when my next period is due next week, but I know I'm pregnant now," Wendy said.

"Jackie always said the same when she fell with Pippa," I replied.

"So you believe I'm not mad then?"

I nodded.

My phone buzzed again.

"Turn the fucking thing off," Wendy said firmly.

I'd never heard her swear before.

Chapter 61

Even though I was at the Holiday Inn before nine, the guy from the SIS was already waiting for me in the lobby. He introduced himself as DS Barry Highams, we ordered coffee and took a table in a dark discreet corner of a very busy hotel. I'd actually completely forgotten that he wanted to speak to me.

"This is about Tony Pascal, right?" I asked.

Barry nodded.

"This will only take a few minutes, I promise. But what I am about to discuss with you can't be repeated or recorded; we'll deal with any disclosure issues but these will be minimalised if you don't put this through the system – not at this stage anyway.

"We have a long-term operation running targeting Tony Pascal and his OCN; we are about to arrest him for money laundering and to freeze his assets with a view to obtaining forfeiture orders. And when I say long-term, this is year four. We've identified his associates, his family members, his bank accounts and assets, both in the UK and abroad. We're not even going to try to prove the substantive offences; he's far too clever to get his hands dirty. So in the first case of its kind, we're just going for straight money laundering."

"And how can I help you?" I asked politely.

"Whatever your team have done over the last few weeks has set some hares running. I want a quick chat to see whether between us, we can identify exactly what you've touched that's so impacted upon our Mr Pascal," Barry explained.

I nodded again.

"Can I assume, although I know you may not be able to tell us, that when you say 'we've set some hares running' you mean their communications have gone very busy?"

"I can't confirm or deny but you're on the right lines. We need to know if two particular phrases mean anything to you?"

"Oh, okay," I replied.

I thought this was very revealing. I had a good idea this was coming from one or more probes. You are allowed to be less secretive about probes than with telephone intercepts, it was just a quirk of the various pieces of governing legislation.

Barry removed a small notebook from his pocket and ruffled through the pages.

"Right, does the following mean anything to you? TT?"

"What, as in Audi TT?" I asked.

"As in 'we need to check on the whereabouts of the TT'. Is an Audi TT involved in your murder?" Barry asked.

"I don't think so, but I can run the search through HOLMES, if you want," I replied.

"What about 'the Lee'?" Barry asked next.

"As in the River Lee?" I asked.

"As in a place certainly. Maybe a club or something?"

"What was the exact phrase? If you can tell us?" I asked.

Barry looked at his notebook.

"I can't read my own fucking writing. I think it says 'make sure the TT's not still in at the Lee'."

"As in Lee Green in South London, perhaps?" I proposed.

"Does that mean anything to you? It's Lewisham, isn't it? I'm a North London boy myself," Barry said.

I shook my head.

"At Lee?" I asked. "As in Attlee House, where our murder victim lived?"

"Could be, I'll have to listen to the tape again," Barry replied. "And finally, what the fuck is the connection between Tony Pascal and the Kiracs? We've been looking at every aspect of the man's life for four fucking years and never a single word about the Kiracs, but in the last week, he's suddenly become paranoid that they're after him because he's pissed them off."

"Okay; that definitely links him to our murder. Although, I need to fill in some of the gaps here so just for a moment, go with the flow. Danny Manning is selling drugs for the Kiracs. He murders Gary Odiham because Gary is selling drugs in his patch, which I assume is Dagenham because that's where the murder took place. Gary is connected to Tony Pascal because he stole his wife's handbag and as a result, had to 'do him a favour'. We don't know what that favour was but maybe the favour was selling drugs for him in Dagenham?" I said.

Barry screwed his nose up dismissively.

"Tony Pascal, drug dealing in Dagenham? Just doesn't ring right to me. Pascal's OCN wouldn't touch low-level street dealers with the proverbial," Barry replied.

"Did your probes ..."

I hesitated to see whether Barry would contradict me but all he said was, "Go on."

"Did your probes pick up anything about the theft of his wife's handbag?"

"Nothing at all at the time. Only your conversation with Tony and his wife," he replied.

"After we'd gone, was there any conversation about it?" I asked.

"No, I don't think there was," Barry replied.

That sort of fitted in with what I'd learnt. Tony Pascal wasn't bothered because he already knew about the theft, not from his wife, who'd actually kept her mouth shut, but directly from Gary himself.

"So that's how you discovered that we were looking at Tony Pascal. You heard us on tape?"

Barry nodded.

"Of course, but your partner did most of the talking; was it DC Dyson?" he asked.

"It was. Was there any reaction to our visit?" I asked.

"No, not really; oh, except he was mightily pissed off with his daughter."

"What for?" I asked.

"I don't think we knew specifically; he did advise her that she should 'put some fucking clothes on before parading around in front of visitors' – those were his exact words. He was fucking steaming with her."

"Did you pick up anything about the murder of the prison officer? At the time, in about November?" I asked.

"A little collateral, nothing of note. The prison officer was dating his daughter, wasn't he? Tony was pissed off that he was fucking his little princess and to make matters worse, he was fucking her about. There was a bit of traffic between him and his missus about it, a bit but nothing more. It was a month or two ago now but I think his daughter complained to his wife that Tim had sent some inappropriate texts to her best friend. It was typical family stuff, you know, nothing of note," Barry replied.

"What was his reaction to the murder of the prison officer?" I asked.

"I don't think there was one," Barry replied.

"What? Not a word?"

"I don't recall anything and I read the transcripts every day," he replied.

I found that interesting.

"Can you do me one favour, Barry? Can you check your records for Friday 10th January, the morning after Gary Odiham's murder? Did Tony Pascal know that Gary Odiham had been murdered? What did he know and when?"

The DS from SIS nodded and made a note in his book. Somehow I thought that fact might be relevant but I couldn't quite articulate why.

~~~

I spent an hour with Barry but by the end of our exchange I don't think I knew a great deal more than I did at the beginning; only the reference to the significance of an Audi TT was completely new information. Apart from the Pascal/Kirac connection, nothing I'd heard seemed to bear any relevance to the murder of Gary Odiham. If anything, I was starting to believe that maybe Tony Pascal was actually a suspect for the prison officer murder, though not himself directly, but one of his minions.

When Barry left, a lady called Sharon came over and introduced herself as the officer in charge of the SO19 team. She was in her early thirties and stunningly attractive with blonde hair and bright blue eyes. I played it cool.

"The night duty team said your witness was in the bar last night and chatting to a couple of guys, business types, who were also staying in the hotel," Sharon said.

"Did they not stop her?" I asked.

"We're here to protect her and her family, not to babysit them. That's your job, I'm afraid. Unless there was an immediate threat to her life, we'd just let her get on with it," Sharon explained.

"Fair enough," I replied. "Right, what's the SP?"

Sharon said that she had four officers deployed inside the hotel and that they were all like her, dressed to fit in with the environment. I was impressed, as I hadn't noticed anyone, but when she nodded towards each of her team who were within sight, I wondered how I hadn't spotted them earlier.

Sharon's instructions were to provide close armed protection until the family was well outside London and we were satisfied that they hadn't been followed. I explained that we would hopefully find somewhere by the end of the day and therefore we'd be looking at a transfer at some point this afternoon. She said all she needed from me was a time of departure and a drop-off point. The sooner I could get her that information, the better. They usually used motorway services as the drop-off point.

An hour before departure she would, she said, brief all of the officers and witnesses taking part. She would utilise one of the many conference rooms at the hotel for this purpose.

Her team would provide the transport, a small coach of some sort, and the driver, and that at the allotted time, we were to board the vehicle which would be immediately outside the hotel. When we'd all boarded, the coach would be escorted by the armed team through London and away. It all seemed relatively straightforward; I mean, what could possibly go wrong?

Chapter 62

By the time I'd met with Barry and Sharon, the rest of my crew had arrived.

There were four of us: Samantha, Julie, Nicola and me. Pod was dealing with Sonia's family and Taff was still tied up with the crime scenes from the shooting.

We had an impromptu mini-team meeting and made sure we were all up to speed with what the day ahead held for us. Nicola and Samantha were tasked with finding a suitable holiday park, preferably a long way out of London, while Julie and I would have the unenviable task of finding out what was happening with our family.

"What time did you leave them? I asked.

"Just before eleven, but we weren't off duty until two," Julie replied.

"What were you doing for three hours?" I asked.

"Cleaning the bleeding parade room at Stokey. The place looked like a war zone when we left. We had to go back and sort it out otherwise we'd never be welcome there again; and they were all so accommodating," Julie explained.

It was nearly eleven when Julie and I steeled our nerves and headed up to the eighth floor and the Manning posse. I confess to being slightly surprised that we'd heard nothing from them all morning.

I knocked at Tracey's door; there was no reply. I called out and knocked again, this time harder.

"Go 'way," Tracey shouted.

"Tracey, it's Chris, open the fucking door, darling," I said.

"'off; I'm tired," she replied.

"Which room's Leigh in? She's the oldest, right?" I asked Julie.

Leigh's room was directly opposite so Julie knocked there.

Leigh opened the door quickly and ushered us in with a sense of urgency.

"I'm in the middle of feeding the baby."

She had left the baby on the bed and was clearly anxious that it would only take a few seconds for him to roll over and fall off.

Julie pointed to the travel cot that was at the end of a second bed.

"I thought I put that up in your mum's room," she said.

Leigh, who was now sitting on her bed feeding the baby from a bottle, looked to the heavens. "Like that was ever going to happen!" she said.

"She's refusing to answer the door; what time did your mum get to bed?" I asked.

"You know she had two men in there last night, don't you? They only went about an hour ago," Leigh replied.

"What?" Julie asked incredulously. "We didn't leave you until eleven and you were all in your rooms."

"And as soon as you did, mum went down to the bar," Leigh explained, "where she got chatted up by two guys. She got pissed; they got pissed. The night manager threw them out the bar and she brought them up here because she's got a load of drinks in the fridge thing. They were fucking about, mum was naked running up and down the corridor, the other guests were kicking off; it was a nightmare."

"How are the others doing?" I asked.

"They're fine; they're watching the telly and eating chocolate out the fridge. I just checked on them. I'm gonna need more milk for the baby and I'm down to my last two nappies. Bobby's going to need nappies too; he needs eighteen months to two years."

"Thank God you're here," I said.

Leigh smiled; I guessed she didn't get many compliments.

I asked Julie and Leigh to make a detailed shopping list of all their requirements over the next week and told her to give it to the two guys downstairs to source and purchase.

It took some shouting, swearing and threatening, but eventually, I got Tracey to open her door. The bedroom was like nothing I had ever seen before. In just twelve hours, she had turned a pristine four-star London hotel room into a scene of complete devastation. Every single item in the courtesy bar had been removed and either drunk, eaten or just dropped and crushed into the carpet. Bedclothes and pillows were everywhere, except on the beds themselves. Towels were strewn about; a hand towel was even lodged in the toilet, making it inoperable. Her large suitcase was empty and clothes thrown just about anywhere that wasn't a cupboard or drawer. Two or three used condoms had been dropped on the floor and a deep cloud of grey tobacco smoke hung in the air of this no smoking room. Just when I thought it couldn't get any worse, I noticed that the smoke detector had been stuffed with toilet paper and there were cigarette burns on the carpet and several articles of furniture.

"What the fuck has gone on in here?" I asked.

"We had a part', your mates and me," Tracey replied.

She was completely pissed, again.

The guys that had been here yesterday really should have had the sense to empty the mini-bar before they left our chief witness.

"You had two men in here last night. Are you seriously telling me they were police officers?" I asked.

"Of course they were," Tracey said.

"Did they show you their warrant cards? Did you see any firearms? The only officers who were here last night were armed, Tracey. If the guys you had back here weren't carrying guns, then they weren't police officers."

"Ooops," she said.

"Fucking hell, Tracey. Look at this fucking room," I said.

"Wot's wron' wit' it?" she asked, looking around.

When I thought about it, it didn't actually look too dissimilar to the state of Tracey's home, so I figured this was what she expected a room to look like.

"Never mind. Listen, Tracey, you gotta sober up. We're moving you all out in a couple of hours. You need to wake up and get your arse in gear."

I then spent a good twenty minutes explaining to Tracey why her dog couldn't come with us, not now anyway, and that she'd be really happy in the lovely kennels we'd found for it. Quite frankly, I couldn't have cared less about the mutt.

I searched the room to make sure there wasn't any more alcohol secreted about the place and then left her with clear instructions to have a shower, get dressed and pack.

I was an idiot. As soon as I left her, Tracey went back to bed so that an hour later, we were no nearer leaving than we had been; in fact, if anything, we were in a worse situation because Tracey seemed to be spiralling deeper into a pit of self-loathing and despair.

Samantha and Nicola had found somewhere to take them, a holiday park in Devon about four hours' drive away, but we'd have to stop regularly with so many young children. Samantha had booked a really nice four-bedroom log cabin; it even had a hot tub.

The site itself had several children's play areas, including a ballpark and a swimming pool, though I couldn't imagine that Tracey had ever possessed the inclination to teach her kids to swim. What's more, because we were out of season, one week in the cabin was the same price as four rooms for one night in the Holiday Inn.

My only reservation was the distance from London. I knew that I'd probably be spending the next six months going back and forward to the place and would have preferred somewhere a little closer, like the Sussex coast.

I spent an hour sat in the car playing the tape of their interview yesterday with Tracey. It was similar to the conversation I'd had with her on Saturday, the one where I lost the tape because of the reference to hearing Gary, but this time Tracey was sober and the guys were able to probe a little more. The only significant development was that Tracey talked about the stabbing being done with an ice pick. Originally, the pathologist had described the object used as 'a single-width implement, possibility a screwdriver'. An ice pick was a single-width implement so that would fit with the finding of the post-mortem but I had heard the term 'ice pick' used before, I just couldn't remember where.

Pod, who'd done the interview with Nicola, had pushed Tracey hard on the issue of Tony Pascal. Listening to her replies, I decided Tracey was simply not bright enough to lie and had clearly never heard Tony Pascal's name before and knew nothing about him.

I thought this was really important, because if Gary's murder was nothing to do with Tony Pascal, then the handbag theft was unconnected and the 'favour' irrelevant.

By the time I'd finished my review of the interview, I came to the conclusion that the motive for the murder was simply that Danny Manning had come across Gary Odiham selling drugs in an area of London where he thought he had the exclusive rights. It was indeed just a turf war.

If I were to guess the missing details, I'd say that the five grand Gary stole elevated him from low-level dealer and at about this time he met Bigga, himself newly arrived on the scene from Jamaica. As a result of this new 'business connection', Gary started selling in Dagenham, not knowing that by doing so, he was straying into Kirac-licensed territory.

What this did mean was that the connection to Tony Pascal, the possible link to police corruption, the 'cleaning' of the victim's flat, the visit of the debt collectors, and, most importantly of all, the Buster issues were all irrelevant.

I got my thoughts clear and my argument ready and phoned the DCI to try to persuade him to drop the CIB angle. This was an important roll of the dice; Buster and his family were due to land back in the UK tomorrow.

Chapter 63

Walking back into the hotel, I felt like I was walking on air. The DCI had agreed that this case was now pretty much in the bag and while he had grave reservations as to whether Tracey would ever make it into the witness box, and even if she did then what kind of witness she would make, he no longer considered there to be a police corruption aspect. He said he would phone Adam Stanley at CIB and have the same conversation. I was absolutely elated.

It took forever to get the Mannings ready to leave. Tracey got gradually more sober as the day rolled on but still did absolutely nothing to control or otherwise parent her six children. The oldest daughter, Leigh, was an absolute star, assuming the roles her mother did not. She was lovely too; it was difficult to know how such a sensible and level-headed young adult could emerge from such a dysfunctional family, but she had.

We met for our briefing with Sharon at five o'clock in the conference room. The first thing Sharon did was to seize our mobile phones. She then took out each battery and SIM card and placed everything in a large rucksack, which she sealed closed.

"It's too easy to track mobile devices with short-range scanners. We'll give them back to you at the drop-off point. The coach will be outside at six. Please get in and sit at the rear. Some of my team will travel with you in the front. We like to keep the whole event low key, so please try to leave the hotel quietly and quickly without disturbing the environment too much. Now I know that's not that easy when you're such a large family, but it's really important."

I looked around the room; the children seemed out on their feet and I guessed they'd been up all night watching TV, playing computer games and generally trashing their rooms. The upside was that with any luck, they'd sleep on the coach.

After the meeting, I had a quick word with the hotel manager and apologised for the damage to the bedrooms, assuring him that the Metropolitan Police would pay for any repairs.

We gathered the family in one room and at five to six, got two lifts down to a packed reception. I placed myself with Tracey. Only Samantha and I were going to get on the coach. Nicola and Julie were going to bring our cars along, otherwise we'd be without any transport when we arrived at the holiday park.

As we passed through the lobby, Tracey made a comment about never having seen so many fit, good-looking young men in one room – the woman was a complete nightmare.

As we got through the revolving door, the coach was only a few paces away, but I was immediately surprised because it was a proper full-length, forty-seater, whereas I'd somehow imagined a minibus. Even more surprising, there were police motorcycle outriders to the front and rear, with their blue lights flashing. So much for leaving the hotel incognito, I thought.

The coach was the height of luxury, with leather seats and sofas; there were even several TV screens. I was impressed.

We did as we had been instructed and went to the rear. Once seated, I pulled across a curtain, which separated the last quarter of the coach. We had our own TV screen and toilet and several large leather settees, and in this section the windows were darkened so no one could see either out or in.

A few minutes later, the engine started and I felt the coach rock as several of the firearms team assumed their seats at the front.

Then the TV screen sparked into life and played this week's Premier League highlights at a volume that was annoyingly intrusive. Several of the kids watched while the younger ones made themselves comfortable. Not five minutes after we got on, the coach moved off accompanied occasionally by the sound of police sirens as we made our way through the North London rush-hour traffic.

Having been on Tracey's case all day, I really wanted to use this time together to bond. I started a conversation telling her how great the holiday park was going to be and how much the kids would enjoy it. She seemed more relaxed than I had seen her, and more sober. Even though she wasn't intoxicated, she still spoke as if she was. It was weird, and although I'd spent more than my fair share of time with London's lowest echelons, I'd never come across anyone who spoke quite as lazily as Tracey.

Right in the middle of a completely innocuous conversation about how the kids would get on with swimming armbands, and completely out of the blue, Tracey said, "Danny ha' a 'and on his arm, you know? He cut it whe' he stab'd the geezer."

"Sorry?" I said.

I wasn't quite sure with the noise from the telly that I'd actually heard Tracey accurately. I leaned into her, putting my ear closer to her mouth.

"Danny says, whe' he wen' ta stab da' geezer, he missed and stab'd his own ar'."

Was that last word 'arm'? I wished she'd speak more fucking coherently. And how do you stab yourself in your own arm? Was Tracey talking bollocks? I thought I'd ask simple questions.

"What did Danny use? Was it a knife?"

"No wa '. An ice pic', I tol' 'em yesterd'," Tracey replied.

"Where is the ice pick now? I asked.

"He drop'd it dayn a dryan," she replied.

"Do you know where?" I asked, more in hope than expectation.

"Yea, he show'd me. I could fuckin' see it, cover'd in bloo' and brains."

"Where? Where is the drain?" I asked.

"In the Hig' Stree' som'where. I can't rememb'," she replied.

"Which High Street?" I asked with mounting excitement.

"Stoke," she replied.

444

"Is it near the police station, the nick?" I asked.

Tracey shrugged her shoulders.

"Tracey, are you telling me that the ice pick which Danny used to murder Gary Odiham is in a drain in Stoke Newington High Street?"

She nodded.

"Are you telling me you've actually seen it there?"

She nodded again.

"Why the fuck didn't you tell us when we were there?" I asked.

"You didn't ask," she replied.

We had to get someone to recover it immediately. I reached for my phone but of course, we'd all given them to Sharon. I pondered briefly whether this could wait until we got to the drop-off point, the Leigh Delamere services near Bath. I decided it couldn't, stood up and pulled the curtain slightly to one side so that I could get a feel for who was where and who would be best to approach.

I glanced for about three seconds and then pulled the curtain quickly back across. Something was dreadfully wrong. We were in fact on a coach full of, to quote Tracey, 'fit good-looking young men' and one old one, a grey-haired, craggy-faced Frenchman, who was very familiar.

We had mistakenly got on the Arsenal football team coach and were now on the way to Highbury for that evening's League Cup game against Middlesbrough.

Chapter 64

My initial plan was to sit tight until the team had got off the coach but that failed when two of the boys started fighting and Tracey screamed at them to desist like a fishwife on acid. About ten seconds later, the Frenchman put his head through the curtain and asked very politely and in his strong accent, "Perhaps you will tell me, who are you?"

I showed him my brief, asked to have a quick word and we stepped to the other side of the curtain, as the two boys, who had momentarily paused their set-to, once again went at each other.

Even though I wasn't a huge football fan, I recognised most of the players' faces, which were now turned to listen to my explanation as to why there was a group of complete strangers on their team bus.

"I am really sorry; we are obviously on the wrong coach. For reasons I can't go into, I am getting this family, who have been staying at the Holiday Inn, to a place of safety. We were being picked up at six o'clock and when we stepped out of the hotel, I assumed this was the transport sent to collect us so we got on, went to the back as we'd been told to, and just waited to set off. I only just looked through the curtains and realised what we'd done. I'm really sorry, I really am."

Fortunately, everyone saw the funny side but we agreed to remain on the coach until it had deposited the Arsenal team.

I didn't learn until later that at six o'clock exactly, the minibus which we were meant to get on, had driven towards the front of the hotel only to realise the Arsenal coach was in the way. The driver had to relocate towards the side of the hotel, but in the few seconds he took to manoeuvre his vehicle and while the front entrance was momentarily out of his vision, we had jumped onto the wrong coach. Apparently, they sat there for twenty minutes assuming that the myriad of children had delayed our exit before the realisation dawned that we were no longer there. They couldn't call us because, of course, they'd taken all our mobiles off us at the briefing.

The whole episode ended up costing us two hours, as we had to arrange for the proper coach, which was a bog-standard twelve-seater hired from Budget, to come to Highbury and collect us. It was a complete debacle. We were so late leaving London that the holiday park was likely to be closed for admissions by the time we arrived. Just as importantly, the small local hotel we had booked for ourselves may well have locked up for the night. To make sure none of this happened, I sent Julie and Nicola straight there on the hurry up, so they could get the chalet keys and hotel rooms sorted in advance of our arrival.

I did manage to get the message to the DCI about the murder weapon and he sent several Onions to see if they could locate the ice pick, but that was going to be challenging as it was dark and cars would be parked over many of the storm drains.

As it was, we arrived at midnight at the holiday site but then we had to unpack and get the kids down and all the time, every ten minutes that went by, Tracey asked me to get her a drink. In the end, I snapped and told her exactly what I thought of her continual nagging. Overhearing my outburst, Samantha asked to have a word, and from the tone in her voice and her body language, I actually thought she was going to give me a bollocking, but I was wrong.

"Chris, if Tracey is a genuine alcoholic, then you can't just not give her anything. It's really quite dangerous; it can, in extreme cases, be fatal."

"Are you kidding me?" I asked.

"No, absolutely not. We really should get a doctor to see her, we can't just leave her like this."

"A doctor? At one o'clock in the morning? In the middle of nowhere, in Devon? Are you shitting me?" I asked incredulously.

I really wasn't in the mood for this. Fuck me, I'd been working solid for seventeen hours; the last thing I was going to do was to wait another two or three hours for a doctor to come out, if indeed they would under these circumstances.

"I've got a better idea," I said.

"Go on," Samantha encouraged me.

"About five miles ago on the A30 we passed an all-night BP garage. They'll sell alcohol. While I'm finishing up here, jump in the car and go and buy one of those small bottles of vodka and some coke. You know, the two-hundred-and-fifty-mil ones. It won't be enough for her to get pissed but it'll keep her alive. What do you reckon?"

I didn't know Samantha quite well enough to be able to anticipate how she'd react to my innovative solution.

"No problem," she replied.

"You know it makes sense," I replied.

My phone rang.

"Nostrils?" I recognised the voice immediately, it was one of the Onions.

"Yes, mate?"

"Bingo," he said.

"Did you just say 'bingo'? The signals not great here, we're in the middle of fucking nowhere," I replied.

"Bingo, house, over 'ere," he said.

"You've got it, haven't you?" I said.

"Oh yes, my son. In a blocked drain right outside the front entrance to Stoke Newington police station. And Nostrils ..."

"Yes, mate?" I said.

450

"It's covered in blood and unless I'm very much mistaken, brains."

"You're kidding me?" I asked.

"No, mate. We have the murder weapon and you have the key witness, all we need now is to find the suspect and it's another clear up for team two."

Despite feeling shattered, the news was elating. In that moment, I knew why I did this job rather than any other.

"You told the DCI?" I asked.

"Oh, yes," he replied.

"Well done, mate; great work," I replied.

I hung up and wandered back into the chalet where Julie and Nicola were still getting everything sorted. I thought the circumstances had presented me with one more golden opportunity. I took Tracey outside, lit a cigarette and handed it to her.

"Nice, innit," she said, referring to the countryside stretching out in the darkness.

"Yeah it's nice, this part of the world. You been here before?" I asked.

She laughed.

"Don' be stupi'. I ain't never been out'a London. Where are we? It too' fuckin' for ever."

"We're in a place called Buckfastleigh. It's in Devon," I replied.

She nodded.

"Chris, I gonna need tha' drin'," she said.

It was just what I wanted her to say.

"Tracey, darling, I'll tell you what. I'll get you a drink, just a small one, if you can tell me where Danny is?"

"I dunno, honest. I dunno. Last time I saw him, he sai' he wa' goin' awa'," she replied.

"Where to?" I asked.

"Didn't mean nuffin to me," she replied.

"So he did say something?" I asked.

She nodded.

"Try to remember, drinkee drinkee," I said teasingly.

"I dunno. The Kiracs had sorte' it ou'. He had to go to the fat koon in 'eaven. Summit like tha'," she replied.

"The fat koon? Is that what you've just said?" I asked.

She nodded.

"That means nothing to me," I said.

"Me, too. Tha' is wot he sai'. He was goin' to the ila' koon."

"Did Danny know where he was going? I asked.

"No, he just sai' the fat koon or ila koon. I thin' he was a bit worried, in case they decided to stiff him," she replied.

I scratched my head; it meant nothing to me.

Chapter 65

I slept deep and long. The knowledge that we had solved that case and that Buster was in the clear meant that, for the first time in ages, I could relax a little. Now all I had to do was to save my marriage and hope that Wendy wasn't pregnant. If those two ships came home I'd be laughing. It was also two hundred and eighty-four hours since my last score, or twelve days. The stomach cramps and diarrhoea had only lasted four or five days and if I am being honest, the whole thing had been so much easier than I'd thought it would be. The fact we'd picked up this job had been really helpful too, because it took my mind off it. This morning felt good; this morning felt like the first day of the rest of my life.

Over a very late breakfast everyone was tired but happy. If the forensics came back on the ice pick, we'd have solved the case itself, leaving us with what was called in the trade, a manhunt. I told everyone about Tracey's claim that Danny was in 'the ila or fuck koon and in heaven' but they looked at me blankly.

We were going to pop back to the holiday park and make sure Tracey had everything we needed, then we would head back to London. Samantha said she thought we'd be back within forty-eight hours and that it might be easier for two of us just to stay down, at least for a few days. She was right. There was no way that Tracey was going to be able to cope and it wasn't fair to leave sixteen-year-old Leigh in charge, even if she was to all intents and purposes the responsible adult.

Julie quickly pointed out that she had other commitments. I didn't blame her. Looking after six children really wasn't her thing. I appreciated Nicola volunteering but explained that we'd probably all have to take it in turns; after all, looking after Tracey was going to be a marathon, not a sprint. Julie thought it might be useful to tell the local Old Bill. She was right of course, and I was disappointed I hadn't thought about doing so earlier.

After breakfast we agreed to meet again in an hour and be packed and ready to go. I had several calls to make, the first to the DCI, which I was going to enjoy immensely. He seemed really happy; he also delivered some more excellent news. Although officially we had to wait for toxicology, the finding of the Sonia Rider post-mortem was that she had died from a heroin overdose and, therefore, her death was no longer being treated as suspicious.

"CIB had someone at the special because of the death after police contact angle, but they're happy that there's no more to it. They'll want to interview you and Pod at some stage, but that's not a priority. They've got more important things to do this morning, as you know, Chris."

I had no idea what he was talking about and told him so.

"About an hour ago, they nicked the DC from Bethnal Green when he landed at Gatwick," the DCI declared.

454

I could barely speak. Why in God's name had they done that? We'd solved this murder and it was nothing to do with Buster bloody Edwards. My mind was racing and the DCI was still speaking, but I wasn't listening.

"Sorry, boss, can you say that all again. My signal is shite, we're in the middle of nowhere."

"I said they're putting him on an ID parade this morning with Mrs Amasanti. That's after they've spun his home address, which they're doing now."

"Fucking hell, boss. I thought you said that you were going to speak to them and tell them that he's not connected to this murder," I said, trying to hide the sheer desperation in my voice.

"I did, but they said they were going to go with it anyway. I get the impression that it didn't really matter about this murder and that they had their own lines of enquiry. They seem absolutely convinced that he was at the victim's address after the murder and to be honest, Chris, I agree. Someone was there; someone claimed to be Old Bill to the debt collector guys. And Mrs Amasanti didn't imagine that she saw someone leaving the address. Oh, and we've had the forensics back from that scene: someone definitely wiped the laptop with polish, Mr Sheen's multi-surface cleaner to be precise. I mean, you've been there, do you honestly think our victim had ever, ever polished anything in his life?"

I was about to contradict the DCI and tell him that I'd never actually been inside the flat, but I stopped myself just in case any of my prints were in there.

I chatted with the DCI about whether we should leave someone with Tracey and about how and whether Witness Protection would be able to assist us, but I lost all my enthusiasm.

When I hung up, I thought through my options. Everything seemed to hinge on whether Mrs Amasanti picked Buster out. He would obviously deny being there and if she didn't identify him, there'd be no evidence and they would have to NFA him, whatever they thought privately. But if she did pick him out, then they'd charge him. It probably wouldn't be straight away because they'd need the Attorney General's consent.

I did toy with the idea of keeping quiet and letting him take the rap, but only for the briefest of moments and then only to try to imagine how I would feel. I remember many years ago, Sarah's boyfriend Paul was going to fit me up, and when Sarah found out about it, she went to CIB to protect me. In so doing, she destroyed her own career and also risked getting herself seriously in trouble, but she'd done the right thing and there wasn't a day that went by when I wasn't grateful to her for what she did. That was real bravery, not a bullshit macho kind of bravery, but proper solid valour. Now, eighteen years later, it was my turn to do a similar thing, but I was actually going to step forward for a man I didn't know and whom I'd never met.

I felt really subdued.

We went back to the holiday park and spent several hours with Tracey, then Samantha and I drove back via Exeter, where we called into the Police Headquarters to let them know what was going on. They were a friendly bunch and put a marker on their system to treat any calls to the holiday park as urgent.

The more time I spent with Samantha, the more I liked her. She was one of those people that you don't think are particularly bright and then they come out with a flash of inspired thinking and you think 'where the fuck did that come from?'.

I did occasionally forget that she was a woman. I couldn't help it; because all my life I'd been wired to know the difference between a man and a woman, the subconscious part of me just could not accept her as female. This fault usually manifested itself by my addressing her as 'mate', which I would never do to a female colleague. Samantha seemed fine with it; I think she knew my heart was in the right place.

We were just passing the Heston Services on the M4. I was having a trip down memory lane, because many years ago something significant had happened there when I was a young sprog on his way to Hendon, when my phone rang. It was Nicola who, with Julie, should have been a couple of hours behind us.

"Hi, Nicola. Where are you?" I asked.

"We're still in bleeding Devon. I put petrol in the car but it's a diesel. We had to wait for the AA to come out but I only put like five quid in before I realised so when he got here, the AA man said it should be all right," she replied.

"So you're on your way, then? I asked.

"No, we've turned round. We're on our way back," she replied.

"What have you forgotten?" I asked.

"Nothing," she replied.

"Has Tracey called? What's fucking happened?" I asked.

"No, she hasn't. We've just realised something that's quite important when we passed a road sign a few miles back," she said.

"What?" I asked.

"Where Danny is," she replied.

"What? How do you know?" I asked.

"Because, babes, we think he might be in Devon, and only about twenty miles away from his missus and our witness," she replied.

"What? How do you know that?" I asked.

"Because we've just realised, well Julie's just realised, 'the fuck koon in heaven' is almost certainly Ilfracombe, in Devon. We just passed a sign for Ilfracombe and the penny dropped."

"Where is that, exactly?" I asked.

"It's on the north Devon coast. It's a little way away from where she is, but too close for comfort."

"Tracey's not going to be going out of the holiday camp, is she? I think we're probably safe but you're right to turn round, sorry. I'll let the DCI know, call me when you arrive," I said.

I checked my watch; it was seven o'clock. I knew that the last thing Nicola and Julie wanted to do was to go back to Buckfastleigh and I really appreciated their professionalism.

I was just about to dial the DCI when he called me.

"Hi, boss; there's been a development," I said.

"Oh, you've heard? Can you believe it? Talk about all happening at once," he said.

"I don't think we're talking about the same thing," I said. "You go first."

"It looks like your man Bigga has been arrested by Immigration; his real name is Sylvester Jackson. He's at Carter Street police station and once they've served the requisite papers, he'll be on the great silver bird back to Jamaica. Get over there will you, see what he's got to say and whether there's enough to nick him."

"Fucking hell, boss," I replied, "isn't anyone else free? I'm out on my feet."

"Sorry, Chris. They're all tucked up. I'm trying to manage about twenty-five different things at once. And I've got CIB breaking my balls about Buster. I'll tell you what, why don't you send Julie and Nicola?"

"Because they're on their way to the fuck koon in heaven," I replied.

Chapter 66

As we drove over to Carter Street nick, which, incidentally, since its rebuild was actually called Walworth Road police station, Samantha and I talked about the feast and famine nature of murder squad work.

Samantha said that in the first month after she'd joined, she'd barely had enough to do to fill two hours work a day and then contrasted that to the last two weeks, where we'd worked almost flat out, with sixteen-hour days and no time off. I said I thought it destroyed your social life but Samantha pointed out that wasn't really an issue for her, as she didn't have one.

She asked me whether I had an understanding wife. I said that I did, but then told her that we were probably getting divorced. It was the first time I'd told anyone and it felt simultaneously a very normal and terribly sad thing to say. I also thought the fact that no one had told her that I had a girlfriend called Wendy really demonstrated just how disconnected she was from the rest of the team.

Samantha told me that the girls had invited her out next week to lunch and asked me whether I thought she should go. I was a little surprised at her question and told her so. I mean, how could she moan about not feeling part of the team, and then turn down an invitation to go to a team social event? She agreed with me, but explained how stressful she would find the whole situation. I didn't quite understand but let the matter pass.

I called Jeff to see if he had any more information on the Bigga arrest; he was in the Peacock and I couldn't hear him until he stepped outside.

"Immigration did some searches yesterday on several council flats which were being illegally subleased by a Nigerian OCN and picked up over twenty-five tenants who were illegals. They're in police cells all over the place, but the Bigga chap is at Carter Street; the DCI said you were on your way."

"We are," I replied, "but how did anyone know he was our man?"

"He told the arresting officer," Jeff replied.

"Why the fuck would he do that?" I asked.

"So they'll let him stay in the country, I assume. You know, if he is a witness in a murder case they'll hardly deport him, will they. And then, I'm guessing, he'll try and claim asylum," Jeff replied.

~~~

Dealing with prisoners is usually a really slow process that requires a mindset immune to the progress of time, a bit like fishing. I had learnt over the years that the worse thing to be, when dealing with prisoners, was in a hurry, because nothing would occur quickly. This particular case, however, was the complete opposite. For a start, our man Sylvester Jackson had already been booked in; secondly, as he was a potential witness, he didn't require a solicitor nor, therefore, did he need to go into a legal consultation period; and finally, and most amazingly of all, Immigration already had an English–Patois translator at the nick.

Within thirty minutes of arriving we had our witness, his interpreter, a platter of jerk chicken from the Jamaican takeaway next to the nick, and we were all ready to go.

I'd interviewed Patois speakers several times. It was the strangest of languages, because unlike French or German, you could understand most of what was being said, particularly if the speaker wanted to make it easy for you.

Sylvester was a very heavily set, Afro-Caribbean man in his late twenties. He had a natural air of intimidation, born no doubt out of the toughest of Kingston ghetto upbringings.

After thanking us for his dinner, the first thing out of Sylvester's mouth was a question as to whether if he helped us, we could stop his imminent extradition. I had learnt over the years that the one thing you didn't do in these situations was lie. So I gave him an honest answer. No, I couldn't stop his deportation, but he might have to come back to the UK on an expense-free trip at a later date to give evidence, if the case went to trial. That seemed to keep him happy.

I asked him what he had to tell us and he spoke through his interpreter uninterrupted for the next ten minutes.

Sylvester said he'd been living in Dagenham at 73 Palmerston Road for about the last four months. He occasionally had friends over for parties and some of them would bring drugs, mainly cannabis, to smoke. He didn't like it, but what could he do to stop it? Shortly after he started having these parties, an Irish guy called Danny came to his house to sell drugs to his guests. He didn't like it, but again, what could he do? This wasn't his country and he thought perhaps that if he said anything, Danny would report him to Immigration. Then about a month ago, he met a guy called Gary, he didn't know his surname. Gary had a business proposition concerning the supply of drugs to his guests, but Sylvester wasn't interested because he didn't want anything to do with drugs. Shortly afterwards, one Thursday night, by chance Gary and Danny were at his house together. Danny said he needed some gear and Gary agreed to go to get some and told him that he'd be back. Seconds after Gary left, Danny did too. As he was leaving, Danny picked up Sylvester's pick from his ice bucket, which was on the bar. Danny said to Sylvester 'I need to lend this, I'll bring it later'. Sylvester had never seen either of them again, but when he heard about the murder he realised that it must have happened after the two had left his house. He heard from a friend of a friend that

Danny had used his ice pick to stab Gary, which had made him very angry.

Sylvester's account was full of evasion, fake indignation and half-truths, which wasn't a surprise. After all, he was hardly going to admit serious criminal offences, was he? But the remaining strands of truth did merge nicely into the account provided by Tracey Manning, and the mention of the ice pick was, well, icing on the cake. We would need to get Sylvester to identify the ice pick as the one taken from his house.

Sylvester revealed one final piece of information, which fitted nicely into the jigsaw. He told us that on the night of the murder, Danny had been with another white male and that the second person was wearing a red coat. This reconciled with the information from the van driver who had nearly run over the two males who were running away from the scene.

Sylvester denied ever hearing the name Tony Pascal, knew nothing about the theft of a handbag and looked completely blank when the name Kirac was mentioned. It was the only time I was actually convinced he was telling us the whole truth.

When Sylvester had finished, through the interpreter I explained I was going to ask a number of questions and invite him to comment. Before the interpreter had said a word, Sylvester nodded; he clearly understood more than he let on.

"Sylvester, I suggest that you were running a shebeen, an illegal drinking club at 73 Palmerston Road."

No, it wasn't a club; he just had a few friends around most evenings, he replied through the interpreter.

"I suggest you allowed people to take drugs at your club; it was one of the main reasons people went there."

No, he told them not to but everyone ignored him, he replied. That was a big lie because no one would ignore Sylvester.

"Danny used to sell drugs in your club," I said.

It wasn't a club, it was his house, but yes, Danny did sell drugs there.

"I think you were fed up with Danny selling drugs in your club and you arranged for Gary to start supplying to your customers?"

Curiously, Sylvester replied 'no comment' without using the interpreter.

I realised that if I progressed this line of enquiry, I really should caution Sylvester and offer him a solicitor. Such a move would, however, just confuse everything, so I decided to call a close to the interview. After all, we had the information we wanted.

I was happy. I'd been right all along about the important part played by the shebeen. What the original connection between Gary and Bigga was, I had no idea, nor did I know where Gary was getting his drugs. Perhaps it was someone like Tony Pascal after all? With that said, it could have been anyone.

It was nearly ten when we pulled out of the back yard of the nick and into the traffic going towards the Elephant and Castle. Samantha was driving, in between yawns.

I gave the DCI a quick call to update him. He seemed amazed that we'd finished so early, pleased with the consistency of the information we'd obtained and how everything was coming together. I suggested that after a decent night's sleep, Samantha and I would get down to Devon to try to trace Danny Manning. He agreed, but what he said next changed my plans completely.

"They're going to charge the DC from Bethnal Green tonight. They reckon they've got him bang to rights."

I felt sick.

Chapter 67

My time of reckoning had arrived.

I sat in the downstairs reception at Jubilee House in Putney waiting for the detective superintendent to come and collect me for the eleven o'clock appointment, which I'd made first thing that morning.

While I was waiting, Barry from the SIS called to say that they'd reviewed the tapes from Friday 10th January (the day of Gary's murder) and he could tell me that Tony Pascal received a call really early on, told his wife that he had to use a secure line to make a call and went out for nearly two and a half hours.

When he returned, his wife asked him whether everything was all right and he replied that he had called in a favour. So it sounded to me like the underworld drums had been beating and Tony Pascal did know about the murder. I asked Barry whether it was on that day that they'd heard the conversation about the Audi and Attlee House. Barry confirmed that it was.

I had decided to tell CIB Detective Superintendent Adam Stanley everything, as there seemed little point in a selective admission. I knew I'd been lucky to get away with being on the gear for so long. I'd probably known on some level that eventually I would come a cropper. I would be suspended by the end of the day and I'd have a few months, probably six, to sort my life out. Perhaps I could write a book? After all, I'd have to find some way of earning a living and I did have a number of great stories to tell.

I hadn't heard from Jackie in days and had spent last night at Wendy's. She was so excited about the possibility that she was pregnant and I have to confess, I was genuinely pleased for her and just hoped she was right. She'd already taken two pregnancy tests; both confirmed that she was pregnant, but it was terribly early days. Rather worryingly, in just two days she'd already managed to buy several things for the baby, including a small plastic bath and a bottle steriliser.

"Hi, Chris," Adam Stanley said, holding out his hand.

"Hi, boss," I said, standing up and shaking it.

He indicated to the security guard to open the side turnstile and let me in and we made idle chit chat while he ushered me into a lift and up to the fourth floor. I realised that he was taking me to the canteen. I'd have rather had had the conversation in a more private location, but I was confident he would relocate us when he realised the gravity of my declaration.

Having got two coffees, we took seats by the window overlooking Putney Bridge. I took a deep breath, but Adam spoke first.

"I guess you're intrigued to find out what's been going on, old sport?" he asked.

I nodded. I might as well let him talk and then interject at the appropriate moment.

"We started to look at DC Edwards because of the information which you provided about the Gary Odiham murder. As I told you previously, he had passed an integrity test at Romford with flying colours so we never suspected that he was a thief. But what was he doing in Gary's flat the night after the murder?"

"Are we absolutely sure he was in the flat?" I asked, absolutely sure that he wasn't.

"Oh yes, no doubt about it, old sport. ID is legally established. Mrs Amasanti picked him out immediately on the ID parade. She confirmed that he was without doubt the person she'd seen leave the flat at six o'clock in the morning after the two bouncer type guys had called. They'd obviously been watching the address, waiting for Gary to appear, without realising that he was never coming home."

"Which, if it's true, also eliminates them as suspects for the murder itself," I added.

"Yes, indeed, Chris. Anyway, we nicked Ronnie Edwards in Arrivals at Gatwick after he and his family landed back from Madeira. Mrs Edwards is really ill; she looked dreadful. We were very discreet about it and gave her and the kids a lift to her parents in Braintree, but she was devastated," the DCI explained.

I felt awful; I really should have stopped this sooner.

"We found a handgun in the garage at his home address in Brentwood, it wasn't particularly well hidden. He obviously wasn't expecting to be caught," the DCI said.

"What? I beg your pardon?" I said.

"We found a Tokarev handgun in his garage; fully loaded, well actually I think one bullet was missing. It was in a tool kit. I assume he put it there as it was the one place neither his wife nor kids would ever look, you know, by accident."

What the fuck was going on?

"Fucking hell," I muttered.

What did this surprising development mean?

"We interviewed DC Edwards under caution and he's put his hands up. He was in a right state, crying his eyes out. Difficult not to feel a bit sorry for him, I don't think he'd any idea it would end up like this. The good news is that I think we'll be able to get him to turn Queen's. I mean, he is just a tiny bit player, but his testimony could send down some very serious criminals. We got him a brief who we knew would give him the right advice and explained that if he wanted to stay out of prison, he had to tell us the truth, the whole truth and nothing but, from the get-go."

Adam continued with his story unaware that I was in a state of total shock and utter bewilderment.

"DC Edwards said that one Friday morning two weeks ago, he got a phone call from his uncle, who had learnt that Gary Odiham had been murdered. DC Edwards immediately knew the name because by sheer coincidence, he had turned his flat over the previous morning.

"His uncle wanted him to go round to the flat just to check that there wasn't a firearm hidden there. He didn't think there would be but he just wanted him to make sure.

"DC Edwards admitted that his uncle paid very well for the occasional favour and that previously he'd done PNC checks and CRIMINT searches for him. Not many and not very often, perhaps one or two a year. In fact, he started to talk about a death by dangerous driving case from a few years ago; two people were run over at a bus stop in Chelsea. Apparently, his uncle wanted the court case scuppered.

"Anyway, I digress. DC Edwards said he thought going to the flat would be money for old rope because by chance he'd only just been involved in a search at the address and was therefore entirely confident there wasn't a firearm there. Of course, he knew he could get his hands on the keys very easily and could even afford to leave the odd fingerprint, as he'd legitimately been in the flat only a few hours earlier."

I was starting to realise that if Buster had actually done this, then I didn't need to say anything, but there were going to be some glaring anomalies, like if all this was true, then why did Buster cleanse the flat of prints?

"Anyway, there was a handgun there, hidden under the pillow on the bed. DC Edwards was really surprised and assumed the occupier had brought the gun home after their search. So he took possession of it, took it home and hid it in his garage. When he told his uncle, he was beside himself with anger ...

"Sorry to interrupt you in full flow, but the uncle is ..." I hesitated.

"Tony Pascal. Tony is DC Edwards' mother's older brother, well half-brother, you know what these families are like."

"Of course. And that's the connection to supplying the City," I said.

"I'm not with you, old sport?" Adam said.

"It doesn't matter for now, please go on. You were saying that Tony Pascal was annoyed but why? I mean, DC Edwards found the handgun? Wasn't that what he sent Buster round there to do, I mean, to recover a handgun?" I said.

"His uncle wasn't annoyed with DC Edwards but with Gary. You see, when Gary Odiham went grovelling to Tony Pascal because he'd stolen his wife's handbag, Tony gave clear instructions that he was to use the money to rent a safe deposit box, in Gary's own name, and then lay the handgun down there. DC Edwards said the arrangements were that if Tony ever needed the firearm, Gary had to go to the box, get it out and deliver it wherever, immediately. Of course, Gary didn't. Instead he decided to hold the handgun himself and keep the money that he would have had to spend renting the box. Apparently, DC Edwards said when his uncle found out, he said that if someone hadn't already murdered Gary, he would have done it himself."

"Hang on. Fuck me. Tony Pascal got Gary to look after his firearm?"

I was desperately trying to remember something Pod had told me about the handgun used to murder the prison officer at the off-licence.

"Yeah. Well Pascal didn't want to keep it himself because of the risk of getting caught with it. As a convicted blagger, he's a prohibited person for life, so he'd be looking at at least five if he got caught in possession," Adam replied.

"What make of handgun was the one you recovered from DC Edwards?" I asked.

"A TT, or to give it its full name, a Tokarev eight millimetre, which had been made safe and then re-bored to a nine millimetre," the DCI replied.

"Are you aware that a Tokarev nine millimetre was used in the Tim Hughes murder, the prison officer from HMP Pentonville who was going out with Tony Pascal's daughter, that was a Tokarev," I said.

"You're kidding me?" Adam replied.

Chapter 68

As soon as I'd told Adam about the link to the prison officer murder, he'd hurried off to make a number of phone calls, but asked me to hang around, as he had one last thing to discuss.

I tried to find my old mate Dave but he was out and about, so I sat there reading an old copy of The Job newspaper and sending a few texts for the best part of an hour. I was just about to give up and set off for Arbour Square, when Adam reappeared.

"Busy?" I said, knowing that all hell would be breaking loose behind the scenes.

"A little," he replied, with a wry smile.

"I'll get off, boss. I need to get to Arbour Square; I've got so much to do. The Gary Odiham murder is now a manhunt, but we've got a good idea where the suspect is so, if it's all right with you …"

"Before you go, Chris. There is one thing that's mystifying me."

"Go on," I said, but I'd suddenly started to worry.

"DC Edwards says that when he went to the flat to look for the handgun, he was in the lounge when someone else came into the flat."

"Did he see who?" I asked, way too quickly.

"No, he was really worried, shitting himself, I think, were his exact words. The lounge door was half closed and he made a pretty futile attempt to hide behind the door in the hope that when the

475

person, whoever it was, entered the room, there was just a chance he could remain out of their view behind it. Anyway, the mystery intruder never entered the lounge. DC Edwards reckons he heard them searching the rest of the flat and then someone else was knocking really hard at the front door. He thought he was going to be caught bang to rights but somehow, and much to his surprise, a few seconds later it all went quiet and he heard the unidentified intruder leave. He waited ten minutes and made his escape. Well that's his account, anyway."

"Did DC Edwards find the victim's stash?" I asked.

"Well, if he did he's not telling us. And when you consider that he's telling us a lot of things about which we had absolutely no idea, on balance I think he's probably being truthful," Adam replied.

"I wonder," I said, tempting Adam to ask me what, which he obligingly did.

"Do you think it could have been Gary's girlfriend who was searching the flat?" I asked.

"Who, Sonia? The one that overdosed at the weekend," he asked.

"Yeah, that would make sense. She could have been searching for, in fact she could have even found Gary's stash," I suggested hopefully.

Of course, my idea was almost perfect as with Sonia dead, no one would ever be able to prove anything different.

"No, that's not right, is it. Remember whoever it was showed out, didn't they. The debt collector guy, Munroe was it, said he saw some bloke holding what he thought was a police warrant card. Though, come to think of it, I'm not certain he knew what he'd actually seen."

"Oh yeah, of course. So it must have been DC Edwards who showed out, mustn't it?" I replied.

"I guess," Adam replied, but I could tell he was unconvinced.

"If DC Edwards was right, and someone else was in the flat, I bet that was Sonia; which is why she was able to deal for a short while after Gary's murder, because she'd recovered his stash. It all makes perfect sense," I said.

I could almost hear his mind ticking over.

"Yeah of course; that does all fit, you're right, old sport. And, yes, of course it was DC Edwards who showed out. That's the only explanation, of course, of course," Adam said.

This time he sounded absolutely certain. Under the circumstances, the detective superintendent had come to the only possible conclusion.

~~~

As I didn't expect to leave of my own volition, when I'd travelled to Jubilee House I'd taken public transport. Now I spurned the

Underground, choosing instead to walk at least part of the way back to Arbour Square nick, because I needed time to get my head around events.

In the end I walked all the way. It took me two and a half hours, but by the time I was back at the office, I'd worked out everything.

The easiest thing to understand was the murder of Gary Odiham, who had been killed by Danny Manning because he'd started to sell drugs in an area of London where Danny was 'licensed' by the Kiracs. I didn't believe much of what Bigga had said but I did believe him when he said the attack didn't take part in the shebeen, so my assessment that the assault had occurred in Palmerston Road within sight of the BP garage had probably been accurate. Gary had run to the garage in the hope that he could get medical attention there, but when the ice pick had entered his brain, he had less than a minute to live.

Danny had been stupid enough to tell his wife, a mentally unstable alcoholic, what he'd done. Whether he was trying to impress her or not, he made an even worse decision when he pointed out to Tracey where he'd discarded the ice pick.

Without Tracey's intervention, the chances were we would never have solved the murder. Now we had the murder weapon, if Danny's prints were on it and Gary's DNA, the case wouldn't be completely reliant on her evidence, which would be good, because I thought she'd make a dreadful witness.

Somehow, we'd also managed to solve the murder of the prison officer, Tim Hughes. Though quite how this had happened was more opaque.

In one of the oddest motives I'd ever come across, Tony Pascal had murdered the prison officer for no more serious a reason than he was mucking his precious daughter around. He'd not involved anyone else but done the deed himself, quietly and effectively. On his motorbike, Tony Pascal had followed the prison officer from HMP Pentonville and then shot the poor lad when he stopped at an off-licence on his way home.

It was the perfect hit except for two small mistakes; firstly, and most crucially, he kept the handgun. Tony Pascal was a fool; he should have thrown it in the Thames, always the safest option. In my experience, however, some villains got attached to their 'lucky' weapons and didn't like to dispose of them, especially if they had the piece for years and successfully used it a couple of times.

That was the favour that Gary had done for Tony Pascal to compensate for stealing his wife's handbag. Tony exploited the opportunity this presented and got Gary to agree to have the firearm 'laid down' at a safe deposit box, which was rented in Gary's name to hide the real owner. This was a fairly safe option, particularly as Tony and Gary were to all intents and purposes unconnected. Besides, Tony could easily make a quick call and order the handgun to be retrieved if it was needed again.

Choosing a drug addict and low-level dealer was Tony's second mistake. Gary never bothered putting the handgun in a safe deposit box; instead, he hid it in his flat alongside his stash.

The arrangements to lay the handgun down were picked up on a telephone call that was intercepted, or perhaps they came up on the probe being run by SIS.

Whoever it was, the chaps who were listening mistakenly thought whatever was being discussed was drugs and not a firearm, probably because they had sufficient information to identify Gary and research would quickly have recognised him as a low-level dealer. The intelligence was passed to Nick Charles, who executed the search warrant but found nothing.

A few hours later, poor Gary was murdered and news of the event soon reached Tony Pascal. He was worried for two reasons; first, just in case Gary hadn't done as he had been instructed and opened a safe deposit box in which to keep the gun, but second, and probably of more concern to Tony, was the thought that the Kiracs might erroneously think that he was trying to muscle in on one of their areas.

Tony called in a favour from his sister's boy and Buster went to Gary's flat to ascertain whether the handgun was still there. So all the time I'd been searching the flat, Buster was hiding in the lounge, which of course, I had never entered.

And what's more, Mrs Amasanti had been right all along; she'd obviously missed me legging it and, in fact, had seen Buster leaving the flat, and had quite correctly identified him as being one of the police officers from the day before.

I had never had much to do with firearms, so when I found and relocated the handgun at Gary's, I didn't recognise the make as a Tokarev. Even if I had, the information wouldn't have meant anything to me. Nor did I know until Adam Stanley told me, that a Tokarev is often referred to as a TT, which is what had come up on the SIS probe.

Sonia had known what was going on. She knew about the handbag theft, which she told us, and she knew that Gary had agreed to hide the firearm, information she was too afraid to impart.

The five grand that Gary stole allowed him to extend his dealing, and one of the mistakes I'd made was originally thinking that Bigga was supplying Gary, when in fact, it was probably the other way around.

There were still one or two things that concerned me, the most significant of which was Gary's mobile phone billing and the presence of an incoming call from my mobile. With that said, if the ice pick came up trumps on the forensics, they would probably NFA any further enquiries on the billing.

It was strange though, and the more I thought about it, the stranger it became. The thing was, for a few days in February a combination of curious circumstances and sheer coincidences had irrevocably linked the lives of eight people. Gary was my drug dealer, but he was also supplying to Bigga, who knew Danny Manning. Gary had stolen Mrs Pascal's handbag, which unwittingly connected him to Tony Pascal and the murder of the prison officer. It also allowed him to escalate his drug dealing, an activity that brought him to his early demise. Sonia was Gary's girlfriend, but because he was murdered and I gave her the money, she overdosed. Buster had just searched Gary's house when his uncle, Tony Pascal, called and asked him to do a favour that, once again, linked directly to the prison officer murder. As a result of everything, Gary was murdered, Sonia dead, Mr Pascal and Danny Manning charged with murder and Buster became the Met's first police officer supergrass. And then there was me.

I knew I didn't deserve to walk away scot-free from the Buster debacle, but in life sometimes you get a mound of excrement and sometimes you get a fortunate break. I'd got the former a few times. I'd been blown up in an IRA bomb, kidnapped by a woman driven insane by the loss of her son and fitted up with racist material, but this time I got the lucky break. I wasn't going to complain; next time, I'd probably get the pile of shit again.

Epilogue

14th June 2003

The Central Criminal Court, London EC1

Practically everything I had done for the last six months had been designed with the sole intention of bringing about this moment.

I was inside the Old Bailey sitting outside court twelve in the communal waiting area. Lounging lazily opposite me was the principal prosecution witness, Tracey Manning, and next to her, her seventeen-year-old-daughter, Leigh.

We were in the modern part of the court under a plain white ceiling and strip lighting. There was a business-like atmosphere, with gowned officials whispering to one another in hushed but urgent tones and then busily going about their business. Occasionally, an usher would step outside his or her court and call a particular name to summon the individual to give testimony. Members of the public in this part of the building were few and far between and fell into two loose categories: witnesses, who always looked nervous, and the victim's closest family, who were usually in a state of permanent shock because most of the victims in these cases had been murdered and their loved ones were in the process of finding out, in the most graphic detail, what had happened to them.

Earlier that morning when I'd gone to the toilet, I had experienced the most surreal of moments, being simultaneously flanked on my left by a former Radio 1 DJ and on my right by a Conservative peer, who were standing both at the urinal and on trial.

Tracey was about to give evidence against her husband, who was standing trial for the murder of Gary Odiham on 10th January 2003 in Dock Lane, Dagenham. My team had been assigned the investigation and after several weeks, during which we'd made little progress, Tracey had picked up her phone, dialled 999 and put her husband in the frame. He had, she said, admitted it all to her and she even told us where the murder weapon was hidden.

That we had managed to get Tracey to this point was nothing short of a miracle, but even under normal circumstances I wouldn't have rated her chances in the box. Some of these defence barristers were almost as clever as they thought they were. In contrast, our poor witness bordered on being educationally subnormal. This morning, the situation was even worse than it might otherwise have been, because Tracey was drunk.

We'd brought her and her daughter Leigh up to London the day before, leaving two of my unfortunate colleagues in Devon to babysit the remaining five children. We'd spent the previous night in a hotel in Enfield. At breakfast this morning, Leigh had arrived to declare that her mum had changed her mind, gone back to bed and wasn't going to court.

I'd dispatched Julie to her bedroom to force our star witness first into the shower, next into clothes, and finally into our waiting car. Leigh then explained to me that the previous evening, after we'd all gone to our rooms, her mum had got up and with her feminine charm, managed to get the night duty manager to open the bar and fire up the Jacuzzi, where she had whiled away the night drinking champagne and having sex. Leigh thought her mum had crawled back into her bed at about five thirty.

I was furious with Tracey, but a bit of me also understood. She simply couldn't deal with the enormity of having to give evidence against her husband, who was not only charged with murder, but who was also a member of London's most feared criminal network. In a strange way, this was a characteristic climax to one of the toughest of journeys.

Just after the murder, we'd taken Tracey and her family into protective custody because her old man, the murderer, was part of a powerful and infamous North London crime family called the Kiracs. We'd relocated her to a holiday site in Devon and two months later moved them again, this time into permanent social housing in Plymouth.

Apart from a few happy memories, the family left behind at the holiday site a bill for fifteen thousand pounds worth of damage to the top-of-the-range luxury log cabin. Every bed was soiled, every carpet needed replacing, every curtain rail was pulled out of the wall and every wall had been drawn on. On top of which, and completely understandably, the owners of the site had charged the Metropolitan Police for lost rent while the chalet was being repaired.

When we delivered them to their new home, a scabby council estate with burnt-out cars and evidence of drug abuse littered in every stairwell and landing, I knew they'd actually be much happier, which in fact they were.

They'd only lasted three weeks in witness protection before they were deemed to have broken too many rules and expelled. At which point, they became my responsibility again. It was probably the most challenging six months of my police career. It had nothing to do with solving crime and everything to do with making sure this star witness stood in the witness box. To that end, all my efforts had been directed.

Although we'd arrived at the Old Bailey later than planned, we actually had plenty of time. The case was listed to start at ten thirty and had done so, but the next forty minutes was spent selecting the jury, and the next hour in opening speeches.

As time edged slowly by, Tracey started to sober up. We got her sandwiches and coffee and delivered repeated assurances that she would be fine and that in a couple of days, she would be able to put her past behind her and get on with the rest of her life. Whenever she went to the toilet, which was every fifteen minutes, I sent my colleague Julie with her to make sure she didn't try to do anything stupid.

Tracey's daughter Leigh was also scheduled to give evidence because she had overheard her stepfather talking about the murder with her mum. Leigh was everything her mother was not; she was calm, sensible and sober, and I anticipated that she would make an excellent witness. I don't know how we would have coped without Leigh over the last six months because to all intents and purposes, this young lady was the matriarch, a role she had assumed at far too early an age. I will always remember her with the greatest respect and fondness.

At about twelve fifteen, the door to court twelve swung open and the usher called 'Tracey Manning' twice. To this day, I have never seen anyone more nervous than poor Tracey at that moment. She went to stand but her legs gave way and she had to be carried the short distance to the court entrance by Julie and her daughter.

Julie sat back down next to me and grimaced.

"She's still drunk; she stinks of it," she said.

"I know. We've done everything we can," I replied.

"I never want to do this again, Chris. This has been the hardest six months of my life. I was not cut out to look after six kids and a bleeding yappy dog. I am meant to be a detective, not a nanny," Julie protested.

I looked around to make sure Leigh hadn't heard and was glad to see she'd wandered off.

"I know, Julie. You've done a fantastic job. I couldn't have done it without you," I said.

"How much will Jeff be able to tell us?" Julie asked.

Jeff was a detective sergeant on our team and he was dealing with the court case in the sense that he was physically sitting in court alongside the CPS representative to respond to questions raised by prosecution counsel. He could do this because he wasn't himself a witness and as the office manager, he had an excellent knowledge of the case.

"Enough," I replied.

The door to court twelve swung open and Tracey stumbled out; she'd only been inside about two minutes! Julie and I jumped up and Tracey started sobbing her heart out. We collected her and sat her down on the nearest chair.

"What happened?" Julie asked.

"They've fuckin' thro' me ou'," Tracey replied, stating the fairly obvious.

I looked across at Julie. We both had a fairly good idea why; the only question that remained was whether the case had also been thrown out, because if that had happened, we had a real problem.

~~~

Sometimes it's great to be wrong and this was just such an occasion. Tracey hadn't been thrown out, she'd been asked to wait outside while the court discussed a legal matter.

Jeff emerged less than a minute later and took me to one side.

"After Tracey had taken the oath, prosecution counsel asked her to identify her husband to the court, which she did by pointing at him in the dock. Then the prosecution asked her when she first met Danny Manning, to which she replied, "the fuckin' day he got ou' o' the nick", and that was the end of that trial. Judge has ordered a new jury to be sworn in tomorrow and instructed witnesses to be back here at midday," he said.

Juries are not allowed to know a defendant has previous convictions, so Tracey's reply, which informed them that he had at least one serious previous criminal conviction because he'd just 'got ou' o' the nick', meant the defendant wouldn't get a fair trial. Most importantly, the case was still on and we had another chance to get Tracey to court sober. The only downside was that we had to go through the difficult last twenty-four hours again, but no matter.

~~~

The trial lasted for only two weeks, which is remarkably short for a murder case. The jury unanimously found the defendant guilty after only three hours of deliberation, another extremely short time period. Danny Manning was sentenced to life imprisonment, with a minimum tariff of fifteen years.

After sentence, and over a pint or two in the Magpie and Stump, the pub just opposite the court, Jeff took me through the highlights of Tracey's evidence.

"Nostrils, I've been Old Bill for twenty-nine years and I've never seen such a performance in the box. Tracey's biggest asset was that she was obviously not bright enough to concoct a lie. Everything she said came across as honest and sincere. She was an outstanding prosecution witness who actually did better under cross-examination than she did during evidence-in-chief."

"You know on that first day, when she mentioned that Danny had been in prison, she was drunk, did you realise?" I asked.

"She was only in the box briefly, Nostrils. She slurs her words so much, it's hard to tell. In fact, it was quite grating to listen to," Jeff said.

"I know; her speech sounded permanently garbled because she never finished her words. If a word had three syllables, she'd only pronounce two," I replied.

"The trial had two outstanding moments," Jeff said. "The first was when defence counsel proposed to Tracey that she'd made the defendant's confession up and that her motive for so doing was because she wanted to get out of an unhappy marriage. 'Are you sayin' I don't luv Danny?' Tracey asked, incredulously. 'I am' replied the defence. 'I fuckin' luv that man', at which point she pointed at the defendant and burst into tears. 'I fuckin' luv ya' Danny. Why's ya do it, darlin'?' I luv ya', babe.'"

"God, I bet that went down like a cup of old cold sick with the defence," I said, laughing.

"He couldn't change the subject quick enough," Jeff replied, "but unfortunately, his next line of questioning was equally ill-judged. He asked Tracey whether she'd spent a lot of time with police officers over the last six months. She agreed that she had. Defence asked her whether she'd become emotionally close to anyone in particular. Fucking hell, Nostrils, I was holding my breath for you."

"And what did she say?" I asked, starting to feel both guilty and nervous, which was quite ridiculous, as I'd done absolutely nothing wrong.

"She said that she particularly liked Chris Pritchard; that she listened to whatever you told her. Well, defence obviously thought he'd spotted an opportunity because his next question was whether you'd ever given her any advice about what to say when she gave evidence," Jeff said.

"Oh my God, what did she say?" I asked.

"She said that you had. Defence nearly shat himself with excitement."

"I haven't," I replied innocently.

"Defence asked Tracey how often you'd given her advice about what to say in the witness box. She replied, every time you'd met. And then clarified her answer with a specific number, she said probably a hundred times," Jeff said.

"I've never given her any advice," I replied indignantly.

"Well, defence then reminded the court that the coaching of witnesses is prohibited and that if it is established to have occurred, the activity would constitute a serious legal breach. The judge didn't like that and reminded counsel to stick with questioning the witness and that it was his responsibility to advise the jury on such matters. But of course, the point had been made and you could feel the tension mount as defence delivered his next question. 'Did this police officer, this Detective Sergeant Christopher Pritchard, tell you what to say?'" Jeff said.

"But I didn't," I protested.

I was sure Jeff was enjoying this; he knew he had started to get me worried.

"Tracey replied that you had told her what to say. I was certain that I actually heard several gasps. Then counsel delivered his killer question. 'Mrs Manning, please tell the court exactly what advice DS Pritchard gave you.' I actually don't think Tracey realised the significance of the exchange, which made her casual, almost nonchalant reply even more devastating. Tracey said, 'He's said da me, no ma'er what 'appens, to tell the truff.',," Jeff explained.

I breathed a slight sigh of relief but this was tempered.

"Defence counsel asked what else you had told her. 'Nothing else' she replied. Defence counsel pressed, pointing out that she'd just told the court DS Pritchard had advised her on a hundred occasions about giving evidence. 'I know, I fuckin' did,' she replied. 'And he told me, no ma'er what, just tell 'em the fuckin' truff.'"

"Quite right, too," I said, now more relaxed than I had been since this part of the conversation had started.

"Nostrils, her reply completely stumped the defence counsel. I think for a few moments he thought about pushing the matter harder, but then wisely decided to let it drop. Tracey's response was priceless. It was perhaps the best reply to a question under cross-examination that I've ever heard. I looked at the jury and several of them were actually grinning."

Before I could milk the moment any further, Jeff's phone rang and he stepped outside to take the call. I checked my watch, it was just gone three and if I got off shortly I'd be able to pick my girls up and take them out to dinner. Their mum, Jackie, and I were separated and I got to see them every Monday and to have them every other weekend – it wasn't ideal but it was what it was.

Jeff came back in and I had just started to tell him that I needed to head off when he interrupted me:

"We've got a new job, Nostrils. The DCI wants us all in."

Printed in Great Britain
by Amazon